THE UNKNOWN
SIGRID
UNDSET

THE UNKNOWN SIGRID UNDSET

JENNY AND OTHER WORKS

EDITED WITH AN INTRODUCTION BY TIM PAGE

WITH NEW TRANSLATIONS BY TIINA NUNNALLY

STEERFORTH PRESS
SOUTH ROYALTON, VERMONT

For information about permission to reproduce
selections from this book, write to:
Steerforth Press L.C., P.O. Box 70,
South Royalton, Vermont 05068

LIBRARY OF CONGRESS CATALOGING-IN-PUBLICATION DATA

Undset, Sigrid, 1882-1949.
  [Selections. 2001]
  The unknown Sigrid Undset : Jenny and other works / Sigrid
Undset ; edited and with an introduction by Tim Page ; new transla-
tions by Tiina Nunnally.— 1st ed.
    p. cm.
  ISBN 1-58642-021-6
  1. Undset, Sigrid, 1882-1949—Correspondence. I. Page, Tim,
1954- . II. Nunnally, Tiina, 1952- . III. Title.
  PT8950.U5 A6 2001
  839.8'2372--dc21

                                    00-012977

FIRST EDITION

CONTENTS

ACKNOWLEDGMENTS

Thanks to my publishers and friends at Steerforth Press, especially Robin Dutcher, Chip Fleischer, Michael Moore, Thomas Powers, and Kristin Camp; to my literary agent, Melanie Jackson; to Anna Lou Dehavenon, Polly Holliday, David Kanzeg, Hilton Kramer, Robert Lantz, Jacqueline Mitchell, Ellis B. Page, Richard and Jean Reynolds Page, Vanessa Weeks Page, Ray Roberts, Edward Schneider, Jack Sherman and Rita Sherman, Charles and Betsy Sigman, Julieta Stack, Terry Teachout, Susan T. Vigilante, Linton Weeks, and Michael Zubal for their various contributions; to Kristin Brudevoll and the Norwegian Literature Abroad office for a translation grant and other assistance that was invaluable; to Cathrine Janicke from Aschehoug Publishing; to Robert Gottlieb and Toinette Lippe from Alfred A. Knopf; and to John Waters for a never-to-be-forgotten evening on the town during my visit to Oslo.

Without the support of my mother, the late Elizabeth Thaxton Page, I would never have been able to pursue the release of the Dawn Powell papers — one single line of which provided the direct impetus for this book. Her gentle spirit lives on in her grandchildren, my sons William, Robert, and John Page.

Finally, all gratitude to Tiina Nunnally for her glistening translations of *Jenny* and the letters to Dea Forsberg. It is our hope that the "unknown Sigrid Undset" will soon receive her due as a heroine of twentieth-century literature.

Tim Page

Sigrid Undset's *Kristin Lavransdatter* is one of those gigantic, once best-selling volumes that can be found in most secondhand book stores, placed high on a dusty shelf with Romain Rolland's *Jean Christophe* and Eugene Sue's *The Wandering Jew.* An epical and encylopedic trilogy set in medieval Norway, *Kristin Lavransdatter* won the Nobel Prize for Literature in 1928 and has remained in print ever since, selling a small but steady number of copies every year. Still, unless a present-day English-speaking reader happens to be of Scandinavian descent, the Catholic faith, or unusually interested in world literature, the name of Sigrid Undset will likely draw a blank.

This lamentable situation has begun to correct itself. During the last decade of the twentieth century essays, dissertations, and at least three full books on Undset and her art have appeared. A new edition of *Kristin Lavransdatter* was recently published by Penguin; Tiina Nunnally's fresh translation eschewed the stilted "olde worlde" archaisms of the Knopf edition, making for a starkly elemental retelling that is infinitely closer to Undset's original style and intention. And now, with the publication of *The Unknown Sigrid Undset,* the author stands revealed as the unsparing, compassionate, and magnificent realist that she was.

The present collection is devoted entirely to Undset's early work and encompasses her first great novel, *Jenny* (1911), two strong and extended short stories, "Thjodolf" and "Simonsen," and a trove of letters addressed to Dea Forsberg (née Hedberg), a childhood friend. Although all of Undset's words preserved here were written before she had passed the age of thirty, there is very little that is stereotypically "youthful" in *The Unknown Sigrid Undset.* On the contrary, she was already a frank pessimist, a fearless chronicler of the human condition who detested cant, frivolity, easy answers, and grafted-on happy endings. That she was also a young woman of few means writing almost a hundred years ago in a remote northern city seems incredible, for we meet her not as a relic but rather a vital contemporary from another land.

———

Sigrid Undset was born in Kalundborg, Denmark, on May 20, 1882. Her father, Ingvald Undset, was a celebrated Norwegian archaeologist, and his book-length study, *The Beginnings of the Iron Age in Europe* (1880), although long since superseded, is still esteemed. Anna Charlotte Gyth Undset, Sigrid's mother, is said to have had a sharp and lively mind; she took a near-colleagial interest in her husband's work, and accompanied him on several expeditions. In 1884 the family moved back to what was then known as Kristiania (the original name, Oslo, would be restored in 1925), where Ingvald had a post at the university museum. It was there that Undset and her two younger sisters grew up.

Both of the elder Undsets were firm believers in coeducation. Ingvald Undset was so taken with young Sigrid's intellectual prowess that he hoped she would grow up to continue his own work. Toward this end, he discussed history, politics, and archaeology with her on an adult level and taught her to read Old Norse. Considering the keen understanding of the distant past that Sigrid Undset would display in her most popular novels, it seems appropriate that one of her favorite playthings should have been a terra-cotta horse unearthed from the ruins of Troy. This precious souvenir was a gift to the family from Heinrich Schliemann, who had discovered the buried (and long-believed mythical) city only a few years earlier.

Ingvald Undset's health was precarious: He had contracted malaria in 1880, and Sigrid's early life was a long witness to his slow decline, which ended in 1893.* After his death the Undset family was impoverished, reduced to living off the minuscule state pension provided for widows. Sigrid Undset grew into a quiet, dutiful, highly serious, and somewhat remote young woman whose closest companions were her books. Of these the anonymous *Njal's Saga,* among the richest works in the neglected early Icelandic canon, made the most profound impression on her. Indeed, Undset later said that *Njal's Saga* had changed her life; many of its virtues — scope, austerity, a wary acknowledgment of fate, and an abhorrence of soft sentimentality — may be found in her own writing.

By the age of fifteen, Sigrid Undset had enrolled in a commercial college; upon her graduation the following year, she would take a secretarial position at

---

*An intricate and somewhat fictionalized interior memoir of the author's childhood — in which Sigrid called herself "Ingvild" — was published in 1934 as *Elleve aar* (once available in English translation as *The Longest Years,* although "Eleven Years" would be more exact).

the Wisbech Electrical Company (a subsidary of a German firm) in Kristiania. From the beginning she hated her job; still, faced with the necessity of making a living, she remained with the firm for more than ten years. Her fellow workers would later describe her "imperturbable tranquillity" at her desk. During one midmorning break she was heard chuckling over something she was reading. "It was a piece she had written herself," according to her first biographer, A. H. Winsnes. "She read it to the others. It was written with such 'warmth and humor', say her colleagues, 'that we could not help interrupting — Good Heavens! Why don't you write instead of sitting in an office?'"

She had often considered this course — as we may read for ourselves in the letters here preserved — but this time she went ahead and settled down to business. By the end of 1901 Undset was in the middle of her first novel, a long historical fiction set in 1340. She finished it in 1904 and took it to Peter Nansen of the esteemed Gyldendal publishing house in Copenhagen. There she was met with a condescending but not wholly dismissive response. "He gave me a friendly pat on my shoulder and said 'Don't attempt any more historical novels. You have no talent for it. But you might try writing something modern. You never know.' Then I came home, my mind awhirl, and wrote *Fru Marta Oulie* [Mrs. Marta Oulie]. That, I felt, should be modern enough."

It was indeed modern and, as it turned out, rather scandalous, cast in the form of a diary, and beginning with the once shocking declaration: "I have been unfaithful to my husband." *Fru Marta Oulie* saw print in the fall of 1907, brought out by the Norwegian firm of Aschehoug, which would be Undset's publisher for the rest of her life. *Fru Marta Oulie* has never been translated into English and it is rarely counted among the author's finest works. (It was read, considered, and finally rejected for this omnibus.) Yet it attracted a good deal of attention at the time, and in certain intellectual circles Undset was hailed as a female counterpart to her countryman Henrik Ibsen.

She followed *Fru Marta Oulie* with a one-act play, some scattered poems, and a collection of gloomy short stories, ironically titled *Den lykkelige alder (The Happy Age)* in 1908. ("Thjodolf," the best of these, is contained in the present volume, while "Simonsen" first saw print in a second collection titled *Fattige skjæbner* [Fates of the Poor], which was issued in 1912.) But it was not until the acceptance of her second novel, *Fortællingen om Viga-Ljot og Vigdis (Gunnar's Daughter,* 1909) that she felt secure enough to quit her job and devote all of her energy to writing.

The Scandinavian countries have an honorable tradition of supporting their artists, and Undset was granted a traveling scholarship in 1910. After some time in Germany, she moved on to Rome, a place she loved and would describe, meticulously and poetically, in *Jenny*. While in Rome she met Anders Svarstad, a gifted painter in his early forties. A passionate affair ensued, despite the fact that Svarstad was a married man with three children. After much commotion and a divorce painful for all concerned, the two were married in Antwerp on June 29, 1912, when Undset was already pregnant with their first child.

By this time *Jenny* had been published, and the young author found herself the center of controversy. One critique (from the newspaper *Morgenavisen*) will serve to sum up the conventional horror:

> This endless carrying on until dawn in cafés and lodgings by ladies and gentlemen, this use of the informal means of address, this cursing, drinking, and cigarette smoking, this kissing in all the corners and even worse — this is a side of the free, artistic life that the vast majority of citizens would rather not know. It can't help but have a nauseating — and common — effect. In general, it cannot be denied that the characters in Jenny move in quite a sultry atmosphere, which gives the book a tinge of shadiness. It is most certainly not suitable for display on the Christmas table among both adults and children.

This sort of conventional assessment might well have been predicted. But Undset found herself attacked from another side as well. As the perceptive scholar Susan T. Vigilante observed in *A Life of Sigrid Undset*:

> Already the most promising woman writer in Norway, Undset had naturally been something of a heroine to Norwegian feminists, who at the time were still deeply engaged in the fight for voting rights. To them, *Jenny* was a betrayal. . . . The depiction of any woman as having a "biological destiny" to bear children and, perhaps worse, a powerful emotional need to rear them seemed to imply that women were not quite the equals of men.
>
> Undset's own life, of course, vindicated all the feminists' important claims about the value of women to society. But the same qualities

that made them want to claim her as one of their own made that claim impossible. The suffragettes were ideologues with the ideologue's longing for simplicity. But Undset was a realist. She would not surrender her tragic sense to their neat certainties. She knew that the struggle between the need to express her talents and the equally powerful imperative to love and protect her children was the central and potentially tragic contradiction in the life of every woman artist. She knew that this contradiction could never be denied or glossed over and would not be made any easier by debates or pamphleteering.

I shall have more to say about *Jenny* presently; in the meantime, let's continue with this cursory biographical introduction. After a year in London and Rome, Undset, Svarstad, and their baby boy, Anders, returned to Kristiania. A daughter, Maren Charlotte, was born in 1915, severely retarded. Shortly thereafter, Undset learned that Svarstad's three children (one of whom was also brain damaged) had been placed in an orphanage; they, too, were admitted into the household. But Svarstad and Undset were both difficult people, shot through with "artistic temperament," and their relationship had become prickly. Moreover, Undset thought Svarstad an indifferent father and a lackadaisical provider. They split in 1919, a month before the birth of Undset's last child, who was named Hans Benedict.

Throughout this time Undset had been working on the first volume of *Kristin Lavransdatter;* it was published in 1920 and immediately acclaimed. But it also reflected some enormous changes that had come over Undset's thinking in the years since she had written *Jenny.* Her deep unhappiness about what was then known as the Great War, combined with her fascination for history and, in particular, for the lives of the saints, helped to lead a gradual, unexpected, and overwhelming religious conversion. Her marriage to Svarstad was formally annulled on November 23, 1924; the following day she was received into the Roman Catholic Church.

This is neither the time nor the place for a lengthy examination of Undset's faith. Most studies place her among the most significant figures in the Catholic literary revival, an assessment with which I would not quarrel. Yet her life story has been too often told as a sort of hagiography, the tale of a long spiritual progression instead of a straightforward narrative of a supremely talented writer who became a devout Catholic in middle age.

The fact is that the works contained in *The Unknown Sigrid Undset* — her finest writings, to my taste — were written at a time when Undset, by her own account, considered herself an agnostic, if not an atheist. For this reason the efforts by A. H. Winsnes and others to find nascent Christian stirrings in a bleak and fundamentally existential novel such as *Jenny* seem exercises in twenty-twenty hindsight. (Some Undset studies do not mention the early works at all.) In no way am I trying to play down the profound faith that informs Undset's later work; I only seek to remind the reader that Undset enjoyed no such consolation when she wrote the works in this omnibus — and there were many paths that she might have taken from here.

In the mid-1920s Undset moved to the pristine village of Lillehammer, some three hours north of Oslo. Here she wrote, gardened, raised her children, and spent the happiest years of her life. In 1928 she won the Nobel Prize for Literature for *Kristin Lavransdatter,* for *The Master of Hestviken* (a gigantic medieval tetralogy), and for her evocative depictions of ancient life in Norway. She spent the 1930s writing — four modern novels (of which two, *The Burning Bush* and *The Wild Orchid,* are paired), autobiographical works, and a variety of essays, including some rather ill-tempered attacks on Protestantism and Lutheranism. She grew to be one of the most famous novelists in the world, and her later books sold many thousands of copies.

Undset's last years were miserable. In April 1940 Germany invaded Norway, and Undset, who had been outspokenly critical of Hitler and Nazism, was advised to flee (her first son, Anders, would be killed at the front only a few weeks later). Under desperate and frightening conditions she traveled through Sweden, the Soviet Union, and Japan (an odyssey recounted in the autobiographical *Return to the Future*), eventually reaching San Francisco. From there she moved to New York, where she lived in Brooklyn Heights and played an active part in the war effort, delivering speeches and lending her prestigious presence to a variety of committees. She continued to write as well, albeit in a diminished capacity; she never finished a novel after leaving Norway.

In August 1945 it was finally safe for Undset to return to Lillehammer. But by then her health was broken and she suffered from chronic bronchitis, among other ailments. It is also possible that she may have been afflicted by depression, as a letter to the writer Hans Aanrud from 1948 indicates:

> I can indeed say that I think the world has become dismal. During
> the war, when I was in America, I had the feeling that I was mak-

ing myself useful and that we could all look to the future with some kind of hopeful expectation. Not that I expected everything to become excellent all of a sudden, or that "the good old days" should return. But neither did I expect "the new age" to be so anemic and feeble, although with so much blood spilled it is not strange that people should suddenly give the impression of being anemic, rebellious and unenterprising. . . .

Undset died in Lillehammer on June 10, 1949, while in the midst of preparing an essay on Edmund Burke, a philosopher who was understandably dear to her. She received a state funeral and was buried next to Anders and Maren Charlotte Undset, her first two children. The Undset house is now owned by the Norwegian government; it has been extensively refurbished and will eventually be open to the public. It is already something of a shrine for her admirers, some of whom travel thousands of miles for the privilege of merely seeing it. For if Undset means anything to a reader at all, it is likely that she means a great deal.

—⟡—

The English translation of *Jenny,* published by Alfred A. Knopf in 1921, was permitted to drop quietly from the Undset catalog in the 1930s, at the very peak of the author's career. The reason for this is still unexplained, for any of her works would by then have had a large following. Perhaps Undset had come to consider the book a "sin of youth" — certainly it had a very different tone and philosophy from most of the works that were now streaming from her pen. Or perhaps the English-speaking Undset disapproved of the wretched translation, which removed long passages of lyrical writing and several of the more "salacious" references. For whatever reason, *Jenny* has always been far and away the hardest to find of Undset's novels in English translation.

And so it is a particular pleasure to present Tiina Nunnally's pristine and authoritative translation of *Jenny.* She has maintained the cadences of Undset's style, restored many passages that were omitted eighty years ago, and set it all down in the most evocative and expressive language. The result is a solemn, brooding masterpiece of the first order. I am surprised to find this *Jenny* reminiscent of nothing so much as the very early Theodore Dreiser (*Sister Carrie* and *Jennie Gerhardt,* in particular) with its sense of intricate, inevitable, irredeemable tragedy. And yet the writer's massive power is unmistakably, even defiantly, female.

We don't really come to know Jenny until about a quarter of the book has run its course. Instead, we are seduced by a beautifully detailed portrait of turn-of-the-twentieth-century Rome, peopled with Bohemians as vividly timeless as those found in Murger and Puccini. But Jenny, once established, is unforgettable. Had there ever been such an acute psychological portrait of a determined woman artist? (Willa Cather's *The Song of the Lark* was still four years off.) Had a woman's sexual yearning ever been portrayed so frankly and so seriously? Those who railed against Undset's "betrayal" of feminism would seem to have had a very simplistic conception of this welcome revolution.

One young writer understood, however. The American author Dawn Powell (1896–1965) came across *Jenny* when she was in her midtwenties, and it made roughly the same impression on her that *Njal's Saga* had made on Undset. In 1953 Powell made a list of the novels that she had liked best, a list I discovered while editing her diaries for publication. Most of her chosen books — by Dreiser, Flaubert, Balzac, Dickens, Gogol, Sinclair Lewis, and George Eliot — were familiar ones (although Powell's championship of the *Satyricon* of Petronius Arbiter was decidedly unconventional for its time). Only the selection of Undset's *Jenny* drew a complete blank. I decided to investigate, and even in the inadequate translation I found the novel extraordinarily rich and moving. Fortunately, my editors at Steerforth Press agreed with me and now, six years later, here is our edition of *The Unknown Sigrid Undset*.

Although they date from approximately the same time that Undset was working on *Jenny*, "Thjodolf" and "Simonsen" were first published in English by Alfred A. Knopf in 1959, a full ten years after Undset's death, as part of a small collection called *Four Stories*. We have retained the original translations by Naomi Walford, which continue to hold up remarkably well, deftly balancing Undset's dark vision with her equally compelling human sympathy. It was Tiina Nunnally's idea to conclude the volume with Undset's never-before-translated letters to Dea Forsberg, which might be fairly described as a "portrait of the artist as a young woman" — stretching, dreaming, trying on philosophies, scrutinizing herself and others, all the while feeling for her destiny as a writer.

Tim Page
Washington, D.C.
October 15, 2000

THE UNKNOWN
SIGRID
UNDSET

JENNY

translated by

TIINA NUNNALLY

PART ONE

I

The music surged up the Via Condotti just as Helge Gram turned onto the street in the twilight. It was *The Merry Widow,* played at a preposterously fast tempo, making it resound like a wild fanfare. And small, dark-haired soldiers stormed past him in the cold afternoon, as if they were no less than part of a Roman cohort which, at a furious double time, was about to fall upon the barbarian hosts rather than peacefully return home to the barracks for supper. Or perhaps that was exactly the reason they were in such a hurry, thought Helge with a smile; for as he stood there with his coat collar turned up against the cold, an oddly historic feeling came over him. But then he began humming along — "No, a man will never understand women" — and continued down the street in the direction where he knew the Corso must be.

He stopped at the corner and looked up the street. So that's how the Corso looked. A ceaselessly flowing stream of traffic in the cramped thoroughfare and a churning throng of people on the narrow sidewalk.

He stood still and watched the stream flow past. And he smiled, because he was thinking that now, every single evening, he could head up this street in the dark through the swarms of people until it became as familiar to him as Karl Johans Gaten back home.

Oh, he had the urge right now to walk and walk, through all the streets of Rome, gladly all night long. He was thinking of the city as it lay below him a short time ago, when he stood on Monte Pincio and watched the sun go down.

Clouds had covered the entire sky to the west, crowded together like small pale gray lambs. And the sun gave them glowing golden-amber edges as it sank behind. Beneath the pale sky lay the city, and Helge suddenly knew that this was precisely how Rome should look — not the way he had dreamed of it, but precisely like this, as it was.

Yet everything else he had seen on this trip had disappointed him because it wasn't the way he had imagined beforehand, as he went about at home, longing to go out and see things. At last, now at last there was one sight that was richer than all his dreams. And it was Rome.

A wide plain of rooftops lay beneath him in the hollow of the valley, a jumble of roofs on buildings that were old and new, tall buildings and low buildings. They looked as if they had been put up quite haphazardly and as big as was needed at the time; only in a few places did the streets cut regular clefts through the mass of rooftops. And this whole world of disorderly lines that intersected each other at thousands of sharp angles lay rigid and motionless beneath the pale sky, in which an invisible sinking sun sporadically ignited a tiny rim of light on the edges of the clouds. The sun hung dreaming under a delicate, whitish mist, into which not a single spurting column of smoke blended, because there were no factory smokestacks in sight, and no smoke came from any of the comical little tin chimneys sticking up from the buildings. Grayish yellow lichen lay on the old, rounded, rust-brown roof tiles, and greenery and small shrubs with yellow flowers grew along the eaves. Around the edges of the terraces stood silent, dead agaves in urns, and from the cornices twining plants spilled in silent, dead cascades. Wherever the upper story of a taller building loomed above its neighbors, dark, dead windows stared out from a red-yellow or gray-white wall — or else they slumbered with closed shutters. But out of the mist rose loggias, looking like the stumps of old watchtowers, and arbors made of wood and tin had been erected on the rooftops.

And above everything hovered the church domes, a countless number of them. The magnificent gray dome far off in the distance, on the other side of the place where Helge caught a glimpse of the flowing river, that was the Basilica of St. Peter.

But on this side of the valley floor, where the dead roofs covered the city — which, on this evening, Helge certainly felt could be called eternal — a low hillside arched its long back toward the sky, and its ridge carried into the distance a lane of Italian stone pines whose crowns spread out into one above the slender pillars of their trunks. And farthest away, beyond the dome of St. Peter's, where the eye stopped, another slope rose up with light-colored villas among the pines and cypresses. Surely that must be Monte Mario.

Above his head hung the thick, dark foliage of the holly oaks, and behind him splashed the jet of the fountain with a peculiarly vivid sound. The water crashed against the stone bowl and trickled innocuously into the basin underneath.

Helge whispered aloud to the city of his dreams, whose streets his feet had never trod and whose buildings concealed not one familiar soul: "Rome, Rome, eternal Rome." And he grew shy before his own lonely being, and afraid, because he was deeply moved, although he knew that no one was there watching him. All the same, he turned around and hurried down toward the Spanish Steps.

Now he was standing here on the corner of Via Condotti and the Corso, feeling an oddly sweet anxiety because he was about to cross through the teeming life of the street and then make his way into the strange city. He would go straight through, all the way to the Piazza San Pietro.

As he cut across the street two young girls walked past him. Those two are undoubtedly Norwegian, it occurred to him at once, and he found the idea amusing. One of them was very blond and wore a light-colored fur.

He suddenly felt happy just from reading the street names on the corners of the buildings, the white inlaid marble plaques with the clean, Roman letters chiseled into them.

The street he was following ended in an open square near a white bridge that had two rows of streetlamps burning a sickly greenish yellow against the vast pale light streaming down from the restless heavens. Along the water ran a low stone parapet, shining wanly, and a row of trees with withered leaves, the bark of their trunks scaling off in big white flakes. On the opposite side of the river, gas lamps burned beneath the trees, and the massive buildings stood black against the sky; but on this side the evening light still flared in the windowpanes. The sky was almost clear now, a transparent blue-green above the ridge with its lane of pines, but a few heaps of heavy cloud banks drifted past, glowing red and yellow, like a portent of storm.

He stopped on the bridge and looked down at the Tiber. How murky the water was! It gushed in torrents, flame-colored from the sky's reflection; it swept branches and planks and debris along with it, there below in its bed of pale stone walls. On one side of the bridge a small stairway led down to the water. Helge thought about how easy it would be to sneak out here one night if things ever became too unbearable. He wondered if anyone ever did.

In German he asked a constable the way to St. Peter's, and the constable replied in French and then Italian, but when Helge kept on shaking his head, he went back to speaking French and pointed up the street the way the traffic was flowing. Helge set off in that direction.

A massive dark wall rose against the sky, a low round tower with notched battlements and the coal-black silhouette of an angel on top. He recognized the contours of the Castel Sant'Angelo. He passed right below it. There was still enough light in the sky that the statues along the bridge looked yellowish in the dusk, and the Tiber's water still flowed with the reflection of red clouds, but the gas lamps were gaining in power and cast arcs of light onto the currents. Behind the Ponte Sant'Angelo the electric trolley cars, with lights shining from their windows, raced across a new bridge made of iron. Blue-white sparks flew from the insulated wires.

Helge tipped his hat to a man. "San Pietro, *favorisca?*"

The man pointed and said a great deal that Helge could not understand.

The street he now entered was so narrow and dark that he actually felt a thrill of recognition — this was the way he had imagined an Italian street would look. And there was one antiques shop after another. Helge peered with interest into the poorly lit windows. Most of it was probably junk. The dirty remnants of coarse white lace hanging there on strings: Was that Italian lace? There were bits and pieces of pottery displayed in dusty box lids, small, venomous-green bronze figures, old and new metal candlesticks, and brooches with clusters of stones that didn't look genuine. Still, he had an absurd urge to go in and buy something — inquire, bargain, make a purchase. He ended up inside a cramped little shop, almost before he knew what he was doing. But it was an amusing place, with all sorts of strange artifacts: old church lamps up near the ceiling, tattered silk with gold flowers on red and green and white backgrounds, rickety furniture.

Behind the counter sat a dark-haired young man, reading. His skin was golden, his chin blue with stubble. He chattered his replies as Helge pointed at various items and said, "*Quanto?*" The only thing Helge could understand was that everything was shamelessly expensive. Of course he ought to wait to buy anything until he spoke the language and could haggle properly.

Over on a shelf stood a number of porcelain pieces: rococo figurines and vases decorated with molded bouquets of roses. But they looked new. Helge picked up a little knickknack at random and set it on the counter. "*Quanto?*"

"*Sette,*" said the man and put out seven fingers.

"*Quattro.*" Helge held up four fingers, wearing his new brown glove. And he suddenly felt happy and confident at this leap into a foreign language. It was true that he didn't understand a word of the clerk's protests, but each time the man stopped talking, he would repeat his *"quattro"* and hold up four fingers.

"Non antica!" he added with a flourish.

But the shop clerk insisted: *"Antica."*

"Quattro," said Helge for the last time. Now the man was holding up only five fingers. When Helge turned toward the door, the man called after him — he gave in. Bursting with joy, Helge accepted the knickknack, which had been wrapped in pink tissue paper.

—✴—

At the end of the street he could glimpse the dark dimensions of the church against the sky. He walked fast. And he hurried across the first section of the piazza, where the shops stood with bright windows and the trolleys raced past. He was headed toward the two semicircular arcades, which seemed to be placing a pair of curved arms around part of the piazza, pulling it into the silence and darkness, toward the magnificent dark cathedral, which thrust across the square its wide stairs, jutting out into a shell-shaped semicircle in the middle.

Black against the dim vault of the sky stood the dome of the church with its ranks of statues: saintly hosts lining the roof of the arcades, with buildings and crowns of trees irregularly piled up on the slope behind. The gas lamps seemed to have little power here; the dark seeped out through the pillars of the arcades, flooding down the steps from the open portico of the cathedral. Helge walked all the way up to the church and peered at the closed bronze doors. Then he went back to the obelisk in the center of the piazza and stood there, staring at the dark cathedral. He tilted his head back and moved his eyes along the slender stone spire that pointed straight up into the evening sky, where the last clouds had settled onto the rooftops in the direction from which he had come, and the first stars were drilling their glittering needles of light through the darkness, which was growing denser.

And his ears were filled once again with the odd crash of splashing water gushing into a stone basin, and the soft trickling of water overflowing from bowl to bowl, into the basin underneath. He moved close to one of the fountains and looked up at the thick white jet that was being forced upward in fierce defiance, bursting apart high overhead, dark against the clarity of the sky, then falling back in the darkness, where the water gleamed white again. He stared until a little gust of wind seized the fountain's column of spray and bent it toward him. The water no longer slammed against the stone basin; it hissed, and he was showered with icy drops in the cold night.

But he stayed where he was, listening and staring; walked on a bit, stopped a moment, walked on again — but very quietly, trying to hear the whispering inside him. Now he was here, he was actually here — far, far away from everything he had been longing so feverishly to leave behind. And he walked even more quietly, treading like someone who had escaped from prison.

There was a restaurant on the corner of the street. He headed toward it, found a tobacco shop along the way, and stopped in to buy cigarettes, postcards, and stamps. While he waited for his steak and drank great gulps of red wine, he wrote cards to his parents. To his father: "I'm thinking of you so much down here tonight," and he smiled sadly — yes, it was true, in spite of everything. But to his mother he wrote: "I've already bought a little gift for you — the first I've purchased here in Rome." Poor Mother. He wondered how she was. He had often been unloving toward her over the past few years. He unwrapped the knickknack — it was probably an eau de cologne bottle — and looked at it. And he added a few lines about how well he had managed with the language and how it wasn't very difficult to bargain in the shops.

The food was good but expensive. Well, as soon as he became familiar with things here, he would no doubt learn how to get by more cheaply. Feeling full and lively from the wine, he set off in a new direction, glimpsing long, low, dilapidated buildings and high garden walls. He passed through a crumbling arched gate and came to a bridge, which he proceeded to cross. A man in a toll-booth stopped him and made Helge understand that he had to hand over a soldo. On the other side stood a large dark church with a dome.

Then he entered a maze of dark, narrow streets. In the secretive dimness he could make out old palazzos with eaves jutting against the sky and windows with grates, standing side by side with miserable hovels and small church facades among the rows of buildings. There was no sidewalk; he stepped on dubious-looking garbage that lay reeking along the curb. Outside the narrow, illuminated tavern doors and beneath the few gas lamps he caught sight of sinister-looking people.

Helge was half delighted and half frightened — as excited as a boy. At the same time he began to wonder how he was going to get out of this labyrinth, and how he would find his way back to the hotel, far away on the other side of the world. He would probably have to splurge on a cab.

He walked down another narrow street, completely deserted. Between the tall buildings, whose walls rose straight up with black window holes carved into them but no cornices, rippled a crevice of sky, clear blue and darkly luminous, while below, on the uneven cobblestones, dust and fluttering paper and shreds of straw drifted along in a little gust of wind.

Two women came up behind him and walked past, right near a gas lamp. He gave a start: They were the ones he had noticed on the Corso that afternoon. The ones he thought were Norwegian. He recognized the light-colored fur the tall girl was wearing.

He had a sudden impulse; he would have himself a little adventure, ask them for directions to see whether they were Norwegian, or Scandinavian, at any rate. With his heart beating a little faster, he proceeded to follow them. He was certain they were foreigners.

The two young women stopped along the street in front of a shop that was closed. A moment later they continued on. Helge considered whether he should say "Please" or *"Bitte"* or *"Scusi"* — or come right out and try *"Undskyld"* — it would be fun if they were Norwegian.

The girls turned the corner. Helge was close behind, gathering his courage to speak to them. Then the shorter one looked over her shoulder and said something in Italian, in a low, furious voice.

Helge was very disappointed. He was just about to say *"Scusi"* and leave, but then the tall girl said to her friend in Norwegian: "Oh, no, Cesca, don't say anything to them — it's much better to pretend you don't notice."

"But I can't *stand* these darned Italian louts who won't ever leave a woman alone," she replied.

"I beg your pardon," said Helge, and the girls stopped and turned around at once.

"You really must forgive me," Helge stammered and blushed, which annoyed him, and he blushed even more in the dark. "But I've just arrived from Florence today, and now I've gotten completely lost in all these twisting streets. And so I thought you ladies might be Norwegian, or Scandinavian, at any rate — I can't manage very well in Italian, and so I thought . . . Would you be kind enough to tell me where I might find a trolley? My name is Herr Gram," he said and tipped his hat again.

"Where are you staying?" asked the tall girl.

"Well, it's a place called Albergo Torino — right near the train station," Helge explained.

"Then he should take the Trastevere trolley over by San Carlo ai Catinari," said the short girl.

"No, it's better to take route number one from the new Corso."

"But that one doesn't go to the Termini," replied her friend.

"Yes, it does. The one that says SAN PIETRO–STAZIONE TERMINI on it does," she explained to Helge.

"That one . . . it goes up around Capo le Case and Ludovisi and then keeps on going all the way around first. It takes at least an hour to get to the station on that one!"

"No, no, my dear — it goes straight there, right up Via Nazionale."

"No, it doesn't at all," said the short girl, stubbornly. "Besides, first it goes around to Laterana too."

The tall woman turned to Helge.

"Just take the first street on the right, over to the flea market. Then take a left at the Cancelleria out to the new Corso. As far as I remember, the trolley stops at the Cancelleria, or right next to it, at any rate. You're bound to see the sign. Then be careful to take the trolley that says SAN PIETRO–STAZIONE TERMINI. It's route number one."

Helge stood there a little dejectedly, listening to the two young women tossing the foreign names back and forth right in front of him. He shook his head. "I'm afraid I won't find it, Frøken. I suppose I'd better just keep walking until I find a cab."

"We'd be happy to go with you to the stop," said the tall girl.

Her friend began whispering crossly in Italian, but the tall girl rebuked her. Helge felt even more dejected by these remarks flying past him, which he didn't understand.

"Thank you, but you really mustn't trouble yourselves; you know, I'm sure I'll find my way back somehow."

"It's no trouble at all," said the tall girl and began walking. "We're going quite near there ourselves."

"You're much too kind. It certainly is hard to find your way around here in Rome, isn't it?" he said, attempting to converse. "At least in the dark."

"Oh, you'll know your way around in no time."

"Well, I just arrived today. I came from Florence this afternoon, on the train."

The short girl said something softly in Italian. The tall girl asked Helge, "Is it cold in Florence right now?"

"Yes, freezing cold. It seems quite a bit warmer here in the city, doesn't it? And here I just wrote home to my mother yesterday, asking for my winter coat."

"Oh, it can get quite bitter here too. Did you like Florence? How long were you there?"

"Two weeks," said Helge. "I think I'm going to like Rome better."

The other girl laughed. The whole time she had been walking along muttering in Italian. But the tall girl told him in her calm, warm voice, "Yes, I don't think there's *any* city that you'll like more than Rome."

"Your friend is Italian?" asked Helge.

"Oh no, Frøken Jahrmann is Norwegian. We just speak Italian to each other so I'll get better at it. She speaks it so well, you see. My name is Winge," she added. "Here's the Cancelleria." She pointed to a large dark palazzo.

"Is the courtyard as lovely as they say?"

"Yes, quite lovely. Now let me make sure you find the right trolley."

As they stood and waited, two gentlemen cut across the street.

"Well, look who's here," said one of them.

"Good evening," said the other. "Shall we go up there together? Have you been over to look at the corals?"

"It was closed," sulked Frøken Jahrmann.

"We ran into a countryman, and we're helping him find the right trolley," explained Frøken Winge, and she made the introductions. "Herr Gram — the painter, Heggen, and the sculptor, Ahlin."

"I don't know whether Herr Heggen remembers me . . . My name is Gram, we met up at Mysusæter three years ago."

"Oh, that's right, of course. And now you're here in Rome?"

Ahlin and Frøken Jahrmann were whispering to each other. Now they came over to the other girl.

"Jenny, I'm going home. I don't feel like going to Frascati after all."

"But my dear — it was your idea in the first place."

"Oh, no, not Frascati. Ugh. Sit there and mope with two dozen Danish women of all ages."

"We could certainly go somewhere else. But here's your trolley, Herr Gram."

"Yes, well, thank you so much for your help. I hope I'll meet you ladies sometime again — perhaps at the Scandinavian Club?"

The trolley stopped in front of them. Then Frøken Winge said, "I wonder . . . maybe you might like to come along with us? We were planning to go out for a bit this evening — drink some wine and hear some music."

"Oh yes . . ." Helge stood there a little uncertain and shy, looking around at the others. "That would be very pleasant, but . . ." and he turned trustingly to Frøken Winge with her bright face and kind voice: "All of you know each other, and . . . well, I'm sure it would be more comfortable if you didn't have a stranger tagging along," he exclaimed and laughed with embarrassment.

"Oh, my dear man," she said with a smile. "It would be so nice. And look, there goes your trolley. You already know Heggen from before, and now you know us. And we'll make sure that you get home properly. So if you're not tired . . ."

"Tired? Oh no! I would love to join you," said Helge eagerly, with relief.

The three others had begun to suggest taverns. Helge didn't know any of them by name; none of them was among those his father had talked about. Frøken Jahrmann rejected them all.

"All right then — we'll go down to Sant'Agostino. You know, the place with the red wine, Gunnar." Jenny Winge started off at once; Heggen followed.

"They don't have music," objected Frøken Jahrmann.

"Yes, they do — the man who squints and that other man are there almost every evening. Let's not stand here talking nonsense."

Helge followed behind with Frøken Jahrmann and the Swedish sculptor.

"Have you been in Rome long, Herr Gram?" asked Ahlin.

"No, I came from Florence this afternoon."

Frøken Jahrmann gave a little laugh. Helge felt sheepish. He walked along thinking that perhaps he ought to say he was tired after all, and leave. As they continued on through the dark, narrow streets, Frøken Jahrmann kept talking to the Swedish sculptor and barely responded whenever he tried to speak to her. But before he had made up his mind, he saw the other couple disappear through a narrow doorway down the street.

2

"What the hell is wrong with Cesca, again tonight? There seems to be no end to her moods. Take off your coat, Jenny, or you'll be cold when you go back out." Heggen hung up his hat and spring coat and dropped into a chair with a woven seat.

"Poor thing, she's not feeling well today — and then this Gram started following us for a bit, you see, until he dared speak to us and ask for directions. That kind of thing always upsets her, and then there's her heart, you know."

"Poor girl. An insolent fellow, by the way."

"Oh, I feel sorry for him. I think he was just walking along, not knowing what to do. He doesn't give the impression that he's used to traveling. You know him?"

"Not that I can remember. But that doesn't mean I might not have met him. There they are now."

Ahlin took Frøken Jahrmann's coat.

"The Devil take me," said Heggen, "you look lovely tonight, Cesca. As cute as a little lizard!"

She smiled happily, smoothing her skirt over her hips. Then she put her hands on Heggen's shoulders. "Move over — I want to sit next to Jenny."

May God save me, how beautiful she is, thought Helge. Her dress was a shimmering leaf-green; the waist of the skirt cinched so high that her full bosom seemed to rise from a stem vase. And the folds of the velvet bodice shone with a golden luster; it was cut very low around her plump, tawny throat. Her hair was quite dark; under her brown plush cloche, little coal-black ringlets dangled around her glowing, peach-blush cheeks. Her face was that of a little girl, with full eyelids above deep-set, dark gray eyes and charming dimples at the corners of her small, dark red lips.

Frøken Winge was certainly an attractive girl too, but she was no match for her friend. She was as fair as the other was dark. Her hair, which was pulled back from her high, white forehead, billowed in golden flames beneath the little gray leather beret, and her complexion was a glowing pink and white. Even her eyebrows and the lashes around her steel-gray eyes were light-colored: a golden brown. But her mouth was too big for her narrow face with its short, straight nose and curving, blue-veined temples, and she was rather pale, but her even teeth gleamed when she laughed. And everything else about her was so lean: her long, slender neck, her arms that were covered with a fine, light down, and her hands, which were long and thin. She was so tall and lanky that her figure seemed almost boyish. She had to be terribly young. There were slender white bands around her elbows and across the neck opening of her light-gray, silky dress, which was lightweight and flowing, gathered both at the breast and around the waist — no doubt to disguise her thinness. Around her neck she wore a string of little pink beads that cast rosy patches of light on her skin.

Helge Gram had unobtrusively sat down at the end of the table and was listening to his new acquaintances talking about a Fru Søderblom, who had been ill. An old Italian man wearing a filthy white apron across his big stomach came over and asked them what they'd like to order.

"Red, white, sour, sweet — what would you like, Gram?" Heggen turned to ask him.

"Herr Gram will have a half liter of my red wine," said Jenny Winge. "It's one of the best in Rome — and that's saying a lot, you know."

The sculptor slid a cigarette case over to the ladies. Frøken Jahrmann took a cigarette and lit it.

"Oh, please, Cesca, no," begged Frøken Winge.

"Oh yes," said Frøken Jahrmann. "I'm not going to get any better if I stop. And I'm in a bad mood tonight."

"But why is that, my dear?" asked the Swede.

"Well, I didn't get that coral necklace, after all."

"Were you planning to wear it tonight?" asked Heggen.

"No, but I'd made up my mind to buy it."

"And tomorrow I'll bet you decide to get the malachite necklace," Heggen said with a laugh.

"No, that's not true at all. But it's insufferably annoying that Jenny and I should dash all the way down there for the sake of those wretched corals."

"Yes, but then you ran into us. Otherwise you would have had to go to Frascati, and you've taken such a sudden dislike to it."

"I would not have gone to Frascati — I can assure you of that, Gunnar. And I would have been much better off. Because now I'm going to smoke and drink and stay out all night, since you've managed to get me out."

"I thought it was your idea."

"The malachite necklace was extraordinarily beautiful, I thought," Ahlin interrupted. "Very expensive."

"Yes, but malachite is much cheaper in Florence. This one costs forty-seven lire. In that place in Florence where Jenny bought her *cristallo rosso,* I could have had one for thirty-five. Jenny only paid eighteen for her necklace. But he's going to let me have the corals for ninety lire."

"I can't make any sense out of your finances," said Heggen with a laugh.

"Well, I don't feel like talking about it anymore," said Frøken Jahrmann. "I'm tired of all this chatter back and forth. But tomorrow I'm going to buy those corals."

"But isn't ninety lire terribly expensive for a coral necklace?" Helge ventured to ask.

"This is not an ordinary necklace, you know," Frøken Jahrmann condescended to reply. "They're *contadina* corals — a thick necklace with a gold clasp and heavy earrings that are long like this."

"*Contadina* — is that a type of coral?"

"Not at all. They're the kind *contadinas* wear, of course."

"I don't know what a *contadina* is," said Helge timidly.

"A country girl, of course. Haven't you seen the necklaces they wear, those heavy, dark red polished corals? Mine are exactly the color of raw beef, and the center bead is this big . . ." She made an egg-sized circle with her thumb and index finger.

"It must be magnificent." Helge grasped eagerly at the thread of the conversation. "I'm not familiar with malachite or *cristalla rosa* — but I think that corals like that would certainly suit you best."

"Do you hear that, Ahlin? And you wanted me to buy the malachite necklace. Heggen's stickpin is malachite — take it off, Gunnar. And Jenny's beads are *cristallo rosso* — not *rosa* — pink rock crystal. You see?"

She handed him the stickpin and the necklace. The beads were warm from the young girl's throat. Helge studied them for a moment. Inside each bead were what looked like tiny fissures that drew in the light.

"But you should wear corals, Frøken Jahrmann. You know, I think you would look like a Roman *contadina* yourself."

"Huh — you hear that?" She gave Helge a little smile and hummed contentedly. "Did you hear that?"

"You have an Italian name," Helge continued earnestly.

"Oh, that's just from the Italian family I lived with last year. They changed the awful name I was given, after my grandmother Fransiska, and so I just kept the Italian version."

"Francesca," said Ahlin softly.

"I'll never be able to think of you as anything but Francesca — Signorina Francesca."

"Why not *Frøken* Jahrmann? Unfortunately we can't speak Italian together, since you don't know the language." She turned to the others. "Jenny and Gunnar — I'm going to buy those corals tomorrow."

"Yes, that's what you keep telling us," said Heggen.

"And I *won't* pay more than ninety."

"Well, you can always haggle," said Helge sagely. "I was in a shop this afternoon over near St. Peter's and bought this for my mother. The clerk wanted seven lire, but I got it for four. Don't you think that was cheap?" He placed the knickknack on the table.

Fransiska gave it a look of contempt. "They cost one and a half at the flea market. I brought back a couple of those for the maids at home last year."

"The man claimed it was an antique," Helge protested meekly.

"They always do when they see that someone doesn't know anything about it. And can't speak Italian."

"You don't think it's pretty?" Helge asked, disheartened, as he wrapped it up in the tissue paper again. "You don't think I should give it to my mother?"

"I think it's hideous," said Fransiska. "But then, I don't know what kind of taste your mother has."

"God knows what I'm going to do with it," sighed Helge.

"Go ahead and give it to your mother," said Jenny Winge. "It will make her happy that you thought of her. Besides . . . back in Norway people do like that kind of thing. Those of us who come down here, we see so much."

Fransiska grabbed Ahlin's cigarette case, but he didn't want her to have it. They whispered fiercely to each other for a moment. Then she flung it away.

"Giuseppe!"

Helge understood that she was telling the bartender to bring her some cigarettes.

Ahlin jumped to his feet.

"Frøken Jahrmann — my dear — I only meant — you know that it's not good for you to smoke so much."

Fransiska stood up; she had tears in her eyes.

"Well, it doesn't matter anyway — I'm going home."

"Frøken Jahrmann — Francesca . . ." Ahlin stood holding her coat, gently imploring her. She wiped her eyes with her handkerchief.

"Yes, I'm going home. My dears, you can see that I'm impossible tonight. No, I want to go home — alone. No, Jenny, I'm not going to let you leave."

Heggen also got to his feet. Helge remained sitting at the table, abandoned.

"Now, you don't think that you're going to be allowed to go home alone at this time of night, do you?" said Heggen.

"Oh, I see — perhaps you're going to forbid me?"

"Yes, absolutely."

"Oh, hush, Gunnar," said Jenny Winge. She dismissed both gentlemen, who sat down and fell silent as Jenny put her arm around Fransiska's waist and drew her aside to speak to her quietly. In a moment the two of them came back to the table.

But after that the group sat there rather dispirited. Frøken Jahrmann was practically reclining in Jenny's lap. She now had her cigarettes and was smoking and shaking her head at all of Ahlin's assurances that his were better. Jenny had ordered a platter of fruit and was eating mandarins, slipping sections into Fransiska's mouth. Oh, how enchanting she looked as she lay there with her small, sad child's face, letting her friend feed her. Ahlin sat and stared at her while Heggen broke up all the used matches into tiny pieces and stuck them in among the orange peels.

"Have you been in town long, Herr Gram?" he asked Helge.

Helge tried to make a joke. "I usually say that I came from Florence this afternoon, by train."

Jenny laughed politely, but Fransiska gave him a wilting smile.

At that moment a bareheaded, dark-haired girl with a dark, stout face came in. She was holding a mandolin in her hand. Behind her minced a short, shabby, but elegant waiter carrying a guitar.

Jenny spoke as if to a child. "Do you see that, Cesca? There's Emilia. Now you'll have your music."

"What fun," said Helge. "Do these street musicians really still go around to the taverns here in Rome?"

The folksingers started in on *The Merry Widow*: "You know that I am respectable." The girl had a strangely shrill, clear, metallic-sounding voice.

"Ugh, no." Fransiska woke up. "Not that song. We want something Italian, don't we? *'La luna con palido canto'* — what do you think?"

She slipped over to the musicians and greeted them like old friends, laughing and gesturing, picking up the guitar and strumming it, humming a few bars of some melody.

The woman sang. Sweet and ingratiating, to the accompaniment of the resounding steel strings, the melody fluttered, and all of Helge's companions sang along with the refrain. It was about *amore* and *bacciare*.

"It's a love song, isn't it?"

"A fine love song," laughed Frøken Jahrmann. "Don't ask me to translate. But in Italian it sounds quite charming."

"Oh, it's not that bad," said Jenny Winge. And she turned to Helge with her obliging smile. "So, Herr Gram, don't you think it's pleasant here? Isn't the wine good?"

"Yes, excellent. And I assume the premises are very typical?"

But he had completely lost his courage. Frøken Winge and Heggen talked to him now and then, but he made no attempt to keep the conversation going. And so they began talking to each other, about paintings. The Swedish sculptor merely sat and looked at Frøken Jahrmann. And the unfamiliar melodies whirled from the clanging steel strings — right past him — with messages for the others. The room where he sat was perfect; a floor of red brick, whitewashed walls and ceiling, the vault of which rested on a thick pillar in the middle. But it was true that the tables were unpainted, and the chairs had green rush seats, and the air was heavy and acidic from the fermented vapor issuing from the wine casks behind the marble counter.

The artist's life in Rome. It felt as if he were looking at a picture or reading a description in a book. Except that he now felt superfluous — so hopeless. As long it was just in books and in pictures, he could dream of being here. But among these people he was certain that he would never be accepted.

Damn it all, it was no doubt better that way. He wasn't much good with other people in general — and definitely not with this sort. See how blithely Jenny Winge was now picking up the heavy opaque beer glass with its dark red wine; the glass had caught his attention. His father had talked about that kind, pointed out to him the glass the girl was holding in her hand, the girl in Marstrand's Rome painting hanging in the Copenhagen museum. It was probably a paltry painting, in Frøken Winge's opinion. Maybe these young girls had never read about Bramante's courtyard in the Cancelleria: "that pearl of Renaissance architecture." They might have discovered it by accident one day when they were at the flea market buying necklaces and other finery. Delighted, they might have brought their friends and shown them this enchanting spot, which they had not spent long years imagining. It was unlikely that *they* had read books about every stone and every site, until their eyes had sickened and they could no longer see beauty in anything unless it was exactly the way they had imagined it back home. No doubt they could look at some white pillars standing against the southern blue sky and rejoice without any pedantic curiosity about which temple to which forgotten god had once stood there.

He had dreamed — and read. And he understood that nothing in reality looked exactly as he had expected. Everything turned so gray and harsh in the clear light of day. The dreams had swathed his fantasy images in a soft chiaroscuro, rounding and closing them off harmoniously, spilling a summer-green over the ruins. He would end up merely walking around to see whether everything was where it should be, all that he had read about. Later he could rattle off all the places in the books back at the private school for young ladies and say that he had seen them — and he wouldn't have a single thing to add about anything he had discovered for himself. He would learn nothing other than what he had already read. Whenever he met living human beings he would always try to select one of the dead, fictitious figures he knew, to see if there was someone they resembled. Because how was he supposed to know anything else about living human beings — he, who had never lived?

But Heggen over there, with his thick red lips — he wasn't the type to dream of some romantic tale like the ones in the Novel Library published by the *Family Journal* if he struck up an acquaintance with a young girl on the streets of Rome one evening.

Gram suddenly began to feel the effects of the wine he had been drinking.

"If you go home to bed now you'll have a headache in the morning," Frøken

Winge told him as they stood outside in the dark street once again. The three others were walking on ahead; Helge followed a few steps behind with Jenny.

"Yes, but Frøken Winge — be quite honest, don't you think I'm an awfully boring fellow to have along?"

"No, my dear. It's just that you don't know us, and we don't know you — not yet."

"I have such a hard time getting to know people — never really do. I shouldn't have agreed to come when you were kind enough to invite me tonight. Apparently it takes practice to have fun." He tried to laugh.

"Yes, I'm sure it does." Helge could hear from her voice that she was smiling. "I was twenty-five years old before I started practicing. And God knows it wasn't easy for me in the beginning either."

"You? I thought you artists always . . . By the way, I didn't think you were even close to twenty-five."

"Oh yes, thank God — I'm much older than that."

"You say 'thank God' about such a thing? And here I am, and a man at that . . . I don't know . . . For every year that seems to drip away from me into eternity . . . without bringing anything but humiliation when I see that other people have no use for me . . . don't want to be around me . . ." Helge stopped, suddenly horrified. He could feel his own voice trembling — and he had an inkling that he must be slightly drunk to be talking this way to a lady he didn't even know. But he went on, in spite of his own shyness. "I think it's utterly hopeless. When my father talks about the youths of his day — evidently they all talked at once about golden illusions and things like that. I've never had a single damned illusion to talk about in all the years I've spent growing up. And those years are gone now — wasted — can never be retrieved."

"That's not true, what you just said, Herr Gram. No years of a person's life are wasted, as long as you're not in a position where suicide is the only way out. And I don't think those who lived in the time of golden illusions were any better off — their youthful illusions robbed them of life. We — most of the young people I know — start off without illusions. We were thrown into the struggle for existence, almost all of us, before we were fully grown. And we saw things right from the beginning that taught us to expect the worst. And then one day we learned that we could manage to reap quite a bit of good out of it. Something happened that made us think: If you can bear this, you can bear the knife. Once you've gained your self-confidence in this way, it's not an illusion that chance circumstances or fellow human beings can plunder from you."

"Oh — circumstances — or chance — can be such that no amount of self-confidence does any good. When they're stronger than you are."

"Yes," she laughed. "Of course — after a ship sets sail, chance may make it go under. One flaw in the casting of a wheel and everything shatters. A collision. But you can't think about that. And you have to make an attempt to conquer circumstances. Most often you'll find a way out in the end."

"I see that you're quite an optimist, Frøken Winge."

"Yes." She walked on for a moment. "I've become one. Now that I've seen how much people can actually endure . . . without losing their courage to keep on fighting, and without becoming demeaned."

"That's exactly what I think they become. Demeaned — or diminished, at any rate."

"Not everyone. And I think the very fact that *some* people refuse to be denigrated or diminished by life is enough to make anyone an optimist. This is where we're going," she added.

"I think it looks more like a *boîte* in Montmartre or somewhere like that, don't you?" Helge looked around.

Lining the walls of the tiny room were upholstered plush benches. There were small marble tables, and on the counter stood two nickel spirit lamps with flames underneath.

"Oh, I think these kinds of places probably look much the same everywhere," said Jenny. "Do you know Paris?"

"No, I just thought . . ."

Suddenly he felt unreasonably annoyed. Here was this little artist girl, who could, of course, romp around in the world wherever she liked — and Lord only knew where they got their money from. It was just as natural for them to have been in Paris as in Dronningen Pub in Kristiania one evening. For someone like this it was so easy to talk about self-confidence. A minor disappointment in love in Paris, which she forgot in Rome — that was doubtless the worst she had ever experienced. And then she felt so damned brave and cocky, grown up enough to face the rest of life.

Her figure was almost gaunt, even though her complexion was fresh and her coloring lovely.

What he wanted most was to talk to Frøken Jahrmann. She was wide awake now, but completely monopolized by Ahlin and Heggen. In the meantime

Frøken Winge was eating fried eggs and plain bread and drinking steamed milk.

"What a peculiar crowd," he turned to her all the same. "Real criminal types, every one of them, if you ask me!"

"Yes, I suppose there are all sorts here. But you have to remember that Rome is a big modern city — there are lots of people who work at night. And this is one of the few places that's open at all hours. Aren't you hungry? I'm going to have some black coffee."

"Do you always stay out so late?" Helge looked at his watch; it was almost four.

"Not at all." She laughed. "Just once in a while. Then we watch the sun come up and go off to have breakfast. And now Frøken Jahrmann doesn't want to go home tonight."

Helge hardly knew himself why he kept sitting there. They drank a bluish green liqueur, which made him drowsy, but the others laughed and chattered. Names of people and places he didn't know swirled past him.

"No, you know what, that Norman Douglas with his sermonizing . . . He can't fool me. I have to tell you, one morning we were alone in the life drawing studio, he and I and the Finn — you remember, Lindberg — and the Finn and I go out to get some coffee — this was in June. When we go back upstairs, there sits Douglas with the girl on his lap. We pretended it was nothing. But he never asked me to tea after that."

"Good Lord," said Jenny. "Was it that bad?"

"In the middle of spring — in Paris," said Heggen with a laugh. "Let me tell you, Cesca . . . Douglas *was* a fine fellow — you shouldn't think otherwise. Talented too; he showed me some charming things from out at the fortifications."

"Yes, and do you remember the one from Père Lachaise, with the violet-pearl wreaths on the lower left?" said Jenny.

"Oh, that's right — it was damned enchanting. And what about the girl at the piano?"

"Yes, but remember that disgusting model?" said Frøken Jahrmann. "It was that fat, middle-aged blonde, you know. And then he made such a show of being so virtuous."

"But he was," said Heggen.

"Ha! And there I was just about to fall in love with him for that very reason."

"Oh, I see! Well, that casts a different light on the matter."

"Yes, he proposed to me so many times," said Fransiska thoughtfully. "And I had actually decided to say yes. But it turned out lucky that I didn't."

"If you had said yes," said Heggen, "then you never would have seen him with the model sitting on his lap."

Fransiska Jahrmann's face changed abruptly. A tremor flashed lightning quick across her supple features. Then she laughed.

"Hmph — you're all alike. I don't trust a single one of you, my boy. *Per bacco.*"

"You mustn't think that, Francesca." Ahlin raised his head from his hand for a moment.

She laughed again.

"You know, I think I need some more liqueur!"

———

Toward morning Helge walked with Jenny Winge along the dark, deserted street. Once, the party in front of them stopped. Two half-grown boys were sitting on a stone stairway. Fransiska and Jenny spoke to the children and gave them some money.

"Beggars?" asked Helge.

"I don't know. The older boy said he sells newspapers."

"The beggars down here, they're mostly phonies, aren't they?"

"I don't know. Maybe some of them are, maybe even most of them. But a lot of people sleep on the street, even now, in the middle of winter. Many of them are crippled and . . ."

"I saw it in Florence. Don't you think it's scandalous? People with horrible sores — or terribly deformed — and they're allowed to go around begging? The authorities should really take care of the poor things."

"I don't know. That's the way things are down here. We're foreigners and can't be the judge. It could be they like it better this way — earn more this way."

"At the Piazzale Michelangelo there was a beggar with no arms — his hands stuck right out of his shoulders. The German doctor I was staying with told me that the man owned a villa at Fiesole."

"Yes, but that's splendid, isn't it?"

"Back home the crippled learn to work," objected Helge. "So they can make an honest living."

"I don't think a villa would ever come of that," she said and laughed.

"Yes, but can you imagine anything more demoralizing than making a living by displaying your disability?"

"I suppose it's always rather demoralizing to find out that you're crippled."

"But still — to make a living by invoking sympathy."

"The person who's crippled knows that he's going to be pitied. And he *has* to accept help — from people or from God."

———◦◦◦———

Jenny climbed a few stairs and lifted the corner of the door's curtain, which resembled a worn mattress. They were standing in a tiny church.

Candles burned on the altar. Their glow splintered across the bronze rays of the halo on the monstrance cupboard, shimmered restlessly over the candleholders and metal objects, and turned the paper roses in the altar vases blood-red and golden-yellow. A priest was standing with his back to them, reading silently from a book; a couple of choirboys tiptoed back and forth, bowing and crossing themselves and making a series of gestures that were meaningless to Helge.

Otherwise the small church room was dark; in two side chapels the flames of tiny night lamps flickered, hovering in their darkly gleaming metal chains in front of paintings that were even blacker than the darkness.

Jenny Winge knelt down on a straw footstool. Her hands lay clasped on the ledge in front of her, and she held her head tilted slightly back so her profile was sharp against the soft golden radiance of the candlelight, which shimmered in the curls of her upswept hair and crept across the slender, naked arc of her throat.

Heggen and Ahlin soundlessly lifted chairs with woven seats from a pile stacked up around one of the pillars.

There was something quaint and poignant about this silent church service before dawn. Gram eagerly followed every movement of the priest up at the altar. A choirboy draped a white robe with a gold cross over his shoulders. Then the priest took the monstrance from the cupboard over the altar, turned around, and held it out to the light. The boys swung their incense vessels; gradually the sharp, sweet smoke drifted over to them. But Helge waited in vain for music or song.

Frøken Winge apparently flirted a bit with Catholicism, since she was kneeling there like that. Heggen sat and stared straight ahead at the altar. He had placed one arm around Frøken Jahrmann's shoulders; she had fallen asleep and was leaning against him. He couldn't see Ahlin, who was sitting behind a pillar; no doubt he too was asleep.

It was actually quite odd to be sitting here with these utter strangers. He felt alone, but this time it didn't distress him. The free, happy mood from the night before had returned. He looked at the others, at the two young women: Jenny and Fransiska. He now knew what their names were, but not much else. And none of them knew what it meant to him to be sitting here — or all that he had put behind him, all the painful struggles he had run from back home, or what obstacles he had fought his way through, what bonds had confined him. He felt a strange, almost superior joy about everything, and he looked at the two women with gentle sympathy. Such children they were, Cesca and Jenny, green and fresh with little self-assured opinions behind their white, smooth, girlish brows. Two lively, pretty girls who moved along their unswerving paths through life, perhaps with a few pebbles to sweep aside now and then, just for a change — but they knew nothing about paths like his. Poor things, how would life go for them if they had to try it themselves?

He gave a start when Heggen touched his shoulder. He blushed; he had dozed off.

"I see you took a little nap too," said Heggen.

Outside, the tall buildings stood silent in the gray dawn, sleeping with closed shutters on every floor. But in a side street a clanging trolley crossed the inter-section, a hansom cab rattled over the cobblestones, and a few frozen and sleepy figures trudged along the sidewalk.

They turned down a street, at the end of which they could see the obelisk in front of the Trinità dei Monte church; it stood white against the dark evergreen oaks of the Pincio. There wasn't a soul in sight, and not a sound but their own footsteps on the cobblestones and a small fountain trickling in a courtyard. Far off in the distance, through the silence, splashed the fountain on Monte Pincio against its stone basin. Helge recognized it, and as they walked toward the sound, a slender, delicate spray of joy shot up inside him — as if his own hap-piness from the evening before awaited him up there at the spurting fount beneath the evergreen oaks.

He turned to Jenny Winge without being aware that his eyes and his voice were pleading for his small joy.

"I stood up here last night and watched the sun go down. I thought it was so strange . . . You see, I've been working for this for years. I had to come here for the sake of my studies. I was supposed to have been an archaeologist, but I had to become a teacher after I finished my secondary exams. I've been waiting for the day when I could come here — preparing myself for it. And then when I stood here, all of a sudden . . . It was as if I was completely unprepared."

"Yes," said Jenny, "I think I understand."

"In fact, from the moment I stepped off the train yesterday and saw the ruins of the baths right across from me . . . the sun above the massive ocher ruins, right in the middle of the splendid new buildings with cafés and cinemas . . . the trolleys in the square and the park and the lovely fountain, which contains such an abundance of water. I thought it was so beautiful with the old walls in the midst of the modern construction and the city traffic all around."

"Yes," she said with joy in her voice and nodded. "I like it too."

"And then I walked downward. All the new and the old interspersed. And fountains everywhere, trickling and gurgling and splashing. I walked straight over to San Pietro; it was dark by the time I reached it, and I stood there looking at the two fountains. I suppose they keep running all night here in the city?"

"All night long; almost anywhere you go, you can hear the fountains. It's so quiet in the streets here at night. At the place where we live, Frøken Jahrmann and I, there's a little fountain down in the courtyard. We have a balcony outside our rooms. On warm nights we sit outside and listen to it trickling until the early hours."

She had sat down on a stone banister. And Helge Gram was standing in the same spot as he had the evening before, once more gazing out at the city, which lay with the mountain ranges behind, light gray and crumbling beneath a sky as bright and clear as above the mountains in Norway. He drank in the icy pure, cold air.

"Nowhere else in the world," said Jenny Winge, "are the mornings like they are here in Rome. I mean, it's as if the whole city were sleeping — a sleep that grows lighter and lighter — and then suddenly it's awake, rested and fresh. Heggen says it's because of the shutters; there are no windowpanes to catch the morning light and blink."

They sat with their backs to the dawn and the golden sky, where the crowns of the stone pines in the Medici garden and the two small towers of the church with the pavilions on top were etched sharp and hard. There was still time before the sun arrived. But the gray blocks of buildings below slowly began to radiate color — as if in some astounding way the walls were illuminated with colors from within. Some of the buildings blushed until they were entirely rose-colored, some turned golden, some turned white. The villas out on the slopes of Monte Mario rose gleaming from the brown grass embankments and black cypresses.

Until all of a sudden a star seemed to wink from somewhere on the heights behind the city; there was a windowpane, after all, that had caught the first rays of the sun. And dark foliage was lit an olive-green over there.

A little bell began clanging down in the city.

Frøken Jahrmann came over and leaned sleepily against her friend.

"*Il levar del sole.*"

Helge tilted his head all the way back and stared up at the cool blue vault of the sky. Now there was a ray of sun touching the very tip of the jet spurting from the fountain; the drops glittered azure and gold.

"Oh, God bless all of you, how dreadfully sleepy I am," said Fransiska Jahrmann, yawning as widely as she could. "Brrr, how cold it is! Jenny, I'm surprised you're not freezing your better part off, the way you're sitting there on that stone. But now I've got to go to bed — *subito!*"

"Sleepy, yes!" Heggen yawned. "We should see about getting home now. Or rather, I'm going to have a cup of steamed milk at my *latteria* first. So, shall we go?"

They sauntered down the Spanish Steps. Helge looked at the tiny green leaves peeking out from between the white stone stairs.

"Imagine that anything can grow here, where so many people go trampling up and down."

"Oh yes — there's always something sprouting here, anywhere there's a bit of earth between two stones. You should have seen it this spring on the roof above our rooms. There's a little fig tree growing from the roof tiles. Cesca is so worried about whether it will make it through the winter, and what it will live on when it gets bigger. She's made a sketch of it."

"I understand your friend also paints, is that right?"

"Yes. She is very talented, Cesca is."

"I remember seeing one of your paintings at the national art exhibition last fall," said Helge, a little embarrassed. "Roses in a copper basin."

"Yes, I painted it down here last spring. I'm not quite satisfied with it anymore, by the way. I was in Paris for two months this summer, and I learned so much in that time. But I sold it — for three hundred kroner; that was the price I listed it for. And in fact, it did have some good qualities."

"Your style is so modern. But I suppose all of you paint that way?"

Jenny didn't reply but gave him a little smile.

The others were waiting for them at the bottom of the stairs. Jenny shook hands with everyone and said good-bye.

"I can't believe it," said Heggen. "Do you really intend to go out and work now?"

"Yes, of course!"

"You're out of your mind, you know."

"Oh no, Jenny, come home with me," fretted Fransiska.

"Why shouldn't I work if I'm not tired? Well, Herr Gram, I assume you'll want a cab to take you home, won't you?"

"Yes. But by the way, isn't the post office open by now? I know it's supposed to be close to Piazza di Spagna."

"I'm going right past it, so you can come along with me."

She nodded one last time to the others, who were starting to turn toward home. Fransiska Jahrmann clutched Ahlin's arm, stumbling with fatigue.

3

"So there was a letter for you," said Jenny Winge. She had stayed in the post office vestibule to wait. "Now let me show you which trolley you should take."

"Thank you, that would be most kind."

The piazza was white with sunshine. The air was morning-cold and still clear. But people and traffic were busily swarming in and out of the narrow streets all around.

"You know, Frøken Winge, I don't think I'll go home — I'm as wide awake as could be. I feel most like taking a walk. But perhaps you'd think it presumptuous of me to ask whether I might accompany you for a while . . ."

"No, not at all. But then how will you find your way back to your hotel?"

"Oh, it shouldn't be hard, now that it's light."

"And besides, you can find a cab just about anywhere."

They entered the Corso. She told him the names of the palazzos — but kept on getting ahead of him because she walked briskly, slipping nimbly among the throngs of people who were already filling the narrow sidewalk.

"Do you like vermouth?" she asked. "I'm going to slip in here and have one."

She drank it down in one gulp, standing at the marble counter of the bar. Helge didn't care for the bittersweet drink, which was mixed with quinine. But it was new to him, and he found it amusing to stop in at a bar in passing.

Jenny headed down the cramped streets where the air was raw and clammy. Only high overhead did the sunlight brush the walls of the buildings. Helge looked all around with alert interest, at the blue-painted carts with the mule teams, whose harnesses had brass fittings and red tassels; at the bareheaded women and dark-haired children; at the small, cheap shops and the stands of fruit and vegetables in the gateways. In one place an old man stood deep-frying clumps of dough on a stove that looked like a tar burner. Jenny bought one and offered a bite to Helge. But he declined. What a strange girl she was. She ate it with relish. He felt nauseated at the mere thought of the fat-drenched balls of dough between his teeth — and the taste of vermouth was still with him — after the various drinks of the night. Not to mention how filthy the old man was.

Side by side with dilapidated, wretched houses, where grayish laundry had been hung out to dry between broken shutters, stood enormous, imposing palazzos with grated windows and overhanging cornices. At one point Jenny took him by the arm — a fiery red automobile came honking out of a baroque portal and turned with difficulty, then sped off, up the narrow street where the center gutter was filled with trash and cabbage leaves.

He walked along, enjoying himself, because it was all so obviously foreign and Mediterranean. And because for years all his experiences had consisted of his fantasies and dreams colliding with an ordinary, petty reality, until finally, to protect himself from the pain, even he had begun to scoff at his dreams and temper his fantasies. So now he tried to remind himself that of course the same types of people lived in these romantic districts as in every other big city: shop clerks and factory workers and typesetters and telegraphists, people who worked every day in stores and offices and with machinery, who were the same as in every other place in the world nowadays. But he thought about this with a strange sense of joy, because these streets and buildings, which resembled what he had dreamed of, were such a tangible reality.

They came out into an open square, where the baking sun was white and gentle after their walk through the narrow streets with the damp, fetid air. Beyond the square, where the earth had been dug up in all directions, and piles of garbage and trash lay among heaps of rubble, stood old, decaying houses, some of them half demolished, with exposed rooms where a wall was missing — and amid them all, ancient ruins.

Walking past scattered buildings that stood as if temporarily forgotten during the ongoing demolition, they came to the piazza of the Temple of Vesta. Behind the big new steam mill and the lovely little old church with its columned vestibule and elegant bell tower rose the Aventine Hill with the cloisters on top, clear against the sunny sky, with dusty gray arches of nameless ruins scattered among the gardens on the steep slopes, and with an abundance of black ivy and naked gray rosebushes and yellow winter-withered reeds.

This was what had always disappointed him — in Germany and in Florence — the ruins he had read about, imagining them standing in a romantic frame of foliage and greenery, with flowers in the wall crevices, the way they looked in the old copperplate engravings or on stage sets. In reality they were dirty and dusty, and yellow pieces of trash and dented tin cans and filth were scattered all around them; a sharp winter air hovered over them, and the vegetation of the south was nothing but grayish black evergreens and bare, thorny bushes and faded yellow reeds.

Now in the sun-bright morning he suddenly understood that even this could be beautiful to someone who was able to see.

Behind the church Jenny Winge turned down a lane between the garden walls. Stone pines rose up on either side, and ivy tumbled over the walls. She stopped and lit a cigarette.

"Yes," she said, "I've succumbed to tobacco, but it's not good for Cesca to smoke because of her heart, so I have to refrain whenever she's watching. Out here I puff away like a steam engine. Here we are."

A small ocher-colored house stood just inside a board fence. In the garden were a table and benches under a couple of large, bare elm trees, along with a gazebo made of rushes. Jenny greeted with familiarity the old woman who came out of the door.

"How about it, Herr Gram — would you like some breakfast too?"

"That might be nice. A little strong coffee, and some bread and butter . . ."

"God bless you — coffee! And butter! Eggs and bread and wine, perhaps some salad and cheese. Yes, she says she has cheese. How many eggs would you like?"

While the woman set the table, Frøken Winge brought out her easel and paints. And she exchanged her long blue evening coat for a smock that was flecked with oil paint.

"Will you permit me to look at your painting?" asked Helge.

Jenny opened up her sketchpad.

"Yes. I'm going to tone down the green — it's so harsh right now. It doesn't have the proper light in it. I think the background is good."

Helge looked at the little picture in which the trees stood like green splotches. He couldn't see anything special about it.

"Oh, here's the food! I'm going to throw the eggs right back in her face if they're hard boiled — I really will. Thank God they're not!"

Helge wasn't hungry. Or at least the sour white wine made his throat burn, and he had a hard time swallowing the plain, unsalted bread. Jenny tore off big pieces with her white teeth, stuffed tiny bits of Parmesan cheese in her mouth, and drank wine. She had already devoured the three eggs.

"I don't know how you can eat that hard bread without butter," said Helge. She laughed.

"I think this kind of bread tastes wonderful. And I've hardly had any butter since I left Kristiania. Cesca and I serve it only to company. We have to live frugally, you know."

He laughed too.

"And what do you call frugal? Beads and coral necklaces?"

"Oh . . . Small luxuries . . . I almost think they're necessities — at least to a degree. No, we live cheaply and eat cheaply — buy silk scarves and then dine on tea and dry bread and radishes for a few weeks."

She was done eating and lit a fresh cigarette. She sat there looking past him with her chin in her hand.

"No, Herr Gram. To starve, you see — well, I've never tried it, but it might come to that one day. Heggen has, though, and he agrees with me. It's better to have too little of the necessities than never to have had anything extravagant. Extravagances — that's what people work for and long for.

"Back home at my mother's, we always had the necessities, though just barely. But anything beyond that was inconceivable. Well, all right, that's the way things have to be; children must have food, of course."

Helge smiled a little uncertainly. "I can't imagine that you're someone who's ever been acquainted with . . . financial difficulties."

"Why not?"

"Well, because you seem so undaunted, so free. You have such strong opinions. When a person grows up in circumstances where everything revolves around making ends meet and is always hearing about it . . . That person doesn't dare acquire any opinions — not in any real way. Because it's so painful to realize that money determines so much what you can afford to think — and want."

Jenny nodded thoughtfully. "Yes, but you shouldn't be that way. Not if you're lively and healthy and capable."

"But take me, for instance. I've always thought I had a talent for scholarly work. And that's the only thing I've ever wanted to do. I've written a couple of short books — of a rather popular nature — but now I'm working on a dissertation: the Bronze Age in southern Europe. But I'm a teacher, you see, and

I have quite a good position. I'm the vice principal of a private school."

"But now you've come down here. To work, if I understood you correctly, late last night," she said with a smile.

Helge didn't reply but went on. "That's how it was for my father too. He was going to be a painter, you see — that was the only thing he wanted to do. He spent a year down here. Then he got married. Now he owns a lithographic business. Has kept it running for twenty-six years — sometimes with great difficulty. I don't think my father feels he's gotten much out of life."

Jenny Winge stared pensively at the sunlight. At the foot of the slope where they sat, rows of garden herbs stood with little innocent tufts of leaves in the gray soil. And above the green meadows gleamed the heaped ruins on the Palatine, faded yellow against the dark foliage. It was going to be a warm day. The Alban Hills, beyond the pines of the distant villa gardens, loomed hazily against the misty blue of the sky.

"But Herr Gram . . ." She took a sip of her wine and continued staring straight ahead. With his eyes Helge followed the pale blue smoke of her cigarette; a gust of morning wind seized hold of it and whirled it out into the sunlight. She had crossed one leg over the other. She had trim ankles in thin, violet-colored stockings, and low-cut, bead-embroidered shoes on her feet. Her smock was open over her pleated, silver-gray dress with the white collar and over the necklace, which cast those rosy specks of light on her milky-white throat. Her leather cap had slid back on her blond, luxuriant hair. "Then at least you must have your father's support. I mean, he understands you — knows that you can't get stuck in that school when you have other work that's important to you."

"I'm not sure. He was very happy that I was coming here. But . . ." Helge searched for words. "My father and I have never been on intimate terms. And then there's my mother. She was afraid. Both that I might overexert myself and because of the finances — that my future would be uncertain. And my father can never take sides against my mother. They're so different, Father and Mother. I don't think she's ever understood him. So she gave all her attention to us children. She was terribly devoted to me when I was a boy, and she was jealous, even toward my father — that he might have more influence on me than she had. Yes, she was even jealous of my work, whenever I shut myself in my room in the evenings to study, you know. And as I said, she was afraid for my health and afraid that I might decide to give up my job."

Jenny nodded a few times thoughtfully.

"It was from them, the letter I received this morning." Helge picked it up and looked at it, but didn't open it. "It's my birthday today, you see," he said, trying to smile. "I'm twenty-six today."

"Happy birthday!" Frøken Winge shook his hand.

She looked at him, almost in the same way she had looked at Frøken Jahrmann when her friend nestled close to her.

She hadn't noticed Gram's appearance before — merely had the impression that he was tall and thin and dark haired, and that he had a little pointed beard. He actually had quite nice, regular features: a high, rather narrow forehead. His eyes were light brown, with an oddly transparent amber sheen. And he had a small, weak, delicate mouth beneath his mustache, with a touch of weariness and sorrow about it.

"I understand you so well," she said suddenly. "I know all about it. I was a teacher myself up until Christmas of last year. I worked as a governess and kept that position until I was old enough to start at a teacher's college." She laughed, a bit embarrassed. "I decided to travel and resigned my job as a schoolteacher when I inherited a small sum from one of my father's aunts. I've calculated that I can make it last about three years — maybe longer. I've undertaken some correspondence lately, and if I manage to sell something . . . But of course my mother doesn't like the idea that I'm going to use up all the money. Or that I resigned when I finally had a permanent position after all those years of struggling with substitute jobs and private pupils. Mothers always seem to think that a steady income —"

"I'm not sure that I would have dared in your situation. To burn all your bridges that way . . . And I realize I'm being influenced by my own home. I couldn't help being afraid about what I would live on after the money was gone."

"Nonsense," said Jenny Winge. "I'm healthy and strong and I have lots of skills. I can sew and cook and iron and wash laundry. And I know languages too. In America or England I'm sure I could always find something to do. And there are plenty of things I could paint. Fransiska . . ." She laughed at the sunlight. "She wants us to go to South Africa and become milkmaids, because she claims that's something she's good at. And then we'll make nude sketches of the Zulu tribesmen — they're supposed to be such splendid models."

"Not exactly trivial plans, either. So you don't consider distance to be a significant obstacle?"

"No, not at all. I know, it's easy to talk. Of course, during all those years at home, I thought it would be completely impossible to go anywhere — even just to Copenhagen, and stay there awhile to do nothing but study and paint. And of course I had a few palpitations when I decided to give up everything and go abroad. My whole family thought it was madness. And I could feel their influence over me; but I'd made up my mind. Because painting is the only thing I've ever wanted to do, and I could see that at home I'd never be able to work with the intensity I needed to. There were so many distractions. But Mamma couldn't possibly understand that I had reached an age where if I was going to learn anything, it had to be now. My mother is only nineteen years older than I am, you see. And when I was eleven, she remarried, and that made her even younger.

"That's the wonderful thing about going abroad — all influences of the people you happen to live with back home are suspended. You have to see things with your own eyes and think for yourself. And you realize that whatever you get out of the trip will depend entirely on you: what you're capable of seeing and comprehending, and how you behave, and who you choose to have an effect on you. And you learn to understand that what you get out of life depends solely on yourself. Yes, a little on circumstances, of course, as you said before. But you find out how, in accordance with your own nature, you can most easily overcome or get around obstacles — both during your travels and in general. You discover that the worst difficulties you encounter are usually things you've brought on yourself.

"People are never alone at home, are they, Gram? That's what I think is the best thing about traveling — being alone and not having anyone around who wants to help or advise. You can't see or be grateful for the good you've gained from home until you're away. You know that you'll never be dependent on your home again, once you've become self-reliant. You can't fully love it until then. You can't love something you're dependent on, can you?"

"I don't know. Aren't you always dependent on what you love? You're dependent on your work, aren't you? And if you're fond of someone," he said softly, "isn't that when you first become truly dependent?"

"Well, yes . . ." She thought for a moment. "But then you've made your own choice," she said briskly. "I mean, you're not a slave; you voluntarily serve something or someone that you value more than yourself. But aren't you glad that you're going to start off your new year alone — free as a bird — and work only on whatever you decide?"

Helge thought about the evening before at Piazza San Pietro. He gazed out at the strange city, at the muted, gray-veiled colors in the sunlight, and at the strange, fair-haired girl.

"Yes, I am."

"Well." She stood up, buttoned her smock, and opened her paint box. "Now I've got to get busy."

"And I suppose you've had enough of my company?"

Jenny smiled. "You must be tired by now, aren't you?"

"Not at all. But I should pay . . ."

She called the woman and settled the bill for him as she squeezed pigment onto her palette.

"Do you think you can find your way back to town?"

"Oh yes, of course. I paid close attention to the way we came. And I'm sure I'll find a cab soon enough. Do you ever come to the club?"

"Occasionally."

"I'd like to see you again, Frøken Winge."

"I'm sure you will." She thought for a moment. "If you'd like . . . You could drop by for tea. We live at Via Vantaggio 111. Cesca and I are usually home in the afternoon."

"Thank you, I'd like that very much." He hesitated for a moment. "Well, good-bye then. And thank you. Thank you for the evening."

He held out his hand. And she grasped it with her slender, thin fingers. "My pleasure."

When he turned around at the gate, she was standing there, scraping at the canvas with her palette knife. She was humming — it was the ballad from the night before. Now it came back to him like an old friend. And he hummed it to himself as he walked down the street.

4

Jenny took her hands out from under the blanket and put them behind her neck. But it was ice cold in the room, and dark; not even a strip of daylight between the shutters. She struck a match and looked at the clock: almost seven in the evening. She could lie here a little longer and doze. She crawled all the way under the blanket again and burrowed her cheek in the pillow.

"Jenny? Are you asleep?" Fransiska opened the door without knocking. She came over to the bed and fumbled in the dark for her friend's face — patting her. "Tired?"

"No, no. I'm getting up now."

"So when did you get home?"

"Around three. I was out on the Prati and took a swim before lunch, and then I ate over at the Ripetta, you know the place. Then I went to bed when I got home. I'm completely rested now — I'm getting up!"

"Wait a bit — it's so cold in here. I'll get in with you." Fransiska lit the lamp on the table.

"You could just call for the signora — oh, come here, Cesca, let me see!" Jenny sat up in bed.

Fransiska placed the lamp on the nightstand and slowly turned in the light.

She had put on a white lace blouse with her green skirt and slung a bronze-colored silk scarf with peacock-blue stripes around her shoulders. Around her neck hung the double row of big, deep-red corals; long polished earrings dangled against her golden-white skin. Smiling, Fransiska pushed her hair aside to show that they were tied around her ears with a piece of darning thread.

"And to think that I got them for eighty-six lire — wasn't that splendid? Do you think they suit me?"

"Splendid. That outfit is so damned . . . you know, I should paint you dressed like that."

"All right. I could sit for you right now. I'm too restless to do any work today. Oh, Jenny . . ." She gave a little sigh and sat down on the edge of the bed. "No, wait — I'm going to do something about the fire."

She came back with embers in a stone crock and knelt down in front of the little stove.

"Just stay where you are, Jenny dear, until it gets warmer. I'll straighten the bed and set the table. And make some tea. Oh, you brought home your study — let me see!"

She leaned the study board against a chair where the light could shine on it. "My, oh my!"

"It's not half bad, is it? I need to make a few more sketches out there. I'm thinking of a large painting. Isn't it a good motif, with all the workers and the mule carts down there in the excavation area?"

"Yes, I think so . . . I think you've got something there. I can't wait to show this to Gunnar and Ahlin. Oh, are you getting up? Well, let me fix your hair then, Jenny!

"God, what wonderful hair you have, my girl. Won't you let me pin it up in a modern style, with ringlets? You will?" Fransiska ran her fingers through the long blond tresses. "Sit still then. A letter came for you this morning. I brought it up. Did you find it? It was from your little brother, wasn't it?"

"Yes, it was," said Jenny with a laugh.

"Was it amusing? Did it make you happy?"

"Of course it was amusing. Oh, Cesca, sometimes I wish . . . that I could just slip home and take a walk across Nordmarken with Kalfatrus. Because he's such a sweet boy, you know."

Fransiska looked at Jenny's smiling face in the mirror. Then she unpinned her friend's hair and started brushing it out again.

"No, Cesca, we don't have time."

"Yes, we do. If they get here early, they can go into my room. It looks like a pigsty, but who cares. But they won't come early. At least not Gunnar — and I'm not going to make any special effort for him. Or Ahlin either. By the way, he dropped by to visit me around noon. I was in bed and he sat and chatted. I sent him out to the balcony while I got dressed. And then we went out and had a fancy lunch at the Tre Re. We spent the whole afternoon together."

Jenny didn't say anything.

"We saw Gram at the Nazionale. Oh, he's so dreadful, Jenny. Have you ever met the likes of him?"

"I don't think he's dreadful at all. He's awkward, poor thing. Just like I was in the beginning. One of those people who wants to have fun but doesn't know how."

"'I came on the train from Florence,'" mimicked Fransiska, and laughed. "Ugh. As if he might have come by airplane."

"You were shamelessly rude to him, my child. That's not right. Actually, I was thinking of inviting him over tonight. But I didn't dare, for your sake. I didn't want to risk having you be impolite toward him when he was our guest."

"There wouldn't be any risk of that. You know that quite well." Fransiska was offended.

"Do you remember the time in Paris when I brought Douglas home with me to tea?"

"Yes, but that was after the episode with the model!"

"Good Lord. Besides, what did it have to do with you?"

"How can you say that? As I said, he had proposed to me. And I had almost decided to accept."

"He couldn't very well know that," said Jenny.

"Well, I hadn't given him a definite no, anyway. And the day before I'd gone out to Versailles with him. And I let him kiss me again and again and put his head in my lap in the park too. And when I told him I didn't love him, he said he didn't believe me."

"Cesca." Jenny caught her eye in the mirror. "You don't know what you're saying. You can be the nicest little girl in the world, when you want to be. But sometimes it seems as if you don't notice that you're dealing with *human beings*. Human beings who have feelings that you *have* to take into consideration. And you *would* take them into consideration if you tried. Because you do want to be sweet and kind."

"*Per bacco*. Are you sure about that? No, just wait, I'm going to show you the roses. Ahlin bought me an armful this afternoon at the Spanish Steps." Cesca smiled defiantly.

"I don't think you should let him do things like that. For one thing, you know that Ahlin can't afford it."

"Is that my concern? Since he's in love with me, he probably finds it amusing."

"I won't even talk about your reputation. Or what it'll be like after these endless escapades of yours."

"No, it's not worth mentioning my reputation. You're so very right about that. My reputation back home in Kristiania . . . I've thoroughly ruined it once and for all." She laughed giddily. "Who cares, anyway. It just makes me laugh."

"But sweet Cesca. I don't understand. You don't care about any of these men. Why do you want . . . And this thing with Ahlin — don't you realize . . . He's quite serious. Norman Douglas was quite serious too. You don't know what you're doing. God forgive me, but I don't think you have the slightest instinct, my child."

Fransiska put down the comb and brush and looked at Jenny's coiffed hair in the mirror. She tried to maintain her defiant little smile. But it faded, and her eyes filled with tears.

"I had a letter this morning too." Her voice quavered. Jenny stood up. "From Berlin — from Borghild. Maybe you should see about getting ready, Jenny. Do you want to put the teakettle on now, or should we steam the artichokes first? They'll be here soon, won't they?"

She moved away, set about straightening the bed.

"We could call for Marietta, but we'd rather do it ourselves, wouldn't we, Jenny?

"Well. She writes that Hans Hermann has gotten married. Last week. I suppose she's quite far along by now . . ."

Jenny put down the matchbox. She cast an anxious glance at Fransiska's small, pale face. Then she cautiously went over to her.

"She's the one he was engaged to, you see. That singer — Berit Eck." Fransiska's voice was barely audible. For a moment she leaned against her friend. Then she went back to tucking in the sheet with trembling fingers.

Jenny stayed where she was.

"But you knew they were engaged — they've been engaged for over a year."

"I know. No thank you, Jenny, let me do it. If you would just put on the tablecloth . . ."

Jenny quietly set the tea table for four. Fransiska spread the coverlet over the bed and brought in her roses. She stood fumbling with the bodice of her dress, then pulled out an envelope and turned it over a few times in her hands.

"She says that she met them at the Tiergarten. She wrote . . . Oh, she can be so cruel, Borghild can." Fransiska rushed over to the stove and tore open the door — tossed the letter inside. She collapsed in the nearby armchair. Then her tears flowed freely.

Jenny went over and put her arm around her neck.

"Cesca — dear little Cesca!"

Fransiska pressed her face against Jenny's arm.

"And she looked so miserable, the poor thing. She was trudging along, holding on to his arm and looking petulant and ill tempered. Yes, I can see it all so vividly. Oh God, the poor girl — to put herself in a position where she's dependent on him in that way. To think she could be such a fool . . . when she knows how he is . . .

"Oh, but just think, Jenny — he's going to have a little baby with someone else. Oh God, oh God, oh God."

Jenny had sat down on the arm of the chair. Cesca snuggled close to her.

"No, I don't suppose I have any instinct, as you say. Maybe I never even really loved him properly. But I wanted so much to have a child with him. And yet I still couldn't persuade myself . . . Sometimes he'd say we should get married — go right to the magistrate. But no, I always refused. They would have been so angry back home. And if we had done it like that, people would have thought that we had to get married. And I didn't want that either. Even though they thought the worst, of course. But I didn't care. I knew that I was completely ruining my reputation for his sake. But it didn't matter to me. Do you understand? It didn't matter.

"But Hans thought I refused because I was afraid he wouldn't marry me afterward. 'So let's just go to the magistrate, you cursed girl,' he'd say. But I wouldn't. He thought it was all pure calculation. 'You're a cold one,' he said. 'But only as long as you want to be.' Sometimes I thought it was true. Maybe it was just that I was scared he was a little too brutish. He hit me sometimes — practically tore the clothes off me. I had to scratch and bite to get away — weep and wail."

"And you still kept on seeing him?" said Jenny gently.

"Oh yes. I certainly did. The landlady refused to clean for him anymore. So I went up there and did it myself. I had a key to his rooms. And I washed the floor, straightened things up, made the bed — God only knows who had been lying in it with him . . ."

Jenny shook her head.

"Borghild was furious about it. She's the one who convinced me that he had a lover. I had my suspicions, but I didn't want to know for sure. Borghild claimed he had just given me a key so that I would come in and surprise them. Then I'd be so jealous that I'd give in, since my reputation was already compromised. But she's wrong about that. I was the one he *loved* — in his own way. He did love me, Jenny. As much as he could love anyone.

"But Borghild was so angry because I pawned the diamond ring that belonged to Great-Grandmother Rustung. No, I don't think I ever told you about that."

She stood up and gave a little laugh.

"You see, he *had* to have money. A hundred kroner. I said I would give him the money. Had no idea where I was going to get it. I didn't dare ask Pappa for even an øre — I'd already spent far too much. So I went to the pawnbroker with my watch and gold link bracelet and that diamond ring. One of those old-fashioned kind, you know, with a cluster of tiny diamonds on a big flat setting. Borghild was so mad because she hadn't inherited it, as the oldest, but Grandmother had specifically said that I was to have it, since I was her namesake. So one morning, you see, I went down there as soon as they opened. Oh, I thought it was so mortifying. But I got the money and went up to see Hans. He asked me where I got it from, and so I told him. Then he kissed me, and he said, 'Give me the pawn ticket and the money, Kitten' — that's what he always called me. I gave them to him. I thought he was going to redeem the ticket, and I told him that he shouldn't. I was terribly touched by it, you see. 'I can take care of this another way,' said Hans, and then he took it and left. I stayed in his rooms and waited for him. Oh, I was so touched, because I knew that he had to have that money. I was going to go back and pawn everything again the next day. I didn't think it would be loathsome anymore — nothing would be loathsome anymore. I was ready to let him have anything he wanted. And then he came back. Do you know what he'd done?" She laughed though she was close to tears. "He redeemed the ticket at the Folkebank and pawned all my things at his 'private banker's,' as he called it. He could get much more for them there.

"Well, we spent the whole day carousing after that, you see. Champagne and everything. And then I went up to his rooms at night and he played — how he played, dear God! I lay on the floor and wept. I didn't care about anything else, as long as he would play like that — and for me alone. Oh, you haven't heard him play. If you had, you would understand everything. But afterward! Yes, then there was trouble. We fought like crazy. Yes, I managed to get away from him. Borghild was awake when I came home. My dress was torn to shreds. 'You look like a streetwalker,' said Borghild. 'And that's probably how you're going to end up.' I just laughed. It was five in the morning.

"But in the end I would have given in, let me tell you. If it hadn't been for one thing. Sometimes he would say, 'The Devil take me if you aren't the only decent girl I've ever met. There's not a man alive who could make you fall.' Wasn't that awful? 'I respect you, Kitten.' Imagine, he respected me because I wouldn't do what he was always begging and threatening me to do. And I, who kept wishing that I dared . . . I wanted so desperately to do anything to please him. If only I could have overcome my dread. He's such a brute, and I knew he had others . . . I just wished he'd stop frightening me — so I could. But then in his eyes I would have fallen.

"That's why I finally broke off with him. Since he wanted me to do something that he would despise me for in the end."

She snuggled closer under Jenny's caresses.

"You love me, don't you, Jenny?"

"You know I do. Dear little Cesca!"

"You're so kind, Jenny. Kiss me some more! Gunnar is too. And Ahlin. I'll behave. I promise you I won't hurt him. Maybe I'll even marry him, since he's so in love with me. Ahlin would never be cruel, I know that. You don't think he would torment me, do you? At least not much. And then I could have some little babies. And you know, one day I'll come into money. And he's so poor. Then we could live abroad. I could work all the time. And he could too. There's something terribly splendid about everything he does, you know. That relief of the young boys playing. And the sketch for the Almquist monument. The composition isn't very original, but my God how charming and noble and serene it is — such wonderful plasticity in the figures."

Jenny smiled a little and smoothed down Fransiska's bangs; they were slightly damp from her tears.

"Oh yes, if only I could work forever. Oh, but Jenny. Those eternal pains in my heart. And my head. And my eyes, Jenny. I'm so deathly tired."

"You know what the doctor said — it's all nerves. If only you'd be sensible."

"Yes, yes. That's what they say. But I'm so frightened. You say I have no instinct. Maybe not in the way you mean, but in a different way I do. I've been a witch this week. I know that. But I've been waiting . . . I could *feel* something dreadful coming. And now you see!"

Jenny kissed her again.

"I was down at Sant'Agostino this afternoon. You know that miraculous Madonna painting? I knelt down and tried to pray to the Virgin Mary. I think it would be good for me to become a Catholic. A woman like the Virgin Mary, for example, would understand me much better. And I probably shouldn't get married, being the way I am. I could enter a convent — in Siena, for instance. I could do copying work in the gallery; the convent could make money on it. When I was copying the angel by Melozzo da Forli in Florence, there was a nun who came every day to work on a copy. And it wasn't bad." She laughed. "Well, actually, it was utterly hideous. But they all said that my copies were good. And they were too. I think I could be happy doing that . . .

"Oh Jenny, if only I felt well. If only I had some peace and weren't so confused and scared inside . . . Then I'd be well. And I could work, do nothing but work. I would be so nice, so nice. God, how nice I would be.

"I'm not always nice. I know that. I give in to all sorts of moods whenever I'm feeling the way I do now. But I'll stop doing that, if only all of you will love me. Especially you. We'll invite that Gram over. The next time I see him I'll go right up to him and act so nice and sweet; you won't even believe it. We'll ask him over and take him along when we go out; I'll gladly stand on my head to please him. Do you hear me, Jenny? You'll be kind to me now, won't you?"

"Yes, Cesca."

"Gunnar doesn't take me seriously," she said thoughtfully.

"Oh yes he does. He just thinks you can be so childish. You know what he says about your work . . . Do you remember what he said in Paris? About your energy — about your talent? 'Both exquisite and personal,' he said. He was certainly taking you seriously then."

"Yes, I suppose so. You know, Gunnar is a splendid fellow. But he was so furious about that episode with Douglas."

"Any man would have been. And I was too."

Fransiska sighed. She sat in silence for a moment.

"Tell me . . . how did you get rid of Gram? I thought you'd never get away from that man — that he would follow you home and be lying here on the sofa, at the very least!"

Jenny laughed. "No. He went with me out to the Aventine and ate break-fast, and then he went home. But you know, I rather like him."

"*Dio mio!* Jenny, your kindness is abnormal. I draw the line at you playing mother to all of us. Or is it that you've fallen in love with him?"

Jenny laughed again. "There's not much hope of that. Though he could eas-ily fall in love with you, of course. If you're not careful."

"They all do. God only knows why. But they get over it soon enough. And then they're mad at me afterward." She sighed.

Someone was coming up the stairs.

"It's Gunnar. I'm going to my room for a bit. I have to bathe my eyes, Jenny. You understand."

She slipped out, whispering hello to Heggen as she passed him in the door-way. He came in and shut the door behind him.

"I see you're looking well, Jenny. For that matter, you always do. What an amazing person you are. And I suppose you worked all morning? What about her?" He tipped his head toward Cesca's room.

"Not good. Poor little thing!"

"I saw it in the paper. I stopped at the club recently. Oh, let me see — are you done with the study? It's enchanting, Jenny. Yes, it certainly is."

Heggen held the painting up to the light and looked at it for a long time.

"Quite enchanting. This part here . . . beautifully placed, Jenny. I think it's very powerful." He continued, "Is she in there crying again?"

"I don't know. But she was sitting here crying. Her sister wrote to her."

"If I ever run into that lout," said Heggen, "I swear I'll find some pretext to give him a good thrashing."

5

Helge Gram sat poring over the Norwegian newspapers in the club one afternoon. He was alone in the dimly lit reading room. Then Frøken Jahrmann
came in.

Helge stood up to greet her.

She came right over and gave him her hand, smiling. "My dear, how are
you? Jenny and I were just talking about you. Couldn't understand why we
never see you. We'd just decided to come up on Saturday to visit you, and take
you out to have a little fun afterward. Have you found a room?"

"No, unfortunately. I'm still staying at the hotel. All the rooms are so expensive that . . ."

"Well, surely it isn't any cheaper at the hotel? You must be paying at least
three francs a day. Yes, I thought so. No, Rome isn't cheap, you know. In the
winter you need a room with sunlight. And since you don't speak Italian . . . If
only you had come to see us — Jenny or I would have gladly gone with you to
look, I can assure you."

"Thank you so much, but I really couldn't trouble you!"

"Trouble? My dear . . . But how are you? Have you met anyone you know?"

"No. I was here at the club on Saturday, but I didn't speak to anyone. I sat
and read the papers. Well, yes, I exchanged a few words with Heggen the day
before yesterday over in the café on the Corso. And I ran into two German doctors whom I knew slightly in Florence. We went out to the Via Appia together
one day."

"Ugh. Do you find German doctors amusing?"

Helge smiled, a bit embarrassed. "Oh, well, we do have quite a few interests
in common. And when you're walking along like that and don't have anyone
else to talk to . . ."

"Yes, but you must get used to speaking Italian. You've studied it, haven't you? If you'd like to take a walk with me, then we can speak nothing but Italian. I'll be your *maestra*. Extremely strict!"

"Thank you so much. But I'm sure you wouldn't find me very entertaining, Frøken Jahrmann — not intentionally, anyway."

"Nonsense. Oh, you know what? There were two old Danish ladies who left for Capri the day before yesterday. I wonder if their room is available — I'm sure it is. A nice little room, and cheap. I don't remember the name of the street, but I know where it is. Shall I take you over there and we can have a look at it? Come along!"

Halfway down the stairs she stopped and looked up at him with a coy little smile. "I was terribly rude toward you that evening we were out together, Gram. I must ask you to forgive me."

"My dear Frøken Jahrmann!"

"Yes, I was. But I was ill. And Jenny certainly gave me a piece of her mind, I can tell you that. But I deserved it."

"My dear, I was the one who intruded on all of you. But it was just . . . I saw you, and I heard you speaking Norwegian . . . I was so tempted to try to talk to you."

"Oh, I know. It would have been such fun — a little adventure. If only I hadn't been so rude. But I was ill, you see. I'm so nervous in the daytime, and I can't sleep, and then I can't work. It makes me impossible."

"You're not well in the daytime, Frøken Jahrmann?"

"No, not at all. And Jenny and Gunnar are working; everyone but me is working. How is your work coming along? Good? Are you happy?"

"Anyway, I'm sitting for Jenny in the afternoons. I have today off. I think it's mostly because she doesn't want me to wander around alone, brooding. So she goes on excursions with me, outside the city walls. She's practically like a mother to me. *Mia cara mammina.*"

"You seem exceedingly fond of your friend."

"Of course I am. She's so kind, so kind. I'm a sickly and spoiled child, you see. Jenny is the only one who can put up with me in the long run. And she's so clever and talented and full of energy. And beautiful. Don't you think she's lovely? You should see her hair when she lets it down! When I'm a good girl she lets me brush it and pin it up.

"This is it," she said.

They climbed a pitch-black stone staircase. "But don't let it bother you. Our entryway is even worse. You'll see when you come to visit us. Why don't you come over some evening? We'll get hold of the others and go out for a real Roman night on the town. I ruined our last one."

She rang the bell at the top floor. The woman who opened the door looked respectable and pleasant. She showed them to a small room with two beds. The window faced onto a gray courtyard in the back with laundry hanging out to dry from the windows, but there were flowers on the balconies, and atop the gray roof stood loggias and terraces with green shrubbery.

Fransiska talked steadily to the landlady as she peeked inside the stove and felt the beds, now and then informing Gram, "There's sun in here all morning. If you take out one of the beds, there's quite a lot of room, actually. The stove looks good. It costs forty lire, not including light or heat, and two for *servizio*. That's cheap. Shall I tell her you'll take it? You can move in tomorrow if you like!

"You don't have to thank me. I think it's fun being able to help you a little," she said on the stairs. "I hope you'll be comfortable here. Signora Papi is very clean, that much I know."

"I gather that's rather a rare virtue in this country, isn't it?"

"Oh, I don't think so. They're no better back home in Kristiania, the people who rent out lodgings. Where my sister and I live on Holbergsgaten . . . I put a new pair of patent leather shoes under the bed, but I never dared take them out again. Sometimes I would take a peek at them, and they stood there looking like two little furry white lambs."

"Hmm," said Helge. "I've always lived at home with my parents."

Fransiska suddenly laughed out loud. "You know, the signora thought I was your *moglie* — that both of us were going to live there. I told her I was your cousin, but I don't think she believed it for a minute. *Cugina* — I don't suppose it sounds very respectable anywhere in the world!"

They both had a good laugh over that.

"Would you like to take a walk?" asked Frøken Jahrmann all of a sudden. "Shall we go out to Ponte Molle? Have you been there? Do you feel like walking that far? We can take the trolley back, you know."

"Yes, but do *you* feel like it? Are you well enough?"

"It's good for me to walk. Go out and walk, Gunnar is always telling me. I mean Heggen."

She chattered incessantly, now and then glancing up to see if she was keeping him amused. They walked along the new road, following the Tiber. The river tumbled yellowish gray beneath the green slopes. There were small clouds, shiny as mother-of-pearl, above Monte Mario's dark thickets, with the yellowish gray clusters of villas among the evergreen trees.

Fransiska waved to a constable and told Gram with a laugh, "Just imagine, that fellow actually proposed to me. I often took strolls here alone, and I used to talk to him. And then he proposed to me. The son of our tobacconist has also proposed to me. Jenny gave me such a scolding. She said it was my own fault, and I suppose she might have been right."

"I think Frøken Winge seems to give you an awful lot of scoldings. She sounds as if she's quite a stern mamma."

"Jenny? No, only when I deserve it. If only someone had done it before . . ." she sighed. "Unfortunately, no one ever did."

Helge Gram felt lighthearted and free as he walked along beside her. There was something so soft about her — her stride, her voice, her face beneath the large plush cloche. It was as if he didn't really care for Jenny Winge when he thought about her right now. She had such self-assured, light gray eyes — and such a voracious appetite. Cesca was just saying that she hardly ever ate anything during the day.

And he said, "Frøken Winge seems to be a most decisive young woman."

"Yes, God knows she is. She has character, that one. Just imagine: She has always wanted to paint. But then she had to become a teacher. And she wore herself out! I know you can't see it now. She's so strong that she always manages to pull herself together. But when I first met her at art school . . . there was something — I don't know — so hard and remote about her; 'armored,' Gunnar says. She was extremely reserved; I didn't get to know her at all until she came down here. Her mother has been widowed twice — her name is Fru Berner — and she has three younger half siblings. Just imagine, they had a cramped two-room apartment, and Jenny slept in the maid's tiny room. She worked, and in her free time she studied and took her exams and helped her mother with the finances and the household. They didn't have a maid. And she didn't have any friends or acquaintances. She seems to close herself off whenever she encounters hardships, refusing to complain. But when things are going well, it's as if she opens her arms to everyone who needs her support."

Fransiska's cheeks were flushed. She looked up at him, wide eyed.

"You see, I've never had any troubles except those I've made for myself. I tend to be hysterical, and so I let my feelings run away with me. But Jenny has talked to me about it. She says the only irreparable troubles that we experience are those we've brought on ourselves. And if you can't train your will to conquer your emotions and desires, and the like, she says . . . If you're no longer master of yourself, you might as well just shoot yourself, Jenny says."

Helge smiled down at her. "Jenny says" and "Gunnar says" and "I had a friend who used to say." How young and trusting she was.

"Yes, but there are different laws that apply to Frøken Winge than to you. Don't you see — as different as the two of you are — even the very idea of living doesn't mean the same thing for two people."

"No," she said quietly. "But I'm so very fond of Jenny. And I need her so much."

They had reached the bridge. Fransiska leaned over the railing. Farther upriver, beneath brownish green slopes, stood a factory, and its tall, slender chimney cast a trembling reflection across the rushing yellow water. Beyond the rolling *campagna,* far inland, rose the Sabine Hills, mud-gray and bare, with bluish clefts, and behind them were snowcapped peaks.

"Jenny painted this, but in strong afternoon light. The factory and the chimney are bright red. And it was after one of those hot days, when you can't see the mountains through the haze, only a few glimpses of white snow high up in the heavy, metallic blue. And with clouds — there are big clouds above the snow. It's beautiful. I'll ask Jenny to show it to you."

"Couldn't we get a glass of wine here?" he asked.

"It'll be getting cold soon, but I suppose we could sit here for a while."

She led the way across the circular plaza on the other side of the bridge. From all the inns she chose a little garden. Behind several shelters with tables and chairs with woven seats stood a bench beneath the bare elm trees. Beyond the garden was a green meadow, and beyond that the heights on the other side of the river rose up dark against the cloud-pale sky.

Fransiska broke off a twig from the elder bushes along the fence. It had tiny, new green buds, which the cold had seared black at the tips.

"See how they put out shoots and then freeze all winter long? But when spring comes, they haven't suffered a bit."

When she put the twig down, he picked it up. And he kept on holding it.

They ordered white wine. Fransiska mixed water with hers and took only a few sips. Then she gave him an entreating smile.

"Would you give me a cigarette?"

"With pleasure — if you think you can handle it."

"Oh . . . I hardly smoke at all anymore. Jenny has almost given it up for good because of me. But tonight I think she's taking her revenge again. She's with Gunnar."

Fransiska smiled in the light of the match.

"But don't tell Jenny I've been smoking — do you hear me?"

"No, of course not." He laughed.

"You know . . ." she smoked thoughtfully. "I so wish that Jenny and Gunnar would get married. I'm worried that they won't; they've been good friends for such a long time. Then it's not easy to fall in love, is it? Not with someone you've known so well from before. And they're actually very much alike. But I've heard that opposites attract. I think it's silly that it has to be that way, but apparently it's true. Yet it would be better to fall in love with someone you felt a kinship for. Then there wouldn't be all the trouble and sorrow that comes with love. Don't you agree?

"Just imagine, Gunnar is from poor farming stock down in Smålenene. But then he came to Kristiania; his aunt who lives on Grünerløkken took him in, because there wasn't enough food to go around back home. He was nine years old at the time, and he delivered laundry for his aunt, who took in washing. Later he was apprenticed to a workshop. Everything he knows and can do, he taught himself. He can't stop reading, because everything interests him so keenly that he has to get to the bottom of it. Jenny says he practically forgets to paint. He's taught himself Italian so well that he can read any book — even poetry.

"Jenny's the same way. She's learned so much just because she found it amusing. I can never learn anything from books — reading gives me a headache. But Jenny and Gunnar tell me things. And then I remember. You must know an awful lot, yourself, Herr Gram. Won't you tell me a little about what you're studying? That's what I like best, having someone tell me things. Then I remember.

"Gunnar's the one who taught me to paint too. I was always drawing as a child; it came so easily to me. Then I met him up in the mountains three years ago. I was staying up there, painting. Well, I knew him slightly from before. I was painting pictures — horribly proper, without a trace of art to them. I could see that myself, but I couldn't figure out why. I wanted my paintings to say something, but I wasn't sure what it was, and I had no idea how to make them do it.

"But then I talked to Gunnar, showed him my work. He didn't have as much skill as I did back then, in terms of technique. He's only a few years older than me. But what he'd learned, he could use. Well, I painted two summer-night pictures. That odd chiaroscuro — all the colors are so deep, but they're also brilliantly intense. Of course the paintings weren't any good. But there was a hint of what I was looking for. I could see that *I* had painted them, and not just any young girl who had a smattering of talent. Do you know what I mean?

"There's a motif out here that I've used — a different road into the city. We'll go there someday. It's a road between two slanting walls — quite narrow. In one place there are two portals in the baroque style, with iron gates. A cypress stands next to each of them. I've done a couple of pen-and-ink sketches and colored them. There's a heavy, dark blue cloud above the cypresses and a clear green sky and a star, with a glimpse of roofs and cupolas in the city far off in the distance.

"It was supposed to show such pathos, you see . . ."

Twilight was quickly closing in. Her face shone pale beneath her hat.

"Shouldn't I . . . Don't you think . . . I've got to get well, I've got to work . . ."

"Yes," he whispered. "Oh yes. My dear . . ."

He could hear that she was breathing deeply. They sat in silence for a moment. Then he said in a low voice, "How fond you are of your friends, Frøken Jahrmann."

"Yes. And I want everyone to be my friend. I would be fond of everybody, you see." She said this quite softly, with a long sigh.

Helge Gram suddenly leaned forward and kissed her hand, which lay small and white on the table.

"Thank you," whispered Fransiska quietly.

They sat in silence.

"We must go, dear sir, it's getting cold . . ."

—◈—

The next day, when he moved into his new lodgings, a majolica vase of little blue irises stood in the sunlight on the table. The signora explained that his cousin had brought it over.

When Helge was alone, he bent over the flowers and kissed them all — one by one.

6

Helge Gram was happy in his room down near the Ripetta. He had a feeling of ease and pleasure as he worked at the little table in front of the window, which faced the courtyard with the laundry and the flowerpots on the balconies. The family directly across had two little children, a boy and a girl, about six or seven years old. Whenever they came out on the balcony they would nod to Helge, and he would wave back. After a while he had started greeting their mother as well. This little nodding acquaintance gave him such a warm, homey feeling. In front of him stood Cesca's vase; he was always careful to keep it filled with fresh flowers. And Signora Papi was good at understanding his Italian. That was because she had had Danish lodgers, said Cesca. Danes weren't good at learning foreign languages.

Whenever the signora had some reason to come to his room, she would always stand in the doorway and chat for an eternity. Mostly about his "cousin" — *"Che bella,"* Signora Papi would say. Once Frøken Jahrmann had come to see him alone, and another day with Frøken Winge. Both times to invite him to visit them. When Signora Papi would finally stop herself with a laugh — here she stood, disturbing his writing — and disappear, then Helge would lean back in his chair with his hands behind his neck. He thought about his room back home, next to the kitchen where his mother and sister always stood talking about him, their voices loud, worried, disapproving. He could hear every word, as no doubt he was meant to. And each day down here was a precious reprieve. Finally, finally he had some peace — to work and work.

His afternoons were spent in museums and libraries. But at dusk, as often as he felt was proper, he would drop by to visit the two women painters on the Via Vantaggio and have tea.

Usually they were both home. Sometimes there were other guests; he regularly met Heggen and Ahlin there. Twice he had found Frøken Winge alone, and once just Fransiska.

They always sat in Jenny's room. It was warm and pleasant, even though they left the shutters open until the last blue tinge of twilight had vanished. The woodstove glowed and crackled, and the teakettle hummed on the spirit stove. He was familiar with everything in the room by now: the studies and photographs on the walls, the vases of flowers, the blue tea service, the book-shelf next to the bed, the easel with Fransiska's portrait. The room was always a little untidy. The table in front of the window was covered with tubes and paint boxes and sketchbooks and scraps of paper. And as Jenny set the table for tea, she would use her foot to shove under the table the brushes and paint rags that littered the floor. There was usually mending and some partially darned socks on the sofa, and she would put them away as she sat down to butter the biscuits, then stand up to move aside a spirit iron that always stood somewhere in the room.

In the meantime he would sit and talk with Fransiska in the corner by the stove. Occasionally Cesca would decide she ought to be domestic, and Jenny was supposed to sit and lounge. But Jenny usually declined. Cesca cleaned like a whirlwind, stuffing all the scattered possessions into places where Jenny could never find them again. Last of all she would pound the missing thumb-tacks into the pictures that hung, crooked and curling, on the walls, using one of her shoes as a hammer.

Gram couldn't figure out Frøken Jahrmann. She was always friendly and nice toward him, but she never took him into her confidence as intensely as she had on that day they went out to Ponte Molle. At times she was so oddly preoc-cupied, as if she took no notice of what he was saying, even though she replied in a manner that was friendly enough. A few times he had the impression that he was boring her. If he asked how she was feeling, she never gave him a straight answer. And once, when he mentioned her painting of the cypresses, she told him, although in a very sweet voice, "You mustn't be angry, Gram, but I don't like talking about my work before it's finished. Not now, at any rate."

He felt some sense of encouragement when he noticed that the sculptor Ahlin didn't care for him. Perhaps the Swede considered him a rival. And besides, he had the impression that Fransiska was no longer interested in Ahlin.

When he was alone, Helge would plan out what he was going to say to Cesca, carrying on long conversations with her in his mind. He longed to speak of that day at Ponte Molle; he wanted to reciprocate, to tell her about himself. But when he met her, he became insecure and nervous. He didn't know how to turn the conversation in the direction he wanted, afraid of seeming importunate or tactless, afraid of doing anything that might make her like him less. Then she would notice his embarrassment and come to his aid, drawing him into the chatter and banter, and it was easy for him to joke and laugh with her. At the time he was grateful to her; she deftly and easily filled all the pauses and helped him get started again whenever he felt tongue-tied. Only afterward, when he was back in his room, would he feel disappointed. Once again there had been nothing but chatter about all sorts of amusing trivialities.

But when he was alone with Jenny Winge, there was always proper conversation about substantial topics. Sometimes he thought it was rather tedious having these serious discussions about abstract matters. But most often he enjoyed talking to her, because the conversation would eventually slip from more general situations to his own. Gradually he ended up telling her a great deal about himself — about his work, about the difficulties he felt he had both with external circumstances and within himself. The fact that Jenny Winge never talked about herself was something he barely noticed, although he did realize that she avoided discussing Frøken Jahrmann with him.

Nor did it occur to him that he couldn't talk to Fransiska the way he talked to Jenny, because in Fransiska's eyes he would have seemed much stronger and more important and confident than he considered himself to be.

———✺———

On Christmas Eve they had all gone to the club together, and afterward to evening mass at San Luigi dei Francesi.

At first Helge thought it was quite moving. The whole church was dimly lit in spite of all the crystal chandeliers, but they were hung so high up in the ceiling. The altar facade was a wall of light — hundreds of wax tapers with soft golden flames. Muted choral songs and organ music streamed through the nave. And besides, he was seated next to a lovely young Italian woman who had pulled her rosary of lapis lazuli out of a velvet-lined jewelry box and was praying most earnestly.

But after a while Frøken Jahrmann began to grumble louder and louder. She was sitting in front with Frøken Winge.

"Come on, Jenny — let's go. You can't really think this sets the proper

Christmas mood. It's just an ordinary concert, a dreary concert. Listen to that fellow who's singing now — no emotion at all — and besides, his voice is completely gone. It's awful."

"Hush, Cesca. Keep in mind that we're in a church."

"I don't care if it *is* a church. This is a concert; we had to buy tickets and programs. A tedious concert . . . it's putting me in a very bad mood."

"All right, all right. We'll leave when this piece is over. But you can at least keep still until then."

"Oh . . . last New Year's Eve," continued Cesca. "I was in Gesu. Now that had atmosphere. *Te Deum.* I was kneeling next to an old farmer from out in the country and a young girl who was ill, but so lovely. Everyone was singing; the old farmer knew the whole *Te Deum* in Latin. That was atmosphere!"

As they quietly made their way out of the crowded church, the *Ave Maria* resounded through the nave.

"*Ave Maria,*" snickered Fransiska. "Do you hear that? The singer doesn't give a damn about what she's singing — it sounds like a phonograph record. I can't bear to hear that kind of music mistreated this way."

"*Ave Maria,*" said a Danish gentleman walking beside her. "I recall a young Norwegian woman . . . How magnificently she could sing that song. A Frøken Eck."

"Berit Eck. Do you know her, Hjerrild?"

"She was in Copenhagen two years ago, singing with Ellen Bech. I knew her quite well. Do you know her, Frøken Jahrmann?"

"My sister knew her," said Fransiska. "Oh, that's right, you met my sister Borghild in Berlin. Did you like Frøken Eck? By the way, her name is Fru Hermann now."

"She was a very sweet girl — enchanting. And unusually promising."

Fransiska fell into step with Hjerrild behind the others.

———

It had been agreed that Heggen, Ahlin, and Gram would accompany the ladies home for a late-night snack; Fransiska had received a Christmas package from home. The table was set with Norwegian Christmas delicacies, decorated with daisies from the *campagna* and candles in seven-armed candelabras.

Fransiska was the last to come in. She had brought the Dane along.

"Isn't this nice, Jenny — that Hjerrild wanted to come too?"

It turned out that there was both beer and gin on the table, as well as Norwegian butter and brown goat cheese and cold wood grouse and head-cheese and smoked ham shank.

Fransiska sat next to Hjerrild. And as soon as the conversation started getting lively around the table, she turned to him.

"Do you know the pianist Hermann, who married Frøken Eck?"

"Yes, very well. We lived in the same lodgings in Copenhagen, and I also just saw him in Berlin."

"What do you think of him?"

"He's a handsome fellow. Enormously talented. He gave me his latest compositions as a gift; they're tremendously original, in my opinion. Yes . . . I like him quite well, indeed."

"Do you have them with you here? Could I see them? I'd love to go up to the club and play them. He was a friend of mine in the old days," said Fransiska.

"But of course! Now I remember — he has your photograph! He refused to say whose picture it was."

Heggen was suddenly alert.

"Yes . . . that's right," said Fransiska feebly. "I think I did give him a photograph."

"Incidentally . . ." Hjerrild downed his drink. "He tends to be somewhat of a brute — can be quite inconsiderate. But perhaps that's what makes him so irresistible to the ladies. Sometimes he was . . . a little too much of the proletarian for my taste."

"That's precisely . . ." she fumbled for words. "That's what I admired about him. That he had fought his way up from the bottom to where he is now. I think a struggle like that would *have* to make you a brute. I mean, don't you think that excuses a lot? Almost everything?"

"Nonsense, Cesca," said Heggen suddenly. "Hans Hermann was discovered when he was thirteen years old and has been helped along ever since."

"Yes, but to have to accept help, and be grateful for everything. And always afraid of being neglected, ignored — reminded that he was . . . well, what Hjerrild just said: a proletarian child."

"I could also claim that I'm a proletarian child."

"No, you can't, Gunnar. I'm convinced that you've always been superior to your surroundings. Whenever you enter a social circle that's higher than the one you were born into, you're always superior to everyone there — more knowledgeable, more clever, with finer ideas. You've always been able to have a strong sense that you fought and worked your way to everything on your own. You've never needed to bow and scrape to people you knew could be looking down on you because of your lowly birth — who were acting the snob by helping out someone brilliant whose reach they didn't understand a whit of — who were deeply inferior to you and yet felt they were better than you — and you had to thank these people even though you felt no gratitude. You can't talk about proletarian feelings, Gunnar, because you've never known what they are."

"But Cesca, someone who accepts that kind of help from people — even though he feels no gratitude — someone like that is an incorrigible lower-class individual."

"But don't you understand, my lad? A person does that when he knows he has talent — maybe even genius — that has to be developed. And besides, you call yourself a social democrat, so I don't think you should talk that way about lower-class individuals."

"A person who has respect for his own talent refuses to prostitute himself. And as far as being a social democrat goes . . . Social democracy means a demand for justice. But justice requires that people like him be subjugated — pressed down to the bottom of society, wearing shackles, with the whip overhead. The true, legitimate lower class *must* be properly subjugated."

"That's a very peculiar socialism," laughed Hjerrild.

"There isn't any other kind — not for grown-ups. I'm not including the naive, blue-eyed souls who believe that all people are good and everything bad is the fault of society. If all people were good, society would be paradise. But it's the proletarian souls that make it bad. They're found at all levels of society, as it now exists. If they're gentlemen, they are cruel and brutish; if they're in service, they are fawning and obsequious — and lazy. For that matter, I've even met them among the ranks of socialists. You know, Hermann calls himself a socialist too. If they can find hands that will lift them up, they seize upon them — and then trample on those same hands later. If they get wind of a troop marching forward, they join up in order to partake of the bounty; but loyalty and a sense of camaraderie are not something they possess. The goal . . . In all secrecy they laugh at it. Justice . . . They fundamentally hate it; they know that if it triumphs, they will suffer.

"It's those who fear justice that I call legitimate proletarians — who must be fought, without mercy. If they gain power over the poor and the weak, they will intimidate and tyrannize them into becoming proletarians too. If they are poor and weak themselves, they don't fight — they beg and wheedle their way forward, and then attack from behind when they see an opportunity.

"It's a society ruled by upper-class individuals that must be our goal. Because upper-class individuals never fight for themselves. They have a sense of their own inexhaustible resources; they shower help on those who are poorer — fight to give light and air to every little ability that is fine and good in the small souls — those who are neither one nor the other: good when they can afford it, bad when the proletarians force them to be that way. The goal is for those to assume power who feel responsible at the thought of every small, good talent that is crushed . . ."

"You don't understand Hans Hermann at all," said Cesca softly. "Oh, it wasn't just for his own sake that he was upset about social injustices. Those small, good talents that were wasted — *he* talked about those too. Whenever we took a walk through the eastern part of the city and saw the pale little children, in those vile, shabby, overcrowded barracks, he said he'd like to burn them to the ground."

"Mere words. If he had to collect their rent . . ."

"For shame, Gunnar," said Cesca vehemently.

"Oh no, he wouldn't have been a socialist if he'd been born rich. But he would still have been a real proletarian."

"And are you so sure that you would have been a socialist," said Cesca, "if you'd been born a count, for instance?"

"Herr Heggen *is* a count," laughed Hjerrild. "And he owns plenty of castles in the air."

Heggen tossed his head back and sat in silence for a moment.

"At any rate, I've never had the feeling that I was born poor," he said, as if to himself.

"Well, well." That was Hjerrild again. "With regard to Hermann's love of children — he doesn't seem to have much love for his own little boy. It was ugly the way he treated Frøken Eck. First he begged and threatened in order to win her. Then, when she was going to have the baby, she had to beg and threaten *him* before he would marry her."

"So they have a little boy?" whispered Fransiska.

"Oh yes. He was born after they'd been married six weeks, right at the time I left Berlin. Hermann had left her and gone to Dresden after they'd been together for a month.

"I don't understand why he couldn't have married her a little earlier. They had an agreement, you know, that they would divorce. That's what she wanted too."

"How awful," said Jenny. She had been listening to their conversation for some time. "To think that anyone would get married with the intention of divorcing afterward."

"Good Lord." Hjerrild chuckled. "When two people know each other inside and out, and realize that they can't get along . . ."

"Then they shouldn't get married."

"Of course not. Free relationships are much more beautiful. But good Lord — she had to. She wanted to give concerts in Kristiania next fall and be able to give singing lessons. She couldn't do that — with the child — if she hadn't been married, poor thing."

"No, no. You may be right. But it's still detestable. I have no sympathy for free relationships, if by that you mean people taking up with each other even though they assume that they'll get tired of it later. Even breaking a perfectly ordinary, platonic, bourgeois engagement . . . I think the person who breaks it off becomes slightly sullied. But if someone has ever been unfortunate enough to make a mistake, and then for the sake of other people acts out a disgusting comedy — a blasphemous wedding, where they stand there making promises that they've decided at the outset not to keep . . ."

—␣⁓␣—

The guests didn't leave until dawn. Heggen stayed behind for a while after the others.

Jenny opened the balcony door to air out the tobacco smoke. She stood there for a moment, gazing out. The whole sky was pale gray with a faint reddish gold tinge just above the rooftops. It was bitterly cold. Heggen came over to her.

"Well, I want to thank you. Another Christmas Eve behind us. What are you thinking?"

"That it's Christmas morning."

"Yes, it's odd, isn't it."

"I was wondering whether they got my package on time back home," she said after a pause.

"Well, didn't you send it on the eleventh? I'm sure they got it."

"I hope so. It was always such fun on Christmas morning to come in and see the tree and all the presents in daylight. I mean, when I was young." She gave a little laugh. "There's lots of snow this year, they said in their letters. The children have probably gone up to the mountains today."

"I suppose so," said Heggen. He stood there a moment, looking outside with her. "Oh, but you'll get cold, Jenny. Good night, then. Thank you for the evening."

"It was our pleasure. Good night. Merry Christmas, Gunnar."

They shook hands. She stayed where she was for a while after he had gone, before she shut the balcony door and went inside.

7

One day during the week of the Christmas holidays, Gram went into a trattoria. Heggen and Jenny were there, but they didn't see him, and as he hung up his coat, he heard Heggen say: "He's a damned lout."

"Yes, he's loathsome," sighed Jenny.

"And it's hell on her health. In this scirocco . . . of course she'll be like a limp rag tomorrow. And she's not doing any work either — just dashing around with that fellow."

"Work? No. But there's nothing I can do. She'd gladly trudge all the way out to Viterbo with him in those skimpy patent leather shoes of hers — in spite of the scirocco and everything — just because that man can tell her about Hans Hermann."

Gram greeted them as he passed. Frøken Winge and Heggen motioned to him, as if expecting him to join them. But he pretended not to notice and went over to the far end of the room and sat down with his back to them.

He understood that they were talking about Frøken Jahrmann.

He couldn't help it. Almost daily he would go over to Via Vantaggio. Now Jenny Winge was almost always home alone, sewing or reading. She seemed glad to see him. He thought that in some way she seemed different lately. She wasn't as bold or definite in her opinions anymore, nor as ready to discuss or lecture. It was almost as if she were a little bit depressed.

One day he asked her whether she was feeling quite well.

"Well? Yes, of course. Why do you ask?"

"Oh, I don't know . . . You just seem so quiet, Frøken Winge."

She had just lit the lamp, and he saw that she was blushing.

"I have to go back home soon. My sister has developed pharyngitis, and

Mamma is in such a state." She stood still for a moment. "I'm a little sad about that. I was planning to stay here at least through the spring."

She picked up her mending and sat down with it.

Helge wondered if it was Gunnar Heggen. He'd never been able to figure out whether there was anything between the two of them. And lately Heggen, whom Helge had heard supposedly had quite a fickle heart, was completely infatuated with a young Danish nurse who was in Rome with an elderly woman she was caring for. It was Jenny's blush that seemed to him quite odd — it was so out of character for her.

That evening Fransiska came home before he left. He had scarcely seen her since Christmas, but enough to notice that she cared nothing for him. It was no longer a question of moodiness or childish caprice. It was simply that she no longer *saw* other people; something or other was completely preoccupying her. Sometimes she walked around as if she were asleep.

But he continued to visit Jenny all the same, both at the trattoria where she usually dined, and at home in her room. He hardly knew why he was doing this, but he felt as if he needed to see her.

One afternoon Jenny went into Fransiska's room to look for a bottle of turpentine. Fransiska was always taking things that she needed from Jenny's room, and she never brought them back. And there was Cesca lying on her bed, muffling her sobs in the pillows. She must have crept upstairs, because Jenny hadn't heard her come in.

"But my dear — what is it? Are you ill?"

"No. Sweet Jenny, just go. No, I don't want to tell you. You'll just say it's my own fault."

Jenny could see it would do no good to talk to her. At teatime she went to her door and called her name. No, thanks, she didn't want anything, Cesca said.

But that evening as Jenny lay in bed reading, Cesca suddenly slipped in, wearing her nightgown. Her face was blotched and swollen from crying.

"Could I sleep in your bed tonight, Jenny? I don't dare be alone."

Jenny made room for her. She wasn't fond of the custom, but Cesca often came in and asked to sleep with her when she was feeling most unhappy.

"No, go ahead and read, Jenny — I won't disturb you. I'll just lie here very quietly next to the wall."

Jenny pretended to read for a little while. Now and then Fransiska would utter a few whimpering sighs. Then Jenny asked her, "Shall I put out the light? Or would you like it to stay lit?"

"No thanks, you can put it out."

In the dark she put her arms around Jenny and told her everything, sobbing.

She had been out to the *campagna* with Hjerrild again. And then he kissed her. At first she merely scolded him a bit, because she thought he was just teasing. But then he turned so loathsome that she felt truly angry. "And then he wanted me to go with him to his hotel tonight. He said it in exactly the same way as if he were asking me to go to a pastry shop with him. That made me furious, and then he got mad too. And he said some horrible, filthy things." She lay quietly for a moment, shivering as if with fever. "Then he said . . . well, you know . . . something about Hans. Hans had talked about me when he showed Hjerrild my photograph — in such a way that Hjerrild thought . . .

"Can you understand it, Jenny?" She pressed closer to her friend. "Because I don't. How can I still be in love with that scoundrel?"

After a pause she said, "But you know, Hans didn't tell him my name. And of course he couldn't know that Hjerrild would meet me. Or recognize me from a photo taken when I was eighteen."

—⁓—

The seventeenth of January was Jenny's birthday. She and Fransiska were going to give a luncheon party out in the *campagna* at a little inn on Via Appia Nuova. They had invited Ahlin, Heggen, Gram, and Frøken Palm, the Danish nurse.

Two by two they walked from the trolley stop across the white road in the sunshine. Spring was in the air. The pale brown *campagna* had acquired a grayish green tint, and the daisies, which had tentatively bloomed all winter, had begun to spread out in silver-glinting patches. And the impatient tufts of light-green buds on the elder bushes along the fences had grown bigger.

Larks hovered and quivered high above in the blue-white sky. And the heat veiled everything; a haze lay over the city and over the ugly, reddish yellow clusters of houses that were spilled across the plain. The Alban Hills, with the white villages on their slopes, could be glimpsed through the fog beyond the mighty arched rows of the aqueducts.

Jenny and Gram walked in front, and he was carrying her light-gray coat. She was radiantly beautiful in a black silk dress; he had never seen her before in anything other than her gray dress or a tailored skirt and jacket. But now he felt as if he were walking beside a new and unknown woman. She looked so soft and round above the slender waist of her shimmering black dress. The square neckline of the bodice was cut low and deep, and her fair skin and hair were dazzling. She was also wearing a large black hat; Helge had seen her wear it before, but hadn't paid much attention. Perhaps it was because of the pale pink necklace that it looked different with that dress.

They ate outside in the sunshine beneath the bare grapevines, which sketched delicate bluish shadows across the tablecloth. And Frøken Palm and Heggen had decorated the table with daisies — although the pasta had been ready for quite some time, and the others had had to wait before those two arrived with the decorations. But the food was good and the wine excellent, and Cesca had selected the fruit in the city and brought it along, and the coffee too. She claimed that she wanted to make it herself to be certain it was good.

After the meal Heggen and Frøken Palm strolled around, studying the pieces of marble — fragments of reliefs and inscriptions that had been found on the property and were plastered into the wall of the building. After a while they disappeared around the corner. Ahlin stayed sitting at the table, smoking with half-closed eyes in the sun.

The inn stood at the foot of a slope. Gram and Jenny wandered upward. She picked some of the little wild morning glories that grew in the reddish yellow sand of the slope.

"There are so many of these on Monte Testaccio. Have you been there, Gram?"

"Yes, several times. I was there the day before yesterday and visited the Protestant cemetery. The camellia trees are bursting with blossoms now. And in the old section I found anemones in the grass."

"Yes, they're coming up now." Jenny gave a little sigh. "There's a place outside Ponte Molle on Via Cassia that's teeming with anemones. Gunnar gave me some blossoming almond branches this morning; they already have them on the Spanish Steps. But I suppose they've been cultivated in a hothouse."

They had reached the top and were walking through the meadow. Jenny looked down as she walked. There were plants sprouting everywhere in the short, scraggly grass. Baking in the sun were rosettes of multicolored thistle leaves and big, silvery gray leaves. They drifted toward a solitary stretch of wall that rose up from collapsed rubble in the middle of the field, formless and nameless.

Pale and gray-green, the *campagna* undulated around them in all directions beneath the bright spring sky and the trilling larks. Its borders were lost in the haze of the sun. Behind them the city became merely a glittering mirage; the mountains and clouds melded together, and the yellow arched rows of the aqueducts emerged from the pale mist, only to vanish again toward town. The countless ruins became nothing but small, shining pieces of wall strewn across the green, and the stone pines and eucalyptus trees near the little rose- and ocher-colored houses looked infinitely lonely and dark and abandoned in the midst of the fair early-spring day.

"Do you remember the first morning I was here, Frøken Winge? I found I was disappointed, and I thought this was because I had longed so much and dreamed so much, that everything I was going to see would be pale and mea- ger compared with my dreams. Have you ever noticed what happens when you're lying in the sun on a summer day with your eyes closed? When you open them, all the colors seem gray and faded for a moment. But that's just because your eyes have grown weak from not being used for a while. They can't imme- diately fathom the abundance of colors that exist; the first impression is imper- fect and meager. Do you know what I mean?"

Jenny nodded, as if to herself.

"Well, it was the same thing for me when I first came here. Rome over- whelmed me. And then I saw the two of you. You walked past me, so tall and fair, but a stranger to me. I didn't pay any attention to Fransiska then — not until we went to the pub. I sat there with all of you, whom I didn't know . . . I had never actually spent any time with strangers before, only in brief encoun- ters on the way home or to school. For a moment I felt so confused; I didn't think I could possibly talk to anyone. And then it all came flooding over me, everything from back home. I almost longed for home — and for the Rome that I had heard about and seen in pictures. My father, you know . . ." He laughed curtly. "I didn't think I could manage anything else. Merely look at pictures, the way others had done, and read what others had written, and sort out and arrange the work of others, and live with fictional characters in books. Sitting there with all of you I felt so desperately alone.

"But then you talked about being alone. And now I understand it.

"Do you see that tower over there? I was there yesterday. It's all that's left of a fortress from medieval times — the age of barons. Actually there are quite a few of these towers still standing, both inside and outside the city. You may see a wall with almost no windows built into the facades of the street — that's a fragment from the Rome of the robber barons. It's the age we know the least about, relatively speaking. But it's what I'm most interested in right now. I find the names of dead people in the archives, but often I know nothing more than their names. I long to know more about them. I dream about Rome in the Middle Ages — when they fought in the streets and bellowed from hot, fiery throats, and the city was full of robber castles. And that's where they locked up their women, daughters of these wild beasts, with their blood in their veins — and sometimes they too would break free and plunge into life as it swirled around the dark red walls. We don't know much about that time. The German professors grow frightened and refuse to be interested in these people, because they're nakedly individuals and can't be turned into abstract ideas.

"Good Lord, what a torrent of life has washed over this land — breaking into waves around each hill with its towns and castles. And yet the peaks still rise above, just as bare and desolate. Look at the endless scattering of ruins to be found out here in the *campagna*. And the mountains of books that have been written about Italy's history — yes, about the history of the whole world. The army of dead people that we know. And yet what a tiny little bit remains after all the waves of life that have washed over this place, one after the other.

"Oh, I think it's so marvelous!

"Think how much I've talked to you, Jenny. And how much you've talked to me. And yet I don't know you at all. Right now, as you're standing here, you should see for yourself how your hair shines . . . You're also a kind of unknown tower for me. And I think that's so marvelous.

"Have you ever thought about the fact that you've never seen your own face? Only a reflection. Your face, when you're asleep, when your eyes are closed — you can't ever see it. Don't you think that's strange?

"On that day it was my birthday. Today it's yours. Now you're twenty-eight. Are you happy about that? You who think that each year a person lives through is a victory."

"That's not what I said. I just said that most often a person has to struggle with a great deal of things in the first twenty-five years, things that you can be glad you've survived."

"But what about now?"

"Now . . ."

"Yes. Do you know for sure what you want to achieve in the next year? How you want to make use of it? Oh, but I think life is so overwhelmingly rich with possibilities. Not even you, with all your powers, could manage to do everything. Don't you ever think about things like that? Doesn't it ever make your heart restless, Jenny?"

She merely smiled. She looked down, and ground out a cigarette she had thrown away. Her ankle gleamed white through the sheer black stocking. With her eyes she followed a grayish white flock of sheep that was running down the slope right across from them.

"Oh, the coffee, Gram! They must be waiting for us . . ."

They walked back toward the inn without speaking. The hillside ended in a steep sandy cliff right above the table where they had been sitting.

Ahlin was leaning over the table with his head buried in his arms. The tablecloth all around him was littered with scraps of cheese and fruit peels among the glasses and plates.

Fransiska, wearing her leaf-green dress, was bending over him with her arms around his neck, trying to lift his head.

"Oh no. Oh, don't cry, Lennart! I'll try to love you — I will gladly marry you. Do you hear me, Lennart? I *will* marry you, but you mustn't cry like that. I do think I can love you, Lennart. If only you won't be so full of despair."

Ahlin sobbed, "No, no . . . not like this . . . then I don't want to do it, Cesca."

—*◇◇*—

Jenny turned around and walked back along the cliff. Gram saw that her entire throat had turned blood-red. The path led along the slope of the hill and down toward the inn's vegetable garden.

There Heggen was chasing Frøken Palm around the little fountain. They were splashing water at each other so the drops glittered in the sun, and she was shrieking with laughter.

Once again a blush suffused Jenny's throat and the nape of her neck. Helge followed her down through the vegetable beds. Heggen and Frøken Palm had made peace over by the fountain.

"The dance continues," said Helge softly.

Jenny nodded faintly with a shadow of a smile.

There was a damper on everyone's mood as they drank coffee. Fransiska tried to make conversation as they sipped their liqueurs. Only Frøken Palm seemed in good spirits. As soon as it seemed proper, Fransiska suggested that they take a walk.

And so the three couples wandered into the *campagna*. The distance between them grew greater and greater, until they lost sight of each other among the hills. Jenny was walking with Gram.

"Where are we actually going?" she said.

"We could go to . . . to the Egeria Grotto, perhaps." It was in the opposite direction from the way the others had gone. But they set off, sauntering over the sunburned hillsides, toward Bosco Sacro. The ancient cork oaks stood there with the sun scorching their dark crowns.

"I suppose I should have brought along a hat." Jenny ran her hand over her hair.

In the sacred grove the ground was littered with discarded paper and scattered refuse. On a stump at the edge sat two women crocheting. Several little English boys were playing hide-and-seek behind the huge tree trunks. Jenny and Gram left the grove and walked down the slope toward the ruins.

"Do we really want to walk down there?" she asked, and then sat down on the ground without waiting for a reply.

"No, why should we?" Helge stretched out in front of her in the short, dry grass. He took off his hat and, propping himself up on his elbow, looked up at her without speaking.

"How old is she, anyway?" he asked suddenly in a quiet voice. "Cesca, I mean."

"Twenty-six." Jenny sat in silence, staring straight ahead.

"I'm not upset," he said softly. "Yes, I'm sure you've noticed . . . if it had been a month ago, maybe . . . She was so sweet and warm and confiding toward me one time. I wasn't used to that. I took it as . . . well, as *Aufforderung zum Tanz* — an invitation to dance. But now . . .

"I think she's sweet. But it doesn't bother me if she dances with someone else."

He lay there looking at Jenny.

"I think it's you that I'm in love with, Jenny," he said suddenly.

She turned slightly toward him, smiled a bit, and shook her head.

"Yes," said Helge firmly. "I think I am. I can't be certain, because I've never been in love before — I know that now. Even though I've been engaged." He laughed quietly. "Yes, that was one of the foolhardy things I did back in my old, foolhardy days.

"But my God, Jenny . . . I must be in love. And *you* were the one I noticed that evening — not her. I saw you first that afternoon; you were walking along the Corso. I stood there thinking that life was new and adventurous, and you walked past me, fair and dignified and a stranger to me. Later, after I'd been wandering around and around in the twilight of the foreign city, I met you again. Yes, I caught sight of Cesca too, so it's not so odd that I was a little confused for a while. But you were the first one I saw.

"And now the two of us are sitting here . . ."

One of Jenny's hands was resting on the ground right next to him. She was leaning on it. Abruptly he gave it a swift caress. After a moment she moved her hand away.

"You're not angry, are you? Because there's nothing to be angry about. Why shouldn't I tell you that I think I'm in love with you? I couldn't help touching your hand — I had to make sure it was real. Because I think it's so strange that you're sitting here. I really don't know you at all. In spite of everything we've talked about. I mean, I know you're clever and clear headed and full of energy — and kind and sincere — but I knew that as soon as I saw you and heard your voice. I don't know any more than that now, but of course there's much more . . .

"Though perhaps I'll never find out about that. But I can see, for example, that your silk dress is burning hot. If I pressed my cheek to your lap, I would burn myself . . ."

Involuntarily she brushed her hand across her silk lap.

"Yes, it's soaking up the sun. And your hair is shimmering. And rays of light are seeping into your eyes. Your mouth is completely transparent; it looks like a raspberry in the sun."

She smiled but seemed a little embarrassed.

"Won't you give me a kiss?" he said suddenly.

She looked at him for a moment.

"Aufforderung zum Tanz?" She smiled faintly.

"I don't know. But you can't be angry just because I ask you for a single kiss. On such a day. I'm just telling you what I'd like. But is there any reason why you couldn't do it?"

She sat motionless.

"Well, if there is some reason . . . Good Lord, I won't try to kiss you, but I don't understand why you couldn't just lean down for a second and give me a tiny little kiss, the way you're sitting there with the sun right on your mouth — Do it just like you give a child a pat and then hand him a soldo. Jenny . . . it would mean nothing to you, but it's the only thing I want . . . Right at this moment it's my greatest wish." He said this with a smile.

All of a sudden she leaned down and did it. Just for a second he felt her hair and her warm lips brush his cheek. And he saw all the movements of her body beneath the black silk, as she bent down and as she straightened up again. He noticed that her face, which was calmly smiling as she kissed him, afterward was confused and alarmed.

But he didn't move, merely lay there and smiled happily at the sun. And she grew calm again.

"You should see this," he said at last, and then he laughed. "Now your mouth is exactly the way it was before. The sun is shining on your lips, right through to the blood. It meant nothing to you. But I'm so happy.

"You must understand that I don't expect you to give any more thought to me. I just want be able to think about you, and I won't mind if you sit there thinking about all sorts of other things. The others may be dancing, but this is much better, as long as I can look at you."

They both fell silent. Jenny sat with her face turned away and looked out across the *campagna* in the sunlight.

As they walked back to the inn, Gram chatted easily and merrily about all sorts of things, telling stories about the German scientists he had met during the course of his work. Now and then Jenny stole a glance at him. He wasn't usually like this — so free and confident. He walked along and looked . . . he was actually quite handsome; his light brown eyes shone like amber in the sun.

8

Jenny did not light the lamp when she came up to her room. In the dark she took off her evening wrap and sat down on the balcony.

Above all the rooftops the sky was velvety black with a swarm of glittering stars. The night was cold.

He had said as they parted, "I may just have to come see you tomorrow and ask you to go out to the *campagna* with me."

But in reality nothing had happened. She had given him a kiss. Though it was the first kiss she had ever given to a man. And it hadn't come about the way she had imagined. It had almost been a joke — the fact that she had kissed him.

She wasn't the least bit in love with him. And yet she had kissed him. She had hesitated, thinking: I've never kissed anyone. And then lighthearted indifference and a sweet weariness had passed through her: Oh God, why be so ridiculously serious about the whole thing? And then she had done it. Why shouldn't she?

No, it didn't matter. He had asked her quite honestly for a kiss, because he thought he was in love with her and the sun was shining. He hadn't asked her to love him, and he hadn't made any further advances — he hadn't demanded anything but one little kiss. And she had given it to him, without saying a word. It was beautiful, that's all. Nothing had happened, she didn't have to feel ashamed about anything.

Good Lord — she was twenty-eight years old. And to herself she didn't deny that she longed for a man whom she could love and who would love her; someone she could nestle close to. She was young and healthy and attractive . . . and warm. And she longed . . . But since she saw things with cold clarity, and since she was not in the habit of lying to herself . . .

Every once in a while she would meet a man and ask herself: Is he the one? A few of them she might have managed to love, if she had made an effort, but that's what it would have taken. If she had helped out by closing her eyes to the one small thing that had aroused a touch of harsh resistance, that she had been forced to quell inside herself. She had never met anyone she simply *had* to love.

And so she hadn't dared. No, she hadn't.

Cesca could let one man after another kiss her and caress her. It meant nothing to her. It touched only her lips and her skin. Not even Hans Hermann, whom she had loved, had been able to warm her strangely thin, chill blood.

Jenny was different. Her blood was doubtless both red and warm. The happiness she longed for should be hot and all-consuming, but it should also be pure and unsullied. She herself would be good and loyal and faithful toward the man to whom she gave herself. There had to be someone who could take her completely, so that no gift within her remained unused, poisoned, or rotting away somewhere deep inside. No. She didn't dare, she refused to be reckless. She refused.

And yet . . . She could understand those who didn't want all the trouble of having to decide. Subduing one urge and calling it bad; coddling another and deeming it good. Rejecting all the small, cheap pleasures — saving up all your powers in anticipation of one great happiness. Which *might* — or might not — come. She was not completely convinced that her path would lead to her goal; occasionally she was impressed by people who quite cynically admitted they were taking other paths and had other goals — and that those who held on to morals and ideals were fishing for the moon in the lake.

One night, many years ago, a man had asked her to go home with him — almost as if he were inviting her to a pastry shop. In reality she hadn't been the slightest bit tempted. And besides, she knew that her mamma was sitting up waiting for her back home, and it would be impossible. She hardly knew the man, didn't like him much, and was annoyed that he was to escort her home that night. So it was not from any sensual inclination . . . It was pure intellectual curiosity that made her, in her mind, experiment with the question for a moment: And *if* I had done it? What would it feel like if I had simply tossed away my will, my self-control, and my old beliefs?

It was this thought that had sent a titillating, lustful shiver through her. Was that life better than her own?

She hadn't been happy about that evening. Once again she had sat and watched the others dance. She had tasted the wine, and the music had blared around her, and she had sat there feeling the bitter loneliness of being young and unable to dance with the others, unable to speak the language of the young or to laugh as they did, though she had tried to smile and talk and look as if she were having fun — once again. And as she walked home in the icy spring night, she knew that she had to be at Kampens School at eight o'clock the next morning to substitute teach. She was also working on a large painting out there in the few hours before she had to go home and tutor her private pupils in math until six o'clock, though the painting remained dead and heavy, no matter how she worked and fumed. Yes, she was working so hard back then that sometimes she felt as if every nerve were quivering with strain. Could she really manage to keep up this deliberate overexertion until the summer holidays?

It was then, for a moment, that she had almost felt enticed by his cynicism — almost, not truly — but . . . She had smiled at the man and told him no — as tersely and matter-of-factly as the way he had asked.

Besides, he was a fool. He began lecturing her, uttering embarrassing flattery and sentimental drivel about youth and springtime, about the right and freedom of passion, about the gospel of the flesh. Then she laughed in his face, quite gently, and hailed a cab that came by.

No, she was old enough to understand those who stubbornly refused to fight for anything in life, who just lay back and let themselves drift. But the greenhorns who babbled on about fulfilling a mission when they were merely satisfying their own desires — those youths who fought for the eternal right of nature when they didn't even bother to brush their teeth or clean their nails — they couldn't fool her.

She supposed she would just have to hold on to her own old moral view, which was essentially based on truthfulness and restraint.

It had begun to take shape after she entered school. She wasn't like the other children in her class, not even in the way she dressed. And her little soul was so very, very different. She lived with her mother, who had been widowed at the age of twenty and had nothing else in life but her young daughter — and with her father, who died before she could remember. He was in his grave and in heaven, but in reality he still lived with them. He hung above the piano and watched everything that she and her mother did, and heard everything they said. Her mother talked to him all the time, and told her what he thought about everything. Father said they should do this, or they shouldn't do that. Jenny talked about him as if she knew him, and in the evening she would talk *to* him, as well as to God, who was someone that was always with her father and who thought the same way he did.

Her first day at school. Jenny remembered it with a smile as she sat there in the dark Roman night.

Her mother had given her lessons, and at the age of eight she entered the third grade. Her mother always explained things using local examples that were familiar to her, so Jenny knew quite well what a "promontory" was. When the geography teacher asked her if she could name a Norwegian promontory, Jenny said, "Nesodden."

The teacher smiled, and the whole class laughed. "Signe," said the teacher, and little Signe stood up and said at once: "North Cape, Stat, Lindesnes." But Jenny smiled, superior and indifferent, in the face of their laughter. That must have been the first time. She never had any friends among the other children she knew before starting school, and she never had any later on, either.

Superior and indifferent, she had smiled at the taunts and scorn of the whole class, feeling a silent and irreconcilable hatred that set in between her — who was not like the others — and all the rest of the children, who for her became a uniform mass, a many-headed monster. The consuming rage she had felt when they tormented her was always concealed behind her disdainful, aloof smile. The few times that she lost her self-control — only once had she almost sobbed her heart out from anguish and bitterness — she had seen them triumph. It was only when she was "haughty," when they were irritated by her stoic insensitivity to whatever they said or did, that she could hold her own among all the others.

In the upper grades she had a few girlfriends. At that age no child can stand to be different from everyone else. She tried to copy them, but she never had much fun with those friends.

She remembered how they teased her when they found out that Jenny, who had turned fourteen, still played with dolls. So she renounced her beloved children, and said the dolls belonged to her younger sisters.

That was when she wanted to go on the stage. She and all her girlfriends were completely theater crazy, selling their schoolbooks and confirmation brooches to buy tickets. Night after night they would sit in the sixty-øre seats in the theater on Bankplassen. But one day Jenny got in trouble by telling them how *she* would have played Eline Gyldenløve.

Her friends howled. What a swelled head she had. They knew she had a wild imagination, but this was too much. Did she really think that she could be an actress? When she couldn't even dance? Oh, it was certainly going to be wonderful to watch her lumber around on stage, tall and stiff and gawky.

But even that didn't make Jenny break off with her friends.

No, she couldn't dance. When she was quite young, her mother used to play dance tunes for her, and Jenny would prance around, curtseying and twirling as she saw fit, and her mother would smile and call Jenny her little wagtail. Then she went to her first school dance, solemn with pride in a new white dress with green flowers — oh, she remembered it well. It was almost ankle length; her mother had patterned it after an old English painting. And she remembered that children's dance. She could still feel that odd stiffness in all her limbs. Never again did it leave her soft, slender body, which turned into a piece of wood whenever she tried to teach herself to dance. She couldn't do it. She wanted desperately to take dancing lessons, but they never could afford it.

She gave a laugh. She was laughing at her friends. She had met two of them at an exhibit the first time one of her paintings was shown, prompting several lines of praise in the newspapers. She was there with several other painters, Heggen among them, although she didn't know him well back then. Her girl-friends had come over to congratulate her.

"You know, that's what we always said in school: Jenny's going to be an artist. We were all so sure that you were going to be somebody."

She had laughed and said, "Yes, I was too, Ella."

———

Alone. She had been alone ever since.

She must have been about ten when her mother met Berner, the engineer. The two of them worked in the same office.

As young as Jenny was, she understood at once. The dead father seemed to slip out of the house. His portrait continued to hang on the wall, but he was dead. She realized what death was. Those who were dead existed only in the memories of other people, who could deliberately extinguish their feeble shadow lives. And then they no longer existed *at all*.

She understood why her mother looked so young and beautiful and happy again. She saw the light that came into her face whenever Berner rang the doorbell. She sat and listened to the two of them talking. They never spoke of things that a child shouldn't hear, and they never sent her away when they were together at home. In spite of her jealous heart, Jenny realized that there was so much that a grown-up mother couldn't talk about to a little girl. And a strong sense of justice surged up inside her; she wasn't going to be angry with her mother. And yet it hurt.

She was too proud to show it. But whenever her mother had a guilty conscience about the child and would nervously and suddenly shower her with tenderness and attention, Jenny would turn silent, cold, and sullen. She was also silent when her mother told her to call Berner "Father," earnestly explaining how fond he was of Jenny. At night she tried to talk to her own real father as she had before; she fervently tried to keep him alive. But she couldn't do it alone. She knew him only from her mother's stories. Little by little Jens Winge died away from her too. And because he had been at the center of all her thoughts about God and heaven and eternal life, these thoughts faded along with his picture. She knew for certain that by the age of thirteen she listened to the religious lessons with a conscious lack of faith. And because all of the others in her class believed in God and were afraid of the Devil, and were also cowardly and cruel and mean — or at least so they seemed to her — religion became something almost contemptible, something cowardly, that was associated with them.

In spite of herself, she couldn't help liking Nils Berner. At first, right after the marriage, she actually liked him better than her mother. He never demanded that his stepdaughter grant him the authority of a father; he treated her with intelligence, kindness, and complete ease. She was the daughter of the woman he loved, and therefore he also loved Jenny.

How much she owed him she didn't realize until she grew up. The way he had uprooted and combated so much in her that was sickly and affected. While she was living alone with her mother in that hothouse air of tenderness and solicitude and dreams, she had always been fearful — afraid of dogs, afraid of trolley cars, afraid of matches, afraid of everything. Her mother would scarcely let her walk alone to school. And she had been so sensitive to physical pain.

The first thing Berner did was to take the little girl along with him out to the woods. One Sunday after another he would take her to Nordmarken — in roasting sunshine, in the springtime damp, in the pouring rains of the fall, and on skis all winter long. And Jenny, who was used to hiding her emotions, tried to conceal both her fatigue and her fear. After a while she felt neither of them anymore.

Berner taught her to use a map and a compass. He consulted with her as he would with a colleague. He taught her to read the signs of the changing weather in the wind and clouds, to tell time and direction by the sun. He acquainted her with the animals and plants. She drew flowers and painted them with watercolors — roots and stems, leaves and buds, and blossoms and fruit. Her sketchbook and his camera were always in their knapsack.

How much love and kindness her stepfather put into this training was something she could measure only now. He had taken a frail little girl as his friend and taught her well — she who was like a blind kitten in the beginning, while he was a renowned skier and mountain climber of Jotunheimen and the Nordland peaks.

He had promised to take her there, as well. That was the summer she was fifteen, at that difficult age. He had taken her along to hunt grouse. Her mother couldn't come with them; she was expecting Little Brother back then.

They stayed at an isolated little hut beneath Rondane. Oh, she'd never been as happy as she was on those mornings when she woke up in her little alcove. She had to get up and make coffee for Berner. And he took her along to the Ronde peaks and up to Stygfjeld and on fishing expeditions, and they hiked down to Fol Valley for provisions. While he was out hunting, she would swim in the icy mountain streams and take endless walks along the autumn-red mountain plateaus, or sit in the door of the hut, knitting and dreaming romantic mountain-girl dreams about a hunter who looked a good deal like Berner, but who was quite young and stunningly handsome. But he would tell her stories the way Berner did in the evening in front of the fireplace — about hunting trips and mountain climbing — and he would promise to give her rifles and take her along to unconquered summits, just as Berner promised.

Oh yes. She remembered the time when she realized that her mother was going to have a baby. How tormented she felt, ashamed and unhappy. She tried to hide her feelings from her mother, although she was not completely successful; she knew that. It was only Berner's fear for his wife, as the birth approached, that changed her feelings. He talked to Jenny about it: "I'm so frightened, Jenny. I love your mother so much, you see." And he talked about how ill Ingeborg had been when Jenny was born.

Her feeling that there was something unnatural and unclean about her mother's condition slipped away as he spoke. But with it vanished the feeling that the relationship between herself and her mother was something mysterious and otherworldly. It became ordinary and matter-of-fact. She had been born, and her mother had suffered pain for her, and she had been little and in need of her mother, and in spite of everything, her mother had loved her. And now a new little child was coming, who would need her mother more. Jenny suddenly felt grown up — with compassion for both her mother and Berner — and she precociously consoled him: "Yes, but you know it usually goes just fine. They almost never die from it, you know."

And yet she had wept from loneliness when she saw her mother with the new little baby, who took all her time and all her attention.

But she loved the child, especially when Little Ingeborg was just over a year old and the sweetest little Tater troll with the blackest hair imaginable, and her mother had another infant.

Jenny never really felt that Berner's children were her siblings. They looked just like their father. Now she characterized her relationship to them as more that of an aunt; she felt almost like a sensible old aunt, both toward her mother and the children.

When misfortune struck, her mother seemed both younger and weaker than Jenny. Fru Berner had become young again in her happy new marriage, though a little weary and worn out and rather sluggish after three childbirths coming one right after the other. Nils was only five months old when his father died.

Berner plunged down Skagastøl Peak one summer and died on the spot. Jenny was sixteen. Her mother's despair was boundless; she had loved her husband, and he had idolized her. Jenny tried to help her mother as best she could. How much she herself grieved for her stepfather, she never told anyone. She knew she had lost the only friend she'd ever had.

After finishing her midlevel exams, she went to art school and helped out at home. Berner had always been interested in her drawings and was the first to teach her a little about perspective and such things, as best he could. He thought she had talent.

They couldn't afford to keep his dogs. The two chubby little puppies were sold, and her mother thought they ought to sell Leddy as well, since she was a valuable animal. She mourned her master terribly. But no one else was to have Berner's dog if they couldn't afford to keep her themselves — that was Jenny's firm decision, and for once she actually had a hysterical fit about it. One evening she took the dog over to Attorney Iversnæs, who was Berner's old friend. He took Leddy up to the mountains on Sunday, shot her, and buried her body next to his cabin.

Just as Berner had treated Jenny like a comrade and friend, she tried to treat his children in the same way. As her half sisters grew older, the relationship between them and Jenny was not intimate — friendly enough but rather distant. And Jenny made no attempt to draw closer. The two of them were sweet little girls, now in their adolescence, with anemia and little infatuations and boyfriends and girlfriends and constant dance parties — merry girls and quite indolent. But little Nils and Jenny had become better and better friends over the years. Kalfatrus was the nickname that his father had given the little tyke, and Jenny had continued calling him that, while he called his sister Indiana.

In all the dreariness of the past few years, her hikes in Nordmarken with Kalfatrus had been the only times when she could catch her breath. Preferably in the spring and fall when there were few people in the woods, and she and the boy would sit in silence, staring at the campfire they had made — or they would lie around babbling their own awful, vulgar language, which they never dared use at home, out of regard for their mother's feelings.

Her portrait of Kalfatrus was the first painting she had been satisfied with. And it *was* splendid. Gunnar swore that it ought to hang in a gallery. She had never painted another that was as good.

She should have painted Berner — Pappa. That's what she had called him when his children started to talk. And then she started calling her mother Mamma. It was her way of confirming to herself the change that had occurred with the mother of her brief childhood and the relationship between them.

Oh, those first days down here. When the terrible strain on her had at last been lifted. It had not been a good feeling. Now she recognized how every nerve inside her had been trembling with overexertion. And she thought she had grown too old to recapture her youth ever again. From Florence she remembered nothing except that she was cold and lonely and incapable of taking in anything new. But then, every once in a while, she would catch a glimpse of the infinite wealth of beauty all around and grow mad with longing to interpret it and immerse herself in it, to be young and to love and be loved.

Those spring days when Gunnar and Cesca took her along to Viterbo . . . The sunshine among the bare oak trees, where multitudes of anemones and violets and primroses bloomed among the pale, withered leaves. The bubbling, stinking sulfur springs that steamed on the faded, steppelike plains outside the city. The land all around the seething springs was white as a corpse from crusted lime. The sunken road out there with its thousands of emerald-green, lightning-quick lizards in the stone walls, the olive trees in the green pastures with the dancing white butterflies. And the old section of the city with its singing fountains and the black medieval buildings and rampart towers. The moonlight there at night. And the yellow, slightly fizzy wine with its fiery taste from the volcanic earth where the grapes had grown.

She was on a first-name basis with her new friends. And at night Fransiska would confide to her everything about her rash young life and finally climb into her bed to be consoled. Cesca would lie there, saying over and over: To think this is what you're like. To think I was always so afraid of you in school. To think you would be so nice!

And Gunnar was in love with both of them. Springtime and the sun made him as lusty as a young faun. And Fransiska let him kiss her and laughed and called him a silly fool.

But Jenny was afraid. Not of him. She didn't dare kiss his hot red lips because she wanted something meaningless, something intoxicating and reckless that would last only these scant hours, while the sun and the springtime and the anemones lasted, while they were here . . . Something with no responsibility. But she didn't dare leap out of her old persona; she sensed that she wouldn't be able to put a lighthearted end to the recklessness — and that he couldn't either. She had watched Gunnar Heggen — the way he treated the other women with whom he had had small flings. He was like them, and yet not entirely. Deep inside he was himself, a man who was better than most women.

Later, he suffered when he fell in love himself. They had become friends — better and better friends. During that wonderful, tranquil time when they worked in Paris, and later, here in Rome.

But this thing with Gram was quite different. He certainly didn't arouse any bold desires or wild longings in her. Good Lord, she liked him well enough. He was far from stupid, as she had first thought. It was just that when he first arrived he had seemed so strained, but that was something she should be able to understand. There was something soft and young and fresh about him that she liked; she felt as if he was much more than two years younger than she was. And what he said about being in love with her . . . That was probably nothing more than a little surge of joy he felt at everything that was new and liberating. No doubt it was completely harmless both for her and for him.

They did love her — everyone back home. Fransiska and Gunnar did too. And yet . . . She wondered whether any of them was thinking about her right now, tonight. She was not at all distressed to know that there was one person who was.

9

She woke up in the morning and told herself that surely he wouldn't come, and that it was for the best, of course. But when he knocked on her door, she was pleased all the same.

"Look here, Frøken Winge, I haven't had any food yet. Do you think you could offer me some tea and a little bread?"

Jenny looked around her room. "But the room hasn't been tidied up yet, Gram."

"I'll close my eyes, and then you can lead me out to the balcony," said Gram, standing outside her door. "I'm awfully thirsty for a cup of tea!"

"Well, all right, just wait a minute . . ." Jenny pulled the coverlet over the unmade bed and cleared off the washstand. And she traded her Frisian jacket for a long kimono.

"So. Come on in and sit outside on the balcony, and I'll make you tea."

She moved a stool outdoors and set out bread and cheese. Gram looked at her bare white arms and the long sleeves of the kimono fluttering around her. The robe was dark blue, sprinkled with yellow and violet irises.

"How charming that gown is . . . It looks like a genuine geisha costume!"

"Yes, it *is* genuine. Cesca and I bought them in Paris, to wear at home in the mornings."

"You know, I find that terribly appealing. That you dress so beautifully even though you're here all alone." He lit a cigarette and studied the smoke. "Back home in the morning . . . oh . . . The maid and my mother and my sister, they all look so . . . Don't you think that women should always try to look as beautiful as they can?"

"Yes, I do. But it's not easy if you have to do the morning chores for a household, Gram."

"Well, at least for breakfast, then. They could pin up their hair and put on something like that, don't you think?" At that moment he rescued a teacup that she was just about to knock over with the edge of her sleeve.

"There you see how practical it is . . . Drink your tea now — you were so thirsty." Just then she discovered that Cesca's pale stockings had been hung outdoors to dry, and rather nervously she moved them inside.

He ate bread and drank tea and explained, "Well, you see . . . I was lying in bed thinking about yesterday until almost dawn. Then I overslept and didn't have time to stop by the *latteria*. I think we should go out along Via Cassia to your anemone place."

"My anemone place . . ." Jenny gave a little laugh. "When you were a boy, Gram, did you also have blue-anemone places and violet places and others that you harvested every year and kept secret from the rest of the children?"

"Of course I did. I know of a birch grove that has such fragrant violets, near the old Holmenkollen road."

"I know that place," she exclaimed triumphantly. "Just to the right of where Sørkedalsveien turns off."

"Precisely. I also had a place at Bygdø, close to Fredriksborg. And one in Skådalen."

"I should go in and get dressed now," said Jenny.

"Put on what you were wearing yesterday, if you wouldn't mind," he called after her.

"Oh, it will get so dusty . . ." she said, but instantly regretted it. Why shouldn't she dress up? That black silk dress had been her best for many years now — she really didn't need to treat it so carefully anymore.

"All right, never mind that! Oh, but it buttons up the back, and Cesca isn't home just now . . ."

"Come out here, and I'll button it for you. I'm an expert; I've buttoned my mother's and Sofie's dresses all my life, let me tell you."

There were only two buttons in the middle of her back that she couldn't reach. So she let Gram help her.

He sensed the faint, mild fragrance of her hair and her body as she stood outside with him in the sunshine and allowed him to button her dress. And he noticed that on one side there were several tiny tears in the silk that had been meticulously mended. His heart filled with an infinite tenderness for her when he saw this.

—⁓—

"Do you think Helge is a nice name?" he asked as they sat and ate lunch at an inn out in the *campagna*.

"Yes, it is."

"Did you know that my first name was Helge?"

"Yes, I noticed it when you signed in at the club." She suddenly blushed a little, wondering if he thought she had made a point of finding out.

"Yes, I think it's nice too. There aren't really many names that are either good or bad, are there? If you know someone with a certain name, it all depends whether you like that person or not. When I was a boy we had a nursemaid named Jenny, and I couldn't stand her. Ever since, I've always thought it was an ugly and plain sort of name; I thought it was absurd that you should be called Jenny. But now I think it's so charming, so blond, somehow. Can't you hear there's something so fair and blond in the sound? Jenny. Someone with dark hair couldn't have that name — like Frøken Jahrmann, for instance. Fransiska suits her perfectly, don't you think? It's so capricious. But Jenny is bright and fresh and clear."

"It's a family name. On my father's side," she said, just for something to say.

"What do you think about Rebekka, for example?" he asked after a moment.

"I don't know. It sounds quite nice, doesn't it? Although perhaps a bit harsh and grating."

"My mother's name is Rebekka," said Helge after a pause. "I think it sounds harsh too.

"And my sister's name is Sofie. She got married just so she could get away from home and have her own place — I'm convinced of that. Isn't it strange that my mother could be so delighted that Sofie was getting married — when she and my father have lived together like cats and dogs? But there was no end to the fuss she made over Curate Arnesen, when he and my sister were engaged. I despise my brother-in-law. I don't think Father can stand him either. But Mother . . .

"*My* former fiancée was named Katrine, but she was always called Titti. I saw that she even used Titti in the newspaper when she was married.

"Hmm . . . well, it was a foolish episode, believe me. That was three years ago. She was a substitute teacher at the school where I work. She wasn't the least bit attractive, but a real coquette toward any male. I'd never met a woman before who wanted to flirt with *me*. You can probably understand that, if you think about the impression I made when I first arrived here. And she was always laughing — it seemed to just burst out of her at the slightest provocation. She was no more than nineteen. God only knows why she chose me.

"And I was so furiously jealous, and that amused her. The more jealous she made me, the more in love I fell. Maybe it was mostly my male vanity; I'd finally won a sweetheart who was enormously sought after. I was so naive back then. And of course I wanted her to give all her attention to me, which was probably quite an impossible demand, considering how I was back then. As I said, God only knows why Titti chose me.

"My family wanted it kept secret, because we were so young. Titti wanted us to make it public. So whenever I thought she was paying too much attention to other people, she would insist that if it was supposed to be secret, she couldn't very well spend all of her time with me.

"Well, then she started visiting me at home, and she and my mother were always quarreling — squabbling worse than . . . Mother outright hated Titti. I suppose it would have been the same no matter who I was engaged to. For Mother, it was enough that she was my sweetheart. So then Titti broke it off."

"Were you terribly upset?" asked Jenny softly.

"Yes. Yes, I was. I really didn't get over it entirely until I came here. But I think it was mostly my vanity that suffered. Don't you think so? If I had loved her properly, then shouldn't I have wished that she would be happy when she married someone else? And yet I certainly didn't."

"That would have required enormously noble feelings," said Jenny with a smile.

"I don't know. Shouldn't you feel that way if you're truly in love? Don't you think so? But do you know what I think is odd? That mothers are always so unkind to their son's sweethearts. Because they certainly are."

"A mother probably thinks that no woman is good enough for her boy."

"Yes, but it's not that way when daughters are engaged. I noticed that quite clearly with the loathsome, flabby, red-haired curate. I've never had much sympathy for my sister. But still, when I think about that fellow . . . Disgusting. The way he used to sit there at home, pawing at her . . .

"No, sometimes I've thought about women who've been married for a while. They end up much more cynical than we men ever do. They don't say so, but I can still feel it — how basically cynical they've become. The whole thing is just business to them. And when the daughter gets married, they're happy that she's roped in a fellow who can take her in tow and feed her and clothe her. The fact that she has to put up with a little married life in return is not something to be taken too seriously. But when a son, in exchange for the same thing, takes on such a burden, they're not delighted at all, of course. Don't you think that's the way it is?"

"Sometimes," said Jenny.

When she was back home that evening, she lit the lamp and sat down to write to her mother. It would be best if she thanked her at once for the birthday greeting and told her how she had spent the day.

And she laughed at her own solemn mood the night before.

Dear God! Yes, of course she had struggled and felt lonely. But they had all had their struggles, most of the young people she had known. Many of them worse than she had. She only had to think about all the young and old women — the teachers at her grade school. Practically every one of them had an aging mother to support, or siblings to help out. Or what about Gunnar . . . or Gram . . . even Cesca — that spoiled girl from a wealthy home. At the age of twenty-one she had cut all ties and ever since pinched and scraped to get by on a meager inheritance from her mother.

And loneliness. Hadn't she chosen that herself? When it came right down to it, wasn't it true that she was not entirely convinced of her own talents? And to hide her doubts she had clung to the idea that she was different, completely unlike everyone else she knew. But she had pushed them all away. Now that she had made some progress, proved to herself that she was good at something, she had grown much more amenable and sociable. She willingly admitted that she had never made an attempt to meet anyone halfway, either as a child or as an adult. She had been too haughty to take the first step.

All the friends she had had — from her stepfather to Cesca and Gunnar — they had all been forced to reach out to her first.

And yet here she went around imagining that she was so passionate at heart. Ha! She, who had turned twenty-eight without having fallen in love — even the tiniest bit. Well, surely she had the right to believe that she wouldn't be a fiasco as a woman if she ever fell for a man — healthy and attractive as she was, with hearty instincts, which her work and outdoor life had trained to be receptive. And of course she longed to fall in love with someone and to be loved in return — to live.

But to go around imagining, out of sheer physical impulse, that she should throw herself into the arms of any man who happened to be nearby at a critical moment — nonsense, my girl. She just didn't want to admit that sometimes she was bored and felt a vulgar urge to make a little conquest and to be wooed like the other young girls — something that she honestly regarded as a shabby pleasure. So she preferred to take a pompous attitude toward this hunger for life and these yearning senses. What rubbish, invented by men because they didn't know, poor things, that women in general are simple and vain and foolish and grow bored without a man to entertain them. That's where the whole myth of the sensual woman came from — but they're just as rare as black swans or disciplined, well-educated women.

Jenny placed Fransiska's portrait on the easel. The white blouse and green skirt now looked harsh and unbecoming. The colors needed to be muted. Her face was turning out well, the pose was good.

But at least this incident with Gram was nothing to take seriously. God knows, she should start behaving naturally, for once. All that nonsense — like with Gunnar in the beginning — about her being afraid that she might fall in love with every new man she met . . . Or he with her. She was almost equally afraid of that, since she was so unused to having anyone fall in love with her; it disconcerted her.

But surely they could be friends; otherwise the world would indeed become terribly disconcerting. She and Gunnar were friends — warm and steadfast friends.

There was so much about Gram that would make it only natural for them to become friends. They had actually shared many of the same experiences.

There was something so young and trusting in his manner toward her. The way he was always saying, "Isn't that true?" and "Don't you agree?"

All that talk yesterday about being in love with her . . . or thinking that he was in love with her, as he said. She laughed a bit to herself. No, a grown man wouldn't talk that way to a woman if he were seriously in love with her and wanted to win her.

He was a sweet boy; yes, he was.

Today he hadn't mentioned a word about it.

She had liked him when he said that if he had truly loved his sweetheart, then he would have wished for her to find happiness with someone else.

10

Jenny and Helge ran hand in hand along Via Magnanapoli. The street was nothing more than a stairway that led down to the Forum of Trajan. On the last step he pulled her close and gave her a lightning-swift kiss.

"Are you mad? Don't you know you can't kiss on the streets here in Rome?"

Then they both laughed. One evening two *guardias* had lectured them on the Laterano piazza. They had been strolling back and forth, kissing each other beneath the stone pines along the old city wall.

The last ray of sun touched the bronze saint atop the Column and singed the walls of the buildings and the crowns of the trees in the gardens up on the slope. The square lay in shadow with its old, dilapidated houses surrounding the excavated forum below street level.

Jenny and Helge leaned over the railing and tried to count the fat, languorous cats that lived among the stumps of gray pillars down in the overgrown site. Now, with the encroaching twilight, they slowly started coming to life. An orange one that had been lying on the base of Trajan's Column stretched, sharpened its claws on the masonry, and then lightly and soundlessly leaped down to the grass, ran across it like a pale shadow, and disappeared.

"By God, if I didn't count twenty-three of them," said Helge.

"I counted twenty-five cats." She turned slightly and shooed away a postcard seller who had come over to them, hawking his wares in a mixture of many different languages.

She leaned over the railing again and stared thoughtfully down at the shadowed grass, sinking into happy weariness after a long sunny day full of countless kisses out in the pale green *campagna*. Helge pressed one of her hands to his arm and patted it. Jenny moved her hand down his sleeve until it was concealed in both of his. Helge laughed to himself, softly and happily.

"Are you laughing, my boy?"

"I was just thinking about those Germans . . ." And then she laughed too, softly and lightly, the way happy people laugh at mere trivialities.

They had walked across the Forum in the morning. And they sat for a while up on the high pedestal of the Column of Phocas and whispered to each other, while below them lay the expanse of ruins, crumbling, gilded by the sun, and with tiny black tourists crawling among the remnants of walls. But off by themselves, seeking solitude in the midst of the crowds of travel groups, was a newly married German couple. He was corpulent, ruddy-faced, and blond, with Lederhosen and a Kodak, and he was reading from a Baedeker to his young bride. She, who was terribly young and buxom and dark-haired, with what looked like an inherited tinge of housewifeliness about her soft, flour-white face, sat down to pose on a fallen pillar, while her husband snapped her picture. And the two sitting up above at the base of the Phocas Column, whispering about their love, without compunction or concern that they happened to be sitting above the Forum Romanum — they laughed.

"Are you hungry?" asked Helge.

"No, are you?"

"No. Do you know what I'd like to do?"

"No, what?"

"Go home with you, Jenny. Have tea in your room this evening. Could we do that?"

"Yes, of course."

They started walking down toward the city. They took the side streets, and they strolled arm in arm.

In her dark entryway he suddenly pulled her to him. His arm was clasped so tightly around her and he kissed her so fiercely and violently that her heart began pounding hard, with fear. And she felt a sudden anger toward herself because she couldn't help being frightened.

"My dear boy," she whispered in the dark because she wanted to force herself to remain calm.

"Not yet," Helge whispered as she was about to light the lamp. And he kissed her again in the same way. "Put on that geisha robe that you looked so sweet in. I'll go out and sit on the balcony in the meantime."

Jenny changed her clothes in the dark. And she put on water for tea and arranged some anemones and almond branches in vases before she called him inside and lit the lamp.

"Oh, Jenny . . ." He pulled her close again. "You're so beautiful. Everything in your room is so beautiful. And it's lovely to be here with you. If only I could stay with you forever."

She placed her hands on his temples.

"Jenny . . . Do you wish that too? For us to be together, always?"

She looked into his splendid golden-brown eyes.

"Yes, Helge. Yes, I do."

"Don't you wish it would never end, this spring down here — our spring?"

"Oh yes." She suddenly threw herself against him. "Oh yes, Helge." And she kissed him, letting her half-open lips and closed eyes beg for more kisses. Because it was as if his words about their spring never ending had awakened a tiny, anguished pang: This spring and their dream *would* end. And underneath lay a little fear that she didn't want to acknowledge, but it had come alive when he said: Do you wish we could be together, always?

"Oh, I wish I didn't have to go home, Jenny," said Helge fervently.

"But I'm going too," she whispered tenderly. "And I'm sure we'll come back here again, Helge. Together."

"So you've made up your mind to go home? Oh, Jenny . . . Does that make you sad? That I've come along and disrupted all your plans?"

She gave him a swift kiss and ran to get the tea water, which was boiling over.

"Well, you know . . . No, I'd half decided beforehand, you see. Since Mamma needs me so badly." She laughed. "I feel almost ashamed. She's very touched that I'm coming home to help her. And here it's just so I can be with my sweetheart. But that's fine. It's cheaper for me to live at home, even though I'll be helping her, and maybe I can earn a little besides. And I still have my money — for the time being."

Helge took the teacup she handed him. And then he grabbed her hand.

"Yes, but . . . The next time you take a trip, it'll be with me, won't it? Because . . . won't you . . . don't you think that we should get married, Jenny?"

His face was so young and his expression so timidly pleading that she had to kiss him over and over again. And she forgot that she herself had been afraid of these words, which had not yet been spoken between them.

"No doubt that would be the most practical thing, my boy. Since we agree that we want to stay together, always."

Helge quietly kissed her hand.

"When?" he whispered after a moment.

"Whenever you like," she said just as softly — and firmly.

Once again he kissed her hand.

"If only it had been possible for us to get married down here," he said a little later in a different tone of voice.

She didn't reply, merely stroked his hair.

Helge gave a little sigh. "But it's not possible. Since we're going back home so soon anyway. And surely it would upset your mother — a quick marriage like that — wouldn't it?"

Jenny was silent. It had never occurred to her that she needed to account to her mother for her marriage. Nor had her mother asked for her daughter's permission to marry again.

"At any rate, I know my parents would feel hurt. I'm not happy about it, Jenny . . . but I know they would. I'd prefer to write home that I've gotten engaged. And since you're planning to go back a little before I do . . . if you could go up and visit them . . ."

Jenny tossed her head, as if she wanted to chase away an unpleasant feeling. But she said, "I'll do whatever you want, my dear — you know that."

"It's not really what I'd like, Jenny. No, it's not. It's been so lovely, all of this — just you and me in the whole world. But it would be rather cruel to Mother, you see. And I don't want to make things any worse for her than they already are. I *don't* feel much love for my mother anymore — and she knows that, and it grieves her so. It's just a matter of a few formalities, after all. And she would suffer if she thought I was trying to keep her out. She'd think it was revenge for that old story, you know.

"But when that's over with, Jenny . . . then we can be married. Then no one else will have any say about it. I wish we could get married soon. Don't you?"

She kissed him in reply.

"Because I long terribly for you, Jenny," he whispered ardently. And Jenny offered no resistance to his caresses. But he let her go — rather abruptly and shyly. And he buttered a biscuit and began eating.

Later they sat next to the stove and smoked — she in the armchair, he on the floor with his head in her lap.

"Isn't Cesca coming home tonight either?" he asked quietly, all of a sudden.

"No. She's staying in Tivoli all week," said Jenny briskly and a little nervously.

Helge stroked her ankle and instep beneath the hem of her kimono.

"You have such beautiful slender feet, Jenny. Oh!" He ran his hand up along her slim leg. And suddenly he pressed her leg violently to his chest.

"You're so lovely, so lovely. And I love you so much — do you know how much I love you, Jenny? I just want to lie here on the floor at your feet. Oh, put your tiny slender shoes on my neck — do it!" Abruptly he threw himself down before her and tried to lift her legs and place her feet on his head.

"Helge. Helge!" His sudden fervor sent a tremor of terror through her. But this was her boy, she reminded herself. Why should she be frightened by what he wanted, since he was the one she loved? His hands were burning hot; she could feel them through her thin stockings.

But when she realized he was kissing the sole of her shoe, she felt a sudden revulsion. And with a bewildering feeling of anxiety and reluctance, she gave a forced laugh.

"No, Helge. Stop it. Those shoes . . . I've been trudging around in these filthy streets with them on."

Helge Gram stood up, sober and humiliated.

She tried to laugh it off. "Just imagine those shoes . . . you know there must be thousands of disgusting germs on them."

"My God! What a pedant! And you're the one who wants to be an artist!" Now he was laughing too. And with exaggerated mirth, to cover up his own confusion, he took her in his arms, and they both laughed with giddy embarrassment. "My charming sweetheart . . . let me smell . . . Oh yes, you smell of turpentine and oil paint."

"Nonsense, my love. I've hardly touched a paintbrush in three weeks. But go ahead and wash up, if you like."

"Do you happen to have any carbolic acid? So I could disinfect myself?" He made a lunge with soapy hands. "Females are chemically free of poetry, my father always says."

"Yes, your father's right about that, my boy!"

"Uh huh, you might as well arrange for a cold-water cure," said Helge and laughed.

Jenny suddenly grew serious. And she went over and put her hands on his shoulders, kissing him.

"I refuse to have you on the floor at my feet, Helge!"

—*∿*—

But after he had left, she felt ashamed. She thought it was probably true that she would have arranged for a cold-water cure. But she wouldn't do it again, because she loved him, after all.

She had made a mess of the evening. She had also been thinking about what Signora Rosa would say if anything happened. Oh, it was so humiliating to think that she was afraid of a scene with an outraged landlady and for that reason had tried to evade her promise to her boy.

Because when she accepted his love and returned his kisses, then she had obligated herself to give him everything that he wanted from her. She was the last person to want to get involved in that game of accepting love and giving a few trifles in return — no more than would allow her to withdraw from the game without losses if she should change her mind.

It was just nervousness, the fear of something she hadn't ever tried before.

All the same . . . She had been happy as long as he hadn't asked for more than she was willing to give. For surely the moment would come when she would wish to give him everything . . .

Oh, it had all happened so slowly and imperceptibly — like the spring here in the south. Just as calmly and steadily, without any abrupt transition. No cold or stormy days that made the heart wild with longing for sunshine, for a deluge of light and consuming heat. None of those eerily bright, endless, devouring spring evenings like back home. When the sunlit day was over, night fell, smooth and serene; cold accompanied the darkness, enticing nothing more than secure and serene sleep between the warm, glossy days. Each day a little warmer than the last, each day with a few more flowers across the *campagna,* which was no greener than the day before — and yet so much greener and softer than a week ago.

But that's the way her love had also appeared. Each evening she had longed a little more for the next sunlit day with him outside the city walls. And little by little her longing turned more toward him and toward his young, warm love. She had accepted his kisses because they made her happy — and day by day their kisses became more plentiful, until at last all speech was silenced between them, and there was nothing but kisses.

She had watched him becoming more mature and manly for each day that passed; the uncertainty seemed to slip away from him, the sudden despondency never overtook him anymore. And she too became more confident, warmer, happier. This was not the cool, stubborn self-assurance of her youth, but rather a heartfelt sense of security. She no longer felt suspicious about any life that refused to obey her dreams; now she confidently met each day with happy anticipation that the unexpected was good and could be turned to good advantage.

Why shouldn't love come like this: slowly, like a warmth that rose higher day by day, taking its time to thaw and warm? Even though she had thought before that it would come like a tempest that would instantly turn her into a different person, someone she didn't even recognize, and over whom her old will had no power.

And Helge . . . He accepted the slow, healthy growth of this love with such infinite gentleness and calm. Each evening as they said good night to each other, her heart was warm with gratitude toward him because he hadn't asked her for more than she was able to give that day.

Oh, if only . . . if only they could have stayed here. Until May, until the summer, all summer long. And their love could have ripened down here until they belonged to each other completely, as naturally as they were now growing closer to each other.

They could live together somewhere up in the mountains during the summer. The actual marriage could always be arranged here in the city afterward — or back home in the fall. And of course they would get married in the customary way, since they loved each other.

When she thought about going home, she felt as if she feared waking from a dream.

But that was nonsense. They were so terribly fond of each other. No, she didn't care for these interruptions with an engagement and visits to family and the like. Yet they were mere trifles, after all.

But she felt an eternal gratitude for this gentle spring down here, which had brought them together so quietly and tenderly — the two of them alone, out in the spring-green *campagna* among the daisies.

—◦◦◦—

"Don't you think Jenny will come to regret the day she got engaged to that Gram fellow?" Fransiska asked Gunnar Heggen. She was sitting in his room one evening.

Heggen twisted and turned the cigar he had in his hand. He discovered . . . it had never occurred to him that there was something indiscreet about discussing

Fransiska's affairs with Jenny. But talking about Jenny's more intimate relationships with Fransiska was a different story.

"Can you fathom what she sees in him?" Fransiska continued.

"Well . . . It's often hard to fathom things, Cesca. Especially what you women happen to see in one fellow or another. I'll be damned if . . ." He laughed a bit to himself. "We go around thinking that we make choices. But you know, we're more like our brothers, the dumb animals, than we like to think. One fine day we have an inclination to fall in love — because of our innate character. And then the place and opportunity take care of the rest."

"Huh," said Fransiska, shrugging her shoulders. "But what about you, Gunnar? You seem to be always so inclined . . ."

Gunnar laughed, almost in spite of himself.

"Or else I've never been — not sufficiently. I've never had that unconditional faith in a woman, that she was the one and only, et cetera. And that's part of love too — because of the innate character of the human being."

Fransiska stared straight ahead, thinking.

"I suppose many times it is. But you know . . . it's possible . . . sometimes you can fall in love with a certain person, not just because it's the right time or circumstances. I . . . I love the man I do because I don't understand him. I couldn't understand how a person could be the way he seems to be. I was always expecting something to happen that would somehow clarify or explain everything about him. I was looking for the hidden treasure, and you know you can become almost obsessed, the longer you look. Especially when I think that some other woman might find it first.

"But there *are* those who love one person and no one else because that person seems perfect to them. Can give them everything they need. Haven't you ever been so in love with a woman that you thought everything about her was right and good and beautiful? So that you loved everything about her?"

"No," he said curtly.

"But that's true love. Don't you think so? And that's how I wanted Jenny to fall in love. But she can't possibly love Gram in that way."

"I don't really know him at all, Cesca. I only know that he's not as dumb as he looks, as the saying goes. Which means that I think there's more to him than our first impression. Jenny must have found out what kind of fellow he is at heart."

Cesca sat in silence for a moment. She lit a cigarette and let the waxed match burn out, thoughtfully fixing her eyes on the flame.

"Haven't you noticed . . . the way he always says 'Don't you agree?' and 'Don't you think so?' and things like that? Don't you think there's something feminine . . . or immature about him?"

"Possibly. But maybe that's exactly what Jenny finds attractive. She's strong and independent herself. Maybe she prefers falling in love with a man who's weaker than she is."

"I can tell you one thing, Gunnar: I don't think Jenny is really so strong and independent. She's had to be that way; back home she had to help and support everyone else, and there was no one to support her. She had to take me under her wing because I'm much, much weaker than she is, and I needed her. There's always someone who needs Jenny. And now Gram needs her. Yes, she *is* strong and confident, and she's aware of that, and no one ever asks for her help in vain. But no one can keep doing that forever, always having to give support and never getting any in return. Don't you see how terribly lonely she must be, when she always has to be the strongest? She *is* alone, and if she marries that man, she always will be. We all talk to Jenny about ourselves, but she has no one she can talk to. Jenny should have a husband she could look up to, someone whose authority she could feel — a man she could tell: This is how I've lived, and this is how I've worked, and this is how I've struggled, because I thought that was the right thing to do. She should have someone who had the right to tell her that she was right. Gram *can't* do that, because he's inferior to her. And then she can't be sure she's right — can she? If she doesn't meet anyone who has the authority to confirm her thoughts? 'Isn't that right?' and 'Don't you think so?' . . . Gunnar, it should be Jenny asking those things now!"

They both fell silent for a long time, and then all of a sudden Heggen said, "It's certainly strange, Cesca. When it comes to your own affairs, you often can't make any sense out of them. But when you talk about other people's relationships, I frequently have the impression that you see things more clearly than any of us."

Fransiska sighed heavily. "Yes, I know. That's why I sometimes think I should enter a convent, Gunnar. Whenever I'm sitting on the outside, observing, I think I understand. But whenever I'm caught up in it myself, I get completely confused."

II

The enormous lobes of the cactus plant were scarred with names and initials and hearts. Helge stood there carving an *H* and a *J*. And Jenny stood with her arm around his shoulder, watching him.

"When we come back here," said Helge, "it'll be a brown scar just like the rest. Do you think we'll be able to find it, Jenny?"

She nodded.

"Among all the other ones?" he said with some dismay. "There are so many names here. But we'll come right out here and look for it — won't we?"

"Yes, we will."

"Don't you think we'll come out here again, my Jenny? And we'll stand here just like we are now, won't we?" He took her in his arms.

"Yes, of course. Why shouldn't we do that, my dear?" With their arms around each other they walked over to the table. Sitting close together, they stared out across the *campagna*.

The sunlight shifted and the deep shadows wandered over the hills in the spring day. Sometimes the light poured out in thick clusters of rays as gleaming clouds drifted across the blue sky, in bright, serene movement. But out on the horizon, where the dark eucalyptus woods near Tre Fontane peeked over the far distant ridge, a pearl-yellow mist seemed to seep upward; at dusk it would no doubt rise up and cover the entire sky.

Far out on the plain the Tiber flowed toward the sea, golden when the sun fell on it, but leaden with the dull sheen of a fish belly when it mirrored the clouds.

The daisies glittered like flakes of new snow all over the hillsides. On the slope beneath the inn's vegetable garden the new wheat was coming up, light green and shiny as silk. In the middle of the field stood two almond trees, their crowns pale pink with blossoms.

"This is our last day in the *campagna,* you know," said Helge. "Isn't that strange?"

"Only for the time being . . ." And she kissed him, refusing to give in to her own despondent mood.

"Oh, Jenny, do you ever think about how . . . when we sit here again, it can't possibly be the way it is now. People are always changing, you know . . . day by day . . . We won't be the same when we sit here again. Next year — next spring — won't be like this spring, Jenny. We won't be *exactly* the same, either. Our love . . . we may love each other just as much, but not in exactly the same way."

Jenny hunched her shoulders, as if she were cold.

"A woman would never say something like that, Helge." And she tried to laugh.

"Do you think what I said is odd? I can't help thinking about it, because I think these past months have changed me so much. And you too. Do you remember that first morning? You said that everything had changed for you the minute you left home. The way it did for me when I came here. You couldn't have fallen in love with me back then, could you, Jenny?"

She stroked his cheek.

"But Helge, my dear boy . . . that's what this big change is all about, of course — that we've fallen in love with each other. And we'll love each other more and more — don't you think? As we change, it just means that our love will grow. Surely there's nothing to be afraid of. We've both become happy people — that's what has changed. Do you remember that day — my birthday? That day on the Via Cassia, the first delicate little threads that began to twine between us? Now the bond has grown so strong, so strong. And it will keep on getting stronger. Surely that's not something to be afraid of, Helge."

He kissed her neck.

"Tomorrow you're leaving . . ."

"Yes. And in six weeks you'll follow."

"Yes. But we won't be here. We can't go out into the *campagna*. It think it's the fact that we have to leave in the middle of spring . . ."

"It's spring back home too, Helge. There are larks there too. Just look . . . Today, with these drifting clouds, it's almost like back home, isn't it? Think about Vestre Aker, Helge — and all of Nordmarken. We'll go up there together. Oh, springtime in Norway . . . with snowy white stripes on all the mountains around the blue, blue fjord, Helge. And those last ski trips in the spring snow

. . . Maybe we can even go skiing together this year. When the snow is so wet that it doesn't clump, and all the streams are rushing and gurgling, and the sky is green and clear at night with shiny golden stars, and the skis scrape and screech on the crusted snow."

"Yes, oh yes." He rocked her in his arms. "But Jenny . . . all of those places . . . Vestre Aker . . . Nordmarken. I've spent so much time up there alone. And that's what I'm afraid of, you know. I think there must be remnants of my old, discarded soul still clinging to every shrub up there."

"Hush, hush, my boy. I think it's going to be splendid. To go with my love to all the places where I've been alone and sad for so many springs."

—◦◦◦—

Hand in hand they walked across the green *campagna*. Now, as dusk was falling, the veil of clouds had spread across the sky, and a spring breeze swept toward them.

Jenny looked at every single thing with tender longing as she said farewell. Down on the road the hay wagons were creaking past, pulled by oxen whose grayish white hides turned into a velvety brown; and in front of the blue-painted grape carts the bells rang from the mules' red harnesses.

Oh, it was all so familiar and dear out here. She had seen it all, day after day, with him — not even realizing that she had paid any attention, but now she suddenly felt that everything had been burned into her mind along with the memories of these days.

The dry, reddish brown earth, with the short, scraggly grass from winter had grown softer and greener from day to day. And the faithful daisies in the meager soil. The mysterious hollows where the ground had collapsed — they had stood before them in wonderment. The thorny hedges along the roads and the shiny, succulent green leaves of the wild callas under the shrubbery.

The ceaseless chittering of the larks beneath the wide vault of the sky, and the countless barrel organs playing for the dances in the distant inns on the plain — the barrel organs with their peculiar glassy sound and always the same little Italian melodies.

Oh, it was so pointless for her to leave all this. Yes, it was.

She walked with him in the flowing spring breeze that soothed her body like a bath, and her body felt like a cool, fresh, succulent leaf, and she longed to give it to him.

—◦—

They said good-bye to each other for the last time in the dark doorway to her building. They didn't want to let each other go.

"Oh, Jenny. If only I could stay with you tonight!"

"Helge." She pressed close to him. "You can!"

He pulled her into a violent embrace. Clung to her hips and her shoulders. But she had begun to tremble as soon as she spoke. She didn't understand why she was afraid — she didn't *want* to be afraid. She regretted it at once when she made a move as if she wanted out of his fierce embrace. But by then he had already released her.

"No, no. I know it's impossible."

"I would like it so much," she whispered meekly.

"Yes, I know." He kissed her. "I know that you . . . But I know that I shouldn't.

"Oh, thank you, Jenny. Thank you for everything. Oh Jenny, Jenny . . . thank you for loving me. Good night now. And thank you, thank you."

—◦—

Cold tears ran down her cheeks as she lay in bed. And she tried to tell herself it was pointless to lie there crying like that — precisely as if something were over.

PART TWO

As Jenny ran across the platform in Fredrikshald to get some coffee in the restaurant, she stopped for a moment. There was a lark trilling above her head.

She half closed her eyes as she sat next to the train compartment window. She was already longing for the south.

The train raced past whimsical little crags of rugged, glazed red granite. The sparkling fjord appeared now and then, in glimpses of unbroken, brilliant azure. Pine trees clung tenaciously to the mountain slopes, with the afternoon sun on their red, ore-colored trunks and dark green, shiny metallic crowns. Everything seemed to be glistening after a bath from the melting snow. Small creeks splashed along the railroad tracks, and the bare crowns of the deciduous trees gleamed against the sky.

This was so different from the spring in the south. And *that* was what she longed for, with its slow, healthy breaths and the gentle joy of its colors. These fanfares of color reminded her of other springtimes, with wilder longings for passionate joys that were not like the serene happiness she now felt.

Oh, the spring in the south, with its calmly growing green on the magnificent plain. And all around it stood the mountains with their steadfast, stern lines. The people had stripped away the forests and built their rampart-cloaked, stone-gray towns up on the heights, planting their silvery olive groves across the hillsides. For thousands of years life had scrambled over the slopes; the mountains had patiently borne those tiny lives on their knees, and yet, with an eternity of loneliness and tranquillity, they had lifted their crests to the sky. Their proud, stern lines and their colors of muted silver and bluish gray and dusty green . . . the ancient towns and the slowly advancing spring . . . In spite of everything that was said about the boisterous life of the south, there the breath of life seemed to be measured out at a calmer, healthier tempo than here. In spite of the spring's dizzying power out there, it still was easier to comprehend that the wave of spring was washing over you — and past.

Oh, Helge. She longed to be down there with him. It was all so far away — and so long ago. Not yet a week . . . but it still felt as if she had dreamed it all. As if she had never even left.

It was strange that she *had* been there. And not here, seeing and sensing all this: the white, peaceful, icy-bright winter receding; the dry, invigorating pale blue air sated with a silvery pure, damp mist in the middle of the day, which hovered and quivered over the fields. The air trembled, all the contours trembled and dissolved, but the colors stood out sharp and blazing — as if naked. Until night came, and everything froze beneath a vault of pale green, corrosive light that lasted an infinitely long time.

My dear, sweet boy, I wonder what you're doing now. I long for you so. I almost can't believe, you see, that you're actually mine. I want to be with you. I don't want to be alone, missing you this whole, long, dreadfully bright spring.

Up through Smålenene watery strips of snow lay at the forest's edge and along the stone fences. The withered brown fields and the plowed-under acres stretched out with their soft colors, and here, where the dome of the sky seemed like a vast arch, the startling bright blue faded gently toward the horizon. The low undulating line of the wooded ridges was off in the distance, but a few freestanding groups of trees in the midst of the fields traced their lacework of branches against the sky.

The old gray farmsteads shone like silver, and the new red outbuildings burned with color. The spruce grove gleamed a lush olive-green, and the birch thicket was reddish violet against it, while the trunks of the aspens were pale green.

Oh yes, this was spring. The feverish colors burn for a brief time until everything turns a shimmering golden green and gleams with the sap of life, only to darken and ripen into summer in a matter of weeks. Spring, when no happiness is bright enough.

Dusk fell as the train raced northward. The last long red rays of sun burst over a mountain ridge. Then the cloudless sky held only a golden sheen, which was extinguished with infinite slowness.

When the train pulled out of Moss, the mountains were pitch-black against the bright green sky. And their reflection was even blacker, a transparent black in the glassy green fjord. A single big golden star hung above the peaks, and its image down below in the water rippled outward like a thin stream of gold.

It reminded her of Fransiska's night paintings. The life of the colors after the sun had set was what Cesca most wanted to paint. God only knew how she was doing. Although lately she had been working steadily. Jenny felt a little pang of conscience. During the past two months she had scarcely seen Cesca, and yet it had occurred to her several times that Cesca seemed to be having difficulties. But all of Jenny's good intentions about sitting down and having a proper talk with her had come to nothing.

———

It was dark when she arrived in the city. They were all at the station to meet her: her mother, Bodil, and Nils.

She felt as if she had seen her mother only a week ago. But Fru Berner wept when she kissed her daughter. "Welcome home, my sweet child. May God bless you!"

And Bodil had grown so tall. She looked trim and chic in her ankle-length tailored skirt and coat. And Kalfatrus greeted her a bit awkwardly.

The air at the train station was unlike anywhere else in the world — with its smell of rank seawater and coal smoke and herring brine.

The hansom cab rattled up along Karl Johans Gaten, past all the familiar buildings. Her mother asked Jenny about her journey and where she had stayed the night. Jenny sat there with an oddly everyday feeling, as if she had never left. The children in the backseat didn't utter a word.

Up on Wergelandsveien, outside a garden gate, two young people stood kissing each other under a gas lamp. High above the bare treetops in the palace park, the sky was deep blue and clear, with a few dewy stars shining. Jenny noticed a scent of moldering leaves gusting toward her — a scent from previous years, full of longing.

The cab came to a halt at the door of their home, a large brick apartment building on Hægdehaugen. The lights were on in the dairy shop on the first floor, and the delicatessen owner peered out when she heard the cab stop, calling hello and welcome home to Jenny.

Ingeborg came rushing down the stairs to embrace her. Then she raced back up again with her sister's suitcase.

The table had been set for tea in the parlor. Jenny saw that her napkin with her father's old silver napkin ring was in its usual place next to Kalfatrus on the sofa.

Ingeborg dashed out to the kitchen, and Bodil followed Jenny to her little room facing the courtyard. It had been Ingeborg's while Jenny was abroad, and she hadn't yet moved out all her things. Pinned up on the walls were postcards of actors, and Napoleon and Madame Récamier hung in mahogany frames on either side of Jenny's old Empire mirror above the chest of drawers on its pedestal.

Jenny washed her hands and face and tidied her hair. Her skin felt so awful after the journey. She patted her face with the powder puff several times. Bodil sniffed at the puff, wondering whether it was scented.

They went in to tea. Ingeborg had baked something warm in shells; she had gone to cooking school in the winter. There, under the lamp, Jenny noticed that both of her younger sisters had their thick curly braids tied up at the nape of their neck with white silk bows. Ingeborg's little tawny face was thinner and paler, but she wasn't coughing anymore.

Oh yes, now she could see it. Mamma had grown older. Or maybe not. Maybe she just hadn't noticed it before, all those years she lived at home and saw her every day . . . not seeing that the delicate wrinkles on her mother's beautiful fair face had multiplied, and that her tall, girlishly slim figure had begun to stoop a bit, or that her shoulders were sharp. From the time she had grown up, she had always been told that Mamma looked like her slightly older and lovelier sister.

They talked about everything that had happened at home during the past year.

"Now why didn't we take an automobile home?" said Nils suddenly. "I think that was awfully stupid!"

"Well, it's too late to have any regrets about that, young man." And Jenny burst out laughing.

Her bags arrived, and her mother and the girls watched breathlessly as she unpacked. Ingeborg and Bodil carried her belongings into her room and put them away in the dresser drawers. Almost with awe they touched the embroidered underwear that Jenny told them she had bought in Paris. And they rejoiced over their gifts: raw silk for summer dresses and strings of beads from Venice. They stood in front of the mirror, draping the silk over their shoulders and the necklaces in their hair.

Only Kalfatrus asked about her paintings and lifted up the lid of the metal cylinder containing the canvases.

"How many have you got, Jenny?"

"Twenty-six. But they're mostly smaller paintings."

"Are you going to have a separate show all by yourself?"

"I don't really know, but I've been thinking about it."

———〰———

The girls had done the dishes, and Nils had made up his bed on the sofa. Fru Berner was sitting with her daughter in Jenny's room with another cup of tea and a cigarette.

"How do you think Ingeborg is doing?" her mother asked anxiously.

"She seems healthy and lively — and she doesn't look so bad either. But of course it's not something to take lightly at her age. We must see about sending her out in the country until she's completely well again, Mamma."

"Ingeborg is always so sweet and nice, cheerful and funny. And so helpful at home. I'm terribly worried about her, Jenny. I think she's been out dancing too much this winter; spent too much time going out and getting to bed much too late. But I didn't have the heart to refuse her anything. Things were so dull for you, Jenny, and I saw how much you missed having any fun or pleasure. I was sure both you and Pappa would approve if I let the child enjoy herself while she could." Fru Berner sighed. "My poor little girls . . . Drudgery and work — that's all they have to look forward to. What am I going to do, Jenny, if all of you go and get sick too? There's so little I can do for you, my children."

Jenny bent toward her mother and kissed the tears away from her beautiful, childlike eyes. Then she leaned close, yearning to show tenderness and receive it, with the memory of early-childhood days and the awareness that her mother had known nothing about her life, about her sorrows before or her happiness now — all of this ran together into a protective feeling of love. Fru Berner pressed her head against her daughter's breast.

"Now, now, don't cry, Mamma. It will all work out, you'll see. I'm going to stay here in Norway for the time being. And thank God we still have some of Aunt Katrine's money left."

"But Jenny, that's supposed to be for your studies. I have to tell you, I've finally come to realize . . . that you mustn't be prevented from working. It was such a joy for all of us when you sold that painting last fall."

Jenny gave a little smile. That painting she had sold, and the few words in the papers about her . . . it was as if her family saw her artwork with completely different eyes after that.

"It will all work out, Mamma. Everything. I'm sure I can earn some money on the side, while I'm home. But I *must* have a studio," she said after a moment. And she added hastily, in explanation, "I need a studio where I can finish my paintings, you see."

"Yes, but . . ." Her mother looked quite horrified. "You *are* going to live at home, aren't you, Jenny?"

Jenny didn't reply at once.

"I don't think that will do, my child," said her mother. "A young girl can't live alone in a studio."

"No, well, I can *live* here," said Jenny.

———*w*———

She took out the photograph of Helge when she was alone. And she sat down to write to him.

She had only been home a few hours. And everything she had experienced down south seemed infinitely far away and strange. Without any connection to her life back here at home, either before or now.

Her letter held nothing but plaintive longing.

2

Jenny had rented a studio, and now she was busy fixing it up and putting everything in order. In the afternoon Kalfatrus came over to help her.

"You've gotten so tall and lanky, Kalfatrus. I was just about to address you as 'Herr Berner' when I first saw you."

The boy laughed.

Jenny asked him all about his activities while she was gone, and Nils told her everything. He and Jakob and Bruseten — they were the two new boys in his class last fall — had been playing savages in the log huts in Nordmarken, and they'd had the best adventures. As Jenny listened to him she wondered whether there would be any more hikes in Nordmarken for her with Kalfatrus.

She strolled through Bygdø in the afternoons — alone in the white sunshine. The fields looked so pale with their dead, yellowish white grass. At the edge of the woods to the north there was still old snow under the iron-black spruce trees. But on the south slope the bare branches of the deciduous trees glowed against the sunny sky, and beneath, in the old damp leaves, downy blue anemones were sprouting. Already there were many birds singing.

She read Helge's letters over and over again; she carried them around with her. She longed for him, sick and impatient — longed to see him and touch him and know for sure that he was hers.

———

She had been home twelve days, and she still hadn't gone over to visit his parents. When he asked her about it for the third time in a letter, she finally made up her mind. Tomorrow she would go.

The weather had changed overnight. A biting north wind had blown in, and with it piercing glints of sun and swirling clouds of dust and scraps of paper in the streets — and then suddenly a hailstorm that was so violent she had to seek shelter in a doorway. The hard white pellets leaped up from the cobblestones around her low shoes and frivolous summer stockings.

Then the sun was shining again.

The Grams lived on Welhavensgaten. Jenny paused for a moment at the corner. The shade was clammy and ice cold between the two rows of dirty-gray buildings. Only on one side did a ray of sunlight touch the upper floor. She was glad she knew that Helge's parents lived on the fifth floor.

This street had been on her route to school for four years. How familiar it looked. The black streaks left by the snow falling from the rooftops all down the plaster ornaments of the facades, and the tiny, dark shops. The windows with their potted flowers in grimy tissue paper and painted majolica vases, and the yellowing fashion magazines leaning against the windowpanes of the seamstress shops; the glimpse of pitch-black courtyards through the building portals. Heaps of filthy snow still lay on the ground, making the air raw in the courtyards. And the trolley droned its way ponderously uphill.

Nearby, on Pilestrædet, stood a soot-gray apartment building with a dark well of a courtyard in back. That's where they had lived after her stepfather died.

She stood for a moment outside the door with the brass plate that said G. GRAM. Her heart was pounding, and she tried to laugh at herself. She was always like this, absurdly anxious whenever she had to step into a situation that she hadn't been able to think through for years in advance. Good Lord — two future parents-in-law were not such terribly significant people, even for her. They weren't going to devour her, at any rate. She rang the bell.

She heard someone coming down a long hallway, and then the door was opened. It was Helge's mother; she recognized her from the photograph.

"You must be Fru Gram. I'm Frøken Winge."

"Oh, is that right? Won't you come in, please?"

She led Jenny through a long, narrow hallway that was cluttered with cupboards and packing cases and overcoats.

"Please come in," said Fru Gram again, opening the door to the living room. The sunlight was dazzling on the heavy moss-green plush furniture. It was not a large room, but it was packed full. There were knickknacks and photographs everywhere, a thick carpet in garish colors covered the floor, and heavy portieres hung in every doorway.

"Oh, would you look at this place . . . I haven't done any dusting in here for days," said Fru Gram. "We don't normally use this room, you see, and I'm without a maid at the moment. I had to get rid of the one I had — the worst kind of slattern, and she was always talking back. Well, so I told her she could just pack her bags, that's what I said. But finding another one . . . No, that's next to impossible, you know — and for that matter, they're all the same anyway. No, the worst thing you can become is a housewife.

"Yes, Helge prepared us for your visit, but we'd actually almost given up hope that you would do us the honor . . ."

As she talked and smiled, she displayed big white front teeth and black holes on either side where her eyeteeth were missing.

Jenny sat and looked at this woman who was Helge's mother.

She had imagined everything quite differently.

She had formed an image of his home and his mother, based on what he had told her. And she had felt sorry for the mother with the beautiful face, who looked like Helge in her photograph. The woman whose husband no longer cared for her, and who had loved her children so dearly that they stood up and rebelled, wanting to get out and away from her tyrannical maternal love, which refused to accept them as anything but her children. In her heart Jenny had sided with the mother. No doubt men didn't realize how a woman was bound to become if she loved someone but her love was never returned — except as the childish love from her children when they were little. No doubt they couldn't understand how that kind of mother would feel as she saw her children growing older and slipping away from her — or that she might rise up in defiance and anger at the inexorable passage of life itself, which meant that a mother's little children grew big and no longer viewed her as all-important, the way they were all-important to her, for all eternity.

Jenny had wanted to love Helge's mother.

But she didn't like her at all. She felt an outright physical antipathy toward this Fru Gram, who sat there chattering away.

Those *were* Helge's features in her photograph. The high, rather narrow forehead and the finely curving nose and the straight, dark eyebrows and the little mouth with the delicate thin lips and the chin that was a bit sharp.

But her mouth gave the impression that everything she said was full of sarcasm; there was a touch of malice and scorn to the fine wrinkles on her face. And her large eyes were an unusually lovely shape with whites that were almost blue — but they were hard and piercing, those big, dark brown eyes. They were much darker than Helge's.

She must have been beautiful once, extraordinarily beautiful. And yet Jenny felt quite certain about something that had once occurred to her: that Gert Gram had probably not married her with joy. She wasn't much of a lady either, judging by her language and bearing. Although it was true that so many proper young women of the middle class turned into real shrews after they had been married for a while — shut up inside a house for several years, bickering their way through life, with maid troubles and housekeeping worries.

"You see, Herr Gram asked me to come over and bring you his greetings," said Jenny. It suddenly felt impossible to call him Helge.

"Yes, he's been spending all his time with you lately. Or at least in his last letters he never mentioned anyone else. Although I seem to have understood that at first he was quite smitten with a little Frøken Jahrmann, isn't that right?"

"My friend Frøken Jahrmann. Yes, in the beginning there was a whole group of us that spent time together. But lately Frøken Jahrmann has been very busy with a major work."

"She's the daughter of Lieutenant Colonel Jahrmann of Tegneby, isn't she? She has money, doesn't she?"

"No. She's paying for her studies with the little she inherited from her mother. She's not on the best of terms with her father . . . or rather, he didn't want her to become a painter, and so she refused to accept any money from him."

"Oh, how silly. My daughter, Fru Curate Arnesen," said Fru Gram, "she knows her slightly. She was here last Christmas. But in her opinion there were other reasons why the lieutenant colonel wouldn't have anything to do with her . . . She's supposed to be quite pretty, but with a rather bad reputation."

"That's not true at all," said Jenny stiffly.

"Oh, it's all well and good for you artists." Fru Gram sighed. "But I don't understand how Helge could get any work done. It seems to me he never wrote about anything but going off with you to one place after another in the *campagna.*"

"Oh, I don't know . . ." said Jenny. It was strangely painful to hear mention of anything down south from Fru Gram's lips. "I think Herr Gram was very diligent. And everyone needs a day off once in a while."

"Yes. Well, we housewives certainly have to manage without, but . . . Wait till you get married, Frøken Winge. But everybody else is always taking days off. I have a niece who was just hired as a schoolteacher. She was supposed to study medicine, but she couldn't handle it and had to give it up and get a teaching certificate instead. Well. She always seems to be taking a day off. You certainly wouldn't want to *overexert* yourself, Aagot, I tell her . . ."

Fru Gram disappeared into the hallway. Jenny got up to look at the paintings.

Over the sofa hung a large *campagna* landscape. It was easy to see that Helge's father had studied in Copenhagen. It was boldly and skillfully drawn, but the colors seemed thin and dry. The foreground was especially dull, with two Italian women dressed in national costumes and miniature plants painted around the toppled pillar. Much better was the posed study underneath, of a young girl.

She had to smile. It wasn't so odd that Helge had found it rather difficult adjusting to Rome, or that he had been a little disappointed, since he had had all this Italian romanticism hanging on the walls back home.

There were many small, neatly sketched brownish landscapes from Italy, with ruins and national costumes. But the study of a priest was good. A few copies — Correggio's *Danae* and Guido Reini's *Aurora* — were quite awful. And several other copies of baroque paintings she did not recognize.

There was also a large, light-green summer landscape. Gram had tried to paint it in an impressionistic style. But the colors were thin and hideous. The one hanging above the piano was better — a glimpse of sunlight above the mountains, and the sky was enchanting.

Next to it hung a portrait of his wife. It was the best of them all. Yes, it really was good. The figure was charmingly drawn. As were her hands. The bright red gown with its flounces, the sheer black mitts. The pale olive face with the dark eyes beneath her bangs, and the tall, pointed black hat with the red bird's wing. But unfortunately she seemed pasted onto the background, which had been brushed in with strokes of a surly grayish blue.

There was a portrait of a child. TEDDYBEAR, FOUR YEARS OLD, it said at the top near the frame. No, good God — was that Helge? That tiny sullen little tyke in the white shirt? Oh, how sweet it was . . .

Fru Gram came in carrying a tray with rhubarb wine and cakes. Jenny murmured something about not wanting to be any trouble.

"I've been standing here looking at your husband's paintings, Fru Gram."

"Yes, well, I don't have much understanding for that kind of thing, but *I* think they're splendid. My husband claims that they're not much good, but that's just something he says. No . . ." She laughed a little bitterly. "My husband is quite a lazy sort, you see. And we couldn't very well live off his painting, not after we got married and had children, so he had to take up something more useful on the side. And then he didn't feel like sitting around and painting in his spare time, and so that's when he decided that he didn't have any talent. But *I* think his paintings . . . They're much more beautiful than all these modern pictures. But perhaps you may have a different opinion, Frøken Winge?"

"Oh no, your husband's paintings are very beautiful," said Jenny. "Especially the portrait of you, Fru Gram. It's absolutely lovely."

"Yes, well . . . But it's not much of a likeness. Gram certainly didn't try to flatter me." She laughed again, that rather bitter, angry laugh. "It's too bad . . . But *I* think he painted much nicer before he started trying to imitate all those others who were considered modern at the time. You know, Thaulow and Krogh, and those confounded . . ."

Jenny drank her rhubarb wine and hardly said a word as Fru Gram talked.

"I'm sorry, I'd like to invite you to have dinner with us, Frøken Winge. But I'm all alone with the housekeeping, as you see, and we're not prepared to have guests. So, unfortunately, I can't. But another time, I hope . . ."

Jenny could see that Fru Gram wanted to get rid of her. And that was perfectly understandable, since she didn't have a maid. She was probably in the midst of cooking. So she said her good-byes.

On the stairs she met Herr Gram. She was sure it was him. In passing she had a fleeting impression that he looked extremely youthful and that his eyes were very blue.

3

Two days later, as Jenny was working, she received a visit from Helge's father.

Now that he stood there with his hat in his hand, she saw that his hair was quite gray — so gray that it was impossible to tell what its original color had once been. But he did indeed look young. His body was slim, a bit stooped, but not with an old man's stoop — more as if he were too slender for his height. And his eyes were young, although they looked tired and sad in his lean, smooth-shaven face. But they were so big and clear blue that they gave him a marvelously wide-open expression, full of wonder and brooding at the same time.

"Well, you see, I wanted so much to meet you, Jenny Winge," he said, giving her his hand. "No, my dear, don't take off your apron. And please tell me if I'm disturbing you."

"Not at all, dear sir," said Jenny happily. She liked his smile and his voice. And she tossed her painter's apron onto the wood box. "Soon the light will be gone anyway. How kind of you to pay me a visit!"

"It seems like an eternity since I've been in a studio," said Gram, looking around. He sat down on the sofa.

"You're not friends with any other painters? None of your contemporaries?" asked Jenny.

"No, none," he said curtly.

"But . . ." Jenny paused to think. "But how on earth did you find your way here? Did you go to my home to ask? Or to the Artists Association?"

Gram laughed.

"No. You see, I saw you on the stairs the other day. And then yesterday, as I was walking to my office, I saw you again. I followed you for a bit, thinking that I would stop you and introduce myself. You came inside here, and I knew that there was a studio in this building. Well, then I decided I would come up and pay you a visit."

"You know . . ." Jenny smiled merrily. "Helge followed me on the street too — when I was with a friend. He'd gotten lost, you see, down in the old section near the flea market. So he came over and started talking to us. He struck up a conversation, to put it nicely. That's how we happened to meet. We both thought he was a little forward. But it looks as if it was from you he learned to be so daring."

Gram frowned and sat in silence for a moment. Jenny had an uneasy feeling that she had said something wrong. She searched for what to say next.

"Would you allow me to make you a cup of tea while you're here?"

Without waiting, she lit the spirit stove and put some water on.

"Well, Frøken Winge, you needn't worry that Helge is too much like me. Fortunately, I don't think he has the least thing in common with his father." He laughed.

Jenny wasn't sure what she should say to that. She busied herself setting out the teacups.

"It's rather empty here, as you can see. But I live at home with my mother."

"Oh, you live at home? Well, this is certainly a fine studio, isn't it?"

"*I* think so."

He sat quietly, staring straight ahead.

"You know, Frøken Winge, I've thought a great deal about you. I gathered from my son's letters that you and he . . ."

"Yes, Helge and I are very fond of each other," said Jenny. She stood with her head high, and looked at him. Gram reached for her hand and held it in his own for a moment.

"I know very little about my son, Jenny Winge. Actually I know nothing at all about him, about what kind of person he is. But since you're fond of him, you must know him well; no doubt better than I do. And the fact that you care for him . . . Well, I take that as proof that I can be happy for him, and proud of him too. I've always *thought* that he was a fine boy — and quite intelligent. And I'm convinced that he's fond of you, now that I've met you. I only hope that he will make you happy, Jenny."

"Thank you," said Jenny, giving him her hand once again.

"Yes . . ." Gram stared straight ahead. "You must know that I'm fond of the boy. My only son. And I think Helge is also fond of me — at heart."

"He is. Helge is very fond of you. Of both you and his mother." She suddenly blushed, as if she had said something tactless.

"Yes, I believe it. But of course he saw early on that his father and mother . . . that they didn't love each other. Helge has had a miserable home, Jenny. I might as well admit it. If you weren't aware of that before, you'll see it for yourself soon enough; I'm sure you're a clever girl. But it's precisely for that reason that I think Helge will understand how much it means for the two of you to love each other. And he'll treat both you and himself very gently."

Jenny poured the tea. "Well, Helge used to come over and have tea with me in Rome in the afternoon. I think it was during those afternoon hours that we really got to know each other."

"And then you fell in love."

"Yes. But not right away. Or rather, I suppose we must have been in love then too. But we just thought that we were very good friends — back then. Of course, afterward, he still came for tea, you know . . ."

Gram smiled, and Jenny smiled back.

"Couldn't you tell me something about Helge, about when he was a boy — a child, I mean?"

Gram smiled sadly and shook his head. "No, Jenny. I can't tell you anything about my son. He was a good boy, and always polite. Diligent in school — no genius, mind you, but consistently smart and diligent. But Helge was quite a reserved child — just as he is as an adult — toward me, at any rate. But I think you should tell *me*, Jenny," he said with a warm laugh.

"About what?"

"About Helge, of course. Yes . . . show me how my son looks in the eyes of a young girl who cares for him. And you're not any ordinary girl, either — a talented artist, and I think you're clever and sweet too. Won't you tell me how you happened to fall in love with Helge? What traits the boy possesses that made you choose him? Tell me."

"Well . . ." Then she laughed. "It's not that easy to say. We fell in love with each other when . . ."

"I see." He laughed too. "It was silly of me to ask, Jenny. Almost as if I'd forgotten what it was like to be young and in love — don't you think?"

"'Don't you think!' Did you know Helge says that all the time? It was actually one of the things that made me love him. He seemed so young. I could see that he was reserved — and then little by little he opened up to me."

"That's something I can easily understand — that people would trust you, Jenny. But tell me more.

"Oh, you don't need to look so shocked. I certainly don't mean for you to tell me your whole love story — yours and Helge's — or anything like that.

"Just tell me a little about yourself — and Helge. About your work, my child. And about Rome. So that, old man that I am, I'll be able to remember how it felt to be an artist. And free. And to be working on something you love. And to be young. And in love. And happy."

———

He stayed where he was for a couple of hours. Then, as he was about to leave, wearing his coat and with his hat in his hand, Gram said in a low voice, "Listen to me, Jenny. Because it won't do any good for me to try to hide from you how things are in my home. It would be better, when we meet there, if you didn't mention that you've met me. So Helge's mother won't find out that I've made your acquaintance beforehand. For your sake too — so you won't be subjected to spiteful and unpleasant remarks. As things stand, if she merely suspects that I like someone — and in particular a woman — it's enough to turn her against the person in question.

"You may think it's odd. But you do understand, don't you?"

"Yes, of course," said Jenny gently.

"Good-bye, then, Jenny. Believe me, I'm very happy for Helge's sake."

———

She had written to Helge the night before and told him about visiting his home. And she had read through the letter with an irksome feeling that the section about meeting his mother was rather meager and terse.

When she wrote to him this evening, she told him all about his father's visit. But then she tore up the letter and started over. It was the part about keeping it from Fru Gram that was difficult to tell him. It was hard to start off having secrets with one person that couldn't be shared with another. She felt almost humiliated, on Helge's behalf, because she had become privy to the misery of his home. She ended up not mentioning it at all in her letter; it would be easier to explain it to him after he arrived.

4

Toward the end of May an unusual number of days had passed without a letter from Helge. Jenny was beginning to feel anxious — had even decided to send him a telegram the very next day if she didn't hear from him. That afternoon she was in her studio when there was a knock at the door. When she opened it, she was grabbed and hugged and kissed by a man standing outside in the attic's dark hallway.

"Helge!" she shouted. "Helge, Helge — let me look at you! Oh, how you scared me, you awful boy! Oh, let me look at you. Helge, is it really and truly you?" She snatched off his traveling cap.

"Now who else do you think it would be?" he said, unruffled and laughing.

"But my dear . . . What's this all about?"

"I'll explain everything," he said but didn't have time for anything else as he nestled his face against her neck.

"You see, I wanted to surprise you." They were sitting on the sofa holding hands and catching their breath after the first jubilant kisses. "And I did surprise you, didn't I? Oh, let me look at you, Jenny. How beautiful you are. My parents think I'm in Berlin right now. I'll check into a hotel tonight and spend a few days here incognito. Don't you think that's a splendid idea? In fact, it's too bad you live at home. Otherwise we could have spent the whole day together."

—✦—

"You know," said Jenny, "when you knocked on the door I thought it was your father."

"My father?"

"Yes." All at once she felt a bit confused herself. It suddenly seemed rather difficult to explain the connection. "Well, you see, your father once paid me a visit, and since then he sometimes comes up here in the afternoons for tea. Then we sit and talk about you."

"But Jenny . . . You didn't write a word about this. You never even mentioned that you'd met Father!"

"No. I suppose I didn't. I wanted to tell you myself. You see, the fact of the matter is that your mother doesn't know about it. Your father thought it was better not to say anything."

"Not even to me?"

"Oh no, no, we haven't talked about that. I'm sure he thinks that I told you. No, it was because your mother wasn't supposed to know that we'd met." She was silent for a moment. "I thought it was . . . well, I didn't want to write and tell you that he and I had ended up keeping something secret from your mother. Can you understand that?"

Helge was silent.

"I didn't really like it myself," she continued. "But you see, he came up here to call on me. And I thought he was terribly nice, Helge. I've grown quite fond of your father."

"Yes, Father can be very charming when he wants to be. And the fact that you're a painter . . ."

"It's for your sake, Helge, that he likes me. I'm sure of that."

Helge didn't reply.

"And you've only seen Mother that one time?"

"Yes. But my dear sweet love, aren't you hungry? Shall I fix you something to eat?"

"That would be nice. But we'll go out and have supper together tonight, won't we?"

—◇—

There was another knock on the door.

"It's your father," whispered Jenny.

"Shhh, be quiet. Don't open the door."

After a moment someone walked back down the hallway. Helge made a little grimace.

"But my own dear boy . . . What is it?"

"Oh, I don't know. I hope we don't run into him, Jenny. We don't want to be disturbed, do we? Or meet anyone?"

"No." And she kissed him on the lips and bent his head down and kissed him behind each ear.

—◌◌—

"I can't believe all this about Fransiska, Helge," said Jenny suddenly as they sat and talked over a glass of liqueur with their coffee.

"Oh yes! But surely you knew about it beforehand. Didn't she write to you?"

Jenny shook her head.

"Not a word. I was so stunned when I got her letter. All it said was that the next day she was marrying Ahlin. I had no idea."

"We didn't either. Of course they were spending a lot of time together. But the thought that they would get married . . . Heggen didn't even know about it until she came and asked him to be a witness."

"Have you seen them since?"

"No. They went up to Rocca di Papa on the very same day, and they were still there when I left Rome."

Jenny sat lost in thought for a moment.

"I thought she was completely preoccupied with her work lately," she said.

"Heggen told us that she finished the big canvas with the portal, and he said it was very good, and she was working on several other pieces. But then all of a sudden she got married. I don't know whether they had been engaged for a while or not.

"What about you, Jenny? You wrote that you were working on a new painting."

Jenny led him over to the easel.

The large canvas showed a street disappearing off to the left, with a row of buildings in sharp perspective — office buildings and warehouses painted grayish green and a dark brick-red. To the right of the street stood several stalls belonging to junk dealers. Behind them the dividing walls of a few big buildings rose against the sky, which was an intense blue. And drifting into the distance were heavy rain clouds — gray-blue like lead and silvery-white. Bright afternoon sunlight fell across the scene, on the stalls and dividing walls, which gleamed reddish gold, and on the burnished green crowns of a few trees just starting to bud; they stood in the lot behind the stalls, with the wall as a partial backdrop. There was an array of workers and carriages and delivery carts in the street.

"I don't have much understanding of this kind of thing. But . . ." Helge pulled her close. "It's very good, isn't it? I think it's beautiful, Jenny — lovely!"

She rested her head on his shoulder.

"While I walked around town, waiting for you, my boy — and before I've always been so melancholy and alone in the springtime — I saw the blossoms of the maples and chestnut trees appearing in the clear, bright foliage against the sooty buildings and red walls . . . and the magnificent spring sky above all the black rooftops and chimneys and telephone lines . . . and then I had such an urge to paint it all. The delicate, bright sprouts of spring in the middle of the dirty, black city."

"Where is this setting taken from?" asked Helge.

"Stenersgaten. Well, you see, your father told me about some pictures of you as a child that he had in his office, and so I was supposed to go over and look at them, you know. And I saw this scene from his office window, and I got permission to set up my easel in the box factory next door. That's where I painted this from. Well, I did have to modify the composition a bit . . . change a few things . . ."

"So you've spent quite a lot of time with my father?" Helge asked after a moment. "No doubt he was very interested in your painting?"

"Oh yes. He came over occasionally to watch, and gave me some advice that was actually quite helpful. He does know a lot."

"Do *you* think Father had any talent as a painter?" asked Helge.

"Yes, I do. The paintings hanging in your apartment aren't very good. But he showed me some studies that he keeps in his office. I don't think your father was a *great* talent, but he did have a delicate and distinctive style. Just a little too easily influenced from all sides. Which I think, in turn, goes along with his great ability to assess and love the good that he sees in what others have done. Because he does have a deep understanding of art, you know — and a love for it."

"Poor Father," said Helge.

"Yes . . ." Jenny caressed her sweetheart. "Things are perhaps much sadder for your father than you — or I — know."

Then they kissed each other and forgot all about Gert Gram.

———

"Your family doesn't know anything about it?" asked Helge.

"No, they don't," said Jenny.

"But what about in the beginning . . . when I sent all my letters to your mother's address? Didn't she ever ask who was writing to you every day?"

"Not at all. My mamma isn't like that."

"*My* mamma," said Helge, suddenly vehement. "Mother isn't really as tact-less as you may think. You're not being fair to my poor mother. I would think for my sake you could stop talking about her that way."

"But Helge!" Jenny looked up at him. "I haven't said a word about your mother!"

"You said: *My* mother isn't like that. You did."

"No, I didn't. I said: My *mother*."

"You said: *My* mother. If you don't like her, that's your own business, although you can hardly have any reason . . . But you could at least keep in mind that it's *my* mother you're talking about. And I love her just the same, no matter what she's like."

"Helge! But Helge . . ." She stopped, because she could feel tears filling her eyes. And it was something so new for Jenny Winge to cry that she held her tongue, ashamed and appalled. But he noticed.

"Jenny! Oh, Jenny, have I hurt your feelings? Oh, my Jenny . . . Good Lord. There, you see — I've barely come back home and it's already starting." He suddenly gave a shout and raised his clenched fists in the air. "Oh, I hate it, I *hate* what's supposedly called my home."

"My boy, my boy — you mustn't . . . Oh, my dear, don't go on like that." She pulled him into her arms, held him close, so close. "Helge! Listen to me, my dear beloved. What does that have to do with *us*? They can't harm *us*." And she kissed him again and again, until he stopped shaking and sobbing.

5

Jenny and Helge were sitting on the sofa in his room. They had their arms around each other, but they weren't saying a word.

It was a Sunday in late June, and Jenny had taken a walk with Helge in the morning and then eaten the midday meal with the Grams, followed by coffee. And all four of them had sat in the living room and struggled through the afternoon until Helge took Jenny into his room on the pretext of asking her to read through something he had written.

"Awful," Jenny said abruptly.

Helge didn't ask what she was saying "awful" about. Wearily he lay his head in her lap, and she patted his hair, then stroked his hand over and over, but she didn't speak.

"Yes," Helge sighed. "It was so much more pleasant in your room on Via Vantaggio. Wasn't it, Jenny?"

From the kitchen came the sound of clattering plates and the crackling of a frying pan — a greasy smell seeped into the room. Fru Gram was cooking a hot meal for supper. Jenny went over to the open window and looked down at the black well of the courtyard for a moment. All the windows opposite belonged to kitchens and bedrooms, with drawn curtains, and in each corner of the courtyard a large window was placed diagonally. Awful. How well she knew that kind of dining room with a single window in the corner, facing a courtyard that was dark and gloomy, with never a hint of sunlight; soot poured in whenever the window stood open, and the smell of food clung to the room.

From a maid's room came guitar music and a full, trained soprano sang:

> Come to Jesus, my friend,
> Come to Jesus, my friend,
> If you knock on the door,
> He will open Heaven to you!

The guitar reminded her of Via Vantaggio and Cesca and Gunnar, who used to lean back in a corner of the sofa with his feet propped up on a chair and strum Cesca's guitar, humming Cesca's Italian ballads. And suddenly she had such a desperate longing for everything down south.

Helge came over to her. "What are you thinking about?"

"About Via Vantaggio."

"Oh yes, it was so wonderful there, Jenny."

Abruptly she threw her arms around his neck and nuzzled her head lovingly against his shoulder. The minute he spoke, it had occurred to her that he was not included in what she had been longing for.

And she raised her face and looked up into his amber eyes and tried to think about all those dazzling sunny days in the *campagna* when he had stretched out in the grass among the daisies and looked up at her.

She was *determined* to shake off the heavy, suffocating feeling of reluctance that overcame her every time she visited his home.

Everything was so unbearable here. From the very first evening, when she was invited over, right after Helge's official return home. Fru Gram had introduced her husband, and then Jenny had to stand there, playing out that comedy while Helge looked on and knew they were deceiving his mother. It tormented her terribly. And things had gotten even worse. She was alone with Herr Gram for a moment, and he mentioned that he had been up to see her one afternoon, but she wasn't home. "No, I wasn't in the studio that day," she told him and immediately turned blood-red. Then he had given her a look of such utter bewilderment that she had said — God knows why this suddenly came out of her mouth — "Well, actually I *was* there. But I couldn't come to the door, because someone was with me."

Gram gave a little smile and then he said, "Yes, I could hear that someone was in the studio." And then in confusion she told him that it was Helge, and that he had been in town for a few days incognito.

"Dear Jenny," Gram had said, and she could see that he wasn't pleased. "You didn't have to hide from me. *I* certainly would have left the two of you alone. Well, well. I won't say another word, but it certainly would have made me happy if Helge had wanted to say hello to me."

She couldn't think of anything to say.

"No, no. Don't worry, I'll make sure that Helge doesn't find out I know about this."

It hadn't been her intention to hide the fact from Helge that she had told her father about it. But then she couldn't bring herself to mention it, afraid that he would be displeased. And it made her nervous and anxious trying to keep track of what one person or another wasn't supposed to know.

Her own family didn't know anything about it either. But that was different. The truth was that she wasn't used to talking to her mother about her personal life. She had never found any sympathy in those quarters, nor had she sought or expected any. And now her mother had all this worry about Ingeborg. Jenny had persuaded her mother to rent rooms near Bundefjord; Bodil and Nils traveled back and forth to school each day, and Jenny lived in her studio and ate her meals in town.

And yet she had never had such good feelings about her mother and her home as she did now. Partly because her mother seemed to understand her a little. Every once in a while, when she noticed that Jenny was having difficulties, she had sincerely tried to offer help and solace — without asking questions. She would have blushed at the mere thought of asking any of her children an importunate question. But this place — Helge's home . . . It must have been utter hell to grow up here. And the discord seemed to hover like a shadow over them, even at other times when they were together. But she was determined to conquer it. Her poor, poor boy.

"My dearest Helge." And all of a sudden she overwhelmed him with caresses.

Jenny kept offering to help Fru Gram with the dishes and with the supper preparations, but every time she was told with a smile, "No, my dear — that's not why you're here. You aren't expected to do that, Frøken Winge."

Maybe she didn't mean it, but Fru Gram's smile was always so spiteful when she spoke to Jenny. The poor thing, she probably didn't have any other kind of smile left.

Gram came home; he'd been out for a walk. Jenny and Helge went into his den with him.

His wife also came in for a moment.

"You forgot your umbrella, my dear, as usual. It's a good thing you didn't get caught in a shower. These men . . . if you don't look out for them . . ." She smiled at Jenny.

"Ah, but you're so good about looking out for me," said Gram. His voice and his bearing were always so painfully polite when he spoke to his wife.

"So you've decided to join him in here too?" she said to Helge and Jenny.

"It's strange," said Jenny, "but I think it's the same in every home: The man's den is always the most comfortable place in the house. It was that way in my family, too, when my father was alive," she added hastily. "I suppose it's because they're furnished as workrooms."

"In that case the kitchen should be the most comfortable room in the house," Fru Gram laughed. "Where do you think the most work is done, Gert? Here in your room or in my . . . well, I suppose you could call the kitchen my workroom?"

"I'll admit that your workroom is without a doubt the most practically furnished of them all."

"Yes," said Fru Gram. "And now I think I may have to accept your kind offer for a moment . . . Would you mind helping me a little, Frøken Winge? Suddenly it's so late."

———— ᨆ ————

They were sitting at the supper table when the doorbell rang. It was Fru Gram's niece, Aagot Sand. Fru Gram introduced Jenny Winge.

"Oh, you're the painter that Helge spent so much time with in Rome. I thought as much," she laughed. "I saw you on Stenersgaten one day in the spring; you were with Uncle Gert, carrying a bunch of artist's supplies — "

"You must be mistaken, dear Aagot," Fru Gram interrupted her. "When did you say that was?"

"The day before the prayer holiday. I was coming home from school."

"Oh yes, that's right," said Gram. "Frøken Winge had dropped her box of paints on the street, and I was helping her pick them up."

"So it was just a little incident that you forgot to confess to your wife," Fru Gram laughed loudly. "I had no idea that the two of you had met before."

Gram laughed too.

"Frøken Winge didn't seem to recognize me. That wasn't exactly flattering, so I didn't want to remind her. Did you really have no idea when you met me that I was the kind old gentleman who gave you a hand?"

"I wasn't sure," she said faintly. She was sitting there blood-red. "I didn't think you recognized *me*." She tried to laugh, but she was painfully aware of the way her voice was quavering and her cheeks were burning.

"Well, just a little incident," Fru Gram laughed. "But that was certainly an odd coincidence."

———— ᨆ ————

"Oh, did I say something wrong again?" asked Aagot. They were sitting in the living room after supper. Gram had retreated to his den, and his wife was in the kitchen. "It's always so awful in this house; you never know when things are going to explode. But please explain, because I don't understand . . ."

"Good Lord, Aagot, just mind your own business," snapped Helge.

"Now, now, be nice, don't bite my head off! Is Aunt Bekka jealous of Frøken Winge? Is that it?"

"You're the most tactless person I've ever known."

"After your mother, you mean — oh yes, that's what Uncle Gert once told me." She laughed. "But that's neither here nor there. Jealous of Frøken Winge!" She peered at the other two with curiosity.

"My dear Aagot, stop meddling in things that only concern those of us who live here," Helge cut her off.

"All right, all right. I just thought . . . oh well, it doesn't matter."

"No, God knows it doesn't."

Fru Gram came in and lit the lamp. Jenny was almost frightened by the closed, hostile face of Fru Gram as she stood still for a moment, staring straight ahead with her hard, flashing eyes. Then she began clearing off the table. She picked up Jenny's embroidery scissors, which had fallen on the floor.

"You seem to be an expert at dropping things. You shouldn't be such a little butterfingers, Frøken Winge. Helge's not as gallant as his father, it seems." She laughed. "Shall I light the lamp for you now, my love?" She walked over to the den, went inside, and closed the door behind her.

Helge listened for a moment — his mother was speaking in a low, furious voice in the other room. Then he slumped forward again.

"Couldn't you just for *once* stop all this foolishness of yours?" For a moment Gram's voice was clearly audible from the den.

Jenny leaned toward Helge.

"I think I'll go home now. I have a headache."

"Oh no, Jenny, don't. There will just be endless scenes after you've gone. Please say you'll stay. It wouldn't do if you suddenly ran off. Mother will be even more annoyed."

"I can't," she whispered, on the verge of tears.

Fru Gram walked through the living room. Gram came in and joined them.

"Jenny's tired. She's going home now, Father. I'll go with her."

"Are you leaving already? Won't you stay a little longer?"

"I'm tired, and I have a headache," murmured Jenny.

"Just stay a little longer," he whispered suddenly. "She . . ." He cocked his head toward the kitchen. "To you she won't say anything. And while you're here, there won't be any more scenes."

Jenny quietly sat down at the table and picked up her embroidery. Aagot was vigorously crocheting a white shawl.

Gram went over to the piano. Jenny wasn't musical, but she could tell that he was, and gradually a semblance of calm came over her as he sat there playing gentle little melodies — for her sake, she thought.

"Do you recognize this one, Frøken Winge?"

"No."

"You don't either, Helge? Didn't the two of you hear it in Rome? In my day they sang it everywhere. I have some sheet music here with Italian songs."

She went over to look at them.

"Is it all right for me to play?" he whispered.

"Yes."

"Shall I play some more?"

"Yes, please."

He brushed her hand.

"Poor little Jenny! But go now — before she comes back."

—⁓—

Fru Gram brought in a tray with rhubarb wine and cakes.

"Oh, how nice of you to play a little for us, Gert! Don't you think my husband plays well, Frøken Winge? Has he played for you before?" she asked innocently.

Jenny shook her head. "I had no idea that Herr Gram played."

"How wonderfully you sew." She picked up Jenny's embroidery and looked at it. "I thought you women artists felt it was beneath your dignity to bother with handwork like this. Such enchanting designs. Where did you find them? Abroad?"

"It's just something I put together myself."

"Oh, I see. Well, then it's easy to make pretty patterns. Look, Aagot, isn't this nice? You seem to be quite a talented girl, Frøken Winge." She patted Jenny's hand.

What loathsome hands she has, thought Jenny. Short, stubby fingers with nails that were wider than they were long and that seemed to dig into her flesh.

———*∿∿*———

Helge and Jenny first walked Aagot over to her boardinghouse on Sofiegaten. Then they continued on together along Pilestrædet in the pale blue June night. After the rain shower there was a cloying scent from the white flower catkins of the chestnut trees along the hospital wall.

"Helge," said Jenny softly. "You *must* arrange things so that we don't have to go with them the day after tomorrow."

"That's impossible, Jenny. Since they invited you to come along, and you said yes. It's for your benefit, you know."

"Yes, but Helge . . . You know it will just be unpleasant. What if we went somewhere alone, Helge? Took an excursion all by ourselves, just the two of us, Helge? Like in Rome?"

"You know there's nothing I'd like better. But it will just cause a lot of trouble at home if we don't join them for that Midsummer outing."

"There's already trouble," she said with contempt.

"Yes, but it will just get worse. Good Lord, can't you put up with it, for my sake? You're not the one who's right in the middle of it all — living in it and trying to work . . ."

He was right, she thought, and she reproached herself bitterly because she wasn't more patient. Her poor boy. He had to live and work in that place, where she could hardly stand to spend even a few hours. And that's where he had grown up and suffered through his entire youth.

"Oh, Helge. I know I'm awful and egotistical." She clung to him — worn out and tormented and humiliated. And she longed for him to kiss her, for them to comfort each other. It was not their concern, after all. They had each other, they belonged together somewhere far away from that atmosphere up there of hatred and suspicion and malice.

The jasmines were fragrant in the old gardens that still lined the street.

"I promise that we'll take an excursion by ourselves, just the two of us, Jenny — some other day," he consoled her. "But to think that you could both be such idiots," he said suddenly. "I can't understand it! Surely you *knew* that Mother might find out — it could happen so easily."

"It's obvious that she doesn't believe the story your father invented," said Jenny meekly.

Helge snorted.

"I wish he would tell her the real truth," she sighed.

"You can count on the fact that he won't. And *you*, of course, have to pretend to go along. There's nothing else you can do. It was so idiotic of both of you."

"I couldn't help it, Helge."

"Huh. I thought I'd told you plenty about how things were back home. You should have put a stop to it after Father came to see you — instead of all those visits in your studio — and those rendezvous in Stenersgaten."

"Rendezvous? I saw that scene and knew that I could paint it — so that's what I did."

"Well, yes, all right. And of course it's mostly Father's fault. Oh!" he exclaimed angrily. "The way he talks to her! You heard what he told Aagot. And then tonight, to you." He mimicked his father, "'She . . . To you she won't say anything.' But she's still my mother, after all."

"You know, Helge, I think your father is much more considerate and polite toward her than she is toward him."

"Oh yes, Father is so considerate! Do you call it considerate, the way he maneuvers to get you on his side? And his politeness . . . You wouldn't believe how I suffered as a child — and as an adult too — because of it. When he would stand there, straight backed, looking so polite, without saying a word. Or if he did speak, it was in such an icy, biting, polite way! I'm almost grateful for Mother's screaming and scolding and fits of rage. Oh!"

"My dear boy!"

"Oh yes, Jenny. It's not *all* Mother's fault, you know. I can understand her. Everybody prefers Father. You do too. And it makes sense; at heart even I do. But that's precisely the reason I can see why she's become the way she is. She wants to be the most important person, you see. But no one sees her that way. Poor Mother!"

"Yes, poor thing," said Jenny. But her heart was ice cold toward Fru Gram.

The air was heavy with the scent of leaves and blossoms as they cut through Studenterlund. In the pale twilight of the summer night they could hear rustling sounds coming from the benches among the trees.

Their solitary footsteps echoed along the deserted streets lined with storefronts, where the tall buildings slumbered with blue reflections in their big, shiny windowpanes.

"May I come up?" he whispered in front of her doorway.

"I'm very tired," said Jenny faintly.

"I would so like to sit with you for a while. Don't you think we need to spend a little time alone?"

She offered no more objections but started up the five flights of stairs ahead of him.

The night looked pale overhead, beyond the big slanting windows of the roof. Jenny lit the seven-armed candelabra on her desk, took out a cigarette, and held it to a flame.

"Would you care to smoke, Helge?"

"Yes, thanks." He took the cigarette from her lips.

"It's like this, you see . . ." he said all of a sudden. "There was once something between my father and . . . a woman. I was twelve at the time. I don't know how much there was to it. But Mother . . . Well, it was an awful period. It was only for our sake that they stayed together — that's what Father himself once told me. God knows I don't thank him for that. Mother is at least honest and admits that she's holding on to him tooth and nail because she doesn't want to let him go."

He threw himself onto the sofa. Jenny sat down next to him and kissed his hair and his eyes. He slid down onto his knees and rested his head in her lap.

"Do you remember the last evening when I said good night to you in Rome, Jenny? Do you still love me just as much?"

She didn't reply.

"Jenny?"

"This hasn't been a good day for us, Helge," she whispered. "For the first time . . ."

He raised his head.

"Are you angry at me?" he said in a low voice.

"No. Not angry . . ."

"What then?"

"No, it's nothing. Just . . ."

"Just what?"

"Tonight," she hesitated, "as we were walking home. You said we'd take an excursion by ourselves — some other day. Things aren't like they were in Rome, Helge. Now you're the one who makes the decisions and tells me what I should or shouldn't do."

"No, no, Jenny . . ."

"Yes, it's true. But you see, I *want* it to be that way. You decide. But Helge, you're going to have to help me out . . . with everything that's difficult."

"And you don't think I helped you out today?" he asked slowly, standing up.

"My dear . . . Yes, of course, there was nothing you could do."

"Should I go now?" he whispered after a moment, pulling her into his arms.

"You should do what you want to do," she said gently.

"You know what I want. But what do you want — most of all?"

"I don't know what I want, Helge." All at once she burst into tears.

"Jenny. Oh, Jenny!" He kissed her gently over and over. But when she grew calmer, he took her hand.

"I'm going now. Sleep well, my love. Don't be mad at me. You're tired, you poor little thing!"

"Say good night to me properly," she begged him, with her arms around his neck.

"Good night, my sweet, beloved Jenny. You're tired, poor thing — so tired. Good night. Good night."

Then he left. And she wept some more.

6

"Here's what I wanted you to see," said Gert Gram, getting to his feet. He had been down on his knees, rummaging in the bottom drawer of the iron cupboard.

Jenny pushed aside the old sketchbooks and moved the electric table lamp closer. He wiped off the dust from the large portfolio and placed it in front of her.

"It's been years since I showed this to anyone, let me tell you. Or even looked at it myself. But I've been wanting to show it to you for a long time. Ever since I first visited you in your studio. That day you were here and looked at the pictures of Helge as a child, I thought about asking whether you'd like to see it. And later on too, when you were working next door.

"Yes, it's strange, Jenny. Whenever I happen to think about it, as I sit here every day in the midst of the usual drudgery . . ." He looked around the small, cramped office. "This is where I've ended up with all the dreams of my youth. They lie there like corpses in their sarcophagi, over in the cupboard, while here I sit: a dead and forgotten artist."

Jenny didn't say a word. Gram sometimes had a way of speaking that seemed to her so sentimental. Even though she knew that the feeling he was expressing was no doubt bitterly true. On a sudden impulse she ran her hand lightly over his gray hair.

Gram bowed his head a bit, as if he wanted to prolong her fleeting caress. Then — without looking at her — he unfastened the ties on the portfolio. His hand was shaking slightly.

She noticed with surprise that her own hands were trembling as she accepted the first page. And it was strange how terribly strained her heart felt. As if she feared some misfortune was about to occur. She cringed at the thought that no one must know about this visit — that she didn't dare tell Helge about it. And she grew dismayed at the very thought of her sweetheart. She had deliberately, long ago, given up wondering what her real feelings were toward him. And she refused to make room for the suspicion that now dawned on her at this very second, refused to be even more alarmed by examining what Gert Gram's true feelings might be toward her.

So she turned the pages in the portfolio containing the dreams of his youth, and it was inexpressibly sad.

He had often told her about this work when they were alone: the illustrations for *Landstad's Folk Ballads*. And she had realized that it was because of this work that he believed he had been born an artist. He himself had said the paintings hanging on the walls of his home were the competent and conscientious dilettante work of a student. But these . . . these were his own.

They looked rather good at first glance, these large pages with their opulent borders of Roman foliage and the precise monk's lettering of the text. The overall color effect was pure and fine — even quite lovely in some places. But the inserted vignettes and friezes with the human figures, as meticulous and accurate as they were in their miniature sketches — how lifeless they were, and devoid of all style! Some were very naturalistic and some so imitative of medieval Italian art that Jenny could even recognize a few specific Madonnas and Angels of the Annunciation beneath the cloaks of the knights and ladies. Yes, even the color effect on the pages of the Hukubal ballad, with its gold and reddish violet — that too she recognized from a certain missal in the Library of San Marco. And how peculiar were the rough-hewn, solidly shaped verses of the ballad as they stood there, printed in the neat typeface of a cloister Latin. In some of the full-page illustrations the idiom and composition were baroque, taken straight from Roman altar paintings. Resonances from everything he had seen and absorbed and loved, that was the melody of Gert Gram's youth. She couldn't find a single note that was his own — only echoes of many other notes; except that these echoes seemed to give everything back with an oddly weak and melancholy tone.

"You don't think much of them," he said with a little smile. "No, I can see that you don't."

"Yes, yes I do. There's so much that is delicate and beautiful about them. You know . . ." She searched a bit for the right phrase. "They just seem a little strange to us, since we've seen the same topics handled differently — and done so well that we can't quite imagine them any other way."

He sat across from her, leaning his chin on his hand. After a moment he looked up — and her heart shrank as she met his gaze.

"Actually, I remembered them as being better," he said quietly, and tried to smile. "As I told you, I haven't taken out this portfolio in years."

"I've never really understood," she said after a while, changing the subject, "why you felt so attracted to that period — the late Renaissance and baroque."

"I can't very well expect *you*, little Jenny, to understand it." He looked into her eyes with an odd, feeble smile. "You see . . . there was a time when I more or less believed in my own talent. But never so unconditionally that there wasn't always a tiny, nagging doubt. Not about being able to realize what I wanted to express . . . but I had my doubts about what it was I actually wanted to portray. I saw that romantic art had finished blossoming and was about to wither — decay and falsehood seemed to have overtaken the entire genre — and yet it was romanticism that had captured my heart. Not just in painting. I longed for the Sunday peasants of romanticism, but I had lived long enough in the country as a boy to know that they didn't exist. And when I went abroad, it was the Italy of romanticism that was my goal. I know full well that you and your generation, you seek beauty in what *is*, both sensual and real. But *I* found beauty only in a reshaping of the reality that others had already abandoned. As you know, the 1880s arrived with their new creed; I tried to accept it with my lips, but my heart rebelled."

"But Gert . . ." Jenny sat up straight. "Reality isn't some kind of precise concept. It appears in different forms to everyone who looks at it. 'There's beauty in everything,' an English painter once told me, 'whether your eyes see it or not, little girl.'"

"Yes, but Jenny — I wasn't capable of seeing reality. I could only perceive its reflection in other people's dreams. I completely lacked any ability to extricate *my* beauty from the multiplicity of reality.

"And I was aware of my own powerlessness. When I arrived in the south, the baroque seized hold of my heart. Can you comprehend such a profound feeling of powerlessness or what agony of soul it provokes, that old cliché? Nothing personal or new with which to fill in the form. Only technique to urge them on — the mad escape into draperies, the obstinate breakneck foreshortenings, the intense effects of light and shadow, the contrived composition. And the emptiness hidden beneath ecstasy. Contorted faces, twisted limbs, saints whose only true passion is the terror of their own devouring doubt, which they insist on blunting with unhealthy exaltation. Yes, it's truly the despair of barrenness, the epigone's work, trying to dazzle — but mostly themselves."

Jenny nodded. "Yes, but Gert, that's your own subjective point of view. I'm not at all sure that the painters you're talking about weren't awfully cocky and self-satisfied."

He suddenly laughed. "Could be. Perhaps it became my obsession because for once, as you say, it was my own subjective point of view."

"But that portrait you painted of your wife — dressed in red — that one's quite impressionistic, and it's very good. The more I look at it, the more remarkable I think it is."

"Yes, well . . . That's just an isolated piece." He didn't speak for a moment. "When I painted it, she was my whole life. I was still so in love with her — but my hatred of her was already boundless."

"Was it her fault," Jenny asked gently, "that you gave up painting?"

"No, Jenny. All the misfortunes that befall us are our own fault. I know that you're not what we call a believer. I'm not either, for that matter. But I do believe . . . in God, you might say, or in a spiritual power, if you will. Which hands out just punishments.

"She was a clerk in a shop somewhere on Storgaten. I happened to see her there. She was astoundingly beautiful; maybe you can still see that. Well, I walked past her one evening as she was leaving the shop, and I spoke to her. Made her acquaintance. I seduced her," he said in a low, hard voice.

"And then you married her because she was going to have a child. That's what I thought. And in return, she has tormented and plagued you ever since, for twenty-seven years. You know what? That's a rather harsh justice you believe in."

He smiled wearily. "I'm not as old-fashioned as you seem to think, Jenny. I don't see anything sinful about two young people giving themselves to each other, whether lawfully or not, if they love each other and feel they belong together. But I really did seduce Rebekka. She was an innocent when I met her — I don't mean just in the purely physical sense. It was clear to *me* how she was; she herself had no idea. I understood how passionate she was, how jealous and tyrannical her love could become. But I didn't care. I was flattered that her wild passion was directed at me, that I possessed this lovely girl so absolutely. And of course it was never my plan to be hers alone, the way I knew she would demand. Not that I was exactly thinking of leaving her . . . But I thought I understood how to assert myself, to keep separate from our relationship those things I didn't want to share — my interests, my work, the very core of my life — even though I knew she would try to take it all. It was damned foolish of me. I knew that I was weak and that she was strong and ruthless. But I figured that her greater ardor would give me an advantage, since I was in some ways relatively coldhearted.

"And I saw that, aside from her great capacity to love, she had little else. She was vain and uncultured and envious and vulgar. We didn't share any sort of spiritual connection, but I didn't miss it. I wanted only to possess her lovely body and enjoy her all-consuming passion."

He stood up and went over to Jenny. He grabbed her hands and pressed them to his eyes for a moment.

"How could I expect that marriage to her would lead to anything but misery? I had to reap what I had sown. And I had to marry her. It was a terrible time. Before, when she came to see me in my studio . . . She was wild and madly wanton, scorning all the old-spinsterish admonitions. She was proud of being my lover — inordinately proud. There was no other life than this life of free love. But when misfortune struck her . . . well, then she began singing a different tune. Then I started hearing about her respectable family in Fredrikshald and her unblemished virtue and good reputation, and I was a scoundrel and a coward if I didn't marry her at once, and so many men had tried to win her, in either one way or another, but she had refused to become engaged or to be seduced. And I had nothing to support a family on . . . I was just a student with a deplorable character and I'd never studied anything but painting. Months passed. I ended up having to go to my old father. So we were married, and two months later Helge arrived.

"My family helped me start up this business. I had dreams of someday becoming a big art-book publisher, and my folk-ballad illustrations . . . But I barely made enough to put food on the table for myself and my family. Once I even had to work out a financial arrangement with my creditors; perhaps you know about that. It was back in 1890. Well, she honestly and truly bore her part of the work and hardships and poverty; she would gladly have starved to death for me and the children. But considering the way I felt about her, it was almost worse having to admit how much she struggled and suffered and sacrificed for me.

"I had to sacrifice everything I loved. Bit by bit she forced me to give up everything I had, except her. She and my father were mortal enemies from the outset. Or rather, he wasn't very enthusiastic about his daughter-in-law, and her vanity couldn't bear it. So she had to sow discord between us. Father was a government official of the old school — a bit narrow-minded, perhaps; a bit rigid and dull — but distinguished and noble and honest, and so warm and gentle and kind at heart. We had always meant so much to each other. Oh, Jenny, you would have loved him. But of course I wasn't allowed to . . .

"And then there was my painting. I realized that I didn't have the talents I had once thought. And I didn't have the strength to keep on trying and trying when I didn't believe in myself. I was tired of struggling to make a living and tired of our marriage, which was becoming more and more of a caricature. She blamed me for it, but secretly she exulted.

"And then there were the children. She was jealous when she saw how I loved them and when she saw how they loved me. She didn't want to share me with the children or to share the children with me.

"Her jealousy has practically become a form of madness over the years. Well, you saw it for yourself . . ."

Jenny looked up at him.

"She can hardly stand it if I'm in the same room with you, even if Helge is there."

She sat in silence for a moment. Then she went over to him and placed her hands on his shoulders.

"I don't understand it. No, I don't understand," she whispered, "how you could bear that kind of life."

Gert Gram bent down and lay his head on her shoulder.

"I don't understand it myself, Jenny."

And when he raised his face for a moment and their eyes met, she put her hand on the back of his neck, and, overwhelmed by an infinitely despairing tenderness and compassion, she kissed his forehead and cheek.

She felt suddenly frightened as she looked down at his face resting against her shoulder with his eyes closed. But then he gently pulled away and straightened up.

"Thank you, little Jenny."

———

Gram put the pages back in the portfolio and cleared off the desk.

"Well, Jenny . . . I hope you will be very, very happy. You're so young and fair, so forthright and lively and gifted. My dear child, you are what I wanted to be. But I never was." He spoke in a low, meditative voice.

A moment later he said calmly, "I think that as long as a relationship between two people is new and . . . they haven't yet grown accustomed to each other . . . there can be so many things that seem difficult. It's my wish that you don't end up living here in town. The two of you should be alone — far away from family and the like — at least in the beginning."

"Helge has applied for that position in Bergen, you know," said Jenny. And once again she had that vague feeling of despair and anguish when she thought about him.

"Don't you ever talk to your mother about these things, Jenny? Why not? Aren't you fond of your mother?"

"Of course I'm fond of Mamma."

"I think it would be good for you to ask her advice, to talk to your mamma."

"It doesn't help to ask other people for advice. I don't like talking to anyone about these matters," she said dismissively.

"No, no. You're . . ." He was standing half turned toward the window.

Suddenly he gave a start and whispered to her in a low, agitated voice, "Jenny — she's down there."

"Who?"

"Her . . . Rebekka."

Jenny stood up. She felt as if she were going to *scream* — out of exasperation, out of disgust. And she started shaking. Every fiber of her being shrank, seeking to protect itself. She *refused* to be mixed up in this, in all that was ugly and repugnant: suspicions, quarrels, hateful words, arguments, scenes, and whatever else. No, she absolutely *refused* to get involved.

"Jenny, you're shaking, my child. You mustn't be frightened. I won't let her do anything to you."

"I'm not frightened — not in the least." All at once she turned cold and hard. "I came here to get you, we spent a few minutes looking at your portfolios, and now I'm going home with you to tea."

"It's not certain that she saw anything."

"And God knows we have nothing to hide, either! If she doesn't know that I've been here, she'll probably find out soon enough. I'm going home with you — do you hear me? We have to do this, both for your sake and for mine."

Gram stared at her for a moment.

"All right. Then let's put on our coats."

When they reached the street, Fru Gram was gone.

"We'll have to take a trolley, Gert. It's late." She walked on a bit farther. Then she said with sudden vehemence, "We have to do it for Helge's sake too. For his sake, it won't do to keep on having all these secrets between us."

—⁓—

Fru Gram opened the door herself. And while Gert Gram offered explanations, Jenny met her hostile eyes unabashed.

"What a shame that Helge has gone out tonight. Do you think he'll be home a little early, Fru Gram?"

"It's odd, my dear, that you should have forgotten about it," Fru Gram said to her husband. "It won't be much fun for Frøken Winge to sit here all evening with the two of us lonely old souls."

"Oh, now that's not true," said Jenny.

"I really can't remember Helge saying anything about going somewhere tonight," said Gram.

"Imagine seeing you without any handwork, Frøken Winge." Fru Gram smiled as they withdrew to the living room after supper. "And you who are always so industrious!"

"No, I didn't have time to go home; I left the studio so late. Couldn't you lend me some work to do, Fru Gram?"

Jenny chatted with her about the price of embroideries both in Norway and in Paris, and about the books she had loaned her. Gram sat and read. Once in a while Jenny could feel his eyes on her.

Around eleven Helge came home.

—⁓—

"What is it now?" he asked as they walked down the steps. "Has there been some kind of scene at home again?"

"Far from it." She sounded angry and annoyed. "Your mother apparently wasn't pleased that I came to visit, accompanied by your father."

"I do think the two of you could have avoided that," said Helge mildly.

"I'm taking a trolley home!" Overwrought as she was, she suddenly lost all control and tore herself away from him. "I can't take any more of this tonight, do you hear me? I refuse to have these scenes with you every time I come over to visit. Good night."

"But Jenny! Jenny . . ." He ran after her, but she had already reached the stop. The trolley arrived just then, and Jenny leaped inside and left him standing there.

7

Restless, she paced back and forth in her studio the following morning. She couldn't even think of doing any work.

Rain was pouring down steadily outside the big slanting window. Occasionally Jenny would stop and look out across the shiny, wet slate roofs and the black chimneys and the telephone wires. Raindrops rolled like pearls down along the curve of the wires, then merged and dripped off, but just as quickly new drops slid into place.

She could go out to Bundefjord to be with her mamma and the children for a few days. She simply *had* to get away from all this. Or, if she had to leave town, she could check in to a hotel somewhere and write to Helge to join her, and she could talk to him in peace.

If only they could spend some time together again — just the two of them. She tried to think about their spring in the south, and she remembered the heat and the green *campagna* and the white flowers and the delicate silver mist on the mountains and her own joy. But she couldn't seem to pull up an image of Helge from those days — the way he had looked to her adoring eyes.

And that time seemed already so far away and strangely isolated in her life. No matter how much she *knew* that there was a connection between then and now, she couldn't *feel* it.

That apartment up on Welhavensgaten . . . no, she didn't belong there. And it was as if *her* Helge had disappeared. But it was unfathomable, it didn't make any sense to her why she should have anything to do with those people . . . ever again.

No. Gram was right. They had to get away from here.

She decided to leave. At once. Before Helge managed to come over and demand any explanations for yesterday.

She had packed her bag and was standing there putting on her raincoat when someone knocked on the door, several times. She recognized Helge's knock.

Jenny froze, waiting until she heard him go away. A little later she picked up her bag, locked the studio, and left.

Halfway down the stairs she discovered there was a man sitting in one of the windows on the landing. It was Helge. He saw her, so she walked down toward him. They stood staring at each other for a moment.

"Why didn't you open the door a few minutes ago?" he asked.

Jenny didn't reply.

"Didn't you hear me knocking?"

"Yes, I did. But I didn't feel like talking to you."

He looked at her suitcase.

"Are you going to visit your mother?"

Jenny hesitated for a bit.

"No. I thought I'd go out to Holmestrand for a few days. I was planning to write and ask you to come too. Then we could be together for a while without anyone interrupting us or making scenes. I'd like to talk to you in peace and quiet."

"I'd like to talk to you too. Can't we go up to your studio?"

She didn't answer at once.

"Is someone up there?" he asked.

Jenny looked at him.

"Someone up in my studio, after I've left?"

"It might be someone you didn't want to be seen with . . ."

She turned bright red.

"Why is that? I couldn't very well know that you'd be sitting here spying on me."

"Dear Jenny, surely you know . . . I didn't mean that there was anything wrong, not on your part . . ."

Jenny didn't say a word but turned to walk back up the stairs. In her studio she set the suitcase down and stood there in her raincoat, watching as Helge took off his own coat and put his umbrella in the corner.

"Father told me about it this morning — that you'd been over to see him, and then Mother walked by outside."

"Yes." She paused. "It's a strange custom you have in your family — going around spying like that. I have to admit that I'm having trouble getting used to it."

Helge blushed.

"My dear Jenny. I *had* to talk to you, and the landlady said she was certain you were here. You *must* know that I don't suspect *you* . . ."

"I don't know what to think any longer," she said, resigned. "I can't take any more of this — all this suspicion and secrecy and strife and ugliness. Good Lord, Helge . . . Can't you at least defend yourself a little?"

"Poor Jenny." Then he got up and went over to the window, standing there with his back to her.

"I've suffered more than you know because of all this, Jenny. It's all so depressing. Because . . . don't you see? Mother's jealousy is not entirely unfounded."

Jenny started shaking as she stood there. Helge turned around and noticed.

"Of course, I don't think Father is fully conscious of it. If he were, he wouldn't allow himself — in that way — to follow his desire to be with you. Although . . . He also talked to me about how we should go away, both of us, away from this town. I don't know . . . Isn't he the one who put the idea into your head about leaving?"

"Going to Holmestrand was my own idea. But yesterday he did talk about how we shouldn't live here in town after . . . after we're married."

She went over to him and put her hands on his shoulders. Her voice was almost plaintive as she spoke.

"Helge . . . my love . . . I have to leave when things get like this. Helge, Helge . . . What are we going to do?"

"I'll leave," he said curtly. And he took her hands from his shoulders, pressing them to his cheeks. They stood like that for a moment.

"Yes, but . . . I have to leave too. Can't you understand? Before, when I thought your mother was just being unreasonable and . . . well, mean — I could just ignore her. But now . . . You shouldn't have said anything, Helge — even if you're mistaken. I can't go over there anymore if I have to worry about whether she might be the least bit justified. I know I'll feel uncomfortable. I can't face her. I'll end up acting like I'm guilty."

"Come here." He led her over to the sofa and sat down beside her. "I want to ask you one thing. Do you love me, Jenny?"

"You know I do," she said quickly, afraid.

He took her cold hands in his own. "I know that you did for a while. And God knows, I never understood why. But I knew it was true when you said it. Your whole manner toward me was full of love and kindness and joy. But I was always scared that the day would come when you wouldn't love me anymore."

She looked up at his white face.

"I'm so terribly fond of you, Helge."

"I know that." He gave her a fleeting smile. "I know you're not the kind of person who would all of a sudden turn cold toward someone you've loved. I know you don't want to hurt me, and that you would suffer too if you stopped loving me. I love you beyond all measure, you see . . ."

He bent forward, in tears. And she took him in her arms.

"Helge. My boy . . . my dear, dear boy . . ."

He raised his head and gently pushed her away.

"Jenny . . . That time in Rome — I could have taken you. You wanted to be mine — completely mine. You were more than willing. There was no doubt in your soul about the happiness it would mean for us to live together. I wasn't as certain. That must have been why I didn't dare . . .

"Later, back here in Norway . . . I felt such longing. I wanted to possess you completely, because I was so afraid of losing you one day. But I noticed you always shied away whenever you saw the — desire — rising up in me."

She looked at him in horror. She hadn't wanted to admit it, but what he said was true.

"If I asked you now. Right this minute. Would you?"

Jenny's lips quivered. Then she spoke, swiftly and firmly.

"Yes, I would."

Helge smiled sadly and kissed her hand.

"Willingly and gladly? Because *you* want to be mine? Because you can't imagine any possible happiness unless you're mine, and I'm yours? Not just because you want to be kind to me? Not just because you don't want to break your promise? Be truthful."

She threw herself across his knees and wept.

"Let me go away! I'll go up to the mountains. Do you hear me, Helge? I want to find myself again. I want to be *your* Jenny, the way I was in Rome. I do want to, Helge. I'm so confused, but I do want to. When I'm feeling calm again, I'll write to you, and then you'll come. And then I'll be your Jenny again, your very own."

"Jenny," said Helge gently. "I'm my mother's son. We've grown apart. We've already grown apart. If you can't convince me that I mean more to you than anything else on earth, that I'm the one and only man for you. That I mean more than anything else. More than your work, your friends . . . I felt you belonged more to them than to me. Just as you're a stranger among the people I belong to."

"I didn't feel like such a stranger with your father," Jenny whispered through her tears.

"No. But Father and I are strangers to each other, Jenny. And there's your work, which I can never fully be part of. I now know that I can even be jealous of that. Jenny, don't you understand? I *am* her son. If I'm not sure that I mean the whole world to you, then I can't help feeling jealous, and worrying that one day someone will come along that you will love more, who will understand you better. I'm a jealous man by nature."

"You *mustn't* be, Helge. Then everything will fall apart. I can't bear to be distrusted. Do you hear me? I could more easily forgive you if you were unfaithful than if you doubted me."

"Well, *I* certainly couldn't." He laughed bitterly.

Jenny brushed her hair back from her forehead and wiped her eyes.

"Helge. We love each other. If we get away from all this — and both of us *want* to — then things will be fine. When two people *want* to love each other and *want* to make each other happy —"

"I've seen too much, Jenny. I don't dare build on what you or I want. There have been plenty of others who based their hopes on good intentions. I've seen what a hell two people can make of their life together. You have to answer my question.

"Do you love me? Will you be mine — like in Rome? Shall I stay with you tonight? Is that what you want more than anything else in the world?"

"I'm so very fond of you, Helge." She sobbed, softly and desperately.

"Thank you," he said. And he took her hand and kissed it. "You can't help it, poor dear, if you don't love me. I know that."

"Helge," she implored him.

"You can't tell me to stay, Jenny, because you can't say that you couldn't live without me. Do you dare take responsibility for all the consequences if you say you love me — just so I won't be upset and leave you right now?"

Jenny sat and stared down at her lap.

Helge picked up his raincoat and grabbed his umbrella.

"Good-bye, Jenny." He took her hand.

"Are you leaving me, Helge?"

"Yes, Jenny. I'm leaving."

"Are you coming back?"

"Not unless you can say what I asked you to say."

"I can't say it right now," she whispered disconsolately.

Helge lightly stroked her hair. And then he left.

———*ᴡᴡ*———

Jenny stayed where she was on the sofa and cried. She cried bitterly and for a long time, without thinking about anything. And in the deep weariness that followed, a weariness from all the petty torments and petty humiliations and petty arguments of the past few months, her heart felt so empty and cold. No doubt Helge was right.

After a while she noticed that she was hungry. When she looked at her watch, she saw that it was six o'clock.

She had been sitting there like that for four hours. When she decided to put on her coat, she realized that she was still wearing it.

Over by the door there was a puddle of water; it had started trickling toward several paintings standing there with their canvas stretchers facing out. Jenny went to get a rag and wiped it up. Then it occurred to her that the water must have come from Helge's umbrella. She leaned her forehead against the door and began to cry again.

8

Dinner didn't take long. She tried to read the newspapers and ignore her thoughts for a while. But it did no good. It would be better just to go home and sit there.

A man was standing on the top landing, waiting. He was tall and slender. She raced up the last steps, calling Helge's name.

"It's not Helge," he replied. It was Helge's father.

Jenny stood breathless before him and stretched out her hands.

"Gert — what is it? Has something happened?"

"Hush, hush, Jenny." He took her hand. "Helge has left. He went to Kongsberg to see a friend, a classmate from school who's a doctor there. To stay with him. Good Lord, child, surely you weren't afraid that something else . . ." He smiled ever so slightly.

"Oh, I don't know . . ."

"But my dear Jenny . . . you're completely beside yourself."

She led the way along the corridor and unlocked her studio. There was still daylight in the room, and Gert Gram looked at her. He too was pale.

"Is it terribly distressing for you, Jenny? Helge said . . . or at least I understood him to say that . . . the two of you had agreed . . . both of you thought that you weren't suited to each other."

Jenny didn't reply. Now that she heard someone else say it, she felt compelled to protest. She hadn't fully comprehended before that it was over. But here he stood and said it: that they had agreed it was best this way, and Helge had left, and the love she had once felt for him was gone — she could no longer find it in her heart — and so it was over. But God in heaven, how was it possible that it could be over when that's not what she had wanted?

"Is it terribly distressing for you, Jenny?" he asked again. "Are you still in love with him?"

Jenny shook her head.

"Of course I'm fond of Helge." Her voice quavered a little. "You don't stop caring about someone you've loved. You can't be unconcerned if you've hurt someone . . ."

Gram didn't speak right away. He sat down on the sofa, turned his hat in his hands, and looked at it.

"I can understand that this is difficult and distressing for the two of you. But Jenny — after you've had time to think it over — don't you think it's best for both of you?"

She was silent.

"I can't even tell you how deeply happy I was, Jenny, when I met you and saw what kind of woman my son had won. It looked as if my boy was going to have everything that I had given up in my life. You were so lovely and wonderful. I had the impression that you were as kind as you were clever and strong and independent. And you were also a gifted artist who doubted neither your purpose nor your talents. You spoke with joy and warmth about your work and with joy and warmth about your sweetheart.

"Then Helge came home. And it seemed to me that you changed — and remarkably quickly. The painful scenes that are a daily occurrence in my home seemed to have much too strong an effect on you. I thought it was impossible for something like . . . an unpleasant future mother-in-law to poison so completely the happiness of a young woman in love. I began to fear there was some deeper trouble that you gradually became aware of. That you realized that your love for Helge was not as strong as you had thought. You realized that you and he were actually not as suited for each other as you had thought. That it had been more of a momentary inclination that had brought you together. Down there in the south, where you two were alone . . . released from all the ordinary bonds back home, alone in new surroundings, both of you young and free, happy to be working . . . both of you doubtless with a longing for love in your souls. Wouldn't that spark a momentary empathy and understanding? Even though that empathy and understanding didn't reach down to the deepest layers of your hearts?"

Jenny was standing over by the window, looking at him. She felt an oddly intense indignation at what he was saying. Good Lord, he was probably right. But he still had no idea, as he sat there laying it all out, what it was that distressed her most.

"That doesn't make matters any better, even if there is some truth to what you're saying. Maybe you're right."

"And yet it *is* better, Jenny, that the two of you have realized this now. Rather than later on, when the bonds were tied tighter and it would be even more painful to undo them."

"That's not it, that's not it!" she abruptly interrupted him. "It's that I . . . I despise myself. To give in to such a trifling attraction, and then to make up lies about it. You should *know* that you can keep your word before you tell someone you love him. I've always despised that sort of careless behavior more than anything else in the world. Now I'm the one who has to bear the shame."

Gram suddenly gave her a sharp look. He turned pale, and then bright red. After a moment he began speaking in a strained voice.

"I said it was best, when two people weren't suited for each other, if they discovered this before the relationship had taken such a firm hold on their lives that neither of them — and especially the woman — could erase the traces. If that's the case, it would be better to try, if they can — with a little resignation but much goodwill on both sides — to establish some sense of harmony. If that turns out to be impossible, they can still . . . I don't know whether you and Helge . . . how far it has gone . . ."

Jenny gave a little scornful laugh.

"Oh, I understand what you mean. For me it's not binding that I *wanted* to belong to Helge — promised him that — but can't keep my word. It's just as humiliating, maybe more, than if I had been his."

"You wouldn't say that if you ever met a man for whom you could feel a deep and true love," said Gram quietly.

Jenny shrugged her shoulders.

"And do you actually believe in a deep and true love, as you call it?"

"Yes, Jenny, I do." Gram smiled faintly. "I know that the very phrase may sound comical to you young people today. But I do believe in it — and with good reason."

"I believe that every person's love is like the individual himself," said Jenny. "The one who is bighearted, and true to himself . . . who doesn't waste his time on frivolous love affairs . . . I thought that I myself . . .

"But I was twenty-seven when I met Helge, and I had never been in love. That was something I regretted, and I wanted to try. *He* was in love, warm and young and sincere, and I was tempted. So I lied to myself, just like all other women. He cast his warmth over me, and I rushed to pretend that I was warm too. Even though I knew that it's impossible to keep up the illusion for long — only until something is *required* of your love. Other women do this kind of thing in all innocence, because they don't know the difference between right and wrong and are always lying to themselves. But I don't have that excuse.

"Oh, in reality I'm just as petty and egotistical and deceitful as other women. So you can be sure, Gert, that I'm not likely to make the acquaintance of your deep and true love."

"Well, Jenny, God only knows," and Gert once again had that melancholy smile. "As you can see, I'm neither great nor strong, and I had lived with lies and ugliness for twelve years, and I was ten years older than you are now . . . when I met someone. Someone who taught me to believe in the feeling that you speak of so scornfully — and I will never doubt it again."

They were both silent for a while.

"But you stayed . . . with her," said Jenny in a low voice.

"We had children. I didn't realize back then that I couldn't expect to have the slightest influence over my own children. Especially when someone other than their mother possessed so completely . . . my heart and my soul.

"She was married too. A bad marriage. She had a little girl. She could have taken the child with her. Her husband was a heavy drinker.

"It was also a form of punishment, you see . . . punishment for the marriage I had gotten involved in — with my wife. Which had never meant anything to me other than sensual attraction.

"Our relationship was too beautiful to be based on lies. We had to hide our marvelous, exquisite love as if it were a crime.

"Oh, little Jenny . . . There is no other happiness, you see."

She came over to him, and he got to his feet. They stood there, close to each other, without moving and without speaking.

"I must go, my dear," he said suddenly, his voice strained and hoarse. "I have to be home at the usual time, you see. Otherwise she'll be suspicious."

Jenny nodded.

Gert Gram walked toward the door, and Jenny followed.

"Don't be afraid that your heart is incapable of loving," he laughed quietly. "I think you have a proud little heart, Jenny — and warm! Will you still count me as one of your friends, dear girl?"

"Yes, I'd like that," said Jenny softly, giving him her hand. And he leaned down and gave it a long kiss — longer than ever before.

9

Gunnar Heggen and Jenny Winge were going to have a joint exhibition that fall, and he was in town for the occasion. He had spent the summer down in Smålenene, painting red granite rocks and green spruce trees and blue sky. Afterward he had gone to Stockholm, and sold a painting there.

"How is Cesca?" asked Jenny. They were sitting in her studio one morning, drinking whiskey and soda.

"Oh Cesca, well . . ." Gunnar took a gulp of his drink, puffed on his cigarette, and looked at Jenny, while Jenny looked at him.

It was so strange to be sitting there with him again, talking about people and things that seemed so distant. As if there were a land far away, beyond all the oceans of the world, where she had once known him and Cesca — lived with them, worked with them, and been happy with them.

That open, suntanned face of his, and his crooked nose. Someone had hit him in the nose when he was a child. That was what saved Gunnar's physiognomy, Cesca once said — otherwise he would have been one of those horribly handsome types. That's what she had said back in Viterbo.

There was some truth to it. Taking his features one by one, he was actually quite a rugged Adonis. With his low, broad forehead beneath the curly brown forelock, his big steel-blue eyes, and his lips so red and full, with shiny white teeth. His skin was tan all the way down his strong, firm neck, and his wide-shouldered, slightly short body was almost brutally well formed and muscular. And yet . . . the sensual mouth and the full eyelids bore an oddly innocent, untouched expression, and his smile could be so exquisitely refined. His hands were the fists of a real worker, with thick sinews and bulky joints on his short fingers, but he moved them in a uniquely lively and graceful way.

He had grown rather thin, but he looked healthy and content, while she felt so worn out and dissatisfied. He had worked all summer, reading Greek tragedies and Keats and Shelley whenever he wasn't painting.

"But I'd like to read the tragedies in the original language," said Gunnar. "So I'm going to have to learn Greek now — and Latin."

"Good Lord," said Jenny. "I'm afraid there are so many things that you absolutely have to learn before you can have any peace in your soul, that in the end you won't have any time to paint — except on your day off."

"Oh, but I have to learn it, Jenny. Because I'm going to write some articles."

"You are! So now you're also going to start writing articles?" She laughed.

"Yes, a whole series about all kinds of things. Including the need to reintroduce Greek and Latin in the schools; we need to see about getting some culture up here in the north too."

"Like hell!" said Jenny.

"Yes, exactly — like hell! Because we can't keep on this way. With our national symbol becoming a porridge bowl with rosemaling and a few carved curlicues — which is supposed to represent a clumsy imitation of the shabbiest of all European styles: the rococo.

"Yes, because that's the way we manifest our nationalism up here, after all. As you know, the best thing you can say about someone in this country — whether he's an artist or a respectable person — is that he broke away! Broke away from a school or a tradition or rules about manners or the concepts that ordinary civilized people have about proper behavior and decency. But just for once I'd like to state that, given our circumstances up here, it would certainly be more admirable if someone tried to make connections and then acquire, trade, and drag home to our cave here in the north a few of the accumulated treasures that are called 'culture' in the rest of Europe.

"But to break off, you see, a tiny section of the whole, literally pinch off a single ornament from an entire style . . . And the same applies to intellectual movements — to whittle and carve them up in such a clumsy and loathsome way so that in the end they become unrecognizable, and then to hail them as original and patently, patriotically Norwegian."

"Yes, well. But those sins were also committed during the period when a classical education was officially established for all institutions of learning up here."

"Yes, I know. But it was only a small piece of classicism. A fragment. A little Latin grammar and a few things like that. Here in Norway, among all the depictions of our precious forefathers, we've never displayed an image that portrayed the whole of what's called the classical spirit. And as long as we don't, we'll remain excluded from Europe. If we don't perceive Greek and Roman history as the ancient historical basis for our own culture, we won't have a European culture. It doesn't make any difference what happened historically in reality — what's important is how it has come down to us. Take, for instance, the wars between Sparta and Mycenæ. They were actually only a few half-savage tribes of warriors who fought with each other a long time ago. But in the story handed down to us, it has become the classical metaphor for what drives sensible people to fight to the last man rather than tolerate any assault on their individuality or their right to govern themselves. Jesus — we haven't fought for our honor in all these centuries. We've just been stuffing our bellies with cartloads of potato cakes and porridge ever since. The Persian wars, of course, were nothing more than trifles. But for a robust people, Salamis and Thermopylæ and the Acropolis meant the blossoming of all the noblest and healthiest instincts, and their words will continue to shine, as long as those instincts have some value and . . . as long as a nation believes it has qualities worth asserting and a past and a present and a future to be proud of. And as long as a poet can write a vivid poem about Thermopylæ and fill it with his own vivid emotions. Leopardi's ode to Italy — do you remember I once read it to you in Rome?"

Jenny nodded.

"It's a bit rhetorical . . . but God save me, it's lovely. Isn't it? Do you remember the part about Italia, the most beautiful of women, who is sitting in chains in the dust, with flowing hair and with tears falling into her lap? And then he wishes he was one of the young Greeks who had set off toward certain death in Thermopylæ, as merry and bold as if going to a dance. And their names are sacred, and the dying Simonides sings his jubilant song from the top of Antelos.

"And all the marvelous ancient stories that are symbols and parables, that never grow old. Just think of Orpheus and Eurydice. So simple: Belief in love wins out over death itself, but a single moment of doubt means that all is lost. Yet here in Norway the story is known only through an operetta.

"The English and the French have known how to use the old symbols to create new and vibrant art. In their countries, during the best periods, people were still being born who had impulses and emotions that were so cultivated that they could be developed strongly enough to make the fates of the Atrides as understandable and gripping as reality. The Swedes too — they still have a vital connection to classicism. Which we've never had. But after all, what kind of books do we read here — and write? Sunny little stories about sexless masquerade figures in Empire costumes, smutty Danish books that couldn't possibly interest any male over the age of sixteen, if he hasn't had to wear a Vita belt. Or else a green youth stands there babbling about the mystical, eternal female to a little chorus girl, who treats him insolently, deceiving him because he doesn't have enough manly sense to realize that the whole riddle can often be solved with a few swats of a cane."

Jenny laughed. Gunnar had begun to pace back and forth.

"I think Hjerrild's actually wrestling with a book about the Sphinx right now. I happened to be slightly acquainted with the lady. Well, it never got so serious for me that I felt like demeaning myself to give her a thrashing. But I'd always been fond of her, enough to think it disgusting. It made me a little sick when I found her out. But I've put it all behind me through my work, you see.

"In general, Jenny, I don't think there's anything you can't forget through your work."

Jenny was silent for a few minutes. Then she said, "So what about Cesca?"

"Oh yes, Cesca! Apparently she hasn't touched a paintbrush since she got married. When I went over to see them, she opened the door herself — they don't have a maid — wearing a rough apron around her waist and holding a broom in her hand. They have a studio and two little closetlike rooms, and of course they can't both work in the studio. And besides, she said the housework takes up all her time. The first morning I was there she kept crawling around on the floor; Ahlin was out. First she swept up with a broom, and then she crept around and dusted under the furniture, looking for little dustballs in all the corners; then she scrubbed the floor and dusted the room, and my God, how clumsily she did everything. Then I went out with her to shop for the midday meal — I was supposed to eat with them — and then Ahlin came home and she was out in the kitchen. And when the food was finally ready, her little curls were damp with sweat. But the meal wasn't bad. And then she washed the dishes — such a clumsy, cumbersome process, running out to rinse each piece under the faucet. Yes, Ahlin and I helped. I did give her a good deal of advice, you know.

"Then I invited them to have supper out with me. Poor Cesca sat there exulting because she didn't have to cook or wash up.

"If they have any children — and I'm certain they will — you can be sure that Cesca will be done with painting. And it's a damned shame. I have to admit, I think it's sad."

"Oh, I don't know. For a woman, having a husband and children . . . At any rate, sooner or later we start yearning for that."

Gunnar looked at her and sighed.

"I suppose as long as they love each other," she said. "Do you think Cesca is happy with Ahlin?"

"I don't know, Jenny. Yes, I think she does love him. At least it was constantly 'Lennart thinks' and 'Do you like the gravy, Lennart?' and 'Would you like?' and 'Shall I?' And of course she's started speaking a dreadful half-Swedish, let me tell you. I have to say, I don't really understand . . . Of course he's so in love with her that he's not tyrannical or brutish — on the contrary. But it's odd how she's become so meek and submissive, our little Cesca. It can't be just all those household worries, although God knows they've taken their toll on her. That's not exactly her forte, and in her own way she's such a conscientious little creature, and they don't have much money, I could see that.

"Maybe . . ." he laughed a bit frivolously, "maybe she came up with some brilliant idea. Spent their wedding night telling him about Hans Hermann and Norman Douglas and Hjerrild and all her other conquests, one after the other. It might have been rather overwhelming."

"Cesca certainly has never tried to hide any of her affairs. He must have known about them beforehand."

"You're right." Gunnar poured himself another whiskey and soda. "But there might have been some small detail that she hadn't revealed, up until then. Something she felt obligated to tell her husband."

"For shame, Gunnar."

"Well, damn it — no one ever really knows what to make of Cesca. Her version of the Hans Hermann story is awfully strange. I'm sure Cesca has never done anything I'd actually call wrong. Damned if I know why it should bother a man if his wife has had a prior relationship — or even several — as long as she was honest and faithful while it lasted.

"Because all that fuss about demanding physical innocence is basically crap. If a woman truly loves a man and accepts his love in return, I think it's tawdry if she leaves the relationship with something she hadn't wanted to give him. Of course I'd prefer it if my own wife had never loved anyone else before me . . .

Well, I suppose it might be different if it's your own wife. So many old prejudices and egotistical vanities can crop up."

Jenny took a sip of her drink. She made a move as if to speak, but refrained.

Gunnar had stopped in front of the window. He was standing with his hands in his pants pockets, his back turned to her.

"No, Jenny . . . I think it's all so sad. I mean, if on a rare occasion you happen to meet a woman who has talents in a certain area — who has known the joy of developing them and working, someone who has energy and so on . . . Who realizes she's an individual and can figure out right and wrong for herself, and who has the will to cultivate some of her abilities and instincts as good and valuable and weed out others as bad and useless . . . And then one fine day she meets a man, and it's good-bye work and development and everything else. She gives up all of herself for the sake of some wretched man. Jenny, don't you think that's sad?"

"Yes, I do. But that's the way we were created — all of us!"

"I just don't understand you. When it comes right down to it, we can't ever get it into our heads that someone who's supposed to be an individual could so totally lack self-confidence. The way all of you do. Women don't have souls — that's a fact. You admit more or less openly that a love relationship is the only thing that interests you."

"There are men who say the same — at least in the way they act."

"Yes, but a decent man has no respect for such . . . skirt chasers. Officially . . . well, we don't like to think of it as anything but a . . . natural diversion, alongside our work. Or rather, a capable man has a family because he thinks he can manage to support more than just himself . . . and he wants to have someone to continue his work."

"Yes, but Gunnar — by nature women are meant for other purposes."

"Oh, hogwash, that's not it at all. If they don't want to be individuals and work, but just females . . . What the hell good is it to produce a bunch of kids if they're not going to grow up to be individuals but just go on reproducing — if the raw goods aren't going to be reworked?"

"That may be true enough." Jenny gave a little laugh.

"Of course it's true. But women . . . Oh, I've seen it ever since I was a boy. When I was going to the workers' academy and other places. I remember a girl I studied English with. She wanted to learn the language so she could talk to foreign sailors. The highest goal any of the girls felt like striving for was the hope of a job in England or America. While the boys, my friends and I, we studied to learn — for the sake of mental gymnastics — trying in every way possible to supplement what we had learned in school. The girls just read for fun.

"Take socialism, for instance. Do you think women have any idea what it is, unless they have husbands who have taught them to understand it? Try explaining to a woman why society should be such that every child who is born has the chance to cultivate his talents, if he has any, and to live in freedom and beauty, if he can stand freedom and has a sense for beauty. Freedom, well . . . Women think it means that they can get out of doing something or that they don't have to behave properly. A sense for beauty . . . That's not something they possess. They just want to deck themselves out with anything that's expensive and hideous, and is considered modern. Just look at the kinds of homes they furnish — the richer they are, the uglier. Has there ever been a fashion, no matter how hideous or improper, that they don't go along with, provided they can afford it? Surely you can't deny this?

"I won't even talk about female morals, because they don't have any. Never mind your morals with regard to us — but among yourselves! The way you talk about each other and attack each other! My God!"

Jenny gave a little smile. She both agreed and disagreed, but she didn't feel like getting into an argument. Still, she thought she ought to say something.

"That was a gruesome salvo — the whole army decimated at once!"

"You'll have it in writing someday," he said contentedly.

"Yes, there's a good deal of truth in what you say, Gunnar. But there are differences among women too — although it may be only a matter of degree."

"Of course there are differences. But I have to tell you that what I said applies to all of you, to some extent. And do you know what's to blame? The central focus for all of you is a man: either one you have or one you lack. The only thing in life that has any real value and importance is something that in reality is never important to you. By that I mean, work. For the best among you, it may be for a while — and then I truly think it's because when you're young and beautiful, you're convinced that 'He' is bound to turn up. But as time passes and he doesn't put in an appearance, and you begin to get on a bit in years . . . Then you start neglecting your work and go around looking worn out and unhappy and dissatisfied."

Jenny nodded.

"Listen here, Jenny. I've always respected you as much as I do any first-class man. And soon you'll be twenty-nine, and it's necessary to reach that age before anyone can begin to work in a more or less independent fashion. You're not going to tell me that now, just as you're about to start your own life in earnest, you want to burden yourself with a husband and kids and a house and everything else that would only end up binding you hand and foot — all those things that would just get in the way of your work?"

Jenny laughed quietly.

"Oh, dear God, my girl! If you had all that, and you were about to die, with your husband and children and everything all around you, and you hadn't made use of the talents that you knew you possessed . . . I'm positive that you'd be filled with regret and dismay — I know you would!"

"Yes, but what if I had accomplished everything it was within my ability to do — what if I knew, as I lay there about to die, that my life and my work would live on long after I was gone, but I was alone — there wasn't a single person who was truly close to me. Don't you think that would also fill me with regret and dismay?"

Heggen sat in silence for a moment.

"Yes. Of course, there's also the fact that being unmarried isn't the same for women as it is for men. It often means that they're excluded from everything in life that people make the most fuss about. That an entire set of organs — spiritual as well as physical — simply withers away, unused.

"Oh, Jenny! Sometimes I almost wish . . . that just for once you'd be a little bit frivolous — so you could be done with all that and go back to working in peace and quiet."

"Women who have been a little bit frivolous, as you call it, Gunnar, are *never* done with it. If the first time was disappointing, then they hope for better luck the next time. Or the next time, or the next. They aren't content with disappointments. And before they know it, there has been a whole series of them."

"Not for you," he said swiftly.

"Thank you. By the way, this is something new that you're preaching. Before, you always said that once women started off on that track, they were ruined — for good!"

"Most women, yes. But some should be able to . . . I don't know. Of course those women who have no solid interests in life other than a man . . . you can't very well keep on changing the focus of your life. But the others, who have some sense of purpose — more than just being female. Why shouldn't you, for example, be true and loyal to a man — even though you both realized that you couldn't give up everything and bind yourself to being merely his wife for the rest of your life? Because love always fades away — sooner or later. Don't let yourself have any doubts about that!"

"Yes, that's something we know — and yet still doubt." She laughed. "No. Either you're in love, and you think it's going to last and it's the only thing worthwhile. Or else you're not in love, and you're unhappy because you're not."

"Oh, Jenny. I don't like it when you say things like that. To feel alive, with all your powers alert, ready to receive and grab hold and reshape and create — to make the most of yourself — to *work* — that's the only thing worthwhile!"

Jenny bent her face to Gert Gram's bouquet of chrysanthemums.

"I'm very happy that you like my paintings so much!"

"Yes, I do like them. Especially the portrait of the young girl with the corals — as I told you."

Jenny shook her head.

"The colors are so beautiful," said Gram.

"But it's not quite right. The shawl and the dress . . . I should have paid more attention to them. But just when I was working on it, so many other things happened — both for Cesca and for me," she said in a low voice.

After a moment she asked him, "Do you hear anything from Helge? About how he's doing?"

"He doesn't write much. He's working on his doctoral dissertation — you know, the work he was researching in Rome. And he says that he's well."

Jenny nodded.

"He doesn't write at all to his mother. And of course she's very hurt by that. It hasn't made her any more pleasant to live with. Well, poor thing. I suppose she really is having a difficult time lately."

Jenny moved the flowers over to her desk and began straightening up.

"I'm glad Helge is working, at least. God knows he didn't have any peace for it this summer."

"You didn't either, poor dear."

"No, I didn't. But the worst thing is, Gert, that I haven't been able to get started again — not yet. And I don't feel the slightest inclination either. I was intending to make some etchings this winter."

"Don't you think, Jenny . . . It's quite reasonable that this kind of disappointment . . . would take some time to recover from. But what about your exhibition? It's been quite successful and so well received. Don't you think that will give you back your desire to work? You've already received an offer for your Aventine painting. By the way, are you going to accept it?"

She shrugged her shoulders.

"Of course. I have to. My family is always in need of money, as you know. And besides, I need to get out and travel. I can tell that it's not good for me to stay here in Norway."

"So you want to travel," Gram said quietly, his eyes lowered. "Yes, I suppose you do. That's understandable."

"Oh, that exhibition." Jenny threw herself with resignation into the rocking chair. "All my paintings, at least the newest ones . . . It's been an eternity since I worked on them. The Aventine painting . . . I finished the study for it on the day I met Helge. I painted it while we were together — the one of Cesca too. And the one from near your office on Stenersgaten I did while I was waiting for him.

"I haven't done a thing since. Not a thing. So Helge's working again . . ."

"It's understandable, my dear, that something like this would leave a deeper impression on a woman."

"Oh yes, yes, yes — a woman, yes. That's the whole key to this wretchedness. Walking around moping and being lazy — bone-lazy! All for the sake of a love that doesn't even *exist!*"

"Dear Jenny," said Gram calmly. "I think it's quite natural. Of course it will take time for you to get through this — and then to get beyond it. Because you *will* get beyond it. And then you'll understand that you haven't been through this experience for nothing. In one way or another, a person's soul is always enriched by his experiences."

Jenny gave a short laugh but didn't reply.

"There were many things you wouldn't have wanted to miss. Isn't that true? All those happy, warm sunny days with your love, down south in that beautiful country, Jenny?"

"Will you tell me one thing, Gert? Is it your personal experience that you've been able to enrich your soul, as you call it, through your own experiences?"

He gave a start, looking a bit pained and almost astonished at her bluntness. It took a moment before he answered.

"That's not the same thing, Jenny. The experiences that are the rewards of sin — and I'm sure you know that I don't mean sin in the orthodox sense; I mean the consequences that come from acting against your own better judgment — those kind never hold any sweetness. Nevertheless, I still think that in some way my experiences may have made my inner life richer and deeper than lesser misfortunes would have done — since it was my fate not to experience great happiness. And someday that may be the case to an even higher degree. I have a feeling, Jenny, that it could possibly lead me to a real understanding of what the true meaning of life is.

"But of course I meant it in a different way as far as you're concerned. Even though your happiness in love turned out to be fleeting, it was still pure and blameless for the time that it lasted, since you believed in it wholeheartedly and without reservations. You betrayed no one but yourself."

Jenny didn't speak. A storm of objections raged inside her, but she had a suspicion that Gram wouldn't understand.

"Do you remember Ibsen's words: And even if I've run my vessel aground, / Oh, how lovely it was to sail."

"Oh, I can't believe you'd repeat those idiotic words, Gert. Let me tell you that nowadays, at least, we have too much of a sense of responsibility and self-esteem for that kind of argument — most of us, anyway. Let me be shipwrecked and sink to the bottom . . . I'll try not to blink, if only I can be sure that I wasn't the one who ran my ship aground. As far as I know, the best sailors prefer to go down with their ship if it's their own fault, rather than survive."

"Well, I happen to be of the opinion that a person usually only has himself to blame for any adversity — in the long run, at any rate." Gram smiled. "But a person can often extract spiritual value from his misfortunes too."

"I agree with the first part. And the second part, but only if the misfortune doesn't entail having your self-esteem diminished."

"But little Jenny . . . you shouldn't take all this so hard. You're terribly upset, and bitter. Yes, I remember very well what you said the day Helge left. But good Lord, child, you can't mean that a person should suffocate all feelings of love before they're born, unless it can be guaranteed at the moment they arise that these same feelings will last until death, withstand all adversity, and endure all sacrifices. That they should even, as if in a vision, grasp and understand the personality of their object — illuminating the most secret depths, so that later on a different view of him or her is completely excluded?"

"Yes, I do," said Jenny fiercely.

"Have you ever felt that way yourself?" asked Gert Gram gently.

"No, but that's still what I believe. I've always known that's the way it should be.

"But when I turned twenty-eight and was still an old spinster and I yearned to love and be loved in return, and Helge came along and fell in love with me . . . then I put aside all demands on myself and *my* love, and took what I could get. Of course, to a certain degree, in good faith. It will be fine, I thought. It will work out. But the internal, positive conviction that it would work out because nothing else was conceivable . . . That's not something I felt.

"Let me tell you what my friend Heggen said to me one day. He has the most genuine and straightforward disdain for women — and rightfully so! We women, we have no self-esteem, and we're lazy too, so that we never seriously make the decision to create our own lives or happiness by working and fighting for it. Secretly we all go around hoping that a man will come along and hand us happiness so we won't have to struggle for it. Those of us who are most feminine, who want only idleness and adornment and amusement, latch on to the man who can provide these things in the greatest abundance. But if one of us has truly human feelings and a longing to be a solid, fine individual — and tries to become that — then we hope at least that a man will meet us halfway and we can stay where we most want to be: in his love.

"We may work for a while — quite honestly and effectively. Even feeling the joy of work. But in all secrecy we're waiting for an even greater happiness, which we won't obtain through honest toil: someone who will appear as a gift.

"Never will we women reach the point where our work is enough for us."

"Do you think that work alone is enough for a man? Never!" said Gram calmly.

"For someone like Gunnar, it is. You can count on him to know how to keep women in their proper place in his life — as mere trifles."

Gram laughed. "How old is your friend Heggen, anyway? I hope for his sake that with time he comes to view the important things in life a little differently."

"I don't," said Jenny vehemently. "And I hope that someday I'll also learn to put all that love nuisance in its proper place."

"Good Lord, Jenny, you talk as if . . . I almost said as if you had no sense, but I know you're smarter than that." Gram smiled sadly. "Shall I tell you a little about what I know of love, my dear?

"If I didn't believe in it, how could I have the slightest kernel of faith in people — or in myself? Can't you understand, Jenny? Oh, God help us . . . maybe you think that it's only women who find life meaningless or feel their hearts frozen and empty when they don't have anything but their work to love? Just their own impulses, and nothing else to rely on! Do you think there's a single soul alive who doesn't have moments of self-doubt? No, child, there has to be another person with whom you can deposit the best of yourself — your love and your trust — and that's the bank you must be able to rely on.

"When I tell you that my life since I got married has been hell, I'm not using too strong a phrase. That I've stuck it out, more or less, has partly to do with the fact that I assume Rebekka's love in some way excuses her. I know that what she now feels — a mean and vulgar joy at her power to torment and humiliate me; jealousy and bitterness — that's the caricature that a betrayed love becomes. Don't you understand that I see in it some kind of validation for my sense of justice — that there's a *reason* for my unhappiness? I betrayed her when I accepted her love without being able to return it wholeheartedly — with the secret intention of giving her a few scraps, the small change of love — when she offered me the best of herself.

"But if life mercilessly punishes every offense against the sanctity of love, then that proves to me that it's the most sacred thing in life. And if someone is true to his own longing for love, then life will reward him with the purest and most magnificent bliss.

"I once mentioned to you that there was a woman I learned to love after it was too late. She had loved me ever since we were children — and I never noticed or wanted to notice. When she heard that I was married, she took as her husband a man who swore that she could save him and put him on his feet if she married him. Yes, I know that you scoff at these types of rescue attempts. But I must tell you, child, that you can't judge, unless you've experienced what it's like when the one you love with all your soul is in someone else's arms, and you feel that your own life is worthless, and you hear a lost soul begging that worthless life for salvation.

"Well, Helene wasn't happy, and neither was I. And then we met and understood each other and found comfort in each other's company. It wasn't what people understand by happiness — and yet it was. We were both bound by ties that we didn't dare break. And I confess that, as my hope of one day making her my wife ever so slowly died out, my love changed. But the memory of her — now far away in another part of the world, devoting herself to easing the burden for her children of living with a father who's nothing but a drunken wreck — I remember her as the loveliest gem of my life. For her sake, over all these years, I've held firm to my belief in the purity and beauty and strength of the human soul — and my belief in love. And I know that the memory of me is what gives Helene the secret power to persevere and endure over there beyond the sea. Because she loves me today as she did in our childhood. And she believes in me, in my talent, and in my love, and that I deserved a better fate. So I still mean something to her, don't you think so, Jenny?"

She didn't reply.

"Happiness is not just being loved by someone, Jenny. The greatest part of happiness . . . is loving someone else."

"Hmm. It must be a paltry kind of love, Gert, to love someone and not be loved in return."

He sat in silence for a moment, his eyes downcast. Until he said, almost in a whisper, "Great or small — it's happiness. To find someone about whom you believe only the best, the very best. Someone about whom you say to yourself: Dear God, let me see her happy, because she deserves it, because she is pure and lovely and warm and noble and talented and good. And you pray to God: Give her everything that I didn't have. I think it's a form of happiness, little Jenny, for me to pray that way for you. No, it's not something to be frightened of, dear . . ."

He was on his feet, and she stood up too and made a gesture as if she were afraid he would come closer. Gram stopped, and then he laughed softly.

"How could you think otherwise — you who are such a clever little girl? Jenny, I thought you understood long before I realized it myself.

"How could it go any other way? My life . . . it's moving toward the end, toward old age, lethargy, darkness, and death. Now I know that everything I've longed for all my life — it will never be mine. Then I meet you. I think you're the loveliest woman I've ever met, and you want the same things that I once wanted and was on my way to achieving. How could my heart do anything else but scream: God, let her reach her goal. God, help her — don't leave her stranded the way I was stranded.

"And you were so sweet to me, Jenny. You came to visit me at my office, and you told me about yourself. You listened to me, and you understood so well, and your beautiful eyes were so full of sympathy and kindness and warmth . . ."

"But dear God, are you crying?"

He grabbed her hands and pressed his lips to them.

"You mustn't, Jenny. You mustn't cry like that. What are you crying for? And you're shaking. What are you crying about?"

"About everything," she sobbed.

"Here, sit down." He knelt down in front of her, and for a second he rested his forehead on her knee. "You mustn't cry about me, do you hear me? Do you think I wish I'd never met you? My dearest girl . . . If you love someone and you wish it had never happened, then you've never really loved — I can tell you that's the truth. Oh no, Jenny. I wouldn't have wanted to miss what I feel for you, not if it cost me my life!

"And you mustn't cry for yourself. You *will* be happy — I'm sure of that. Someday . . . of all the men who will love you, one of them will kneel down before you as I'm doing now, and he'll say that it means life itself to him to lie at your feet, and you will think the same. And then you'll understand that to be with him — even if it's in the poorest hut and for a single, brief moment after a day filled with the dreariest, heaviest toil — that is happiness. Much, much greater happiness than if you became the greatest artist who ever lived — or if you achieved all that can be achieved of honor and fame. That's what you believe too, isn't it?"

"Yes," she whispered tearfully.

"And you mustn't be afraid that you won't have the happiness you deserve. That's it, isn't it, Jenny? You feel you're struggling to be a good and capable person and a true artist, but at the same time you're also longing to meet someone who will tell you that it was right for you to struggle, and that he loves you for it."

Jenny nodded. And Gram reverently kissed her hands.

"That's what you are, you know — you're everything that is good and fine and proud and lovely. I'm telling you that now, but one day a man who is younger and better and stronger than I am will tell you the same thing, and you will be happy — very happy. Aren't you a tiny bit glad that I'm telling you this? Glad to hear that you're the best and sweetest and most wonderful little girl in the world? Look at me, Jenny. Can't I make you a little happy by telling you that you will have the greatest joy in life because you deserve it?"

She looked down into his face and tried to smile. Then she bowed her head and ran her hands over his hair.

"Oh, Gert — oh, Gert — I couldn't help it! I didn't want to hurt you. I couldn't help it, could I?"

"You mustn't be sad about that. My dear . . . I love you because you're the way that you *want* to be — and the way that I once wanted to be too. You mustn't be sad, even if you think you've caused me sorrow. Some sorrows are good, blessedly good, I can assure you."

She sat there quietly weeping.

After a while he whispered, "May I come to see you, once in a while? If you're feeling sad, won't you send word to me? I would so like to try to help my little girl. Jenny?"

"I don't dare, Gert."

"Dear little friend, I'm an old man. I could be your father."

"For . . . for your sake, I mean. It wouldn't be right for me to . . ."

"Oh yes, Jenny. Do you think you would be any less in my thoughts if I didn't see you? I just want to see you — talk with you — try to help you a little — may I? Oh, may I please?"

"I don't know, Gert. I don't know. Oh, dear man, go now — you must go. I can't anymore . . . It's so awful . . . Go now."

He stood up quietly.

"I'll go then. Good-bye, Jenny. But child . . . you're quite beside yourself."

"Yes," she whispered.

"I'll go. May I come back sometime? I'd like to see you before you leave. After you've calmed down . . . and this no longer frightens you. There's no reason why it should, Jenny."

She stood in silence for a moment. Then she suddenly pulled him close and brushed his cheek with her lips.

"Go now, Gert."

"Thank you. God bless you, Jenny."

—⁓—

Afterward she paced back and forth in the room. She couldn't understand why she was shaking so badly. And deep inside she felt — no, it couldn't be happiness, but she thought it had been good to hear what he said as he knelt before her.

Oh Gert, Gert! She had always regarded him as a weak person, someone who had allowed himself to be conquered and trampled like those who are defeated. And then all of a sudden she learned that deep inside he had great strength and confidence — and he had stood there like a rich man who knows that he can help and wants to do so. But she was confused and uncertain and sick with longing in the depths of her being, behind the armor of opinions and thoughts that she had shaped for herself.

And then she had asked him to go. Why? Because she was so boundlessly poor, and because she had expressed her need to him, thinking that he was equally poor. But then he had shown her that he was rich and gladly offered her a little help from his riches. And she had felt humiliated and asked him to go. That must be it.

To receive help from someone's love without giving in return — that had always seemed to her so pathetic. Because she had never thought that she would be the one who needed that kind of help.

He hadn't been able to do the work he wanted to do. The love he bore in his heart had not been allowed to flourish. And yet he did not despair. That must be the joy of a believer. It didn't matter what you believed in, as long as you had something beyond yourself in which to put your faith.

Because it was impossible to live if you had only yourself to believe in, only yourself to love.

She had always considered the possibility of voluntary death. If she died right now . . . Well, there were many people she cared about who would be sad, but there was no one who couldn't live without her. No one who would grieve so much at her loss, that she might feel obligated to drag through her life for their sake. Her mother and her siblings . . . If they didn't find out that she had taken her own life, then after a year their sorrow would be only a gentle melancholy whenever they thought of her. Cesca and Gunnar would probably grieve the most because they might understand that she had been unhappy, but she stood only on the periphery of their lives. The person who loved her most would no doubt grieve the most, but she had nothing to give him. He could love her just as much if she were dead. His happiness came from the fact that *he* loved her; he had the capacity to find happiness within himself.

If it was true that she lacked that ability, then nothing would help. Work couldn't fulfill her, so she longed for nothing beyond it. And why should she go on living because they said she had talent? No one had as much joy from looking at her art as she had from creating it. And that joy wasn't great enough to satisfy her.

And it wasn't just what Gunnar had said — that her virtue plagued her, to put it bluntly. That could easily be remedied. But she didn't dare, because she was afraid that what she longed for might come to her afterward. And the worst thing would be to share life with another person but deep inside feel just as lonely as before. Oh no, no. To belong to a man, with all the subsequent types of intimacy, both physical and spiritual . . . and then one day to see that she had never known him, and he had never known her, and neither of them had ever understood a word the other person said . . .

Oh no. She kept on living because she was waiting. She didn't want a lover because she was waiting for her master. And she wouldn't die, not right now, not while she was waiting.

No, she refused to throw her life away just yet — for any reason. She *couldn't* die like this — so poor that she didn't have a single beloved thing to say good-bye to. She didn't dare, because she still believed that someday things would be different.

So she had to try painting again. Presumably it would be an utter disaster, since she was walking around sick with love.

She laughed.

That's what was wrong with her. The object of her affection hadn't yet appeared, but the love was there.

———

In the slanted window the sky was darkening to a violet blue. Jenny went over and looked out. Slate roofs and chimneys and telephone wires. The silent world outside was spreading frosty gray into the twilight. And from the streets billowed a reddish gleam, coloring the icy fog. The clatter of carriages and the shriek of trolleys on the tracks sounded so harsh on the bare, frozen street.

She didn't feel like going home to have dinner with her mother. But that was what they had agreed. Jenny closed the damper on the stove, put on her coat, and left.

Outside, the cold was dank and clammy. The fog reeked of soot and gas and frozen dirt. What a hopelessly dreary street it was. It started in the center of town, where the trolleys clanged and the shops stood with their glittering store windows, crowded with people streaming in and out. But the street led down to the lifeless gray walls of the fortress, and all along it the buildings were gray and dead — whether they were new office structures made of steel and glass, where the work unobtrusively fluttered in and out on pieces of paper, pored over by unobtrusive, busy young people in the serene white light behind the large windows, where people talked to other people through a telephone receiver; or whether the buildings were the old ones that still remained from the days when the town was small. Low and grayish brown, with smooth facades and mesh gratings on the office windows; occasionally a little window with curtains and potted plants belonging to a humble home — peculiarly lonely homes along this stretch where most of the buildings were deserted at night.

Even the shops were not the kind with people streaming in and out. They were businesses selling wallpaper and plaster rosettes for the ceiling or stoves and fireplaces; furniture stores with mahogany beds and varnished oak chairs that looked as if no one would ever sit on them.

A little boy was standing in a doorway — a little street urchin, blue with cold, holding a big basket in his arms. He was watching a couple of mongrels that were fighting in the middle of the street, making the dank icy dust fly all around. He flinched when the dogs came tumbling close to him.

"Are you afraid of dogs?" asked Jenny.

At first the boy didn't reply. But she said, "Would you like me to walk past them with you?" and then he slipped in beside her, but still said nothing.

"Which way are you going? Where do you live?"

"On Voldsgaten."

"Have you been out doing the shopping? All the way out here? A little boy like you? How clever you are!"

"We shop at Aases on Strandgaten 'cause Pappa knows them," he said. "But the basket is so heavy that . . ."

Jenny looked up and down the street; there were only a few people around.

"Come, little one, let me carry it for you for a while."

The boy handed over the basket a bit reluctantly.

"Now take my hand and I'll walk with you past those dogs. Oh, how cold you are. Don't you have any mittens?"

The boy shook his head.

"Here, put your other hand inside my muff. You don't want to? Maybe you think it wouldn't do for a boy to be walking around with a muff?"

She thought about Nils when he was small. She had longed for him so often. Now he was a big boy and had so many friends; he was almost at the age when it wasn't acceptable to be seen trudging around with his older sister. He seldom came to visit her. First she had been gone a year, and then there were those months when she was so preoccupied with Helge, and she and Nils seemed to have drifted far apart. Later on, when he got older, maybe they would be friends like they were before; no doubt they would be, since they loved each other. But right now, at this age, she knew that he was having too much fun without her. Oh, if only Nils were still a little boy, then she could have taken him on her lap and told him stories while she bathed him and dressed him and kissed him. Or if he were a little older, like when she took hikes with him in Nordmarken, with the peak of Slakteren in the distance and the road full of adventures and strange events.

"What's your name, little boy?"

"Ausjen Torstein Mo."

"How old are you, Ausjen?"

"Six."

"So you don't go to school yet, do you?"

"No, but I'm going to start in April."

"Do you think it will be fun to start school?"

"No, because the teachers are all so mean. And Oskar already started, so I won't get to be in the same class as him because Oskar will be in second grade."

"Oskar is your friend?" asked Jenny.

"Yes, they live on the same street as us."

There was a little pause, and then Jenny started talking again.

"Don't you think it's a shame that we haven't had any snow? There's that hill down by Piperviken that you can go to. Do you have a sled?"

"No, but I have ice skates and skis too."

"So it would be nice if we had some snow."

They had reached Stortingsgaten. Jenny let go of his hand and then looked at the basket. But it was very heavy, and Ausjen was so small. She kept on carrying it, even though it wasn't particularly pleasant to be seen walking along with a poor little urchin. What she really wanted to do was take him to a pastry shop, but she would be embarrassed if she met anyone she knew.

But once they came to dark Voldsgaten, she took his hand again and carried the basket all the way to the tiny house where he lived. She gave him ten øre when she said good-bye.

In Homansbyen she bought chocolate and red mittens, which she planned to send to Ausjen.

Good Lord, if she could give someone a little joy. A little unexpected joy . . .

She would try to get him to pose for a couple of hours a day. Although he might be too young to stand for very long.

His poor little fist . . . it had felt so warm in her hand. And it had done her good to walk along holding his hand.

Yes. She would try to paint him. He had a lively little face. And she would give him milk with a dash of weak coffee and plenty of sandwiches, and then she would work while she chatted with Ausjen.

PART THREE

I

On a fair and mild May afternoon, as dusk approached, a sunny haze lay over
the dark blocks of buildings; the bare walls turned reddish gold, and the factory chimneys were liver colored in the glow of the sun. The outline of the city,
with its high rooftops and low rooftops on buildings both big and small, stood
silhouetted against a sky that was a grayish violet, heavy with dust and smoke
and vapor.

The little tree next to the red wall had tiny, bright yellowish green leaves
that the light was shining through, the same as it had the year before.

Jenny noticed the dappled light along the edges of the junk dealers' stalls —
how soft and glittering it looked. And in some places the flakes of soot drifting
down the walls of the shop buildings were pitch-black, while in other places
they seemed to form a delicate silver membrane that shimmered.

She looked up at the sky. All morning she had wandered around Bygdø, and
there the vault of heaven had hovered dark blue and hot above the golden-olive
spruces and the amber-colored buds of the leafy trees. But here the sky above
the tall buildings and network of telephone wires was turning a pale blue
behind the fine, opal-white veil of haze. It was actually much more beautiful
like this. Gert couldn't see it. For him the city was merely filthy and ugly and
gray — it was the city they had cursed, all those youths of the 1880s, who had
been confined here to do hard labor. At this very moment he was probably
standing up there, looking out at the sun, but he wouldn't notice the play of
light over the contours and shadings, because for him it was merely a touch of
sunshine outside his prison window.

She stopped a short distance from his doorway and, out of habit, looked up
and down the street. There was no one she knew — workers heading toward
Vaterland or toward the center of town. It was past six o'clock.

Jenny ran up the stairs — those hideous iron stairs that echoed between the bare brick walls whenever they had stealthily slipped out of his rooms up there, on those late-winter nights. It felt as if the cold, raw air never left these walls.

She walked briskly down the corridor and knocked three times on his door.

Gram opened at once. He pulled her close with one arm and as they kissed, he locked the door behind her with his free hand.

Over his shoulder she saw the fresh flowers on the little table with the carafe of wine and the imported morels in a cut crystal bowl. There was a faint haze of cigarette smoke in the room. And she knew that he had been sitting there since four, waiting for her with all of these things he had arranged for her benefit.

"I couldn't come any earlier, Gert," she whispered. "I'm sorry you had to wait."

When he released her, she walked over to the table and bent over the flowers.

"You won't mind if I take two of them for my dress, will you? Oh, I always feel so pampered when I'm with you, Gert." She held out her hands to him.

"When do you have to leave me, Jenny?" he asked as he kissed her arms ever so gently.

Jenny bowed her head slightly.

"I had to promise to be home this evening. Mamma always sits up to wait for me, you know, and she's been so tired lately. Right now she needs me to help her in the evenings with all sorts of things," she said quickly.

"You have to understand that it's not easy to get away from home," she whispered, entreating him.

His head drooped under her outpouring of words. When she came over to him, he took her in his arms so that her face was hidden against his shoulder.

She couldn't tell a lie, the poor thing — not well enough that he believed her for a single pitiful second. That brief, brief time last winter . . . those first blue-green spring evenings . . . Back then she had always been able to get away from home.

"It's too bad for us, Gert. But it's difficult right now since I'm living at home; I'm sure you can understand that. And I have to, you know, both because Mamma needs the money and because I have to help her. You agreed that it would be best if I moved back home, didn't you?"

Gert Gram nodded. They had sat down on the sofa, close to each other. Jenny's head was resting against his chest so he couldn't see her face.

"You know . . . I was out at Bygdø today, Gert. I walked around the same places where we used to go. We should go out there together again, don't you think? How about the day after tomorrow, if the weather holds? I'll think up some excuse to tell my family so we can stay together all evening. Would you like that? You're sad that I have to leave again so soon, aren't you?"

"My dear Jenny, I've told you a thousand times . . ." and she heard in his voice that he was once again sitting there with his most melancholy smile. "I'm grateful for every single second of time that you're willing to offer your friend."

"Don't say that, Gert," she begged him anxiously.

"Why shouldn't I say it, when it's true? My beloved little girl, do you think I will ever forget that everything you've given me is a lavish act of mercy? And I'll never comprehend how you could offer me . . ."

"Gert. Last winter, when I realized that you cared for me — how much you cared for me — I said to myself that it couldn't go on. Then I realized that I couldn't live without you. And then I became yours. Was that an act of mercy? When I couldn't let you go?"

"But that's exactly what I mean by an inconceivable mercy, Jenny — that you have come to love me in that way."

Silently she nestled close to him.

"My young, lovely, little Jenny."

"I'm not young, Gert. When you met me, I had already started growing old, without ever really being young. I thought *you* were young — much younger in your heart than I was, because you still believed in everything that I ridiculed and called childish dreams, up until you made me believe in their existence: love and warmth and all those things."

Gert Gram laughed quietly to himself. Then he whispered, "Perhaps my heart wasn't any older than yours. At least I felt as if I'd never had any youth; but deep inside, I stubbornly kept hoping that someday, just once, I would feel its touch — the touch of youth. But my hair had turned white in the meantime."

Jenny shook her head. And she lifted her hand to stroke the top of his head.

"Are you tired, little Jenny? Shall I take off your shoes? Would you like to lie down and rest?"

"No. I want to sit here like this. It feels so good."

She tucked her legs up underneath her and curled up in his lap.

Gert put his arm around her. With his free hand he poured the wine and held the glass to her lips. She drank greedily. Then he fed her cherries, taking the stones from her mouth and putting them on a small plate.

"More wine?"

"Yes, please. Oh, I want to stay here with you. I'll send a message with an errand boy, saying that I ran into Heggen. I think he's in town. But I'll have to go home before the trolleys stop running. Unfortunately."

"I'll send the message for you." He laid her gently down on the sofa. "Just lie here and rest. My dear one!"

After he had gone, she unbuttoned her shoes and pulled them off. She drank some more wine. Then she stretched out on the sofa, buried her head in the pillows, and pulled the blanket over her.

She did love him. And she wanted to be with him. When she sat here and snuggled close to him, resting in his embrace, then she felt happy. He was the only person in the world who had ever taken her on his lap to warm her and hug her and call her his little girl. Yes, he was the only person who had ever been really close to her. So why shouldn't she be his?

When he simply wanted to take her in his arms and hug her so that everything else was blocked out and all she felt was him holding her and warming her . . . That's when she was happy. Oh no, she couldn't lose him. And why shouldn't she give him what little she had, since he gave her something that she couldn't live without?

She would let him kiss her, do with her what he liked. As long as he didn't speak. Because then they would drift far apart, since he talked of love, but her love was not what he imagined. And she couldn't explain it in words. She merely clung to him, and it had nothing to do with mercy or a lavish gift. It was simply a poor, little, imploring kind of love, and he shouldn't thank her for it; he should just be fond of her without saying a word.

When he came back she was lying there, staring with wide-open eyes. But she closed them under his quiet, adoring caresses and smiled. Then she threw her arms around his neck and clung to him. The faint violet cologne he wore smelled so lovely and fresh. And she gave a little nod as he lifted her up with an inquisitive glance. He wanted to say something, but first she placed her hand over his mouth, and then she kissed him so that he couldn't speak as he gently carried her into the room next to his office.

—⁂—

Gert followed her to the trolley. For a moment Jenny stood outside on the step of the trolley and watched him go, as he walked down the street in the blue May night. Then she went inside and took a seat.

Gram had left his wife at Christmastime. Now he lived alone on

Stenersgaten, where he had a room in addition to his office. Jenny understood that he intended to ask for a separation after some time had passed and Rebekka Gram finally realized that he wasn't coming back. No doubt it was his nature to do it this way; forcing an abrupt break was not something he could manage.

Whatever else he might be planning for the future, she didn't dare ask. Was he thinking that they should get married?

She couldn't deny that never for a single second had she ever wanted to bind herself to him for good. And that was why she felt such bitter, hopeless humiliation, such shame, whenever she thought about him and she wasn't with him to hide herself in his love. She had deceived him — all along she had deceived him.

"But that's exactly what I mean by an inconceivable mercy, Jenny — that you have come to love me."

Yes, but could she help it if he thought of it that way?

He wouldn't have made her his lover if she hadn't wanted it herself — if she hadn't let Gert know that she wanted it. Oh, God. When she realized that he longed . . . When it tormented her every time they were together, aware of his desire and seeing how he fought to hide what he was too proud to reveal. Yes, she had seen that he was proud — too proud to beg for what he had once offered to give, perhaps also too proud to risk facing her refusal. And when she knew at heart that she couldn't turn away his love, couldn't lose the one person who loved her . . . Was there anything else for her to do but offer him what she had, since she had accepted something from him that she couldn't do without? If she was to think of herself as an honorable person?

But then she had been forced to use words that were stronger and more ardent than she felt. And he had believed her and taken her at her word.

And it happened over and over. Whenever she came to him, unhappy, dejected, tired of thinking about how this would all end, and she saw that he understood . . . Then she would again say those warm words and feign stronger emotions than she felt. And he would believe her at once.

He knew no other kind of love than one that was inherently happy. Unhappiness in love — that came from the outside, from the cruelty of fate or a harsh justice seeking revenge for an old wrong. She knew what he feared: that her love would one day die when she saw that he was too old to be her lover. But he would never suspect that her love had been *born* sickly, containing within it the seed of its own death.

It would do no good for her to try explaining this to him. Gert wouldn't be able to understand.

She had sought shelter in his arms because he was the only one who had offered this to her. She had felt so terribly alone. When he offered her love and warmth, she hadn't had the strength to turn it away.

Even though she should have known that she shouldn't accept it; she wasn't worthy of his love. No, he wasn't old. His was the passion of a twenty-year-old combined with a childish faith and a devout adoration; it was the warmth and kindness of a grown man — all the love that one man's life could hold, now overflowing on the borders of old age. And it should have fallen on a woman who could return his love, who could have experienced with him, in the brief years it would last, the entire lifetime he had longed for and dreamed of and hoped for. Who could have lived with him in such a way that she was bound to his side by thousands of happy memories when old age came. With steadfast love, as the one who had been the wife of his youth and manhood, and was now aging alongside him.

But she . . . If she wanted to try to be . . . What could she give him, if she tried? She had never been able to give him anything — she had only taken. If she tried to be . . . She couldn't fool him, wouldn't be able to make him believe that the longings of her life would be quelled forever by the love of youth.

He would tell her to leave. She had loved and given, and now she loved him no more and should be free. That's how he would see it — never understanding her grief because she had been *unable* to give anything, anything at all.

Oh, how he tormented her when he spoke of her gifts. Yes, she had been a virgin when she became his. He always remembered that, as if he used it to measure how infinitely deep and great her love was, since she had granted him the purity of her youth.

The purity of her twenty-nine years. Oh yes, she had saved it like a white bridal gown, and it was neither used nor sullied. And in her longing and anguish that she might never wear it, in despair at her own icy loneliness, at her inability to love, she had clung to it, crushing it and mauling it with her thoughts. Wasn't the person who had lived a life of love purer than she, who had only brooded and brooded and kept watch and yearned, until all her faculties were paralyzed with longing?

And then she had become his. What a small impression that had made on her. Not that she was cold. Sometimes his love had moved her. But she feigned heat when she was merely lukewarm. And when she wasn't with him, she scarcely thought about it, but confessed to a modest yearning for his sake. Yes, she had offered him pretense, over and over, in return for his genuine passion.

And yet . . . there had been a time when she wasn't just pretending — or rather, if she lied to Gert, then she had also lied to herself. She had felt a storm inside her; it must have been sympathy for him and his fate, and a rebellion against her own. Why were they both, in their own way, being ravaged by longing for something impossible? And it was because of her emerging fear of where it would all lead — everything she had thrown herself into — that she had exulted in her love for him. Because she couldn't help falling into this man's arms, no matter what madness she knew it would be.

That was when she would sit in the trolley in the evening and gloat, looking at all the sleepy, tranquil, middle-class faces. She was coming from her lover's arms, and the tempest of their fate was whirling around them both. They had been forced to go out in it, and they didn't know where it would take them, and she had been proud of her fate, because misfortune and darkness threatened.

But now she merely sat and longed for the end. Made her plans to go abroad, to flee from it all. She had accepted Cesca's invitation to Tegneby as a way to prepare for the break.

It was better for Gert, at any rate, that he was alone now. If she had been the reason why he ended his marriage with that woman . . . well, at least she had done one good thing for him.

—⁓—

Two young housewives were sitting across from Jenny. They probably weren't any older than she was, but looked disheveled from trudging around in a marriage for several years. Three or four winters ago they might have been stylish office girls who wore nice clothes and went on sports holidays with their suitors in Nordmarken. Yes, now she was certain that she recognized one of them from there; they had stayed overnight at the same place on Hakloa one Easter. Jenny had noticed her back then because she was an excellent skier and her trim figure looked so pretty and chic in her sports attire.

She still looked well dressed. Her tailored suit was the latest style, but it didn't fit properly. Her figure was no longer firm. She had grown plump and flabby at the same time that her shoulders and hips were sharp. And her face looked old, with bad teeth and peevish lines around her mouth, beneath a large hat with an abundance of ostrich feathers. She was chattering on, and her friend was listening intently, but she was lolling, sluggish and pregnant, with her knees spread, and her hands in a huge muff resting on her stomach. Her face was actually quite pretty, but stout and flushed, with a double chin.

"Yes, well, I have to lock up the cheese in the buffet. If it gets put in the kitchen, there's only the rind left in the morning — a big Swiss cheese that costs nearly three kroner."

"Yes, I know how that is."

"Oh, but listen to this! She's crazy about eggs, like you wouldn't believe! A few days ago I went into the maid's room — she's such a pig, and it always smells so awful in there. Hasn't made her bed in I don't know how long. 'But, Solveig,' I say and lift up the blanket, and there I find three eggs and a paper bag full of sugar in the middle of that filthy bed. Can you believe it! So she tells me that she bought them herself, and I suppose she was right about the sugar."

"Do you think so?" said the other woman.

"Yes, oh yes. It was in a paper bag, after all. But she took those eggs. Well, I gave her a good tongue-lashing, I can tell you. But just listen to this. Last Saturday I come out to the kitchen, we're going to have rice pudding, and there's the pot on the stove, starting to burn, and the girl's sitting in her room crocheting, so I start calling for her while I stir the pudding, and what do you think I find with the spoon? An egg! Can you believe it? She's boiling herself an egg in the rice pudding! Well, I just had to laugh, but have you ever heard of anything so disgusting? I gave her a piece of my mind, you can be sure of that. I don't know what you may think, but . . ."

"Oh, I know, those maids. Let me tell you what *mine* did a few days ago . . ."

⁓

No doubt as young girls they had also longed for love — their own love. A strong, handsome man with a good job, a man who would take them away from the monotonous workdays at the office or shop and put them in a little home with three rooms filled with all their own things, where they could spread out the little embroidered cloths with roses and bluebells into which they had sewn all their girlish dreams.

And they had probably had girlish dreams about love. These days they would smile haughtily and state with satisfaction, to those who now dreamed the same dreams, that things weren't like that at all. They were proud of belonging to the initiated who knew how things really were. Perhaps they were even content.

Yet there was happiness in being discontent. Happy was the person who didn't give up in resignation when life offered impoverished circumstances, who still said: I believe in my dreams, and I refuse to call anything happiness but the happiness I demanded. And I still think that kind of happiness exists. If it doesn't exist for me, then I was the one who was lacking; I was the one who failed as a virgin, who didn't have the strength to keep watch and wait for the bridegroom. But the wise virgins will see him and enter into his house and dance . . .

—⁓—

A candle was burning in her mother's bedroom when Jenny came home. She had to go in and tell her a little about the party at Ahlström's studio and how Heggen was doing.

Ingeborg and Bodil were asleep in the dim light with their black braids spread out over the pillows.

It was no trouble for Jenny to stand there and tell her mother lies. She had always done so, from the time she was a schoolgirl and had to give merry reports about children's parties where she had sat all alone and watched others dance. Unhappy and alone, a little girl who couldn't join in the dancing or talk about anything that the boys would find amusing.

When Ingeborg and Bodil came home from dances, their mother would sit up straight in bed, asking questions and listening and laughing, looking flushed and young in the lamplight. They could always tell their mamma the truth, because it was full of merriment and laughter. Sometimes they might keep back some small detail that was so delightful they wanted to keep it all to themselves. But what did that matter, since their smiles were truthful?

Jenny kissed her mother and said good night. In the living room she happened to knock down a photograph. She picked it up, and even in the dark she knew which one it was. It was her real father's brother, with his wife and little girls. He had lived in America, so she had never met him. He was dead, and the picture stood there though no one ever paid any attention to it. She wiped off the dust every day without looking at it; it was just another knickknack.

She went into her little room and began unpinning her hair.

She had always lied to her mother. Because how could she have been truthful without causing her mother sorrow? And for no good reason.

Mamma would never understand. She had been through both happiness and sorrow from the time she was quite young. She'd been happy with Jenny's father and grieved over his death and then kept on living for her child's sake, and was content. Then she had met Nils Berner, and he had filled her life with new happiness and new sorrow. And then she again kept on living through her children. It was the happiness of motherhood: her children. It was an emptiness that was tangibly filled, a happiness that was paid for with all-too-real suffering, that was physically much too small and warm in her arms to be doubted. Yes, it must be wonderful to love your child. That kind of love was so natural that there was nothing to brood about. A mother never doubted that she loved her children or that she wished the best for her offspring and acted on their behalf, nor that her children returned her love. And so bountiful is nature's mercy toward mothers that it's against the deepest instincts of children to confide their most bitter or incurable sorrows to their mothers. Illness and money worries are the most they ever hear about. Never what is beyond repair: shame or defeats in life. Even if her children scream that it's true, a mother will not believe they are beyond repair.

Mamma would never know of her sorrows; nature itself had raised a wall to prevent it. Never would Rebekka Gram hear even a tenth of what her children had suffered for her sake. And Fru Lund had wept so terribly over her handsome Einar when he died. She still felt a deep and wistful grief for the boy and dreamed of the rich future that had been torn away from him. His mother was the only one who didn't know that he had shot himself because he didn't want to lose his mind.

Nor did maternal love stand in the way of other happiness. She had known mothers who took lovers and believed that their children didn't know. There were those who divorced and found happiness in other ways. It was only when the new love turned out to be disappointing that they had any regrets or complaints. Her mother had adored her, and yet her love still had room for Berner, and she had been happy with him. Gert had loved his children, and a father's love was more reflective, more understanding, less instinctive than a mother's. And yet he had scarcely given a thought to Helge all winter long.

2

Jenny had picked up the mail from the stationmaster. She gave Fransiska the newspapers and her letters and opened the one addressed to herself. Standing on the coarse gravel of the platform in the full glare of the sun, she glanced through Gert's long letter. She read his loving words at the beginning and end, but skipped the rest. It was just full of lengthy comments on the general topic of love.

Jenny stuck the letter back in its envelope and put it in her handbag. Oh, those letters from Gert . . . She hardly felt like reading them. His words merely showed her that they didn't understand each other after all. She had sensed this when they talked; when they wrote, it became painfully clear.

And yet there *was* an essential affinity between them. Why couldn't they find some kind of harmony?

Was he stronger or weaker than she was? He had lost again and again, becoming resigned and allowing himself to be swayed from all directions; yet he kept on hoping and kept on living and kept on believing. Was that weakness or vitality? She didn't understand him.

Was it the age difference, after all? He wasn't *old*. But his youthful feelings were from a different time. He belonged to a youth that had now died out — a youth with more vigorous beliefs, more naïveté. Maybe she was naive too, with her beliefs and her goals. But if so, it was in a different way. Words change their meaning over the course of twenty years. Was that ultimately what it was?

The gravel glittered red-violet, and the grayish yellow paint of the station building blistered in the sun's glare. Everything went black for a moment as she raised her eyes from the ground. It was odd how she couldn't seem to stand the heat this year.

Across the countryside the haze of heat shimmered above the mown meadows and glittering fields, all the way up to the edge of the woods, which stood black-green against the summer-blue sky. The crowns of the few leafy trees near the farms had already turned dark.

Cesca was still reading her letter. It was from her husband. She stood there in a white linen dress that was dazzling against the blue gravel of the platform.

Gunnar Heggen had placed his bags on the backseat of the landau. He patted the horse and murmured to it while he waited for the ladies.

Cesca put her letter away and raised her head, shaking it a bit, as if chasing a thought from her mind.

"Oh, you must excuse me, my boy. Let's go now." She and Jenny sat up front; Cesca was going to do the driving. "It's so nice that you could come, Gunnar! Isn't it going to be fun for the three of us to be together again for a few days? Lennart sends his greetings to both of you!"

"Thank you. Is he well?"

"Oh yes. Everything's fine. What a stroke of luck that Pappa and Borghild decided to go away. I'm all alone on the estate right now with Jenny, you see, and old Gina would be willing to stand on her head for us. This is lovely!"

"Yes, it's good to see you again, girls!"

He laughed merrily at both of them. But Jenny imagined that she caught an oddly serious glint in his eyes. And she knew that she looked worn out and faded, while Cesca, in that cheap, store-bought linen dress, resembled an adolescent who was starting to get old without ever having grown up. Cesca seemed to have shrunk somehow in the past year, but she chirped and chattered without stopping — about what they would have for lunch and about whether they should drink their coffee in the garden and about all the liqueurs and whiskey and seltzers that she had bought.

When Jenny went up to her room that night, she sat down on the window ledge and let the fresh breeze, which was fluttering the curtains, caress her face. She was quite drunk; incomprehensible as that may seem, it was a fact.

She couldn't understand how it had happened. One and a half whiskey and sodas and a couple of small glasses of liqueur was all she had drunk, and that was after supper. It's true that she hadn't eaten much, but she didn't have much of an appetite lately. And she had also had some strong coffee.

Maybe it was the coffee — and the cigarettes. Although she was smoking less these days than she had in the past.

At any rate, her heart was pounding furiously, and unpleasant waves of heat were washing over her, making her sweat. The scene she was looking at outside was slowly turning before her eyes — back and forth — the grayish lawns and the pale, glistening flower beds and the dark crowns of the trees in the garden against the almost white night sky of summer. And the room was whirling around her. Whiskey and liqueur rose up into her throat. How revolting!

Water spilled over the side as she filled the washbasin. She was moving unsteadily too. But this is scandalous, Jenny *mia.* You must be losing your grip, my girl, if you can't handle alcohol anymore. Before, she'd been able to drink twice as much without any effect.

First she held her hands in the water up to her wrists. Then she bathed her face for a long time. She took off all her clothes and wrung water from the wet sponge over her whole body.

God only knew whether Gunnar or Cesca had noticed. Although it wasn't until she came upstairs that she noticed it herself. Thank God that at least the lieutenant colonel and Frøken Borghild weren't home.

She felt better after she had washed. She put on her nightgown and sat down in the window again.

Her thoughts tumbled wildly among fragments of the day's conversation with Gunnar and Cesca. In the midst of this, she still couldn't get over her surprise at the fact that she was drunk! She had honestly never been drunk before; normally she barely noticed it, even if she had a great deal to drink.

But now it seemed to be over; she felt listless and sleepy and cold. And she stood up and fell into the big canopy bed. Just think if she woke up with a hangover in the morning . . . That would be a new experience, at any rate.

But no sooner had she settled herself on the pillows and closed her eyes than a vile, nauseating heat washed over her, making the sweat break out all over her body. The bed rocked like a ship at sea, and she felt seasick. She lay still for a moment, trying to win control over that abominable sensation — I won't, I won't. But it didn't help; her mouth filled with water. She barely managed to reach the chamber pot before she vomited.

My God, could she really be that drunk? It was getting downright embarrassing. But surely it was over now. She cleaned up, drank some water, and lay down again. Surely she could sleep now.

But after she had been lying there for a while with her eyes closed, the sea swells began again, along with the sweats and the nausea. It was puzzling, because by now she was quite clearheaded. Nevertheless, she had to get up again.

The moment she was back in bed, the thought occurred to her.

Nonsense. She lay there pressing the back of her head against the pillow. That was impossible. She refused to consider it. But she couldn't help it. She lay there and thought back: She hadn't been feeling well lately . . .

She was tired and worn out, of course. Exhausted and nervous. That must be why she hadn't been able to handle the little amount she'd had to drink tonight. She could certainly understand why people became teetotalers, after a few nights like this.

She would *not* think about the other possibility. If that's what it was, she'd know soon enough. She wouldn't torture herself by worrying before it was necessary.

Jenny undid her nightgown and ran her hand over her breasts.

She had to go to sleep. But now, of course, she couldn't stop thinking about that foolishness. Oh . . . And as tired as she was . . .

In the beginning she hadn't been able to avoid thinking about whether there might be consequences, and she had even been fearful a couple of times. But she had taken her own fear in hand and forced herself to look at it sensibly. What if it did happen? For the most part, it was nothing but meaningless superstition, this terror of having a child. These things happened, and why should it be any worse for her than for all the working-class women who had to manage alone with a child? Most of the fear was left over from the time when an unmarried woman in those circumstances had to go to her father or relatives and confess that she had enjoyed her pleasures and now they would have to pay the costs — with no possibility of ever finding anyone else to pay for her keep. And so they had good reason to take offense.

But no one had any right to take offense on her account. Of course her mamma would be upset. But good Lord, when a grown person tried to live life according to her own conscience, her parents shouldn't have any say in it. She had tried to help her mother as best she could, never bothering her with her own sorrows, never sullying her reputation for some frivolous reason, carrying on or carousing. But at the point where her own notion of right and wrong diverged from that of other good folks, she would have to follow her own path — even though it would hurt Mamma if decent people gossiped about her.

But if her relationship with Gert was sinful, at least the sin was not that she had given too much, but rather too little. And no matter how it all turned out, she would suffer — and she had no right to complain.

Surely she should be able to support a child as well as all those girls who didn't have even a tenth of her abilities. She still had a little money put aside, so she could go away. If she had chosen a meager way of earning a living . . . well, many of her peers had to support both a wife and child on it. Besides, almost from the time she was grown up, it had been necessary for her to help others.

Of course it would be best if she could avoid it. Up until now everything had been fine.

She wouldn't think about it.

Gert would probably be in despair.

Oh, but my God . . . if it was true . . . now! If only it had happened while she still loved him — or thought that she loved him. And she could have left him believing that. But now . . . now that everything between them had crumbled to bits, eaten away by all her pondering and brooding . . .

She had come to realize, here at Tegneby during these past weeks, that she wouldn't be able to continue. She longed to get away, to new relationships, new work. Yes. Her longing for work had come back; she was done with that sickly urge to cling to someone, to be pampered and coddled and called his little girl.

She had cringed in pain when she thought about the breakup. And that she would have to hurt him. But good Lord, she had given to him for as long as she could. Gert had been happy for the time it lasted. And at least he had escaped that demeaning enslavement with her — his wife.

And she had resigned herself. Work and loneliness would be her life. She knew that she couldn't erase those months from her life. She would remember them and the bitter lesson they had taught her: The love that was enough for many people was not enough for her. For her, it was better to be without than to settle for too little.

Oh yes, she would certainly remember them. But muted and reshaped in the memories of that brief happiness mixed with pain, and that bitter, remorseful anguish. Over time she would no doubt try to erase part of the memory of the man toward whom she had committed a bloody wrong.

But now she might be carrying his child.

It couldn't be possible. It was pointless to lie there brooding about it.

But if it were true . . .

Jenny fell asleep at last; by that time the light was already starting to come up outdoors. She slept heavily and without dreams. But when she sat up, jolted wide awake, it wasn't much lighter. The sky was a little more yellow above the treetops in the garden, and the birds were chirping sleepily outside.

And the same thoughts returned at once. Jenny realized that she wouldn't be able to sleep anymore that night. Resigned, she gave up and went back to turning the thoughts over and over in her mind.

3

Heggen left, and Lieutenant Colonel Jahrmann and his eldest daughter returned. Then they left again to visit Fransiska's married sister.

Cesca and Jenny were once more alone at Tegneby. Each of them kept to herself, lost in her own thoughts.

Jenny was now certain that she was pregnant. But she hadn't yet comprehended what this actually meant. If she tried to look ahead to the future, her imagination went on strike. But her state of mind was actually much better now than during those anxious weeks when she was constantly waiting to see if she could be mistaken.

She consoled herself that things would work out for her just as they had for so many others. She had been talking about going abroad ever since last fall. Paris had occurred to her as a vague possibility . . . to go there and seek out a *sagefemme* . . . But she couldn't make herself consider it.

She didn't know whether she was even going to tell Gert about her condition. She didn't think she would.

When she wasn't thinking about herself, she was thinking about Cesca. There was something about her that wasn't as it should be, although she was sure that Cesca was fond of Ahlin. Was it that he no longer cared for her?

Jenny could see that Cesca had had a difficult time during the first year of her marriage. She seemed to have become so small and dispirited. They were terribly poor, and Cesca had sat on Jenny's bed in the evenings and complained for hours about her household troubles. Stockholm was very expensive, and it was hard to cook cheap meals if you hadn't learned how, and all the housework seemed so burdensome if you had been brought up as idiotically she had. And it was depressing that the minute the work was finished, it had to be done all over. As soon as she had cleaned the house, it was dirty again, and as soon as she was done with a meal, the dishes needed to be washed. And then it was just a matter of cooking another meal and getting more plates dirty and washing the dishes again. If Lennart tried to help her, he was just as clumsy and impractical as she was. And then there were her concerns about him. He hadn't been awarded the monument job, he never received any appreciation, and yet he was so gifted. But he had too much dignity, both as an artist and a person. There was nothing to be done about it; she certainly wouldn't have wanted him to be any different. And then there were the lengthy illnesses he had suffered in the spring; he had spent two months in bed with scarlet fever and pneumonia and their aftereffects. That period had no doubt taken a heavy toll on Cesca.

But there was something else that Cesca wasn't talking about; Jenny could sense it. Yet Jenny knew that she couldn't be the same toward Cesca as in the past. She no longer had the calm heart or the open spirit that could take in other people's sorrows and offer comfort. And she felt terrible that she couldn't help Cesca.

Cesca had gone to Moss one day to do the shopping. Jenny hadn't felt like going along, so she stayed home and spent the day in the garden, reading in order not to think and then settling down with a complicated knitting pattern because she couldn't keep her thoughts on her novel. But she lost track of the count and had to unravel it and start over, forcing herself to pay attention.

Cesca didn't come home for lunch as she said she would. Jenny finally ate alone and then whiled away the afternoon — smoking, although the cigarettes didn't taste good, and knitting, even though she let her work fall to her lap every other minute.

Finally, close to ten o'clock, Cesca came driving up the lane. Jenny went out to meet her, and as soon as she climbed up beside her in the landau she could tell that something had happened. But neither of them said a word.

Not until after supper, as they drank a last cup of tea, did Fransiska say quietly, without looking at Jenny, "Do you know who I met in town today?"

"No, who?"

"Hans Hermann. He's staying at Jelø. There's a rich old woman there, a Frøken Øhrn, that he's visiting. Apparently she's taken him under her wing for a while."

"Is his wife with him?" asked Jenny after a moment.

"No. They're divorced now. Poor thing, she lost her little boy in the spring; I saw it in the paper."

Then Cesca proceeded to talk about other matters.

———

But after Jenny had gone to bed, Cesca came tiptoeing into her room. She crept up into the canopy bed and sat down at the foot with her legs tucked up and her nightgown pulled down over them. With her arms wrapped around her knees she sat in the dim whiteness of the bed, her little black-haired head looking like a dark shadow against the light draperies.

"Jenny, I'm going home tomorrow. I'll send Lennart a telegram early in the morning, and then I'll leave around noon. But of course you can stay here as long as you like. You mustn't think that I'm being inconsiderate, but I don't dare do anything else. I have to leave at once."

She sighed heavily.

"I can't understand it, Jenny. I talked to him, and he kissed me, but I didn't slap him. I listened to everything he said, but I didn't smack him right in the face. I *don't* love him — I know that now, and yet he has some kind of power over me. I'm frightened, you see. I don't dare stay here, because I don't know what he might make me do. When I think about him right now, I hate him; but I feel like I'm paralyzed whenever he speaks. Because I can't understand how someone can be so cynical — so brutal — so *shameless!*

"He can't seem to comprehend that there's anything called honor or shame; he never takes them into account, and he doesn't think anyone else does either. He assumes that it's nothing but sheer calculation when the rest of us think about right and wrong. I feel hypnotized by him.

"Just imagine . . . I spent the whole evening with him, and I listened to everything he said. Oh God. He talked about how I was married now, and so I didn't need to play hard to get or worry so much about my virtue or anything like that. He also hinted that he was free now and that I might be allowed to hope, or at least that's what I thought. He kissed me in the park, and I felt like I wanted to scream with utter revulsion, but I couldn't make a sound. Oh God, I was so scared. And then he said he would come out here the day after tomorrow — they're having some big party tomorrow. And the whole time he had that smile on this face that used to frighten me so much in the old days.

"Don't you think I should leave, Jenny, since I feel this way?"

"Yes, I do, Cesca," said Jenny.

"I know I'm such a *goose*. But you see . . ." Suddenly she exclaimed fiercely, "I don't dare trust myself. But you can be sure of one thing — if I had been unfaithful to Lennart, by God, I would have gone straight to him and told him, and then I would have killed myself at once, right before his eyes."

"Do you love your husband?" Jenny asked gently.

Fransiska hesitated for a moment.

"I don't know. If I loved him properly, the way you're supposed to, then I probably wouldn't be afraid of Hans Hermann. Don't you think that then I would have slapped Hans when he behaved that way and kissed me?

"But in any case, I know that if I had wronged Lennart in some way, I wouldn't want to go on living. Can you understand that? When my name was Fransiska Jahrmann, I was quite careless with it. But now my name is Fransiska Ahlin. And if I had cast even a shadow of suspicion on that name — his name — then I would deserve it if he shot me down like a mad dog. That's not something that Lennart could ever do, but I could, I know I could."

Abruptly she released her limbs from their hunched position and crept over to nestle close to Jenny.

"You believe me, don't you? You don't think I'd want to live if I did anything dishonorable, do you?"

"No, Cesca." Jenny pulled her close and kissed her. "I don't think you would."

"I don't know what Lennart thinks. He doesn't understand me, you see. But when I get home, I'll tell him everything. The whole truth. Then whatever happens, will happen."

"Cesca," said Jenny softly. But then she decided not to ask her whether she was happy.

But Cesca started talking again. "I've had such a difficult time, you see. It hasn't been easy for me, I can tell you. I was so foolish when I got married — in so many ways.

"I agreed to marry Lennart because Hans started writing to me after he was separated, and he wrote that now he *had* to have me, but I was afraid of him, and I didn't want to get tangled up in that whole mess again. Well, I told Lennart all about it, and he was so sweet and wonderful and he understood everything, and I thought he was the most magnificent man in the world. And he *is*, I know he is.

"But then I did something horrible. And Lennart couldn't understand it, and I know that he has never forgiven me. Maybe it's wrong of me to talk about this, but I can't figure it out, Jenny. I *have* to ask someone if this is something that a man could never forgive. And you must tell me truthfully — do you hear? — tell me truthfully if you think this is something that can't ever be made good again.

"On the afternoon after we were married, we went up to Rocca di Papa. And you know how terrified I've always been of all that, and I was filled with dread. So that evening, when Lennart led me into our room and I saw the big white double bed that I was supposed to sleep in, I burst into tears, and Lennart was so sweet. And he said that I wouldn't have to do it until I wanted to myself.

"That was on Saturday. And it wasn't very enjoyable after that — or at least I could see that Lennart didn't think so. Otherwise I would have been thrilled to be married in that way. And every morning when I woke up, I was so grateful, but I wasn't allowed so much as to kiss my own husband.

"Then on Wednesday we went up to the top of Monte Cavo. And it was splendid and lovely up there; this was right at the end of May, with dazzling sunshine. The chestnut trees were pale green and had just started to blossom, and the goldenrod was blooming like mad all over the slopes, and along the road there were big clusters of white flowers and lilies. And the air was slightly hazy with sunlight — it had rained earlier in the day — and Lago Nemi and Lago Albano were silvery white below us at the foot of the wooded slope, with those small white villages all around, and the entire *campagna* and Rome, off in the distance, were cloaked in a thin veil of fog, and far beyond was the Mediterranean Sea, like a dull golden rim on the horizon.

"Oh, it was all so lovely, so lovely, and I thought that life was marvelous, except that Lennart was sad. And I thought he was the most splendid man on earth, and I felt such boundless love for him, and I suddenly thought that the rest was just my own foolishness. Then I threw my arms around his neck and said: 'Now I want to be yours, completely yours, because I love you.'"

Cesca paused for a moment, sighing heavily.

"Oh God, Jenny, the poor boy was so happy." She swallowed her tears. "Yes, he was happy. 'Now?' he said. 'Here?' And then he picked me up and wanted to carry me into the woods. But I resisted and said, 'No, tonight, tonight.' Oh, Jenny, I don't know why I said that, when actually I wanted to do it. It would have been so beautiful there, deep in the woods, in the sunlight. But I pretended that I didn't want to; God only knows why.

"And then that evening, after I'd gone to bed, and I'd had all those hours of waiting for it, and Lennart came in . . . Well, then I started shrieking again.

"He ran out and was gone all night. I lay there wide awake. I don't know where he went. And then we went back to Rome the next morning and stayed in a hotel. Lennart had reserved two rooms, but I went to him in his room . . . There was nothing beautiful about it.

"And ever since, things haven't been good between Lennart and me. I realize that I offended him terribly. But you must tell me, Jenny, whether you think this is something that a man can't possibly forget — or forgive."

"He should be able to see, afterward," said Jenny quietly, a bit hesitant, "that back then you didn't understand what . . . feelings you were offending."

"No." Cesca shivered. "But I do now. I understand that it was something pure and beautiful that I sullied. But I didn't know that before. Jenny, can a man's . . . love . . . ever recover?"

"It should. You've shown him since then that you want to be his good and faithful wife. All winter long you worked and toiled without complaint. This spring, when he was sick, you watched over him night after night, nursed him week after week."

"That was nothing," said Cesca earnestly. "He was so sweet and patient, and he helped as best he could with my toil, as you call it. And while he was sick, some of our friends occasionally came over and helped keep watch. That week when it looked like he might die, we also had a nurse, but I stayed up with him myself because I wanted to, you see, even though I didn't have to."

Jenny kissed Cesca on the forehead.

"But there's one thing I haven't told you, Jenny. Yes, I know that you warned me about not having the instincts for it, and Gunnar was always scolding me . . . And remember how Frøken Linde once even came right out and said that if you got a man all worked up, he would go to someone else?"

Jenny went stiff with terror as she lay there.

Cesca nodded into the pillows.

"Well, I asked him about that . . . on the morning after . . ."

Jenny lay there, speechless.

"I can understand that it's something he can't forget. Or forgive either. But if he would only relent a little bit — and remember how utterly foolish my ideas were about all that. But ever since . . ." she fumbled for words. "There has been such . . . discord . . . between us, about everything. It's as if he doesn't *want*

to touch me, and if it does happen, it's against his will, and afterward he's angry
with both of us. Even though I've tried to explain it to him. I honestly don't
understand what's so special about it all anyway. But I don't have anything
against it anymore. If it will make him happy . . . Anything that makes Lennart
happy I consider good and beautiful. He thinks it's a sacrifice, but it's *not* — on
the contrary. Oh, how I've cried in my room night after night and day after day,
and I've tried to entice him, Jenny, the little bit that I could — but he pushed
me away.

"I'm so fond of him, Jenny. Tell me, isn't it all right to love a man in that way
too? Can't I say that I love Lennart?"

"Yes, of course, Cesca."

"Oh, I've been so full of despair. But I can't help it if that's the way I am, can
I? And then whenever we go out with the other artists, he's always in such a
bad mood. He doesn't say anything, but I can see that he thinks I flirt with
them. And he might be right, because I'm always in good spirits when I can eat
out and I don't have to cook or wash dishes for one night, and I don't have to
be afraid of ruining the meal, which Lennart has to eat anyway because we
can't afford to throw it out. And sometimes I was also glad I didn't have to be
alone with Lennart, even though I'm fond of him and he's fond of me. I know
he is, but if I ask him, he says I should know that he is, and then he laughs in
a strange and bitter way. But he doesn't trust me, because I can't love in a sensual way and yet I'm still a flirt. Once he told me that I don't know what love
is, and that it was probably all his fault for not being able to arouse me, and
someone else would probably come along and . . . Oh God, how I cried.

"And now this spring. Well, you know how poor we are. Gunnar helped me
sell that still life that I had in the exhibition three years ago. I got three hundred kroner for it. We lived on that money for months, but Lennart didn't like
having to use money that I had earned. I don't see what the difference is, since
we care for each other . . . But he went around saying that he had dragged me
down into misery. And we have debts, of course. One time I wanted to write to
Pappa and ask him for a few hundred kroner. But Lennart wouldn't let me. I
thought he was being unreasonable. Borghild and Helga have lived at home
and Pappa has always supported them, and he paid for their expenses abroad
too, while I've had to pinch and scrape to get by on the tiny inheritance from
Mamma ever since I came of age, because I didn't want to accept a single øre
from Pappa after what he said to me when I broke up with Lieutenant Kaasen,

and there was all that talk about me and Hans. But now he regrets what he said, and he admits I was right. It was mean of Kaasen and everybody back home to try to force me because he had tricked me into that engagement when I was seventeen and didn't know that marriage was not the way it's described in those cursed adolescent stories. But when I began to have an inkling, I knew I would rather kill myself than marry him. And if they had forced me into it . . . Oh yes, I would have been quite a wife . . . I would have taken all the lovers I could find, out of pure spite, to get back at all of them. Pappa sees that now, and he said he'll give me money whenever I like.

"But when Lennart was so sick and miserable, and they said he *had* to go out to the country to recuperate . . . and I was so tired and miserable myself. Well, then I told him that I needed to go to the country to rest because I was going to have a baby. Then he let me ask Pappa for money, and we went to Värmland and everything was lovely, and Lennart regained his health, and I started painting again. But then he realized that I wasn't pregnant after all. And when he asked me if I had been mistaken, I told him I had lied because I didn't want to hide the truth from Lennart. But I could tell that it made him angry.

"I can see that he doesn't really trust me, and it's so awful. If he understood me, he would have to trust me, don't you think so?"

"Yes, I do, Cesca."

"Well, I did say it once before, that I was going to have a baby . . . Last fall, when he was discouraged, and things were so bad. I did it so he would be happy and be nice to me — and he was. Oh, you wouldn't believe how lovely it was. It *was* a lie, but just think . . . in the end I almost believed it myself. I thought God would make it happen so that I wouldn't have to disappoint Lennart. But He didn't.

"I feel so desperate because I don't have any children. Jenny, do you think it's true, what some people say . . ." she whispered in a quavering voice, "that a woman can't have a child if she doesn't feel any . . . passion?"

"No," said Jenny harshly. "I'm sure that's utter nonsense."

"I know everything would be all right if I had a baby. Lennart wants one so badly. And I . . . well, I think I'd turn into an angel out of sheer joy if I had my own little child. Can you imagine how wonderful that must be?"

"No, I can't," Jenny whispered in a strained voice. "If you love each other, that should help overcome any number of difficulties."

"Oh yes, you're right. If it wasn't so embarrassing I would go to a doctor. As a matter of fact, I think I will one day. Don't you think I should? If only I wasn't so shy; but that's silly. And besides, it's my duty now that I'm married. I could go to a woman doctor — someone who's married and has children and everything. Oh, just imagine having a tiny little baby all your own . . . How happy Lennart would be."

Jenny clenched her teeth in the dark.

"Don't you think I should leave tomorrow?"

"Yes, I do."

"And I'm going to tell Lennart everything. I don't know whether he'll be able to understand — not that I really do, myself. But I insist on always telling him the truth. Don't you think I should, Jenny?"

"If you think it's the right thing to do, then you must do it. Oh, Cesca . . . You should always do what you think is right — don't ever do something if you're not sure it's right, Cesca."

"Yes, how true! Well, good night, then, dear Jenny. And thank you." She gave her friend a sudden, fierce hug. "It's so lovely to talk to you. You understand me so well. You . . . and Gunnar. Both of you have always set me on the right track. I don't know what I'd do without you."

She stood beside the bed for a moment.

"Couldn't you come to Stockholm in the fall? Won't you? You can stay with us . . . I'm getting a thousand kroner from Pappa because that's what Borghild is getting for her trip to Paris."

"I don't know, Cesca. I'd like to, but . . ."

"Oh, you must come! Are you sleepy? Should I go?"

"I'm a little tired, yes." She drew Cesca close and gave her a kiss. "God bless you, my child!"

"Thank you." Cesca padded across the floor in her bare feet. Over by the door she said in a sad, little-girl voice, "Oh, how I wish Lennart and I could be happy!"

4

Gert and Jenny walked side by side down the sloping path beneath the scraggly spruce trees. He paused once to pick a few tiny, shriveled strawberries, ran after her, and popped them in her mouth. She gave him a little smile in thanks, and he took her hand as they continued down toward the sparkling blue water glimpsed through the trees, with the sun arcing overhead.

He looked happy and young in his light summer clothes. A panama hat entirely hid his hair.

Jenny sat down at the edge of the woods, and Gert stretched out before her in the shade of the tall weeping birches.

It was roasting hot and still. The grassy hillside down to the water was scorched yellow. Out toward Nesodlandet there was a bank of metallic blue haze, and along its edge glided a few clouds, smoky yellow and white. The fjord was pale blue with rippled stripes from the current; the sailboats out on the water were motionless and white, and the smoke from the steamboats hung on forever, like gray streaks in the sultry air.

But the water murmured quietly over the stones on the shore, and the slender branches of the weeping birches swayed gently above their heads, so that a few leaves, yellowed by the heat, drifted down.

Gert brushed one away that was caught in her blond curls; she had taken off her hat. He looked at it.

"Isn't it strange how little rain we've had this year? It's fine for you ladies who can wear such thin dresses. But that dress makes it look like you're almost in mourning . . . If you weren't wearing those pink beads . . . But it suits you beautifully!"

It was a plain white dress with little black flowers, loose fitting and gathered with a tight black silk belt. The straw hat she was holding in her lap was black with black velvet roses. But the pale pink crystal beads gleamed against the glowing skin of her throat.

He leaned forward so he could kiss her foot right above the edge of her shoe. And he slid two fingers up along the delicate arc of her instep in the sheer stocking, then grabbed hold of her ankle.

After a moment she carefully moved his hand. He grabbed her hand and held it, smiling up at her. She smiled back, then turned her head away.

"You're so quiet, Jenny. Is it the heat that's bothering you?"

"I suppose so," she said. And they both fell silent.

Some distance away, where the garden of a villa reached down to the water, several half-grown youths were making a ruckus out on the pier of a bathing hut. And a gramophone inside the house was singing nasally. Now and then a gust of music could be heard from far away at the seaside resort.

"Gert . . ." Jenny suddenly took his hand. "After I've been to visit Mamma for a few days . . . and after I come back to town . . . I'm going to go away."

"What do you mean?" He propped himself up on his elbow. "Where are you going?"

"To Berlin," said Jenny. She could feel that her voice was quavering.

Gert looked up into her face, but he didn't say a word. She didn't speak either.

Finally he said, "When did you decide this?"

"Actually it's been my plan all along, you know. That I should go abroad again."

"I see. But . . . I mean, how long have you known that you . . . When did you decide that you would leave now?"

"I decided this summer, at Tegneby."

"I wish you had told me before, Jenny," said Gram. Even though his voice was low and calm, it cut right through her soul.

She sat in silence for a moment.

"I wanted to tell you in person, Gert. Not in writing, but in person. When I wrote to you and asked you to come to see me yesterday, I wanted to tell you. But I didn't manage . . ."

His face had turned a stony gray.

"I understand. But God in heaven, child, how you must have suffered," he suddenly exclaimed.

"Yes," said Jenny calmly. "Mostly for your sake, Gert. I don't ask you to forgive me . . ."

"Forgive you? Oh, dear God — can *you* forgive *me*, Jenny? Because I knew this day had to come."

"We both did," she said in the same tone of voice.

All of sudden he threw himself facedown on the ground. She bent over him and placed her hand on the back of his neck.

"Little, little, little Jenny. Oh, little Jenny. What have I done to you?"

"Dear . . ."

"My little white bird. And I've touched you with my hideous filthy fists, besmirched your white wings . . ."

"Gert." She took his hands, speaking quickly and firmly. "Listen to me. You've always been good to me — I'm the one who . . . I was so tired, and you let me rest; I was cold and you gave me warmth. I *had* to rest and I *had* to get warm, and I had to feel that someone cared for me. Dear God, Gert, I didn't want to deceive you, but you couldn't understand . . . I could never make you realize that I loved you in a different way, with such a poor kind of love. Can't you understand . . ."

"No, Jenny. I refuse to believe that an innocent young girl would give herself to a man if she didn't think that her love would last."

"But that's what I'm asking you to forgive. I knew you didn't understand, but I accepted everything you gave me just the same. And then it began to torment me. It got worse and worse, and I realized that I couldn't go on. I *am* fond of you, Gert, but if all I can do is take, with nothing genuine to give in return . . ."

"Was that what you wanted to tell me yesterday?" asked Gert after a moment.

Jenny nodded.

"And instead . . ."

She turned bright red.

"I couldn't do it, Gert. You were so happy when you arrived. And I could see that you'd been longing and waiting . . ."

He raised his head abruptly.

"You shouldn't have done that, Jenny. No. You shouldn't have given me . . . out of charity . . ."

She hid her face. She remembered those agonizing hours she had spent in her dust-filled studio, in the sunbaked, close air, restlessly cleaning and straightening up, waiting for him while her heart cringed with torment. But she couldn't tell him that.

"I wasn't sure of myself, either . . . when you came. I thought for a moment . . . I wanted to try . . ."

"Charity." He shook his head in pain. "That's what it was all along, Jenny — everything you gave me."

"Gert. The fact is that I accepted charity from *you* — the whole time — don't you see?"

"No, I don't," he said vehemently. And he lay back down with his face to the ground.

After a while he lifted his head.

"Jenny . . . is there . . . someone else?"

"No," she said fiercely.

"Do you think I would reproach you if there was? A young man . . . your equal? It would be easier for me to understand *that*."

"Can't you see . . . I don't think there has to be anyone else."

"No, no." He put his head down again. "But it would have seemed more natural to me. And when I happened to think about what you wrote . . . that Heggen was at Tegneby and had now gone to Berlin . . ."

Jenny turned blood-red again.

"If that were true, do you think yesterday I would have . . ."

Gram didn't reply. After a moment he said in a weary voice:

"Then I don't think I understand you, after all."

She had a sudden urge to hurt him.

"I suppose you might actually say that there's someone else, or rather a third person . . ."

He looked up with a puzzled expression. Then he suddenly grabbed hold of her.

"Jenny — dear Jesus — what do you mean?"

She already regretted her words, and blushing she said swiftly:

"You know . . . my work . . . my art."

Gert Gram was now kneeling before her.

"Jenny — is there anything — in particular? You must tell me the truth — don't lie. Is there anything . . . wrong . . . with you? Tell me."

For a moment she tried boldly to look him in the eye. Then she bowed her head. And Gert Gram sank forward with his face in her lap.

"Oh God. Oh God. Oh God, God, God . . ."

"Gert. Dear, dear Gert. Oh no, Gert . . . You annoyed me with your questions about someone else," she said humbly. "I shouldn't have said it. I wasn't planning to tell you — not until afterward."

"I would never have forgiven you," said Gram, "if you hadn't told me.

"But you must have known for some time now," he said suddenly. "Do you know . . . how far along you are?"

"Three months," she said curtly.

"But Jenny . . ." He took her hands and said, aghast, "Now you can't possibly . . . break things off with me . . . not like this, I mean. We have to stay together *now*."

"No, we can't." She caressed his face. "Oh no. If this hadn't happened I might have kept on . . . for a while. But now I *have* to face up to things — and accept the facts."

He lay quietly for a moment.

"Listen to me, dear. You know that my wife and I were separated last month. In two years I'll be free. Then I'll come to you. I'll give you — and the child — my name. I ask nothing from you — do you understand? *Nothing*. But I *demand* my right to restore your good name. That much I owe you. God knows I'll suffer enough because it can't be done any sooner. But I ask for nothing — nothing at all. You aren't bound to me in any way, old man that I am . . ."

"Gert. I'm glad that you've separated from her. But let me say this once and for all: I'm *not* going to marry you if I can't be your real wife. It's not because of the age difference between us, Gert. If I didn't feel that I've never been completely yours, Gert, the way I should be, then I would stay with you, as your wife while you were young and as your companion when you were old — even as your nurse, gladly and willingly. But I know that I can't be for you what a wife should be. And I refuse to make a promise that I can't keep — either before the pastor or the mayor — just because of what people might say."

"Oh, but Jenny . . . This is madness."

"You'll never get me to change my mind," she said quickly.

"Yes, but what will you do, child? No, I can't let you . . . What will become of you? Little Jenny, you must know, you must let me help you. Jenny, dear God . . ."

"Hush now, my dearest friend. You can see that I'm quite calm about the whole thing. It's probably not as terrible as we think, when it comes right down to it. Luckily I still have a little money."

"But Jenny — all those people, who will be so ugly toward you, who will try to shame you."

"No one can do that. There's only one thing I'm ashamed of, Gert — that I let you squander your love on me."

"Oh, what nonsense you're talking. No, you have no idea how . . . heartless people can be — how maliciously they'll treat you, insulting and hurting you."

"I don't care about that, Gert." She gave a little laugh. "I'm an artist, after all — thank God. And they expect us to cause a minor scandal now and then."

He shook his head. And all of a sudden, desperately regretting that she had told him and that she might have hurt him, she pulled him close.

"My dear Gert — you mustn't be unhappy, do you hear me? You can see that *I'm* not. On the contrary — sometimes I'm glad. When I truly try to understand what it means, that I'm going to have a child — my own sweet, lovely little baby — I can hardly comprehend it. I think it will be a great joy — so great that I can't even imagine it yet. A tiny little human being who is all my own — someone I will love and live for and work for. And you know . . . sometimes I think that only then will there be any purpose to my life and my work. Don't you think that then I'll be able to create a name for myself that will be good enough for my child? It's just that I can't yet fully grasp what it will be like, and that's why I'm a little discouraged right now, plus the fact that you're so sad.

"Oh Gert, I may be poor and dreary and egotistical and all that, but I'm still a woman, and I *have* to be glad that I'm going to be a mother."

"Jenny." He kissed her hands. "My poor brave little Jenny. It's almost worse for me that you're taking it this way," he said quietly.

Jenny smiled wanly.

"Oh, I think it would probably be much worse for you if I took it any other way."

5

Ten days later Jenny left for Copenhagen. Her mother and Bodil Berner went to the station with her in the early-morning hours.

"Oh, you have all the luck, Jenny," said Bodil with a big smile on her soft little face. And then she yawned so wide that tears came to her eyes.

"Well, I suppose someone has to have luck." Jenny laughed along with her. "You're not doing so badly yourself, you know."

But she could feel over and over how she was about to burst into tears as she kissed her mother good-bye. And she stood at the compartment window, staring at her. She felt as if she had never really seen her mother before.

That slender, frail, slightly stooped figure. Her hair hardly looked as if it had any gray in it at all, as blond as Fru Berner was. And there was something so strangely untouched and girlish about her features, even though she had a good many wrinkles by now. But only the years and not life itself seemed to have furrowed her face, in spite of everything that she'd been through.

When she eventually found out about this . . . No, Jenny could never have mustered the courage to tell her mother and then watch how she took the blow. Her mother, who didn't have the slightest suspicion, wouldn't have been able to understand at all. If she hadn't been able to go away . . . Jenny knew that she would have sooner killed herself. It wasn't love — it was cowardice. Because eventually she would have to tell her — and from a safe distance she could probably do it.

As the train gave a lurch and began pulling away, she saw Gert. He was walking slowly along the platform. From behind her mother and sister, who were waving their handkerchiefs, he waved to her. He was very pale.

———

It was the first of September. Jenny was sitting at the train window, looking out.

What a beautiful day it had turned out to be. The air was clear and cool, with the sky dark blue and the clouds so white. The dew lay heavy and gray on the lush green meadows, shimmering with late-blooming oxeye daisies. After the hot summer the birches at the edge of the woods had already turned completely yellow, and across the forest floor the huckleberry branches were coppery red. The clusters of berries on the mountain ash trees were blood-red, but where there was richer soil, the leaves were still a deep green. What magnificent colors.

On small rises in the meadows stood the farmsteads, old and silvery gray, or new and shiny white or yellow, with red outbuildings. All around them stood crooked old apple trees with yellow and glassy green fruit visible in the dark foliage.

Time after time tears filled her eyes. When she came back — *if* she ever came back here . . .

The fjord gleamed blue outside Moss. The town, with its red factory walls, stood along the canal and there were small, brightly painted wooden houses in all the gardens. She had often thought, when she traveled through, that she should come here some summer to paint.

The train raced past the little country station that was the stop for Tegneby. Jenny looked across the fields: There was the road. The estate was far off in the distance, beyond the small spruce forest.

There was the church tower. Strange little Cesca, who spent so much time in churches. She would sit there feeling safe and secure in the bygone atmosphere of some sort of higher power. She believed in something, although she wasn't sure exactly what, but she had created a kind of god for herself.

She was glad that Cesca now seemed to be getting along better with her husband. She wrote that he had not understood, but he'd been extraordinarily kind and sweet all the same, and he believed that she would never do anything wrong — not intentionally.

Odd little Cesca. Things *had* to work out for her in the long run. Cesca was honest and good. Precisely what Jenny herself was not — neither one of them to any significant degree.

As long as she didn't have to see her mother's tears, it didn't bother her to cause her sorrow. Which merely meant that she was afraid of scenes.

And Gert. Her heart cringed. A physical sense of nausea flooded over her — a despair and loathing so intense that she felt utterly exhausted, on the verge of complete indifference to everything.

Those horrible last days in Kristiania with him. Finally she had been forced to give in.

He was coming to Copenhagen. And she had to promise to stay somewhere out in the country in Denmark, where he could come to see her. God only knew if she'd ever manage to break things off with him.

She'd probably end up giving him the child and then leaving everything behind. Yes, because it was all a lie, what she had told him about being happy and all the rest. At Tegneby she had sometimes felt that way, because then she had only thought about the child being hers — not his. But if there was going to be a living link between her and her ignominy . . . then she wanted no part of it. She would end up hating the child; she hated it already, whenever she thought about those last days in town.

The pathetic urge to sob her heart out had vanished. She felt dry and hardened, as if she would never cry again.

———

A week later Gert Gram arrived. By then she was so worn out and resigned that it seemed almost possible for her to be in good spirits. If he had suggested that she move to his hotel, she would have done so. And she persuaded him to go with her to the theater and out to eat in the evenings, and even take an excursion to Fredensborg one day in the fine weather. She could see that it did him good whenever she was cheerful and lively.

She scarcely thought about anything anymore; it took no effort for her to stop thinking. In reality her mind was exhausted. Like a constant, murmuring reminder she simply noted that her breasts were tender and swollen and that her corset plagued her.

Jenny had taken lodgings with a widowed schoolteacher in a village in western Sjælland. In the evening Gram accompanied her there and then returned to Copenhagen. At last she was alone.

She had rented the room sight unseen. Back when she was living and painting in Copenhagen, she had once visited that village with some of her friends. They had eaten a meal at the inn and gone swimming down by the dunes. And she remembered how beautiful it was; so when a Fru Rasmussen from the village answered her ad with an offer to house the young woman who was waiting to give birth, Jenny had accepted.

She was actually quite happy. True, the widowed schoolteacher lived in a tiny and dismally ugly yellow-brick house on the outskirts of the village, near the dusty main road, which wound endlessly through the open, cultivated fields. But Jenny liked her room with its sky-blue wallpaper and Exner lithographs on the wall and the white crocheted coverlets everywhere: on the bed and on the American rocking chair and on the dresser, where Fru Rasmussen had set a big bouquet of roses on the day she arrived.

Outside the two small windows, the road ran past the house and the little front garden where roses and geraniums and fuchsias bloomed, unaffected by the dust powdering them. Across the road a bare ridge rose up from the field. Hearty, brightly colored fall flowers tumbled amid the blackberry brambles along the stone walls that divided up the hillside into squares of white stubble and bluish green fields of turnips and brownish green pastures, lined with creaking, windblown willow shrubs. When the evening sun disappeared from Jenny's chamber, flames of red and gold would cover the sky above the ridge and the slender branches of the willows.

Beyond her room there was a tiny doll-sized kitchen with a red-brick floor, facing the yard where the widow's chickens clucked and the doves cooed. A narrow hallway divided the house in half. On the other side was Fru Rasmussen's parlor with flowers in the windows and crocheted doilies everywhere; daguerreotypes and photographs hung on the walls, and a small bookshelf held religious books with black pasteboard bindings, issues of the magazine *Frem* going back several years, and Gyldendal's series of books in deluxe bindings. Beyond was her own small bedroom, where the air was always strangely heavy and filled with an indecipherable smell, although it was spotlessly clean. She couldn't hear if her lodger occasionally wept through the night across the hallway.

Fru Rasmussen herself was not a bad sort. Tall and lean, she shuffled quietly around wearing some kind of felt slippers. She always had a worried expression on her long, yellow, horselike face, framed by her gray-streaked hair, which was swept back into odd little wings over each ear. She rarely spoke, except for a few anxious inquiries about whether Frøken Winge was pleased with the food and her room. Even when Jenny sometimes joined Fru Rasmussen in the parlor after dinner with her handwork, they would sit in silence. Jenny was particularly grateful that Fru Rasmussen never mentioned her condition; only once, when Jenny went out with her painting equipment, had she timidly asked whether Frøken Winge really thought that would be wise.

Jenny worked eagerly in the beginning, standing behind a stone wall with her portable easel, which kept threatening to topple over in the wind. Below the wall, the yellow stubble remaining from an endless field of rye sloped down toward a marsh where the cotton grass was turning pale along blue water holes, and velvety-black peat stood in piles on the lush green, grassy bottom. Beyond the marsh the land undulated with turnip fields and meadows and stubby acres of rye surrounding chalk-white farmsteads in lush, dark green groves, leading down to the sparkling blue fjord. The shoreline arced and curved, pale yellow with sand and short, bleached grass. To the north the heather-brown hillside, with a windmill on top, faced the blue fjord with steep yellow bluffs. And the shadows and light shifted across the open landscape as the clouds wandered across the wide and eternally restless sky.

When Jenny felt tired, she would lie down right next to the wall and stare up at the sky or out at the fjord. She didn't have the strength to stand for long, but that only prompted her to work harder. She finished two smaller paintings up at the wall and was quite pleased with them. She painted one down by the main road, where the low whitewashed houses, with thatched roofs reaching down to their windows and rambling roses and dahlias outside, stood around a velvet-green village pond, and a red-brick church with its stepped-gable tower loomed above the foliage of the parsonage garden. But it made her nervous whenever people came over to watch; the tow-headed children would crowd around her while she painted. So when that painting was finished, she moved her easel back out to the stone wall facing the sea.

But then came the rain in October. It poured down, one week after another. Every once in a while it would clear up slightly, and a sickly yellow streak of light would appear between the clouds above the hill with the sorry-looking willow hedge, and the puddles on the road would gleam for a while. Then it would rain again.

Jenny borrowed Fru Rasmussen's Gyldendal novels and *Frem* magazines and learned to knit lace for her landlady's curtains. But she didn't get much done, whether it was reading or knitting. She would sit in the rocking chair near the window all day long without even bothering to get properly dressed, merely wrapping herself in her faded kimono.

She suffered terribly as her pregnancy became more and more visible.

—⁓—

Then Gert Gram sent word of his visit. And no more than two days later he drove up in the early-morning hours in the midst of a downpour. He stayed a week. He took a room at the Railway Hotel five kilometers away, but he spent all his days with her. When he left, he promised to come back soon, perhaps even six weeks later.

Jenny lay awake every night with the lamp burning. The only thing she knew for sure was that she couldn't do that again. It had been too awful.

Unbearable, all of it — from his first sympathetic, worried glance when he saw her, wearing a new dark blue maternity dress, which the village seamstress had made for her. "How beautiful you are," he told her; he thought she looked like a Madonna. Oh yes, a lovely Madonna. His tentative arm around her waist, his long, careful kisses on her forehead; she felt as if she would die of shame. Oh how he had tormented her with his loving concern for her health and his admonitions to get plenty of exercise. Whenever the weather cleared, he would drag her outside to take a walk, and she was supposed to cling to his arm for support. One evening he took a surreptitious look at her handwork, no doubt expecting her to be hemming diapers.

He didn't mean any harm by all this. But there was no hope that things would be any better when he came back — on the contrary. And she couldn't stand it anymore.

One day she received a letter from him, saying that she should see about consulting a doctor.

That same evening she wrote a short letter to Gunnar Heggen, telling him that she was expecting a child in February and asking him to find her lodgings in a quiet place in Germany where she could stay until the birth.

Heggen answered her at once:

> Dear Jenny,
>
> I have put an ad in a few newspapers here, and I will send you the replies as they arrive so you can look at them yourself. If you like, I would gladly go out and look at the place for you before you rent it. It would be my pleasure, and you must know that I am completely at your disposal. Tell me when you leave and how you plan to travel and whether you would like me to come and meet you, or if there is anything else I can do to help. I was terribly sorry to receive your news, but I know that you are relatively well prepared to withstand

any trouble. Please write to me if there is anything more I can do for you. You know that I would be happy to help. I hear you have a fine painting in the state exhibition — Congratulations.
Greetings from your devoted friend,
G. H.

Several days later a whole packet of letters arrived. Jenny spelled her way through a number of the replies, written in dreadful Gothic script. Then she wrote to Frau Minna Schlessinger who lived close to Warnemünde, and rented a room as of November fifteenth. She informed Gunnar of her decision and then gave notice to Fru Rasmussen.

Not until the last evening did she write to Gert Gram.

> My dear friend,
> I have made a decision that I fear will hurt you, but you must not be angry with me. I'm so tired and nervous. I know that I was unreasonable and unpleasant toward you when you were here, and that is not how I want to be. For this reason, I don't want to see you until it's all over and I'm back to normal. I'm leaving tomorrow morning to go abroad. I don't want to give you my address just yet, but you can send me letters c/o Fru Fransiska Ahlin, Varberg, Sweden. I will write to you through her for the time being. You must not worry about me. I feel healthy and in good spirits, but my dear, I beg you, please don't try to contact me in any other way. And don't be too angry with me, for I think this will be best for both of us. And try not to be too sad or anxious, for my sake.
> Yours,
> Jenny Winge

Then she moved in with another widow in another little house; this one was red with whitewashed window frames. It stood behind a small garden with tiled pathways and seashells lining the flower beds, where asters and dahlias stood, black and rotting. Twenty or thirty similar houses stood along the narrow street, stretching from the railway station down to the harbor, where the sea crashed white over the long stone breakwaters. Some distance away on the pale shore, where heaps of seaweed floated in, stood a small resort hotel with closed shutters. And endless roads led inland, with bare, bristling poplars sway-ing in the wind, past tiny stone farmhouses with a patch of garden in front and a few tall black haystacks, and then on through countless black fields and marshes. In the morning the countryside was sometimes covered with slushy gray new snow that would vanish as the day wore on.

Jenny took walks along the roads, going as far as she could, and then went back home and sat in her little room, which this time was filled with precious knickknacks: painted plaster reliefs of castles and merry tavern scenes in brass frames. She didn't even have the strength to remove her wet footwear, but Frau Schlessinger would take off her boots and stockings, talking all the while, admonishing Jenny to take heart, and telling her about all the fellow sufferers who had stayed with her, and how so-and-so was now happily married — yes, she was!

She had been there a month when Frau Schlessinger came rushing in, excited and beaming. A gentleman had come to call on her.

Jenny was paralyzed with fear. Then she managed to ask what the gentle-man looked like. Quite young, said Frau Schlessinger, and she smiled slyly: *Wundernett* — very handsome. Then it occurred to Jenny that it might be Gunnar. She stood up, but then threw a blanket around her shoulders, wrapped herself up in it, and sank into the deepest armchair.

A delighted Frau Schlessinger strode out to get the gentleman. She led Gunnar to Jenny's room and lingered in the doorway for a moment with a happy smile before she left.

He squeezed her hands so hard that it hurt. But he laughed heartily.

"Well, I thought I ought to look in and see how you were doing. I think this is a rather dreary part of the world that you've chosen, but at least it's invigor-ating." He shook a few drops of water from his felt hat, which he was holding in his hand.

"But you must have tea — and something to eat!" Jenny made a move as if to get up, but then stayed where she was and said with a blush, "Maybe you'd be kind enough to ring for me . . ."

Heggen ate like a wolf, talking incessantly. He was enthusiastic about Berlin; he lived up in Moabit in a working-class section, and he spoke with equal delight about German social democrats and militarism. "Yes, there's something so splendidly masculine about it, you know. And besides, each depends upon the other." He had taken a tour of several big factories, and he'd also been forced to take in a little nightlife after meeting a Norwegian engineer who was there on his honeymoon, as well as a Norwegian family with two charming and winsome daughters. And the young ladies were, of course, burning to see a little depravity close up. So they had been to the National and the Riche and the Amorsaalen; the ladies had enjoyed themselves immensely.

"But then we ended up quarreling. You see, I suggested to Frøken Paulsen that she might come home with me late one evening . . ."

"Oh, Gunnar . . ."

"Yes, damn it all, I was a bit drunk, as you might guess, and it was all just a lark, you know. Of course I didn't expect her to agree — I would have been in real trouble if she had. Might have had to marry a girl who thinks it's fun to go nosing about in things like that . . . No thanks. No, I just thought it was amusing to see her virtue so outraged. Well, there was no danger anyway; those types of girls don't give up their jewels until they've secured payment."

Suddenly he blushed. It occurred to him that Jenny might find it tactless of him to be talking this way to her — now.

But she just laughed. "Oh, you're quite mad, my boy!"

Her strained, painful shyness had gradually left her. And Heggen kept on chattering away. A couple of times, when she wasn't looking, he let his gaze rest anxiously on her face — dear God, how thin and hollow eyed she looked, with lines around her mouth. The sinews in her neck stood out sharply, and several ugly stripes were etched into her throat.

The rain had stopped, and she agreed to take a walk with him.

In the sea fog they walked along the deserted country road with the wind-blown poplars, Jenny heavy and weary.

"Why don't you take my arm," said Gunnar casually, and she did.

"I think it's horribly depressing here, Jenny. You know . . . wouldn't it be better if you came to Berlin?"

Jenny shook her head.

"But you have the museums there, and plenty of other things. And someone to keep you company. And you don't care about going to the National anyway. Why don't you take a little trip there to cheer yourself up? I think it must be so boring here."

"Oh no, Gunnar . . . surely you understand . . . not now."

"You look so pretty in that coat," he said a bit hesitantly.

Jenny bowed her head.

"I'm such an idiot," he exclaimed suddenly. "Forgive me! You must tell me, Jenny, if I'm upsetting you."

"No, not at all." She looked up. "I'm glad you're here!"

"I know it must be awful." His voice had a different tone to it. "Yes, Jenny, I realize that. But I'm serious. For you to stay here, under these circumstances . . . I think you're just making it worse for yourself. I think you should go somewhere that's not so . . . bleak!" He looked out at the dark stretches of meadow and the rows of poplars vanishing into the mist.

"But Frau Schlessinger is very nice," said Jenny evasively.

"Yes, the poor thing, I'm sure she is." All at once he laughed. "Evidently she suspects that I'm the culprit!"

"I know," said Jenny, and laughed with him.

"Oh, to hell with it." They walked a little farther. "Jenny . . . have you given any thought to what you're going to do . . . in the future?"

"I don't really know yet. Do you mean with . . . the child? Maybe let Frau Schlessinger look after it, for the time being. I know she would take good care of it. Or maybe I'll adopt it." She laughed. "Sometimes people 'adopt' children like that. You know, I could call myself *Fru* Winge — and I wouldn't care what people think."

"And you're still determined, as you said in your letter, to break off any connection with . . . the man in question?"

"That's right," she said harshly. "It's not the same man I was . . . engaged to," she added after a moment.

"Oh, thank God!" He said this with such fervor that she couldn't help smiling. "You know, Jenny, he wasn't worth reproducing — not for you, at any rate. By the way, I saw recently that he was awarded a doctoral degree. Well, at least it could have been worse — you know, I was afraid that . . ."

"It's his father," she said suddenly.

Heggen stopped dead.

When she burst into tears, wild and shrill, he put his arms around her and pressed his hand to her cheek as she went on sobbing against his shoulder.

She told him everything as they stood there. Once she looked up at his face — it was quite pale and contorted — and then she wept some more.

When it was over, he tilted her face up for a moment.

"Dear Jesus, Jenny — how you've suffered! I can't comprehend . . ."

—◊◊◊—

Heggen stayed in Warnemünde for three days. Jenny didn't fully understand why she felt so much better after his visit. But the unbearable feeling of humiliation was gone; now she could face her situation with much greater calm and acceptance.

And Frau Schlessinger walked around with a happy and knowing smile, even though Jenny had explained that the gentleman was her cousin.

He had offered to send her books, and a whole crateful had arrived, along with flowers and candy at Christmastime. Every week he wrote her long letters about all manner of topics, with clippings from Norwegian newspapers. For her birthday in January he came to visit in person and stayed two days, leaving behind a couple of the season's newest Norwegian books.

But right after his visit, Jenny fell ill. She was miserable and in pain, tormented and sleepless toward the end. Up until then she had given little thought to the actual birth and had felt no sense of dread about it. Now, when she was in constant pain, she was gripped by a great horror of what she would have to endure. By the time of her confinement, she was utterly worn out from fear and lack of sleep.

It was a difficult birth. And Jenny was closer to death than to life when the doctor, who had been called in from Warnemünde, finally stood with her son in his bloody hands.

6

Jenny's son lived for six weeks. Exactly forty-four and a half days, she told herself bitterly as she thought back, over and over again, to that brief period when she knew what it was to be happy.

She didn't cry during those first days afterward — but she hovered around the dead child and whimpered deep in her throat. And she picked him up to hold him close.

"Little boy — Mother's lovely little boy — I won't let you . . . do you hear me? Little boy, I won't let you die, do you understand?"

The boy had been tiny and frail when he came into the world. But both Jenny and Frau Schlessinger thought he was healthy and doing splendidly. Then one morning he fell ill, and by noon he was dead.

When he was buried, Jenny began to cry and couldn't stop. She sobbed almost constantly, day and night, for weeks on end. And she fell ill with an inflammation in her breasts, so that Frau Schlessinger had to call the doctor, who had to operate. The physical pain and the despair of her soul merged into one on those terrible fevered nights.

Frau Schlessinger lay in bed in the next room. But when she heard the awful, stifled, animal-like moans coming from the young woman's room, she rushed in, horrified, and sat down on a chair beside her bed. "*Um Gottes Willen, Fräulein . . .*"

She set about nursing Jenny, patting her thin, clammy hands with her own, which were plump and warm. And she chided her. It was God's will, and perhaps it was best for both the boy and the young lady. Frøken Winge was still so young. Frau Schlessinger had lost both of her own children: little Bertha when she was two, and Wilhelm when he was fourteen — such a fine boy. And yet they had been born of a lawful marriage and were supposed to lend her support in her old age. But this little boy, he would have been a chain around the young lady's leg — and the young lady was so young and pretty. But dear God yes, he was sweet, the little angel, yes, it was hard to bear.

Frau Schlessinger had also lost her husband, yes she had. And many of Jenny's fellow sufferers who had stayed with Frau Schlessinger, and whose babies had died . . . well, some of them had even been glad. Others had given them up for adoption in order to be rid of them — no, it wasn't pleasant, but what could you say? And some had cried and wailed just like Jenny — but with time they recovered. Most of them were married now, and quite happy. But she had never seen the likes of Frøken Winge's despair — *Herrgott im Himmel* . . .

That her cousin had gone south, first to Dresden and then to Italy, at the very time of the boy's death, Frau Schlessinger in her heart blamed largely on Jenny's despair. Well, that's the way men were, after all . . .

Later on, the memory of those dreadful, anguished nights was inextricably linked in Jenny's mind with the image of Frau Schlessinger sitting on a stool next to her bed, as the lamplight splintered in the tears trickling from her kind little eyes and dripping down her round red cheeks. And her mouth, which never stopped talking even for a moment, and the wisps of hair escaping from her thin gray braid, and her white bed jacket with the notched trim and her pink-and-gray-striped flannel petticoat with the embroidered scallops at the hem. And that little room with its plaster reliefs in brass frames.

She had written to Heggen of her great joy. And he had replied, saying he wanted to come to see the boy, but it was a long journey, and expensive, and he was also just about to leave for Italy. But she and the prince were welcome to visit him there, and Congratulations! When the child died, Heggen was in Dresden. He sent her a long, consoling letter.

She had written a few lines to Gert as soon as she could manage it. At the same time she gave him her address, but asked him not to come until the spring — by then the boy would be big and handsome. Right now only his mother could see that he was lovely. When she had recovered from the birth, she wrote him a longer letter.

On the day the child was buried, she wrote again, telling him in a few words of the death. She also wrote that she was planning to leave for the south that very evening, and that he shouldn't expect to hear from her until she was feeling steadier. "You mustn't worry about me," she wrote. "I'm relatively calm and composed right now, but immeasurably sad, of course."

This letter crossed in the mail with one sent by Gert Gram, which said:

My little Jenny!

Thank you for your last letter. First, let me say, since you seem to be reproaching yourself with regard to our relationship: Dear sweet girl, I would never reproach you, and you mustn't do so either. You have never been anything but good and kind and loving toward your friend. Never will I forget your tenderness and your warmth during that brief period when you loved me — your sweet youth and your delicate and gentle affection during the short time of our happiness.

Our happiness had to be brief; both of us should have known that. I *ought* to have known; you *could* have known, if you had thought about it. But what do two people think about when they are drawn to one another? Do you think I blame you because one day you stopped loving me? Even though it caused me the bitterest suffering in my far-from-happy life? And it was doubly bitter for me when I also learned that our relationship had produced consequences for which you would have to pay for the rest of *your* life.

But now I see from your letter that these consequences — which have doubtless caused me more despair than they have you, no matter what anguish and physical pain you may have suffered — they have now brought you a deeper joy and happiness than anything else you have ever encountered in life. Maternal joy now fills you with peace, contentment, and vitality, and you feel that with the child in your arms you will have the strength to face any difficulties, financial as well as social, that the future may bring to a young woman in your position. To hear this makes me happier than you could ever imagine. For me this is once again proof of the existence of eternal justice, which I have never doubted. For you, who erred simply because your heart was warm and tender and thirsting for tenderness, for you this mistake, which caused you so many anguished hours, will in the end bring you everything you longed for, only better and more beautiful and purer than you have ever dreamed of, now that your heart is completely filled with love for your child. And later it will bring you even more, as the little boy grows up, begins to recognize his mother, clings to her, and can return her love, stronger and deeper and more deliberately for each year that passes.

And for me, who accepted your love even though I should have known that a love relationship between us was neither possible nor natural — for me these months have brought unspeakable suffering and sorrow. And a sense of loss, Jenny — a sense of loss that you can't possibly imagine, the loss of you and of my youth, of your beauty and your blessed love. And every little memory of these things has been embittered with regret and the ever-nagging questions: How could I let her do it? How could I accept her love? How could I believe that happiness was possible for me with her? And I did believe this, Jenny, no matter how mad it may sound, because you made me feel so young. Keep in mind that I had to give up my own youth when I was much younger than you are. I wasn't allowed to taste the youthful joy of work or the joy of love, and I myself was to blame. And this was revenge. My dead youth came back to haunt me when I saw you — my heart felt no older than yours. And Jenny, nothing in the world is more terrible than a man who is old when his heart is young.

You write that you would like me to come and see our child someday when the boy is a little older. Our child — how preposterous that sounds. Do you know what I keep thinking about? Do you remember old Joseph on the Italian altarpieces? The man who is always standing in the background or off to one side, tenderly and sadly gazing at the holy child and the lovely young mother, those two who are completely absorbed in each other and who pay no attention to his presence. Dear Jenny, please don't misunderstand me. Of course I know that the little infant now lying on your lap is also my flesh and blood, and yet . . . When I think of you now being a mother, I feel excluded just like poor old Joseph.

But that is no reason for you to hesitate about accepting my name as my wife and the protection this will lend you and the child, any more than Mary hesitated about confiding in Joseph. In fact, I don't think it's right for you to willfully deprive the child of his father's name, to which he is entitled — no matter how much self-confidence you may have. With this kind of marriage, of course, you would remain as free and independent as ever, and whenever you wish, it could be legally ended. I urgently ask that you consider this. We could be married abroad; then, if you wish, steps could be taken toward obtaining a divorce a few months later, and you would never even need to return to Norway, much less live under the same roof with me.

About myself there isn't much to tell you. I've rented these two small rooms up here on Hægdehaugen, quite close to the neighborhood where I was born and lived until I was ten, when my father became sheriff of Numedal. From my window I can see the tops of the two big chestnut trees outside the door of my childhood home. They haven't changed significantly. Up here the evenings are already getting longer and lighter and more springlike, and the bare brown branches of the trees are silhouetted against the pale green sky, where a few golden stars are sparkling in the sharp, clear air. Night after night I sit here by the window and stare outside, dreaming and remembering my whole life. Oh, dear Jenny, how could I ever forget that between you and me there was an entire lifetime, a life nearly twice the length of your own, and more than half of it spent in uninterrupted humiliation, defeat, and pain.

That you can think of me without anger or bitterness is more than I ever hoped for or expected. I can't tell you how much good it has done me to see the joy expressed in every line of your letter. May God bless and keep both you and the child. I wish for both of you all the happiness in the world. I am so inexpressibly fond of you, little Jenny, who was once mine.

Your devoted,

Gert Gram

7

But Jenny stayed on with Frau Schlessinger. It was inexpensive, and she didn't know where else to go.

Spring was in the air, and across the vast open vault of the sky drifted heavy clouds, rimmed with sun, burning with gold and blood that were mirrored in the restless sea in the evenings when she walked along the breakwater. The dreary, dark countryside turned light green, and the poplars were reddish brown with young shoots and a mild scent. Violets and tiny white-and-yellow flowers teemed along the railroad embankment. And at last the plain became lush and green, and colors burst forth along the culverts, and sulfur-yellow irises and big white Queen Anne's lace were reflected in the puddles of the marshy peat. One fine day the sweet fragrance of hay drifted over the land, blending with the salty smell of seaweed from the shore.

The resort hotel opened, and summer guests appeared in the little cottages near the breakwater. Children swarmed over the white beach, tumbling on the sand and splashing bare legged through the water while mothers and nurse-maids and servant girls wearing Spreewälder costumes sat and sewed and kept watch at the edge of the grass. The bathing huts were brought down to the water, and little German girls shrieked and shouted around them. Pleasure boats were moored at the breakwater, and visitors came out from the city. In the evenings dance music was played at the resort, and people flocked to the small pine woods to take a stroll near the place where Jenny, earlier in the spring, had lain in the scruffy grass and listened to the lapping of the waves and the gusts blowing through the windswept trees.

Now and then one of the women would give her a curious and sympathetic glance as she walked along the beach in her black-and-white summer dress. The guests in town had, of course, heard about the young Norwegian woman who had given birth to a child and now mourned his death so terribly. And there were those who found the story more touching than scandalous.

But for the most part she took her walks inland, where no summer guests ever went. On a rare occasion she would go all the way out to the church and the cemetery where her son was buried. She would sit and stare at the grave. She hadn't made any arrangements to have it tended, but sometimes she would pick a few wildflowers along the way and place them there, although her imagination refused to connect that small gray mound, covered by weeds and straw, with her little boy.

In the evenings she sat in her room and stared at the lamp, with a piece of handwork that she never touched. And she always thought about the same thing: the days when she had her son. Those first days and that languorous, peaceful joy, as she lay in bed recovering; then later, when she was out of bed, and Frau Schlessinger showed her how to bathe and dress and take care of him; and the time they went to Warnemünde together to buy soft fabric and lace and ribbon, and she came home to cut and sew and design and embroider — her son was to have the finest clothing instead of the pitiful store-bought garments she had ordered from Berlin. And she had bought a silly watering can, with pictures on the green-painted metal: a lion and a tiger standing between palm trees near a sky-blue sea, eyeing with horror the German gunboats steaming toward the empire's African possessions. She thought it was so amusing, and she would give it to her little boy to play with when he was old enough, someday in the far distant future. First he would have to discover his mother's breast, which he now blindly suckled, and his own tiny fingers, which he still couldn't untangle when he laced them together. Soon he would recognize his mother, and peek at the lamp and his mother's watch when she dangled it in front of him; there was so much for the little boy to learn. Oh God.

She had put all his things away in a drawer. She never looked at them, but she still knew what each item looked like and how it felt in her hands: the soft, smooth linen and the rough wool and the half-finished jacket made of green flannel on which she had embroidered buttercups — the one he was going to wear when she took him outdoors.

She had started a painting of the beach with children dressed in pink and blue on the white sand. And a couple of well-meaning women came over and looked on, trying to make her acquaintance. "*Wie nett!* How pretty!" But she wasn't satisfied with the sketch and didn't feel like finishing it, nor starting another.

Then one day the resort hotel closed, a storm swept in from the sea, and the summer was over.

Gunnar wrote from Italy and urged her to come south. And Cesca wanted her to come to Sweden. Her mother, who knew nothing, wrote to say that she didn't understand why she was staying there so long. Jenny did consider leaving but couldn't convince herself to go, even though, little by little, a vague sense of longing was awakening in her. She was starting to feel nervous about her own idleness. She had to make a decision, even if it was only to jump into the sea from the breakwater one night.

Then one evening she took out the crate of Heggen's books. Among them was a volume of Italian poetry: *Fiori della poesia italiana*. The kind of book meant for tourists, with an inlaid leather binding. She leafed through it to see if she could remember any of her Italian.

The book fell open of its own accord to Lorenzo de' Medici's carnival ballad and a folded piece of paper with a message written by Gunnar:

"Dear Mother, I can now tell you that I have arrived safe and sound in Italy and am doing splendidly in every way, and that . . ." The rest of the page was scribbled with vocabulary words. Next to the verbs, all of the conjugations had been listed. And there were words written in the margins of the book as well, crowded in next to the carnival poem that was both melancholy and merry. "How lovely is youth, which flees so quickly."

Even the most common words had been written down. Gunnar must have tried to read the poem just after he came to Italy, before he had learned the language. She looked at the title page: G. HEGGEN, FIRENZE, 1903. That was before she knew him.

She turned the pages, reading a bit here and there. There was Leopardi's hymn to Italy, which Gunnar was so wild about. She read through it. The margin was black with vocabulary and blotches of ink.

It was like a greeting from him — more heartfelt than any of his letters. He was calling to her, young and healthy and confident and vigorous. He was asking her to come back to life — and to work. Oh, if only she could pull herself together enough to start working again. She had to try; she had to make a choice, whether she wanted to live — or die. She would go back south where she had once felt so free and strong . . . alone, with her work. She felt a longing for that, and for her friends, those trustworthy companions, who never got so close that it hurt, but lived side by side, each preoccupied with his own concerns — and with those things that belonged to all of them: faith in their own abilities, joy in their work. She wanted to see the land down there again, the mountains with their proud, severe lines and the colors scorched by the sun.

A few days later she left for Berlin. She spent several days in the city, going to the galleries. But she felt worn out and lost, like a stranger. Then she continued on to München.

In the Alte Pinakothek she saw Rembrandt's holy family. She didn't think of it in terms of painting — instead she stared at the young peasant woman sitting there with her shift still pulled away from her breast, heavy with milk, and looking at her child, who had fallen asleep. She was holding one of his little bare feet, caressing it. He was an ugly little urchin, but bursting with health, and he slept so soundly and was sweet and lovely all the same. Joseph was peering at him over the mother's shoulder. But he was not an old Joseph, and Mary was not an ethereal, heavenly bride. Rather, he was a strong, middle-aged craftsman, she was his young wife, and the child was their pride and joy.

That evening she wrote to Gert Gram. A long letter that was tender and sad, but she was saying good-bye to him forever.

The next day she bought a ticket straight to Florence. At dawn she was sitting by the compartment window after a sleepless night on the train. Streams splashed white down the forested mountain slopes. The light began to rise, and the towns she passed looked more and more Italian in character. Rust-brown and mossy-gold roof tiles, loggias on top of the houses, green wooden shutters with reddish yellow brick walls, baroque church facades, stone bridges arching over the river . . . The station signs were in both German and Italian. Vineyards surrounded the towns, and gray castle ruins stood atop the mountain crags.

They reached Ala. She stood at the customs counter, looking at the groggy first- and second-class passengers, and feeling so absurdly happy. She was back in Italy. The customs official smiled at her because she was blond, and she smiled back because he assumed she was some sort of chambermaid for a wealthy family.

The mountain ranges fell away, mud-gray with blue shadows in the clefts; the earth shone rust-red, and the sun blazed white and hot.

But Florence was bitterly cold and gray during those November days. Tired and chilled, she wandered through the city for two weeks — her heart cold to all the beauty she saw, which made her melancholy and dejected because it did not warm her as it had before.

One morning she left for Rome. The fields were white with rime all through Tuscany. Later in the day the frosty fog lifted, and the sun shone. And once again she saw the place she had never forgotten: Lago Trasimeno was pale blue, surrounded by mist-shrouded mountains. Jutting out into the water was a promontory with towers and battlements of a little stone-gray town. A lane of cypress trees led out to it from the station.

But she arrived in Rome during a fierce rainstorm. Gunnar was on the platform to meet her. He squeezed her hands as he welcomed her, and he steadily talked and laughed as they clattered off in a cab to the lodgings he had found for her, through the rain that poured down from the sky and splashed up from the cobblestones.

8

Heggen was sitting on the outer side of the marble table, taking almost no part in the conversation. Now and then he would glance over at Jenny, who sat squeezed into the corner with a whiskey and soda in front of her. She was talking in an excessively high-spirited way to a young Swedish woman sitting across from her and paying no attention whatsoever to those seated on either side of her: Dr. Broager and the little Danish painter, Loulou von Schulin, who were both trying to attract her notice. Heggen saw that she had had too much to drink — again.

They were a small group of Scandinavians and a few Germans who had met at a taverna and now, late at night, had ended up here, in the far corner of a gloomy café. The entire party was feeling the effects of the liquor and was unwilling to heed the café owner's urging to leave. It was well past his legal closing time and he could be fined two hundred lire — yes, he could!

Gunnar Heggen was the only one who would have been more than happy for the symposium to come to an end. He was the only one who was sober and in a bad mood.

Dr. Broager kept on pressing his black mustache to Jenny's hand. When she pulled it away, he merely tried to do the same to her bare arm. He had managed to put his other arm behind her on the sofa, and they were sitting pressed so close into the corner that it was futile to try to escape. And besides, her resistance was at a low ebb, and she laughed, unperturbed by his forward behavior.

"How loathsome!" said Loulou von Schulin, hunching her shoulders. "How can you bear it? Don't you think he's disgusting, Jenny?"

"Yes, I suppose he is. But you can see for yourself that he's just like a fly — it won't do any good to chase him away. Now stop that, Doctor!"

"Oh, how can you stand that man!" said Loulou in the same tone of voice.

"Never mind! I can scrub myself with soap when I get home."

"So!" Loulou von Schulin leaned toward Jenny and stroked her arm. "Let's take care of those beautiful hands. Look!" She lifted one of them into view on the edge of the table. "See how lovely it is?" She unfastened the kelly-green automobile veil from her hat and wrapped it around Jenny's arms and hands. "Wrapped in mosquito netting — just look!" and quick as lightning she stuck out her little tongue at Broager.

Jenny sat there for a moment with her arms swathed in the green veil. Then she unwrapped it and put on her jacket and gloves.

Broager sank into a semi-doze. But Frøken Schulin raised her glass.

"*Skål,* Herr Heggen!"

He pretended not to hear. Not until she said it again did he pick up his glass. "Forgive me. I didn't notice . . ." He took a sip and then turned away again.

A few of the others smiled. Since Heggen and Frøken Winge lived right next door to each other on the top floor of a building somewhere between Via del Babuino and the Corso, everyone assumed that they were involved with each other. As for Frøken Schulin, after a brief, lawful marriage to a Norwegian writer, she had left her husband and child and gone out into the wide world, where she had reclaimed her maiden name, the title of Frøken, and the role of painter, while she cultivated friendships with other women, about which there was a great deal of lurid gossip.

The café owner came back to the group and urgently negotiated to get them out the door. The two waiters had turned out the gaslights in the rest of the room and were standing expectantly near their table. There was nothing else to do but pay up and leave.

Heggen was among the last to exit. Over on the square in the moonlight he saw Frøken Schulin take Jenny's arm. They ran for a vacant cab that the others had already piled into. He raced toward them and heard Jenny shout from a distance: "You know, that place on Via Panisperna," and then she leaped into the overcrowded cab and landed on someone's lap.

But there were ladies who wanted to get out, and ladies who wanted to get in; people kept jumping out one door and into the other. The coachman sat motionless on the box, waiting, and the old nag slept on, its head drooping toward the cobblestones.

Jenny was standing on the street again, but Frøken Schulin stretched a hand out to her — there was plenty of room.

"I feel sorry for the horse," said Heggen curtly. Then she fell in beside him and they proceeded to walk, the last of the crowd who hadn't found room in the cab. The carriage rolled slowly along ahead of them.

"You can't tell me you really want to spend more time with these people — and trudge all the way out to Panisperna just for that?" said Heggen.

"Oh, I'm sure we'll find a vacant cab somewhere."

"I don't know why you bother. They're all drunk as goats — every single one of them," he went on.

Jenny laughed mirthlessly.

"Well, I suppose I am too."

Heggen didn't reply. They had reached Piazza di Spagna. She stopped.

"You don't want to come along, Gunnar?"

"I will if you really want to keep on . . . otherwise no."

"You don't have to come for my sake. I can manage to find my own way home, you know."

"If you're going, then I'm going too. I won't let you wander around with all those drunks."

She laughed, that same slack, mirthless laughter.

"Damn it all, you're going to be so tired tomorrow that you won't even be able to sit for me."

"Oh, I think I'll manage to sit for you . . ."

"I don't believe it. Besides, I won't be able to do any proper work if we're going to be out carousing all night long."

Jenny shrugged her shoulders. But she started heading toward Babuino, in the opposite direction from the others.

Two *guardias,* wearing cloaks, passed them. Otherwise there wasn't a soul in the deserted square. The fountain murmured in front of the Spanish Steps, bathed white in the moonlight and surrounded by the park's evergreen shrubbery, black and glinting with silver.

Suddenly Jenny said in a harsh and scornful voice, "I know you mean well, Gunnar. It's nice of you to try to take care of me. But it won't do any good."

He walked on without speaking.

Then he said, "No, not unless you want it to."

"Want!" she mimicked him.

"Yes, I said 'want.'"

Jenny took a quick, deep breath, as if she were going to answer, but then restrained herself. Loathing rose up inside her; she was quite drunk, and she knew it. The last thing she needed to do was to start shrieking — wailing and howling and babbling, maybe even sobbing. Drunk. In front of Gunnar. She bit back her words.

They reached the door to their building. Heggen unlocked it, lit a waxed match, and began lighting their way up through the endless, dark, stone stairwell.

Their two small rooms were the only ones on the top floor. A little hallway led past their doors and ended in a marble stairway leading up to the flat roof of the building.

At her door Jenny held out her hand.

"Good night, then, Gunnar. Thank you for the evening," she said in a low voice.

"It was my pleasure. Sleep well."

"You too."

———

He opened the window in his room. Directly across, the moon was shining on an ocher-colored wall with closed shutters and black wrought-iron balconies. Monte Pincio loomed behind with its dark clusters of foliage glittering against the moon-blue sky. Stretched out below were old moss-covered roofs, and on a lower terrace, where the coal-black shadow from his own building ended, someone's wash had been hung out to dry, pale as corpses.

Gunnar stood leaning on the windowsill, dejected and ill at ease. God take him if he was usually so prudish, but to see Jenny like that . . . It was awful.

And he was the one who had dragged her into it in the first place. To cheer her up. She had been moping around like an injured bird for those first few months. And of course he had thought that the two of them could have a little fun at the others' expense by taking a look at those . . . buffoons. He never suspected that it would turn out like this.

He heard her leave her room and go up to the roof. Heggen hesitated for a moment. But then he followed.

———

She was sitting in the only chair up there, behind the little arbor made of corrugated sheet metal. The doves were cooing in their sleep in the dovecote on top.

"Haven't you gone to bed yet?" he asked in a low voice. "You'll be cold . . ."

He brought her shawl from the arbor and handed it to her, then he perched on the brick wall between the flowerpots.

For a while they sat in silence and stared out across the city, where the church domes floated in the haze of the moon. The outline of the distant heights was completely blurred.

Jenny was smoking. Gunnar lit up a cigarette too.

"By the way, I can tell that I can't stand any more of it — liquor, I mean. It goes straight to my head," she said, as if in apology.

He saw that she was quite sober now.

"I think you should stay away from it for a while, Jenny. And stop smoking too, or at least cut back. You've been complaining about your heart, you know."

She didn't reply.

"I know that in general you share my opinion about those people. I don't understand why you want to demean yourself by spending any time with them at all . . . in that way."

"Occasionally," she said quietly, "a person needs to feel . . . anesthetized, to put it bluntly. And as far as demeaning myself . . ." He looked down at her pale face. Her blond hair shimmered in the moonlight. "Sometimes I think . . . Although now, at this moment, I feel ashamed. But right now I'm unusually sober, you see." She laughed a bit. "Sometimes I'm not — even if I haven't had anything to drink. And that's when I feel the urge to join in with all that."

"It's dangerous, Jenny," he whispered. And after a pause he said, "I have to tell you, I think it's disgusting what went on tonight. I've seen a few things in my day . . . and what all of this can lead to. I'd hate to see you hit bottom and wind up like Loulou."

"Don't worry, Gunnar. That's not how I'm going to end up. As a matter of fact, I don't have the energy for it. I'll put a stop to it long before that happens."

He sat quietly and looked at her.

"I know what you mean," he murmured finally. "But Jenny . . . other people thought they could do the same. But once you've let yourself slide . . . then you can't 'put a stop to it,' as you call it."

He slipped down from the wall, came over, and took her hand.

"Jenny . . . you won't do it anymore, will you?"

She stood up with a laugh.

"Not for the time being, at any rate. I think I'm cured of the urge to go out carousing for quite a long time."

They stood there for a moment. Then she shook his hand.

"Good night then, my boy." From the stairwell she said, "And I'll sit for you tomorrow."

"Good, thank you."

Heggen stayed behind for a while, smoking and shivering and thinking, before he went back down to his room.

9

She sat for him the next day after lunch, right up until it started to get dark. Whenever she took a break, they would exchange a few casual remarks as he continued to work on the background or washed his brushes.

"So!" He put down his palette and began straightening up his box of paints. "That's enough for you today."

She came over to him, and they stood there for a moment, looking at the painting.

"The black is rather nicely done, don't you think so, Jenny?"

"Yes, I do. I think it's going to be splendid."

"Yes . . ." He looked at his watch. "It's almost time for dinner. Shall we go out together?"

"I'd like that. I just have to go in and change my clothes. Will you wait for me?"

A few minutes later, when he knocked on her door, she was dressed and putting on her hat in front of the mirror.

How beautiful she is, he thought as she turned to face him. Slender and fair in that tight-fitting steel-gray dress. She looked so ladylike — elegant and aloof, reserved and stylish. He wouldn't have believed what he'd been thinking lately.

"By the way, didn't you agree to go out to see Frøken Schulin this afternoon, to look at her work?"

"Yes, but I'm not going." She turned bright red. "To be honest, I'm not interested in cultivating her friendship. And her paintings don't amount to much, do they?"

"No, Lord only knows! I just don't understand why you put up with her advances last night. I'd rather eat a plateful of live worms than . . ."

Jenny laughed. Then she said in a serious voice, "Poor thing — she must be genuinely unhappy."

"Oh, I don't know . . . unhappy . . . I met her in Paris in 1905. The worst thing is that apparently she's not at all depraved by nature. Just ignorant. And vain. And right now *that* happens to be fashionable. If it was considered modern to be virtuous, she'd be sitting on a pedestal right now, darning children's stockings, maybe even spending a little time painting dewy roses. And she would have been the most respectable of all the ordinary Johanne Louises on Dannevåg — and happy as well. But when she ended up down here, having fled her middle-class roots, she wanted to be in the thick of things, a free woman and a painter . . . and she thought she ought to take a lover, for the sake of her own self-respect. And then, unfortunately, she finds herself an idiot who gets her in the family way and is old-fashioned enough to want to marry her, which is so passé, and then he demands that she take care of the child and the household."

"But you can't know . . . It might also be partly Paulsen's fault that she left him."

"Of course it was his fault. He was old-fashioned, as I said, and had a taste for domestic tranquillity — and no doubt he gave her too little love and no beatings whatsoever."

Jenny smiled sadly.

"I see, Gunnar, that you seem to think it's damned easy to deal with life."

Heggen straddled a chair and rested his arms on the back.

"Since there are so few things for us to hold on to in life that are certain, they *are* easy to deal with. You have to take your bearings and make your decisions accordingly. And deal with all the uncertainties as best you can, as they come into play."

Jenny sat down on the sofa and rested her head in her hands.

"I no longer have the sense that there's anything in life that I can deal with adequately — so that I could use it as a basis for my decisions, or as a way to get my bearings," she said calmly.

"I don't think you really mean that."

She merely smiled.

"At least not always," said Gunnar.

"I don't suppose anyone always has the same view of things."

"Oh yes, they do, if they're sober. As you said last night, sometimes a person isn't sober even without anything to drink."

"Now . . . when I'm occasionally feeling sober . . ." She broke off and fell silent.

"You know as well as I do. You've always known it. In the long run, whatever happens to a person, he brings it on himself. You're master of your own fate — as a rule. Once in a while you're not, because of circumstances you can't control. But it's a vast exaggeration to claim that this is often the case."

"God knows, my life hasn't gone the way I wanted it to, Gunnar. And yet I've been following my own will for so many years . . . and lived according to my own wishes . . ."

Both of them fell silent for a while.

"One day," she said hesitantly, "I made a slight change in course. It seemed to me so difficult and harsh, living the life I thought was the most worthy — it was lonely, you know. So I veered away for a moment, wanting to be young and to play a little. And then I was caught in an undertow that carried me off, and I ended up in circumstances that I never for an instant imagined it would be possible for *me* to be anywhere near."

Heggen didn't speak for a moment.

Then he said softly, "There's a poem, by Rosetti. He's actually a much better poet than painter.

> Was that the landmark? What, — the foolish well
> Whose wave, low down, I did not stoop to drink
> But sat and flung the pebbles from its brink
> In sport to send its imaged skies pell-mell,
>
> (And mine own image, had I noted well!) —
> Was that the point of turning? — I had thought
> The stations of my course should raise unsought,
> As altarstones or ensigned citadel.
>
> But lo! The path is missed, I must go back,
> And thirst to drink when next I reach the spring
> Which once I stained, which since may have grown black.
> Yet though no light be left nor bird now sing
> As here I turn, I'll thank God, hastening,
> That the same goal is still on the same track."

Jenny didn't say a word.

"'That the same goal is still on the same track,'" Gunnar repeated.

"Do you think it's so easy," asked Jenny, "to find your way back to the goal?"

"No. But don't you have to try?" he asked, almost childishly.

"What kind of goal did I have, anyway?" she exclaimed fiercely. "I wanted to live in such a way that I would never have to be ashamed, either as a human being or as an artist. Never do a single thing that I didn't think was right. I wanted to be honest and steadfast and kind, and never have another person's pain on my conscience. So what was the crime that started it all? That brought on everything else? The fact that I longed for love, without having any specific man I longed for? Was that so strange? That I wanted so much to believe, when Helge appeared, that he was the one I had been longing for? Until in the end I believed it was true? That was the beginning, from which everything else followed. Gunnar . . . I *did* believe . . . that I could make them happy. Yet I caused nothing but harm."

She had stood up and was pacing back and forth.

"Do you think the spring you're talking about . . . do you think it will ever be pure and clean again for someone who knows that she was the one who muddied it? Do you think it's easier for me to resign myself now? I longed for what every girl longs for. And I still long for it . . . for the same thing. Except that now I know that behind me I have a past that makes it impossible for me to accept the only happiness I care about — because it's supposed to be fresh and healthy and pure, and I'm none of those things anymore. I'll keep on dragging around these longings that I know are impossible — and it will cost me my life, what I've been through these past few years."

"Jenny." Gunnar was on his feet too. "I think it still all depends on you — because that's the way it *has* to be. Either you decide to let these memories destroy you, or you decide to take them as a lesson — no matter how terribly harsh that may sound. And the goal you had before . . . well, I think that was the right one — for you."

"But can't you see it's impossible, my boy? It's buried deep inside me like an acid, and it's eating away at the person I once was. I feel as if I'm crumbling from the inside. Oh . . . And that's not what I want, it's not. But I have an urge to . . . I don't know . . . To make all these thoughts stop. To die. Or to live — in an insane and odious manner — to sink down into wretchedness that's even deeper than this. And let myself be pulled down into the dirt so far that I know the next step will be the end. Or . . ." She was speaking in a low, wild voice, as if choking on screams. "Throw myself under a train — knowing in those last few seconds that soon, very soon, my whole body, my nerves and heart and brain — everything — will be crushed into one big trembling, bloody pulp."

"Jenny!" He cried out. His face had turned pale. And with difficulty he whispered, "I refuse to listen to you talk that way."

"I'm hysterical," she said, as if to reassure him. Nevertheless, she went over to the corner where her canvases stood, and she practically yanked them along the wall, with the painted sides face out.

"You can't very well make things like this be the purpose of your life. Smearing oil paint on canvas. You can see for yourself, that's all they are now: dead blobs of paint. Dear God, you saw how hard I worked those first few months — like a slave — but I can't even paint anymore."

Heggen looked at the paintings. Now he felt as if he was once again on firm ground.

"Go ahead and tell me your honest opinion of that . . . that filth over there," she dared him.

"Well, they're not particularly good — I'll admit that." He stood with his hands in his pockets and looked at them. "But it's something that can happen to any of us — periods when we can't work. For that matter, I think you ought to know that it's something that will pass — at least for you. I don't believe that people can lose their talent, no matter how unhappy they may have been.

"And besides, you've been away from your work for a long time. You have to immerse yourself in it again, regain mastery of your materials — surely you know that. Life drawing, for instance — it's been nearly three years since you sketched a nude. That's not something that goes unpunished, I know that myself . . ."

He went over to the shelf and rummaged among Jenny's old sketchbooks.

"Just think of the work you did in Paris — let me show you . . ."

"No, no — not that one," said Jenny quickly, reaching out for the book.

Heggen stood with the closed book in his hand and looked at her in astonishment.

Then she turned her face away. "Never mind, you can look at it. I was just trying to draw the boy's face one day."

Heggen slowly turned the pages. Jenny had gone back to sit on the sofa, as before. For a few moments he looked at the small pencil sketches of the sleeping infant. Then he gently put the book aside.

"I'm so sorry you lost your little son," he said quietly.

"Yes. If he had lived, nothing else would have mattered, you know. You talk about will — but your will can't keep your child alive. And so . . .

"I don't have the strength anymore to try to be anything, Gunnar, because I thought that was the only thing I was good at — and cared about — being the mother of my little boy. He was someone I could love. Maybe I'm an egotist at heart, because every time I tried to love the others, my own self felt like a wall between us. But my son was mine. If I'd been allowed to keep him, I would have been able to work. Oh, how I would have worked.

"I had made plans. I thought about them in the fall when I came here; I had decided to take him to Bavaria in the summer. I was afraid the sea air in the north would be too cold for him. He was going to lie in his baby carriage and sleep under the apple trees — and I was going to work. Don't you see? I don't know anyplace in the world where I could go that I haven't dreamed of visiting with my son. There's nothing good or beautiful in the world that I didn't think about him learning or seeing while he was with me. I don't own a single thing that wasn't his too — my red blanket I used to wrap around him. The black dress that I'm wearing while I sit for you was the one I sewed in Warnemünde after my confinement. I designed it like that so it would be easy to nurse him. There are milk stains on the lining . . .

"I can't work because I'm obsessed with him. I long for him so much that I feel paralyzed. At night I bunch up my pillow and hold it in my arms and cry for my little boy. I call to him and talk to him whenever I'm alone. I wanted to paint him so I would have pictures of him at every age. He would have been a year old by now — imagine that. He would have been teething and starting to crawl — able to stand up and maybe even take a few steps. Every month, every day I think: Now he would be so many months old . . . and I wonder how he would have looked. All the old women who walk around with a bambino in their arms . . . all the children I see on the street . . . And then I think how mine would have looked when he was that old."

She fell silent for a moment. Heggen sat quietly, leaning forward.

"I didn't know it was like that, Jenny," he said softly, his voice gruff. "I realized that it must have been awful. But I thought that . . . in a way . . . it was best it happened like that. If I had known how things stood, I would have come north to see you."

She didn't reply, but kept on with her own thoughts.

"And then he died. Such a tiny, tiny little thing. It's just selfishness on my part that I begrudged him that: to die before he could have any inkling of understanding. All he could do was peer at the light — and cry whenever he needed to be changed or was hungry. And he would try to suckle my cheek as readily as my breast. He didn't even know me — at least not properly. I suppose tiny sparks of awareness had started to awaken inside his little mind . . . but just think that he never knew I was his mother . . .

"He never had a name, poor thing, except his mother's 'little boy.' I have no memory of him except a purely physical one." She lifted her hands, as if pulling the child into her arms. Then they fell, empty and lifeless, to the table.

"That first sensation, when I touched him, felt his skin against mine . . . It was so soft, a little damp — like something inside me. The air had scarcely touched it yet, you see. I think people often find a newborn infant rather disgusting if it's not their own flesh and blood. And his eyes . . . they didn't have any specific color yet. They were dark, though I think they would have been grayish blue. The eyes of an infant are so strange — I almost said mysterious. And his tiny head . . . when he lay there nursing at my breast, pressing the tip of his nose flat, and I could see his pulse throbbing in the crown of his head, and his downy hair — he had so much hair when he was born — dark hair. And I thought he was so lovely.

"Oh, his tiny little body. I never think of anything else. I can feel his hands in mine. He was so round — plumper in the middle, you know. And his bottom was so comically pressed together, and a little pointed. And of course I thought that was enchanting too. Oh yes, how sweet I thought he was, my little son.

"And then he died. I had spent so much time looking forward to all the things yet to come, that now I don't think I paid enough attention to everything I had while he was mine . . . or kissed him enough, or looked at him enough — even though I did little else during those few weeks.

"And then there was nothing left but loss. You can't imagine what it felt like. As if my whole body ached with the loss of him. I had an infection in my breast, and it felt as if my loss erupted into pain and fever. I missed him in my arms and in my hands and against my cheek. Several times during the last weeks, he would close his hand around my finger when I put it near. Once, all on his own, he grabbed hold of a lock of my hair that had come unpinned. Those sweet, sweet hands of his . . ."

She put her head down on the table, sobbing so hard that she was shaking.

Gunnar had stood up; he hesitated, irresolute, with tears in his throat. Then he suddenly moved to her side; swiftly and shyly, he kissed her hair.

She stayed where she was for a while, weeping. But finally she stood up, went over to the washstand, and began to bathe her face.

"Oh God, yes, how I miss him," she said after a moment, her eyes red from crying.

"Oh Jenny . . ." He couldn't find anything else to say. "I didn't know how things were — you must believe me."

She came back and for a moment put her hands on his shoulders.

"I know, Gunnar. You mustn't take what I said before too seriously. Sometimes I don't know what I'm saying myself. But you can understand . . . for the boy's sake, if nothing else . . . to give in to such follies isn't something I would do.

"Actually, I want to try to make the best of life — you must know that. Try to work again, even though it won't be any good at first. But there's always the consolation that no one lives any longer than he wants to . . ."

She put on her hat again and found a veil for it.

"Let's go out and eat. It's so late — you must be hungry."

Gunnar Heggen's young face turned blood-red. Now that she mentioned it, he could suddenly feel how famished he was. And he was ashamed to have such a feeling just then. He wiped the tears from his hot, wet cheeks and picked up his hat from the table.

10

Without discussing it, they walked past the restaurant where they usually ate and where there were always many Scandinavians. They continued on in the twilight, toward the Tiber and across the bridge, and entered the old Borgo district. Right near Piazza San Pietro there was a little café in an inn where they had eaten a few times before when they came from the Vatican. That's where they went.

They ate without speaking. Jenny lit a cigarette when she was finished. And she sipped her red wine and rubbed the fragrant mandarin peels between her fingers.

Heggen sat and smoked, staring into the distance. They were almost alone in the place.

"Would you like to see the letter I got from Cesca today?" Jenny said all of a sudden.

"Yes, I would. I noticed there was a letter to you from her. Is it from Stockholm?"

"Yes. That's where they are now, and they'll stay there for the winter." Jenny took the letter out of her bag and handed it to him.

> My dear sweet Jenny!
> You mustn't be angry with me because I still haven't thanked you for your last letter. I've been meaning to write every day, but nothing ever came of it. I'm so glad you're back in Rome and you're painting and you have Gunnar to keep you company.
> We're back in Stockholm now, living in the same place as before. It was impossible to stay at our cottage after it turned cold because it was so drafty and the only room we could really keep warm was the kitchen. If only we could afford to buy that little house someday, but it's too expensive because we'd have to make so many repairs and fix up the barn for Lennart's studio and put in woodstoves and

all sorts of things, but we've rented it for next summer, and I'm glad, because that's the place in the world where I feel happiest. You can't imagine anywhere as beautiful as the west coast. It's so desolate and poor and weatherbeaten, with its gray hills and storm-ravaged thickets along the cliffs and all the honeysuckle vines and the little hovels and the sea and the magnificent sky. And I'm told that the paintings I did out there are good, and Lennart and I had such a lovely time. Nowadays we get along so well together, and whenever he thinks I'm acting strange, he just kisses me and calls me a little mermaid and sweet things like that, and as time passes I think I'm going to end up terribly attached to him.

But now we're back in town, and this time there won't be any trip to Paris, but that doesn't matter. I think it's almost heartless of me to write to you about this, Jenny, because you're a much better person than I am, and it was so sad and cruel that you lost your little boy. I don't think I deserve to be this happy or to have my deepest wish fulfilled, but I'm going to have a baby. In only five more months. I could hardly believe it at first, but now it's definitely true. For the longest time I tried to keep it from Lennart. I was so ashamed about deceiving him twice before, and I was afraid I might be mistaken, so at first I denied it when he started having suspicions, but finally I had to admit it was true, although I still can't really grasp that I'm going to have a little one. By the way, Lennart says that he'd rather have another little Cesca, but he's just saying that to console me beforehand if it turns out that way, because I'm sure he'd prefer to have a son. But you know, if it's a girl, we'll love her just as much, and besides, after we've had one, we can always have more.

I'm so happy right now that it almost doesn't matter to me where we are. I don't feel the least longing for Paris. Just imagine, Fru Lundquist asked me whether I was annoyed about the baby coming and ruining our Paris trip. Can you understand people like that? And she has two of the loveliest little boys in the world. But they're left to fend for themselves whenever they're not over here visiting us, and Lennart says that she'd gladly give them to us, and if I could afford it, I'd take them. Then our little one would have two sweet big brothers to play with as soon as he arrives. It's going to be fun to show them their little cousin. They call me their aunt, and I think that's such a dear custom.

But I must close now. Do you know what else makes me happy? That under these circumstances, Lennart can't possibly be jealous, can he? But as a matter of fact I don't think he will be anymore, because now he knows that he's the only one I've ever really loved.

Do you think I'm being cruel to tell you so much about all this and how happy I am? But I know that you wish me well.

Give my greetings to everyone I know down there, and in particular to Gunnar. You're welcome to tell him about this if you like. And take good care of yourself. In the summer you must come and visit us!

Much love from your devoted and faithful little friend,

Cesca

P.S. I've just decided: If it's a girl, she's going to be named Jenny. No matter what Lennart says. And by the way, he sends you his greetings.

Gunnar gave the letter back to Jenny, who put it away.

"I *am* glad," she said quietly. "I'm glad for every person I know who is happy. At least *that* much is left of my old self — if nothing else."

—⁓—

Instead of walking back toward town, they wandered across Piazza San Pietro toward the cathedral.

In the moonlight the shadows stretched pitch-black across the square. White light and murky dark patches played ghostlike over one of the curving arcades. The other one stood in utter darkness; only the row of statues on its roof had flickerings of light along its contours. And the facade of the cathedral lay in shadow, but overhead the dome glittered in places, as if it were wet.

The two fountains sent their white spray, sparkling and frothing, up toward the moon-blue sky. Swirls of water shot up, then splashed down on the porphyry basins, trickling and dripping back into the bowls.

Gunnar and Jenny slowly walked toward the cathedral in the shadows of the arcade.

"Jenny," he said suddenly. His voice sounded quite calm and ordinary. "Will you marry me?"

"No," she said just as calmly, and then laughed.

"I'm serious."

"Yes, but I'm sure you realize that I don't want to."

"But why not?" They continued on toward the cathedral. "As far as I can see, right now you don't seem to think your life is worth anything. From what I understand, sometimes you even contemplate killing yourself. But if you feel so resigned, why couldn't you just as well marry me? You could try it — I know you could!"

Jenny shook her head.

"Thank you, Gunnar, but I think that would be taking our friendship too far." All at once she grew serious. "First of all, you must know that I wouldn't accept. Second, if you actually did persuade me to accept this as a last resort, I wouldn't be worth the effort it took for you to stretch out your little finger to rescue me."

"It's not friendship, Jenny." He hesitated for a moment. "The fact is that I've . . . grown so fond of you. It's not a matter of helping you out — well, yes, I do want to help you. But it's because I now understand that . . . if anything happened to you . . . I don't know what I would do. I can't bear to think about it. There's nothing in the world that I wouldn't do for you — because I love you so much, you see."

"Oh no, Gunnar . . ." She stopped and gave him a frightened look.

"Of course I realize that you're not in love with me. But that doesn't mean you couldn't marry me — just as well as do anything else . . . since you're tired of it all anyway, and you feel like you've given up." And his voice was now filled with fervor and emotion, and he exclaimed, "Because I know you would come to care for me, I'm sure you would — since I care so much for you!"

"You know I'm fond of you," she said somberly. "But that's not the sort of feeling that would satisfy you in the long run. I'm not capable of any strong or absolute feelings."

"Of course you are. Everyone is. *I* was convinced that I would never experience anything but these . . . minor affairs. I didn't truly believe that anything else existed." He lowered his voice. "You're the first woman I've ever loved."

She stood still, speechless.

"That word, Jenny . . . I've never said it to anyone before. I felt a certain shyness — a certain reverence — for it. I've never loved any other woman.

"I was always in love with something else — some individual part of the woman. The way Cesca's lips turn up when she smiles, that unconscious air of refinement she has. Something that would set my imagination in motion, that would prompt me to make up stories about women — stories that would include me. I fell in love with one woman because she was wearing such a stunning deep-red silk dress the first time I saw her — it was almost black in the folds, like the darkest roses. I always imagined her wearing that dress. And you, that time in Viterbo . . . You were so delicate and quiet and reserved, as if you were wearing gloves that covered you completely, to the very tips of your fingers, in both a physical and spiritual sense. And you had a glint in your eye whenever the rest of us started laughing, as if you wanted to play too but couldn't or didn't dare. Back then I was in love with the idea of seeing you lighthearted and laughing.

"But I've never before truly loved . . . another living soul."

He looked away for a moment and stared at the jet of the fountain glittering in the moonlight. And he felt this new emotion rise up and glitter inside of him and his mind was filled with new words that ecstatically poured from his lips.

"Do you understand, Jenny? My love for you is so great that everything else seems unimportant to me. I'm not sad that you don't love me — because I know that you will someday. I'm convinced my love will make you love me. I have time to wait, because it's wonderful loving you this way.

"When you talked about letting yourself be pulled down, or throwing yourself in front of a train . . . then something happened to me. I didn't fully understand what it was, I just knew that I couldn't bear to hear you say that. I knew that I couldn't let that happen — it felt as if it was my own life. And when you talked about your child . . . it hurt me terribly that you had suffered so much and that I couldn't help you, and . . . well, I didn't know it then, but maybe it was also because I wanted you to care for me. And I understood everything, Jenny. Your boundless love and your dreadful sense of loss — because that's how I feel about you too. And then, as we went out, and as we sat in the trattoria over there . . . I suddenly understood it all. How immeasurably dear and precious you are to me.

"And now it seems to me that I've always felt this way, you know. Everything I remember about you is part of it — part of why I love you. Now I realize why I've been so depressed ever since you arrived. I could see that you were suffering, because at first you were so quiet and sad, and later because of all those wild outbursts. I remember that day on the road near Warnemünde; I can see you standing there, crying. That too is part of why I love you.

"The other men you've known, Jenny . . . even your son's father . . . Oh, I know what it was like. You talked and talked to them about all your ideas but it never went beyond talking about ideas, even when you tried to make them see how you felt . . . because they couldn't understand how you were. But I understand. What you said that day in Warnemünde, and what you said today — you know you could only say those things to me. Those are things that only I could understand. Isn't that true?"

She nodded her head in agreement, surprised. It *was* true.

"I know I'm the only one who truly understands you, and I know exactly how you are. Oh . . . And that's why I love you. Even if your soul were covered with blotches and bloody wounds, I could only keep on loving you and kiss them all away until you were pure and healthy again. My love demands nothing of you, Jenny, except that you be the way you want to be and have to be in order to feel happy. No matter what terrible things you might do, I would merely think that you were ill, that something foreign had crept into your soul. If you betrayed me, if I found you lying drunk in the gutter . . . you would still be my beloved Jenny. Do you hear me?

"Won't you be mine? Surrender yourself to me . . . sink into my arms and let me make you mine. You will be healthy and happy again. Right now I don't know exactly how I'm going to do it, but I know that I'll find a way through my love. So that each morning you will wake up a little happier, and each day will be a little brighter and warmer for you than the day before, and your sorrow will be a little easier to bear. Why don't we go to Viterbo, or somewhere else? Oh, give yourself to me . . . I'll take care of you as I would a sick child. And by the time you're well again, you will end up loving me . . . and you know that the two of us can't live without each other.

"Do you hear me, Jenny? You're ill. You can't take care of yourself. Just close your eyes and give me your hands, and I will make you well with my love. Oh, I know that I can."

Jenny turned her pale face toward him. She was leaning against a pillar, standing there and smiling wanly in the moonlight.

"How could I possibly commit such a great wrong and sin against God?"

"Do you mean because you don't love me? But I'm telling you it doesn't matter. Because I know my love is strong enough that someday you will, if only you allow yourself to surrender to it for a while."

He put his arms around her, kissing her face over and over, smothering her with kisses.

She stood there powerless. But she managed to whisper after a moment, "Don't do that, Gunnar. Please don't . . ."

Reluctantly he let her go.

"Why shouldn't I?"

"Because it's you. If it was someone else . . . someone I didn't care about . . . I don't know whether I'd bother to resist."

Gunnar took her hand, and they walked back and forth in the moonlight.

"I understand. When you had your little son, you thought your life had found some meaning again — after everything else seemed so meaningless. Because you loved him, and he needed you. And when he died, you stopped caring about yourself, because you thought you were worthless."

Jenny nodded and said, "There are a few people I care enough about that it would make me sad to know they were unhappy, and glad if things went well for them. But *I* can't bring them either greater joy or sorrow. That's the way it has always been. And that's what has secretly made me so unhappy and full of longing in the past . . . that there I was, but my existence had nothing to do with anyone else's happiness. And that's what I wanted, Gunnar — to make someone else happy. You talked about work, but I never believed that was enough, because it's so selfish. The deepest joy it holds is your own happiness while you're doing the work — and you can't share that with anyone else. But the only true joy is one you can share with others. Except for what you might feel for a few moments when you're young. And I suppose I've had that feeling whenever I thought I was getting closer to the way I wanted to be. But only abnormal people accumulate riches for any other purpose than to spend them. Among women, at any rate. I think a woman's life is meaningless if she can't make someone else happy. But I've never been able to do that; I've only brought sorrow to others. The meager joy that I gave could have been given by anyone at all, because they only loved me for what they imagined me to be, not for what I was.

"And after my little son died, I decided it was good that no one was close enough to me that I might cause them any great sorrow. There was no one who thought I was indispensable.

"But now you tell me all of this. You've always been the one person I didn't want to get tangled up in my confused life. In some ways I've always been more fond of you than anyone else I've known. I thought it was good that we were friends, the way we were. So that love or anything else dangerous or distressing couldn't come between us. I thought you were too good for anything else. Oh, dear God, I wish nothing had changed . . ."

"But I have the feeling now that things have never been any different," he said quietly. "I love you. And I think you need me. I'm convinced I can make you happy again. And if you were, then you would make me happy too."

Jenny shook her head.

"If only I still had even the smallest scrap of faith in myself . . . then maybe. But Gunnar, when you say that you love me . . . I know that what you love about me is dead and gone. And so it doesn't make any difference — you're in love with something that you've dreamed I possess . . . maybe something I once was or might have been. It doesn't matter. One day you'll come to see me the way I am now — and then you too will be unhappy."

"No matter how it turns out, I would never think of it as a misfortune that I love you. I know better than you do that in the state you're in now, it would take only a little push for you to fall . . . into something that was sheer madness. But I love you, because I can see the entire path that has led you this far, and if you fell, I would just come after you and try to carry you back in my arms, and love you all the same."

When they reached the hallway outside their rooms later that night, he took her hands.

"Jenny . . . wouldn't you rather that I slept with you tonight? Instead of lying there alone? Wouldn't it be nice to fall asleep in the arms of someone who loves you more than anything else in the world . . . and then wake up like that in morning?"

She looked up, smiling oddly in the yellow glow of the candle.

"Maybe tonight. But not in the morning."

"Oh, Jenny." He shook his head. "I might come to your room tonight all the same. I think I have the right . . . I wouldn't be doing anything wrong. I know it would be best for you if you were mine. Will you be angry — will you be sad — if I come?"

"I think I would be sad . . . afterward. For your sake. Oh no, don't do it, Gunnar. I don't want to be yours — when I know that I could just as easily belong to someone else."

He gave a laugh that sounded both playful and pained.

"Then I ought to. Once you were mine, you couldn't belong to anyone else. I know that much about you, Jenny. But since you ask me not to . . . Well, I can wait.

"But be sure to lock your door," he said, and laughed again.

II

All day long the weather had been gloomy, with cold, pale gray clouds towering high up in the sky. Now, toward evening, a few thin, brass-colored stripes appeared on the horizon in the west.

Jenny had gone out to Monte Celio in the afternoon to do some sketches. But nothing much had come of it; she merely sat and brooded on the wide stairway outside San Gregorio, looking down at the grove where springtime buds had started to appear on the tall trees beneath the dull gray sky, and a profusion of daisies shone on the green lawn.

She walked back along the lane that wound its way past the south slope of the Palatine. The ruins rose up, a faded gray, toward the palm trees of the cloister on top. All along the hillside clung evergreen shrubs, almost black and powdered with lime dust.

Outside the Arch of Constantine, on the piazza with the deserted ruins of the Colosseum and the Palatine and the Forum all around, several freezing postcard vendors hovered. There were very few tourists out that day. A couple of tiny, shriveled old ladies were haggling in broken Italian with a man peddling mosaics.

A little boy, no more than three years old, tugged at Jenny's coat and held up a tiny bunch of pansies. He had exquisite dark eyes and long hair, and he was all dressed up in a national costume with a pointed felt cap, velvet jacket, and sandals over his white wool socks. He hadn't yet learned to talk properly, but he asked her for a soldo.

Jenny gave him a coin, and his mother immediately appeared at his side and, with a nod of thanks, took it for safekeeping. She had tried to give her own attire the look of a national costume, with a red velvet bodice laced up over her soiled, checkered blouse and a cloth folded into a square on her head. In her arms she held an infant.

Three weeks old, the mother said when Jenny asked. Yes, the poor thing was ill.

The child was no bigger than Jenny's son had been at birth. His skin was red and rough and scaly. He was breathing noisily, as if his air passages were filled with mucus, and his eyes stared listlessly from beneath inflamed, half-closed lids.

Yes, she took him every day to the clinic, said the mother. But they said he was going to die. And it was probably best for the poor thing. The woman looked tired and sad; she was hideous and toothless.

Jenny felt the tears rise up in her throat. That poor little baby. Yes, it probably would be best for him to die. Poor dear. She reached out to stroke the tiny, ugly face.

She gave the woman some more money and was just about to leave. At that moment a man walked past. He greeted her, paused for a moment, but then continued on when Jenny didn't return his greeting. It was Helge Gram.

She was too startled to speak to him. She crouched down in front of the little boy with the flowers and took his hands, pulling the child closer and talking to him as she tried to quell the terrible trembling that had seized hold of her body.

For a moment she turned her head to look in the direction Helge had gone. He was standing and looking at her from over by the steps that led from the piazza, past the Colosseum, and up to the street.

She stayed where she was, squatting down and talking to the woman and child. When she looked up again, he was gone, but she waited until long after his gray hat and coat had disappeared.

Then she practically ran toward home — through the back streets and alleyways, afraid that at every corner she turned he would be lying in wait.

She ended up all the way over behind Monte Pincio, and there she had supper in a trattoria where she had never been before.

After she had sat there for a while and taken a few sips of wine, she felt calmer.

If she did happen to meet Helge and he spoke to her . . . well, of course, it would be awkward. And naturally she would prefer to avoid it. But if it did occur, there was no reason to be afraid. The two of them were finished with each other. Whatever had happened after they parted, he had no reason to call her to account. And if he did, he had no right to do so. Whatever he might know, and whatever he might say . . . she knew full well what she had done. She had had to answer to herself — and nothing could compare with that.

Was there anyone she needed to fear? No one could do her more harm than she had already done to herself.

But it had certainly been a bad day. One of those days when she didn't feel quite sober. Now things were better.

Yet no sooner was she outside than the vague, anguished fear seized hold of her again. And it lashed at her so fiercely that she raced along without thinking, clenching her fists and talking to herself out loud.

All at once she tore off her gloves because she was burning hot. And only then did she remember noticing that one of them had a wet spot on it from when she patted the sick child. She threw the gloves away in disgust.

When she reached home, she stood in the hallway, hesitating. Then she knocked on Gunnar's door. But he wasn't in. She went up to the roof to look for him, but no one was there.

She went to her room and lit the lamp. With her arms folded she sat and stared at the flame. She got up and roamed around restlessly, then sat back down in the same place.

Nervously she listened to every sound in the stairwell. Oh, if only Gunnar would come. Oh, please don't let that other person come . . . But he didn't know where she lived. But he might meet someone and ask. Oh, Gunnar, Gunnar, please come!

Then she would go right up to him, throw herself in his arms, and ask him to take her.

Because from the moment she looked into Helge Gram's amber eyes, her whole past, everything that had begun under the gaze of those eyes, had risen up before her. It had all come back to her: the loathing, the doubt about her own ability to feel, to decide, to choose — the suspicion that she might want after all what she said she didn't want. And she saw herself the way she had looked back then — full of lies and dreams and so weak — while she went around pretending to herself that she insisted on feelings that were pure and strong and absolute, while she claimed she wanted to be honest, diligent, courageous, self-sacrificing, and disciplined. She allowed herself to be buffeted by moods and impulses that she didn't bother to fight, even though she knew she should — feigning love so that she could claim a place in life for herself, a place she could never have won if she had been honest.

She had wanted to change herself so that she could slip in among other people, although she had always known she would remain a stranger because she was not one of them. But she couldn't bear to be alone, trapped by her own nature. She had violated her own nature. And her relationship to those people, who were so profoundly different from her, had become detestable and perverse. And now, afterward . . . her own innermost soul had been destroyed by it, every anchor she had within herself had failed . . . and crumbled. She was disintegrating from the inside.

If Helge came . . . if she met him . . . then she knew that the despair, the loathing she felt for her own life, would overwhelm her. She didn't know what would happen, only . . . that if she had to stand face-to-face with all of it again, she wouldn't be able to bear it any longer.

Oh, Gunnar. She hadn't thought about whether she loved him or not during all these weeks he had begged to make her his own — just as she was. And swore that he could help her . . . to build up again everything that had been destroyed within her.

Sometimes she wished he would take her by force. Then she wouldn't have to decide. Because it didn't matter what he said — if she chose to be his, then the last remnants of her pride told her that she was responsible. Then she would *have* to become what she had once been — what he believed she was and what he believed she could be again . . . whether she had the strength or not. She would have to work her way up from the mire into which she had sunk — and under a whole new life bury everything that had happened ever since she gave Helge Gram that kiss, which had betrayed all her beliefs and her entire life up until that spring day out in the *campagna*.

Did she want to be Gunnar's? Was it true that she loved him because he was everything she had ever wanted to be? Because his whole being called to everything inside her that she had once chosen and cultivated and tended . . . every single ability of hers that she had once thought worthy of developing?

The love she had sought on all the wrong paths, driven there by her unwholesome longing and feverish restlessness . . . was it nothing more than closing her eyes and surrendering to him, the only one she trusted, the one that all of her instincts regarded as her conscience and rightful judge?

But she couldn't do it — during all these past weeks she hadn't been able to do it. She thought instead that she should try on her own to extricate herself from this impasse. She needed to feel that it was her own will, from the old days, that had regained control of her shattered soul. So that she would recover a tiny bit of self-respect and faith.

If she was going to keep on living, then Gunnar meant life itself to her. A few words he had scribbled on a piece of paper . . . a book that brought her a message from the very core of his being . . . that was what had awakened inside her the last flickering impulse to live, back when she was dragging around like a maimed animal after the death of her child.

If he came now, she would let him take her. Carry her for the first stretch of the way. Later she would try to walk herself.

And for her soul, which was crumbling as she sat there waiting, it was now clear:

If he came, she would live. If the other man came, then she would have to die.

And when she heard footsteps on their way up, and it was not Gunnar who knocked on her door, she bowed her head and, trembling, walked over and opened the door to Helge Gram. She felt as if she were letting in the fate she had conjured up for herself.

—⁓—

She stood staring at him as he stepped into the light and put his hat on a chair. Once again she didn't return his greeting.

"I knew you were in town," he said. "I arrived the day before yesterday. From Paris. I saw your address listed at the club, and I thought about paying you a visit someday. Then I saw you on the street this afternoon. I recognized your gray fur coat from far off." He was speaking quickly, as if out of breath. "Aren't you going to say hello to me, Jenny? Are you angry that I've come?"

"Hello, Helge," she said, shaking the hand he offered her. "Won't you sit down?"

She took her place on the sofa. She listened to her own voice — it sounded quite calm and matter-of-fact. But in her mind she had that same peculiar, delirious sense of terror.

"I had an impulse to come and see you," said Helge, sitting down on a chair nearby.

"That was nice of you," said Jenny.

They sat in silence for a while.

"So you're living in Bergen now," she said at last. "I read that you received your doctorate. Congratulations."

"Thank you."

There was another pause.

"You've been living abroad for so long . . ." he said. "Sometimes I thought about writing to you, but I never did. I see that Heggen lives here in the building too."

"Yes. I wrote to him, asking him to find me a place — a studio — but they're expensive and difficult to find here in town. But this room has very good light . . ."

"I see you have a number of paintings over there."

He stood up, walked partway across the room, but then came back at once and sat down. Jenny bent her head — she could feel his eyes fixed on her.

Then he started talking again, and they tried to carry on a conversation. He asked about Fransiska Ahlin and other mutual acquaintances. But the conversation soon died, and he sat silently staring at her, as he had before.

"Did you know that my parents are divorced?" he asked suddenly.

She nodded.

"Yes." He laughed a bit. "They stayed together for the sake of us children as long as they could. Went around grinding and scraping against each other like two millstones, until everything of value to us had been ground to powder between them. I guess there wasn't anything left to grind up, so the mill stopped.

"Oh yes, I remember when I was a boy. Whenever they talked to each other . . . they didn't exactly fight. But there was something about their voices . . . Mother would lose her temper and start berating him, and end up in tears. Father would be calm and composed — but there was an edge to his voice, a hatred so cold and hard that it cut right through you. I would lie in my bed, tormented by what I suppose I could call 'my obsession.' Thinking what a relief it would be to take a knitting needle and stick it straight through my head, in one ear and out the other. Those voices were causing physical pain in my eardrums, you see — a pain that seemed to spread all through my head . . .

"Well, that was in the beginning. Now they've done their duty as parents. And it's over."

He nodded to himself a few times.

"It was so ugly. The hatred, I mean. Everything that comes near it turns ugly. I went to visit my sister last summer. We never had much sympathy for each other, but . . . It was disgusting to see her with that man. Sometimes he would come over and kiss her — take his pipe out of his mouth with those thick, moist lips of his and kiss his wife. Such a pompous preacher in the pulpit and a glutton at home. Sofie would turn quite pale sometimes when he touched her.

"And you and I. Afterward I thought it was inevitable that it all fell apart, everything between us that was so delicate, soft, and springlike . . . it all froze to death in that atmosphere. After I left you, I regretted it. I wanted to write, but do you know why I didn't? I got a letter from Father, and he told me that he had been over to see you. It was his way of chiding me, you know, of trying to make me rekindle my relationship with you. So I didn't write; I had a superstitious terror of taking any advice from him.

"But I've been longing for you and dreaming about you the whole time, Jenny. I kept going over and over my memories of you. Do you know where I went first, here in Rome, yesterday? I went out to Montagnola. I found our initials on the cactus."

Jenny was very pale, sitting with her hands tightly clasped.

"You look exactly the same. But you've lived through three years that I know nothing about," said Helge softly. "Now that I'm here with you again, I can't comprehend it. It feels like it couldn't be true — all those things that happened since we last parted in Rome.

"And perhaps you belong to someone else by now . . ."

Jenny didn't reply.

"Are you . . . engaged?" he asked quietly.

"No."

"Jenny . . ." Helge bowed his head and she couldn't see his face. "Do you know . . . all these years . . . I've thought . . . dreamed about . . . winning you back. I imagined us meeting again . . . and that we would understand each other. After all, Jenny, you said I was the first person you had ever loved. Is it impossible?"

"Yes, it is," she said.

"Heggen?"

At first she didn't answer.

"I've always been jealous of Heggen," said Helge quietly. "I was afraid that he was the one for you. When I saw that he was living in the same building . . . So the two of you are . . . fond of each other?"

Jenny still didn't speak.

"Are you fond of him?" Helge asked again.

"Yes. But I don't want to marry him."

"Oh, in that way, then," he said harshly.

"No." She gave a fleeting smile. Weary and resigned, she bowed her head. "I can't bear having a relationship with anyone — not anymore. I can't bear anything. I wish you would leave, Helge."

But he stayed where he was.

"I can't understand that everything could be over. I never believed it, and now that I see you . . .

"I've thought over and over that it was my own fault. I was so timid — never knew what was right. It could be different. I've thought about that last night we were together in Rome. I always thought that moment could be retrieved. I left that time because I thought it was the right thing to do. Surely that can't be the reason I lost you.

"Back then," he lowered his eyes, "I had never touched a woman before. I was terrified because of what I'd witnessed at home. Dreams and fantasies . . . sometimes it was sheer hell . . . but the terror was always stronger.

"But now I'm twenty-nine years old. And I haven't experienced anything beautiful or happy, except for that brief springtime with you. Can't you understand? I've never been able to stop thinking about you. Don't you see how much I love you — the only happiness I've ever known? I can't lose you — not now."

She was on her feet, trembling, and he stood up too. Involuntarily she took a few steps back.

"Helge . . . there was someone else."

He stood still and looked at her.

"So . . . was there someone else? It could have been me, but it was someone else? But I have to have you — I don't care about that. I want you to be mine, because you once promised me . . ."

Frightened, she tried to slip past him, but he violently pulled her into his arms.

It felt as if several moments passed before her mind registered that he was kissing her on the mouth. She thought she was resisting, but she stood almost lifeless in his embrace.

She wanted to tell him to stop. She wanted to tell him who the other man was. But she couldn't, because then she would have said that she had had a child. And the moment she thought about her son, she realized that she couldn't bear to mention his name — not in the midst of all this. She had to keep her child out of the desolation that she knew was coming. And this felt to her like a gentle caress from the dead little boy, and it warmed her heart and did her good — so that for a moment her body grew soft and pliant in his arms.

"You're mine — I'm the one you belong to, Jenny — yes, yes, yes," Helge whispered to her.

She looked up into his face for a moment. And then she tore away from him and ran to the door, calling loudly for Gunnar.

He came after her and took her in his arms again.

"He can't have you — you're mine, mine . . ."

Then they struggled, without speaking, right there at the door. For Jenny it was clear that everything depended on her being able to open the door and escape to Gunnar's room. But since she could feel Helge's body against her, more passionate and stronger than her own, and he was holding her tight with his arms and knees, then it seemed there was nothing else she could do but surrender. And in the end she gave herself to him.

———

In the gray light of dawn, as he was getting dressed, he kept coming over to her bed to kiss her.

"You marvelous creature! How marvelously lovely you are, Jenny. And now you're mine. Now everything will be good again — don't you think so? Oh, how I love you.

"Are you tired? You must sleep . . . I'm going now. I'll come up to see you later in the morning. Sleep well, my sweet, beloved Jenny. Are you so tired?"

"Yes, very tired, Helge." She lay with her eyes half closed, looking at the pale morning light that Helge had let in through the shutters.

Then he kissed her. He had put on his coat and stood with his hat in his hand. Even so, he knelt down before her bed and put his arm under her shoulders.

"Thank you for last night, Jenny. Do you remember that I said the very same thing on that first morning in Rome? Out at the Aventine. Do you remember?"

Jenny nodded into the pillows.

"Sleep well. Give me one more kiss . . . So, good night, my lovely Jenny!"

Over by the door he stopped.

"Oh, that's right . . . the front door — is there a key? Or is it one of those ordinary, old-fashioned kinds with a latch on the inside?"

"Yes, it's the ordinary kind," she said. "You can unlock it from the inside."

—⁓—

She stayed in bed with her eyes closed. But she saw her own body as it lay under the blanket, white, beautiful, and naked — an object that she had flung away, just as she had thrown away the spotted glove in the afternoon. It was no longer hers.

Then she gave a start — she heard Heggen come up the stairs, slowly, and open his door. He paced back and forth for a while, then he went back out and up the steps to the roof. Now she could hear his swift footsteps pacing over her head.

She was certain that he knew. But it made no impression on her weary mind. She no longer felt any pain. It occurred to her that everything must seem to him as inevitable and unavoidable as it did to her.

What she was about to do was not something that she had any sense of deciding. It had to happen, just as the other had happened — as an unavoidable consequence of her opening the door to Helge last night.

Jenny stuck her foot out from under the blanket. She lay there looking at it as if it were a foreign object that didn't belong to her. It was pretty. She bent it so that the instep arched. Yes, it was pretty, with white and blue veins, and a delicate pink at the heel and toes.

She was so tired. It was good to be tired like this. As if she had been in pain, but now it had gone. While he was with her, she had merely felt that she was being crushed down into darkness, that she was sinking and sinking — and it was a sensual pleasure to perish in that way — robbed of all will, to let herself sink away from life — down to the bottom, where it was quiet. She had a dim sense that she had returned his caresses and clung to him. Now she was tired, and what she had left to do, she would do without thinking.

She stood up and got dressed. After she had put on her stockings, camisole, and petticoat, she stuck her feet into a pair of bronze-colored slippers that she wore indoors. She washed herself and then pinned up her hair in front of the mirror — without noticing her own reflection.

Then she went over to the little table where she kept her painting equipment. She rummaged in the box of etching tools. In the night she happened to think about the sharp, triangular scraper. Sometimes she used to play around by setting it against her artery.

Jenny picked it up and looked at it — tested it against her finger. Then she put it back and picked up a pocketknife. She had bought it in Paris; it had a corkscrew, a can opener, and many different blades. One was short, sharp, and wide — that's the one she opened.

Then she went back and sat down on the bed. She placed her pillow on the edge of the nightstand, rested her left hand on it, and slashed the artery.

Blood gushed out, striking a little watercolor she had pinned up on the wall over the bed. She lay down, automatically pulling her feet out of her slippers, and stretched out on the bed. When she noticed how the blood was spraying all around, she stuck her wounded hand under the blanket.

She had no thoughts and no fear — merely felt that she was surrendering to the inevitable. Even the pain in the cut wasn't bad — sharp and clear, as if concentrated in a single spot.

But after a moment an odd, unfamiliar sensation came over her — a fear that grew and grew. Not a fear *of* anything — it was merely a feeling of terrifying fear in her heart — as if she were being smothered. She opened her eyes — but black spots drifted before her gaze. And she couldn't breathe — the room was falling in on her from all directions. She tumbled out of bed, blindly staggered toward the door and up the stairs to the roof, until she collapsed on the top step.

———

Helge had met Gunnar Heggen just as he came out the front door. They had looked at each other as they both tipped their hats. Then they passed by without saying a word.

But that encounter had sobered Helge. And coming as it did after the intoxication of the night, his mood abruptly changed. What he had experienced seemed to him suddenly unbelievable, incomprehensible. And eerie.

This meeting with her, which he had dreamed about all these years . . . The woman he had dreamed of . . . She had scarcely said a word — just sat there, mute and cold. And then all at once she threw herself into his arms. Wild and mad, but without a word. Now he suddenly remembered that she hadn't spoken — no response to all his words of love last night.

An eerie stranger . . . His Jenny. And instantly he knew that she had never been his.

Helge walked and walked through the morning-quiet streets. Up and down the Corso.

He tried to remember her. To separate the memories from the dreams. To remember her from that time when they were engaged. But he couldn't hold on to her image — knew all of a sudden that he had never been able to. There had always been something in the background that he couldn't see, although he knew it was there.

He knew nothing about her. Heggen might be with her right now — he didn't know. There had been someone else . . . she told him that herself. Who was it? How many others? What else didn't he know but had always sensed?

And now, after this . . . he couldn't let her go now, he knew that, now more than ever before. But he didn't know her. Who was she, this woman who held him in her power? Who had been in all his thoughts for three years?

And it was terror and rage that drove him as he raced back to the door of her building. It stood open. He ran up the stairs. She would have to answer him — he wouldn't let her go until she told him everything.

———

Her door was open. He looked inside — the empty bed and the bloody sheet and the blood all over the floor. And he turned around and saw that she lay curled up at the top of the stairs and that there was blood on the white marble steps.

Helge screamed and raced up the stairs — lifted her up, held her in his arms. He felt her breasts limp against his hand. There was a last, tepid trace of warmth hidden along the edge of her corset, but her arms and hands hung down cold. And he understood, with a physical sense of horror, that this body — which only a few hours ago he had held in his arms, hot and trembling with life — was now a corpse, and soon she would be carrion.

He sank to his knees with her and screamed wildly.

Heggen tore open the door to the roof. His face was white and haggard. Then he saw Jenny.

He grabbed Helge and flung him away — knelt down beside her.

"She was lying here . . . when I came back, she was lying here . . ."

"Run and get the doctor — quickly." Gunnar had ripped open her underclothing — felt inside — put his hands to her head — lifted her arms and looked at the wound. Then he tore the light blue silk ribbon from her bodice and bound it tightly around her wrist.

"Yes, yes, but where does he live?"

Gunnar uttered a scream of fury. Then he said in a low voice, "I'll go. Carry her inside . . ." But he picked her up himself and moved toward her door. When he saw the bloody bed, his face contorted. Then he turned and shoved open the door to his own room. He lay her down on his untouched bed. And he dashed out.

Helge had walked at his side with his mouth agape, as if frozen in a shriek. But he had stopped at Gunnar's door. When he was alone with her, he went over and touched her hand with his fingertips. Then he fell to the floor, with his head resting on the edge of the bed, and sobbed shrilly, convulsed with horror.

12

Gunnar walked along the narrow, grassy road between the high, brightly whitewashed garden walls. On one side were the barracks. There must have been a terrace somewhere, because high above his head stood several soldiers, laughing and chatting. At the corner a sprig of yellow flowers bobbed, growing from a crack at the top of the wall. But on the other side of the road the mighty old stone pines by the Cestius pyramid and the dense cypress trees in the new section of the cemetery towered against the blue and silver-clouded sky.

Outside the gate a young girl was sitting in the grass crocheting. She opened the gate for him and curtseyed in thanks for the coin he gave her.

The spring air was damp, clear, and mild. Inside the cemetery, in the intense green shade, it was as humid and hot as in a greenhouse. And the white narcissus along the border of the pathway had a torrid and sultry scent.

The old cypresses stood close together, forming a grove around the grave sites, which were dark with the clinging vines of periwinkles and violets and lay in terraces along the ivy-clad old city wall. The monuments to the dead gleamed — small marble temples and white angel statues and big, ponderous sarcophagi. Moss tinged them green and shimmered on the trunks of the cypresses. Here and there a white or red blossom still remained in the shiny dark foliage of the camellia trees, but most of the flowers lay brown and withered on the damp, black soil, from which a rotting, clammy smell rose up toward him. He happened to think of something he had read — that the Japanese didn't like camellias because the blossoms fell off whole and fresh, like decapitated heads.

Jenny Winge was buried in the far corner of the cemetery, near the chapel. It was at the very edge of the light green, daisy-covered hillside, where there were still only a few graves. Cypresses had been planted along the perimeter of the lawn, but they were still tiny, looking like toys with their sharp, dark green crowns atop erect, twining brown trunks that resembled pillars in a cloister arcade.

Her grave was out in the meadow, set slightly apart from the others. But when it was dug, the grass around it had been flattened with earth. It was a pale gray, because the sun shone here, and the dark cypress grove stood like a wall behind it.

Gunnar covered his face with his hands and knelt down, bending forward until his head was resting on the withered wreaths.

He felt the weariness of spring in all his limbs, and with each heavy beat of his heart, his blood pulsed sick with sorrow and loss. Jenny — Jenny — Jenny — he heard her bright name in the springtime chirping of every bird, but she was dead.

She was lying down there in the dark. He had snipped off a lock of her hair and he carried it inside his billfold. He could take it out and let it glitter in the sun — but those meager little glints were the only sparks that the sun could now light on her thick, luxuriant curls.

She was dead and gone. There were a few of her paintings left, and there had been a brief notice about her in the newspapers. And there was a mother and sisters who mourned their own Jenny — but the real one they had never known; they knew nothing about her life or her death. And there were others, who stared in bewilderment after the Jenny they had known; they could guess at a little, but they understood nothing.

The Jenny who lay here was his alone.

———

Helge Gram had come to him. He asked questions and spoke of what he knew, and he moaned and begged.

"I don't understand anything. Don't you see? Explain it to me, Heggen. *You* seem to understand. Can't you tell me what you know?"

He had not replied.

"There was someone else. She told me that herself. Who was it? Was it you?"

"No."

"Do you know who it was?"

"Yes, but I won't tell you. It won't do you any good to ask, Gram."

"But it's driving me mad — do you hear me, Heggen? I'll go mad if you don't explain it to me."

"You have no right to know Jenny's secrets."

"But why did she do it? For my sake? For his? For yours?"

"No. She did it for her own sake."

Then he had asked Gram to leave. He was gone now. They hadn't seen each other since.

It was up in the Borghese Gardens that Gram had approached him, a few days after the funeral. Gunnar was sitting there in the sunshine. He was very tired. He was the one who had made all the arrangements and made the necessary explanations on all sides — at the inquest about the suicide, at the funeral. To Fru Berner he had written that her daughter had died suddenly of a heart attack. But there was something about all of this that had done him good. The fact that no one knew of his grief. The fact that the real reason — the only one that could possibly be true — he had hidden from everyone. It had made his sorrow sink so deep inside him that he would never tell it to anyone else. It was his alone. And it would be the innermost core of his soul for as long as he lived.

It would color his being and become colored in turn. It would rule his life — and be ruled in turn — changing color and shape but never erased. Every hour of the day it would be different, but always present, and it would be that way forever.

But he remembered that on the morning when he ran to get the doctor, while the other man was left alone with her . . . at that time he had wanted to tell Helge Gram what he knew, and say it in such a way that the other man's heart would turn to ashes, just as his own had done.

But in the days that followed, everything he knew had become secrets between him and the dead woman. They were the secrets of their love. Everything that had happened had occurred because of the way she was, and it was because of the way she was that he had loved her. Helge Gram was an unimportant and chance stranger to both him and to her, and Gunnar had no need to seek vengeance on him, just as he felt no compassion for Helge's grief or his horror at the unfathomable nature of what had occurred.

For people like them it was quite natural. Everything had happened because of the way she was. One day her soul was bound to sway and bend wildly in a gust of wind because it had grown up so slender and straight. He had believed that she could grow the way a tree does; he hadn't understood that she grew like a flower, a delicate and succulent stalk, striving to reach the sun and to open all of its heavy buds, full of longing, into bloom. She was just a little girl. And it would be to the eternal sorrow of his soul that he hadn't seen this until it was too late.

Because she couldn't pull herself back up once she had been broken. She was like a lily, which can no longer sprout from the roots if the first shoot has been severed. There was nothing supple or vigorous about her. But he loved her just as she was.

And just as she was, she was his alone. He was the only one who knew how fair and delicate she was — so strong and erect in her striving, and yet so frail and brittle — with her sensitive dignity from which no blemish could ever be removed because it had etched its mark too deep.

And now she was dead. And he had been alone with his love for so many days and nights. And he would be alone with it for all the rest of the days and nights of his life.

And there had been nights when he stifled his despairing screams in the pillows of his bed. She was dead, and he had never possessed her. And he was the one she should have loved; he was the one she should have belonged to. And she was the only one he had ever loved. She was dead, and her lovely, slender white body, which held her soul the way a velvet sheath holds a slim and fine sharp blade . . . he had never touched it, never seen it. Others had, but without knowing what a wondrous and rare treasure had fallen into their hands. And now it lay buried in the ground, and it would become hideously, hideously changed, disintegrating and decaying, until at last it was no more than a handful of earth in the earth.

Gunnar shook with sobs as he knelt there.

Others had possessed her. And they had sullied her and destroyed her, and they hadn't known what they were doing. But he had never possessed her.

As long as he lived, there would be moments when he lamented as he did now, because this was true.

Yet he was the only one who possessed her now. Only in his hand did her golden curl shimmer. And she herself lived inside him now — her soul and her image were mirrored in him, as clearly and steadily as in still water. She was dead; her sorrow was no longer part of her, but it was part of him — there it lived on and would never die until he himself was dead. And because it was alive, it would grow and change. He didn't know how his sorrow would look in ten years, but it might grow into something great and lovely.

As long as he lived, there would be moments when he felt a strangely profound and deep joy because this was true.

But during those morning hours when he walked around on the roof terrace above her, as she ended her life . . . He dimly recalled what he had been feeling. He had raged at her. Because she could do something like that . . . He had begged and implored to be allowed to help her, to carry her away from the precipice where she had strayed . . . but she had turned him away and thrown herself off before his very eyes — just like a woman — stubborn, irresponsible, foolhardy, headstrong.

But when he saw her lying there . . . that too he had raged about, in despair. He wouldn't have let her go. No matter what she had done — he would have absolved her . . . helped her, offered her his trust, even his love.

As long as he lived, there would be moments when he would reproach her for choosing to die. Jenny, you shouldn't have done it. And there would be moments when he felt that she had to do it, because of the way she was. That too was why he loved her — forever, as long as he lived.

Only one thing would never happen: He would never wish that he hadn't loved her.

How he had wept — desperately — and would weep again, because he hadn't loved her long before. Because during all the years he had lived side by side with her, when she was his friend and companion, he hadn't seen that she was the woman who should have been his wife.

But the day would never come when he wished that he hadn't seen — even if it was only to see that it was too late.

—⁂—

Gunnar raised himself up to a kneeling position. From his pocket he took out a little flat cardboard box and opened it. Inside lay a tiny bead from Jenny's pink crystal necklace. When he was clearing out her things, he found the necklace in the drawer of the nightstand. The string was broken. He had taken one bead and kept it.

He took a little earth from the grave and put it into the box. The bead rolled around, becoming completely covered with gray dust, but the clear rose color gleamed through, and the delicate fissures in the crystal sparkled, refracting the sunlight.

He had packed up all of her things and sent them home to her family; meticulously gathered all her letters and burned them. In a sealed cardboard box lay her baby's clothes. He sent them to Fransiska, because one day Jenny had talked about wanting to do that.

He leafed through her portfolios and sketchbooks and then packed them away. But first he carefully cut out the pages with the drawings of her son and tucked them into his billfold.

They were his. Everything that she had kept for herself — now it was all his.

———

There were reddish violet anemones growing on the lawn. Without thinking he went over and picked them.

Oh, springtime, springtime . . .

He remembered the last time he had been back home to Norway in the springtime. That was two years ago.

He had hired a cart and a red mare at the local station. The man who owned them was an old classmate of his. And he drove out along the country road on a brilliantly sunny morning in March. Beneath the light blue sky the fields were pale yellow with old grass. Wherever the rocky ground poked up through the earth, small thickets of juniper and birch and mountain ash with shiny bare branches stood outlined against the sky. The manure heaps scattered over the plowed fields shimmered like yellowish brown velvet. Farmsteads appeared, one after another, with the familiar barn contours, with yellow and gray and red buildings, surrounded by apple orchards and lilac bushes. All around the farm-land stood the forest, olive-green with a springlike violet sheen over the birch groves. A single strip of snow lay greenish white in the shadows to the north.

All over the countryside that day he could hear the murmur of invisible larks singing.

He came upon a pair of towheaded children who were trudging along the road carrying a dinner pail. Wearing shabby clothes and thin shoes, they plod-ded through the mud.

"Where are you headed, little children?"

They stopped and stared at him with suspicion.

"Are you taking dinner to your pappa?"

Reluctantly they admitted that they were — a bit surprised that a stranger would know this.

"Climb on up and I'll give you a ride."

He hoisted them up into the cart.

"Where does he work, your pappa?"

"At Brustad."

"Oh, Brustad, yes . . . isn't that over near the school?"

And that's how the conversation proceeded. The foolish, ignorant grown-up man asking one question after another — the way adults always talk to children. The grown-up asks and the youngsters, who possess so much knowledge, consult each other by mutely rolling their eyes and then hesitantly offer as much as they think would be suitable.

After he set them back down they padded hand in hand across the field beneath the reddish brown willows, past a rushing streambed. He watched them go for a moment, then turned the cart around and continued on his way.

Back home they had prayer meetings in the evening. His sister Ingeborg would sit next to the old birch cupboard in the corner and follow along, her pale face ecstatic and her steel-blue eyes shining, as a shoemaker from Fredriksstad talked about mercy. Then she would jump up and testify — trembling with fervor.

Ingeborg, his beautiful, merry sister. How lively she had once been, so fond of dancing and fun. And fond of reading and learning. When he was working in town he used to send her books and pamphlets, and the *Social Democrat* newspaper twice a week. She wanted to know and learn about everything. Then when she was thirty years old, she had a conversion. Now she spoke in tongues.

She had bestowed all of her love on their little nephew, Anders, and their little foster child, a girl from Kristiania born out of wedlock. With blazing eyes she would tell them about Jesus, the friend of all children.

The next day it snowed. He had invited the children to the cinema in the little town a few miles away.

They trudged along the stone wall between the spruce forest and the fields. Everything was grayish white from the slushy March snow — only their footprints left dark traces behind them. He tried to converse with the children; he asked them questions, and they answered in a reticent and reserved fashion.

But on the way home it was the children who asked the questions, and he answered them candidly, magnanimously, feeling flattered. They had seen pictures of cowboys in Arizona and coconut harvesting in the Philippines. And he eagerly did his best to give them proper answers and not be stumped for a reply.

—◇◇◇—

Oh springtime, springtime . . .

And it was a spring day when he had traveled to Viterbo with Jenny and Fransiska.

She had sat there so erect, dressed in black, staring out the train window. How big and gray her eyes were — he remembered that.

Storm clouds swept a ragged, dull black veil of rain over the *campagna,* where there were no ruins for the tourists to see, merely a few crumbling, shapeless, nameless walls spread out at great distances from one another; and here and there a little tenant farm with a couple of stone pines and pointed haystacks near the house. Flocks of sheep huddled together in the valley where small thickets of wild roses grew along the streambed.

Later the train headed through mountains and woods, past towering oak trees where white and blue and yellow flowers bloomed in the old withered leaves like back in Norway. White anemones and blue and sulfur-yellow primroses. And she longed to get out and pick some, she said — to sink down and down under the falling rain, under the dripping branches, into the drenched leaves. "This is just like spring back home," she said.

It had snowed there — slushy gray spring snow filled the ditches, gathering in bright stripes along the fallen branches. The flowers bowed down with their petals stuck together, wet and heavy with sleet.

Lively little streams trickled down the slopes and slid under the railroad bed. But here they were rusty red from the earth.

Then a shower pounded against the compartment windows, darkening them, and the smoke from the locomotive was swept toward the ground. The weather cleared a bit, and breaks in the clouds appeared over the valleys and wooded slopes, where the mist poured down the mountainsides.

Some of his things were in one of the girls' suitcases. By the time he remembered this in the evening, they had already begun to undress. They were laughing and chattering in their room when he knocked on their door. Jenny opened it a crack and handed him what he asked for — she was wearing a bright Frisian jacket with short sleeves, so her slender white arm was bare. And he was tempted to shower it with kisses, but he ventured only a single fleeting one, and so playfully that it seemed almost apologetic.

Back then he was in love with her. Back then he was intoxicated with the spring and the wine and the rain merrily pelting down, and the brief glimpses of sun and his own youth and vitality. He had the urge to invite her out to dance, that tall blond girl who laughed so cautiously, as if she were trying out a new art that she had never practiced before. The girl whose gray eyes stared, somber and full of longing, at all the flowers they passed — and she wanted so much to pick them.

Oh, dear God, for everything that might have been . . . Dry, bitter sobs shook him once more.

———

It also rained the day they went up to Montefiascone — so hard that it splashed back up from the cobblestones around the raised skirts of the two women and their slender ankles and feet. But how they had laughed, the three of them, as they waded up the steep, narrow street, with the rainwater gushing toward them like waterfalls.

And when they reached La Rocca, the fortress in the middle of the old city, the clouds let up.

All three of them leaned over the parapets and looked at Lago Bolsena, which lay black and deep below the green slopes with the olive groves and vineyards. The clouds hovered low over the ridges surrounding the lake. But then a shiny silver strip of light raced across the dark mirror of the water, and then widened and turned blue, and the fog rolled back and slipped into hollows and clefts, as the outline of the mountains around the lake emerged. The sun broke through the clouds, and they sank down and hung golden and leaden blue around the base of the smaller peaks, crowned by the stone-gray hill town. To the north a towering, cone-shaped peak appeared, far in the distance. Cesca claimed it was Monte Amiata.

Across the newly washed, blue spring sky rolled the last traces of rain clouds — heavy and silver rimmed, dissolving in the sun. The storm fled westward, turning the sky dark where the high plain of Etruria sank down, brownish black and desolate, toward the distant pale yellow, glowing strip of the Mediterranean.

Bleak and vast and severe, the land stretched outward — rather like the high mountain landscape back home, in spite of the gray olive groves and grapevines that meandered among the rows of elm trees on the green hills below, around the lake.

In the little park surrounding the fortress ruins the evergreen oaks dropped their old iron-black leaves from their branches, which bore fine new shoots. There were hedges of some kind of evergreen shrubs with leathery leaves. The new young leaves of springtime were an unnatural, glittering golden green.

He had crouched down in the shelter of the hedge with her and held out his coat so she could light a cigarette. The spring wind was icy and sharp and pure up there, and she shivered a little in her wet clothing; her cheeks were red, and the sun shone on her damp, golden hair, which she brushed out of her eyes with one hand.

That's where he would go. Tomorrow he would go up there.

That's where he would greet the spring — the freezing, naked, expectant spring with all the flower buds blinded by rain, shivering with cold in the wind — but blooming nevertheless.

———

Springtime and Jenny — now they had become one for him. Oh yes . . . she who stood there, cold and laughing in the shifting weather and wanted to gather up all the flowers in her arms.

Oh, my little Jenny, you weren't allowed to pick the flowers you wanted, and your dreams never blossomed — but now they will be my dreams.

And when I have lived enough to be as filled with longing as you were . . . maybe I will do as you did and say to my fate: Give me a few of my flowers, I will be content with much fewer than I asked for when I began my life. But I won't die the way you died, because you couldn't be content after all. I will simply remember you and kiss your bead and your blond hair and think: No, she couldn't live unless she was the best and dared to demand the best as her right. And then maybe I will say: Thank heaven that she chose to die rather than to keep living like that.

But tonight I will go to Piazza San Pietro and listen to the ecstatic music of the fountains that are never silent, and dream my own dream.

Yes, Jenny, because now you are my dream, and I have never had any other. Oh, the dream, the dream . . .

But if your child had lived, he wouldn't have become what you dreamed of when you held him in your arms and you put him to your breast, Jenny. Something good and splendid he might have become — or something mean and ugly — the only thing he wouldn't have become was what you dreamed.

No woman has ever given birth to the child she dreamed of while she was pregnant. No artist has ever created the work he envisioned at the moment of conception. And we live one summer after another, but none of them is the one we longed for when we bent down and picked the wet flowers beneath the storm clouds of spring.

And no love is ever the way we dreamed of it, when we kissed each other for the first time. If you and I had lived together . . . we might have been happy or unhappy; we could have caused each other inexpressible joy or pain. Now I will never know how our love might have been if you were mine. The only thing I know is that what I dreamed that night as I stood with you, with the fountains splashing in the moonlight — that's not how it would have been. And that is bitter.

And yet . . .

Dear God, I don't wish that I had never dreamed that dream. I don't wish that I didn't have to dream what I'm dreaming now.

Jenny, I would give my life for you to meet me up there at the fortress and be the way you were back then and kiss me and love me — for one day, one hour . . . I think over and over about how it would have been if you had lived, if you had once been mine . . . I can't ever stop thinking about that. It was such a boundless joy, Jenny, that was wasted. Oh, you're dead, and I am so bereft, so bereft because of it. I have only my poor dreams about you. And yet . . . If I measure them against the wealth of others, then my poverty is so abundantly, gloriously rich. Even if it would save my own life, I wouldn't want to stop loving you and dreaming about you and grieving as I am grieving now.

—⁓—

Gunnar Heggen wasn't aware that, as the immeasurable storm filled his heart, he had raised his arms to the sky and was whispering to himself out loud. He was still holding in his hand the anemones that he had picked, but he didn't know it.

The soldiers on the barracks wall laughed at him, but he didn't notice. He clutched the flowers to his breast, and he whispered softly to himself as he slowly walked from the sunlight at the grave toward the dark cypress grove.

THJODOLF

translated by

NAOMI WOLFORD

1

"Sound, healthy 6-weeks baby boy of cultured parents offered to childless couple in comfortable circumstances, to bring up as their own. One definitive payment. Write Box:... 'Conscientious.'"

"It's not easy for me to keep him here, you see," said Frøken Erdahl, passing two gnarled, skinny fingers over her small yellow, old face. She looked down at the sleeping baby in its improvised cot of two armchairs pushed together.

The visitor made no reply; she just breathed out as if the heat of the room oppressed her.

It was stiflingly hot in there, and rather dark. The frosty fog hung thick in the courtyard outside, and in the building at the back the windows showed merely as little dark patches. The room was very small. Piles of sewing lay on the table in the window by the sewing machine, as well as on the round, spindle-legged table under the hanging lamp and on the shabby daybed along the wall.

"No, it's not at all easy." Frøken Erdahl sighed. "It's wretched pay working for these shops — and then you have to have a fire all day and keep yourself in food and the place clean and all that. I never used to do seamstress work at home like this, you know; unless it might be a bit of work now and then for the people in the other apartments here and so on — in the evenings, or in the summer when my employers were in the country. I've got my regulars, you might say, like the Hansens on Underhaugsveien: I've been doing their sewing now for twenty-five years — twenty-five years last April it was. And it takes a lot of time looking after such a tiny mite, doesn't it, what with the bottles to clean and the washing and all that.

"Otherwise I'd like to have kept him. I've gotten really quite fond of him.

"Small thanks I'd have got for it, though, mind you! Believe me, Fru Johansen, I've done my share of helping that brother of mine and his children one time and another. It was me paid for Fanny to go to the trade school — that's the child's mother — and this is what I get for it.

"Such a nice, pretty girl she was — and then to go off and do that. Well, see for yourself." She took a photograph from the console table and handed it to the visitor.

Fru Johansen glanced at it and gave it back to Frøken Erdahl without comment. "What about the father?" she asked. Her voice was low and rather husky. "Can't he pay anything toward it?"

"Who, him?" Frøken Erdahl snorted contemptuously. "Him, with a wife and five children? First he told Fanny he was divorced, then he said he was going to be — but he'll take care not to do that, you may be sure. She's got a little soap business on Herslebsgaten, you see, so she's the one who keeps him and the children. If he got a divorce he'd have to pay alimony. *Oh* no. And how Fanny could behave like that with a person she knew nothing about — well, it's a mystery. Though of course he comes of decent enough people — he graduated from high school and all that. I know that's so, because the Stenders where I work sometimes — they knew about him. He's the son of a doctor where Fru Stenders comes from, and she knew one of the boys had gone to the bad and that he was here in town soliciting advertisers. That was quite true, she told me."

"It's my husband," Fru Johansen said, as quietly as before. "I'd gladly take a child for nothing, but my husband says when they get bigger it means expense — and there's plenty of people willing to pay up to a couple of thousand to get them into a good home — decent people, I mean. So he says five hundred would be the least he could take, he says —"

"There was a woman from out in Våler — she'd have taken him for three hundred," said Frøken Erdahl. "But somehow I didn't care for her physiometry . . ."

Frøken Erdahl glanced at her visitor, not quite knowing what to make of her. Fru Johansen was pretty in a way, but her narrow face was very pale and the skin was taut over her cheekbones. The big steel-gray eyes were deep set and the pale, thin-lipped mouth turned down at the corners. When one looked at her closely one noticed quite a few gray strands in her dark brown hair, which was parted above the white forehead and drawn smoothly back into a large, braided bun. Otherwise she might have passed for a young girl — of the kind that is never really young.

An orderly sort of person, at any rate; Frøken Erdahl could see that. Her clothes were old fashioned in cut, but of good material and in good condition. She wore a long, narrow coat, and though her muff and stole were out of date in style, they were of good fur, the seamstress noted. The ostrich feather in the little blue hat was fresh and thick, and at her throat, where she had loosened her outer clothes, there was a line of white and an old-fashioned brooch.

These seemed likely to be quiet, pious people, and comfortably off. They had a house of their own, Fru Johansen had mentioned. It would be a good thing if she could place Thjodolf with them, poor little mite; she was very fond of him, but she longed to get all this over and be rid of Fanny and her affairs.

Meanwhile Helene Johansen was hesitating. There was another thing that Julius had told her she must find out: whether the child was quite healthy and wouldn't bring any filthy disease into the house. But she didn't quite like to ask about this.

"He sweats a lot, doesn't he?" was all she said, as she gently passed her hand over the bedclothes.

"They need to be kept warm, you know, these tiny babies," said Frøken Erdahl, bending over the child.

The baby opened a pair of big, dark eyes; his face twisted and reddened and he screamed.

"There, there — Auntie fetch his bottle then — there, there, shhh — shhh —"

Helene sat down again and looked at the screaming baby. Then, with hesitant little movements, she laid her muff, handbag, and stole on the table and picked the baby up in unaccustomed hands. He was wet. She wrapped him in the shawl that had lain over him and placed him in her lap. When she turned him over on his face and rocked him, he stopped crying.

"Was that better then, was it?" she whispered. "That better, little man?"

Gently she supported the soft little face with her work-roughened hand.

"Was you Helene's own boy, then — did you like that, eh?"

2

Helene walked quickly up Vogtsgaten. She was shivering a little, after sitting so long with her coat on in Frøken Erdahl's hot room.

She was deep in her own thoughts, unaware that she sensed as something familiar the gray dampness of the street and the day. An aunt of her mother's had lived on Thorshaugsgaten, and that had been almost the only place Helene had had to go to in the days when she had worked in Kristiania.

The frosty fog bit rawly at her face, and it was tiring to walk, for the pavement was slippery and uneven. Out in the roadway the snow had been churned up into brown sugar. In the lightlessness of the day, people looked black and bundled up as they trudged toward her; the houses, soaring into the fog, looked even darker and dirtier than they were, and the frosted windows of the shops shone oily yellow, for their lamps were lit, although it was the middle of the day. Without knowing it, Helene took in all the street noises: the trolley groaning up the hill, the tinkling of the harness bells as the horses struggled heavily upward over the difficult surface, the cold, hard ring of picks on the sheet ice of the pavement, and the whining voices of schoolchildren as they swept past her in flocks.

She went into a grocer's and bought two wreaths of spruce fir set with little colored everlasting flowers. Dusk was already falling when she reached the cemetery. The side path lost itself in the fog; it lay white, without footprints in the snow, between the two rows of rime-gray birches. The mist stood like a wall before and behind her as she walked. The grave she was heading for was the third from the big yellow wooden crate covering the memorial to the Solum children. Helene laid her wreaths on the little white mound and then for a while she remained standing by it — a narrow black line in the fog.

She hadn't seemed to grieve terribly deeply over Tulla then, ten years ago. It had been so odd and strange in the maternity hospital — embarrassing too. She had hated it there. And when she had gone back to her home in Drøbak, nothing of what she had been through had seemed real anymore — she hadn't felt as if she'd had a baby at all. No one down there had seen it, except Julius the first time he came to visit her, and that was the day after, when Helene had been so ill that she couldn't take anything in properly. And when he came the second time, Tulla was dead.

But later, as the years passed and she had no more children ... life grew ever quieter and more desolate. For the past few years Julius had worked as engineer aboard a freighter on the fjord. He came home only for a day every week or so. Because of this she had really missed her mother-in-law after her death four years ago, and that was something Helene never had expected. Not that there was any harm in the old creature; they had been quite good friends — only she was so affected and silly. How *could* an old woman behave like that! Amanda said she hadn't been exactly an angel in her young days — she'd been up to all sorts of things, it seemed. But she was very kind, poor old soul. And now Amanda had gone too; she and her husband had moved to Odda. Helene had never liked Amanda much; she used coarse expressions and was silly and affected with Julius. But now Helene missed her friend. Weeks passed without her having to open her mouth except when she went shopping.

She would love to adopt little Thjodolf. Just that particular baby; not some better-class child whose parents would pay two thousand kroner to get rid of him, but this poor little wretch who was in the way where he was. Poor little thing — and how good he was to stop crying when she picked him up. Thjodolf — what a nice name! Helene said it aloud to herself once or twice as she walked back through the cemetery.

If only she could borrow the few hundred kroner. Julius need never know. She had earned a certain amount these past years by doing crochet work and embroidery for people in Drøbak, and she could easily earn much more: get work from shops in Kristiania perhaps — embroider names on trousseaux and do crochet work: that was in fashion now. And she worked beautifully and quickly. Should she go to Fru Lund and ask her advice? Perhaps the son — he was a lawyer now — would tell her how to set about getting a loan.

But when she was sitting in the trolley on her way back into town she felt she couldn't talk to the Lunds about it. She had never asked them for anything in her life — she had never asked anyone for anything. Fru Lund was kind; she had always tried to treat Helene well; but it was odd: Although they could be as good as possible to a servant, they never really thought about what sort of life she was leading, or how she felt about things. True, Fru Lund had some-times said: "Is anything wrong, Helene? You look so sad," but she didn't say it in a way to make Helene feel able to talk to her about things she couldn't even sort out properly for herself. No, she couldn't go to Fru Lund with this new idea. It was so difficult to explain too . . .

For it would be really ungrateful of her to complain. She and Julius were doing well; they had their own house, and Helene knew that few homes were as pretty and clean and well cared for as hers. Her summer boarders were always saying so. They wanted to copy her curtains and mats and everything; they praised her house and garden and her housekeeping, and said how charm-ing and comfortable it was there. And her husband — well, she had no right to grumble about him either. Julius was kind, and usually behaved himself when he was at home. He was a bit careless with money, but she always got as much as she needed from him, and sometimes he had brought her fine presents — especially in the early days. And if he did carouse a bit with the boys now that he was out and away so much — well, one had to remember that a man like that came up against plenty of temptation. And another thing: Amanda had probably been right when she said that it was stupid of Helene to be so quiet and serious. Julius liked gaiety and fun, and he was the kind that could always find it too.

Helene suddenly felt that there were tears in her eyes. She rose abruptly and went out onto the platform; at the next stop she got off and walked on into town.

Yes, it was her own silly fault. She had been so bad at mixing with people; she had always gone about on her own. Her old home down in Smålenene was remote — almost forgotten; she had left it at eighteen. Her parents were dead now, and strangers were living there. All her brothers and sisters were in America. An unhappy love affair had driven her to Kristiania. What happened to her is what often happens to a girl who respects herself and thinks herself above some things: The boy found another girl who wasn't above anything at all . . . In her two first situations she had had a dreadful, dreadful time; it was nothing but drudgery from early morning until late at night, enduring vulgar, senseless abuse and never hearing a kind word. So when she had gone to the widow lady, Fru Lund, she had stayed for ten years. Fru Lund was kind and just — indeed she was; so they all were, for that matter. You couldn't count poor Frøken Lovisa; it was only natural that she should be fretful, with that injury, and Erna was just a little chit of a girl when Helene was there. As soon as Fru Lund found out that Helene knew nobody in Kristiania and never made any friends, she offered her extra money to work on confirmation dresses for the little girls in her free time. Helene enjoyed earning more, and enjoyed hearing Fru Lund say: "Oh, what beautiful work, Helene! How clever you are with your hands!" And when she sat all alone in the maid's room in the evenings, she felt deep, quiet joy at the sight of all the fine white things emerging from her handiwork. Often she sat up far too late because she wanted to see what something looked like when it was finished — the embroidery or the lace that she was working on.

It was so quiet, so very quiet, working like that at night, with no sound but the ticking of the alarm clock, the gentle whisper of the paraffin lamp, and her own breathing. Now and again she had to straighten her back and breathe out; it was like a sigh. She herself didn't know what she was so deeply sad about; it was as if she were yearning for something. Not the sort of thing the other girls she knew were so taken up with; she didn't care about being with them because they teased her and called her stupid and strange. Sometimes she had gone out with them and met their sweethearts, but she was no more cheerful for that. She had been to lectures and meetings too, and was none the happier. She visited the old people in Thorshaugsgaten — and came back so miserable that she could have lain down and cried.

Then came *the* summer. The Lunds went to Drøbak, for Frøken Lovisa was to take the baths. They had rented the house of Hermansen the fisherman, just above where she lived now. Helene got to know the old woman first — she always used to sit in the doorway, and when Helene went by, she called to her and asked questions. Then she took to running over, and would stand by the hour talking to Helene through the kitchen window. One evening Helene met Julius. How all the rest came about she never really knew. She met him on her way to fetch the milk or when she was carrying water. And when he came, and smiled, and showed those white teeth in that handsome brown face, saying: "Out walking, then, Frøken?" it was as if something was tickling her inside, and she couldn't help smiling. She heard laughter rippling forth in her own voice — she heard herself laughing; yes, she, who couldn't remember when she had last laughed, had to laugh at Julius until many a time her stomach actually ached with it. One Sunday afternoon she went sailing with him; there should have been others with them, but they never turned up. There was a fairly brisk wind when they came out on the water and she was frightened; yet she knew that never in her life had she known anything as glorious as that trip. At night she would stand with Julius under the great linden trees; the fjord glimmered white in the summer night, and there was a good smell of leaves and dust and water. When she came back into her room above the scullery where she slept and saw what time it was, she was horrified; but she never found it easy to leave him.

Then came the night when he went up with her to her room. And she remembered how he had pleaded, pressing her close to him, bending her over backward, kissing her; she had begged him to release her and go. But then, when for a moment he loosened his hold — just the tiniest bit — her heart sank like lead; she turned cold with dread lest he should leave her, and dared no longer resist.

The next morning she went about with bowed head, in deadly fear. She felt that everyone must be able to see by looking at her what had happened. She felt that her shame must be written on her face. But when she took Erna her coffee — Erna always came down too late for breakfast — the half-grown girl looked suddenly into her face: "Why, Helene, what on earth's happened to you? You're beaming all over. Have you come into a fortune, or something?" Helene began to cry as soon as she was back in the kitchen; yet she knew that it was as Erna had said.

She could no longer understand how that could have been her, the way she was that summer and autumn; she had seemed utterly unaware of anything but Julius. They went on meeting in Kristiania; when he came to her, her conscience troubled her, yet she felt proud and triumphant too. She was beside herself with shame and fear when she found she was going to have a child, and spoke sharply enough to Julius when she told him about it. All the same, she hadn't really meant all she said. It was rather that she wanted to make *him* say something — she didn't know what. Certainly not what he did say, though he offered her marriage at once; to give him his due, he never tried to get out of it. (She should think not — the very idea! She knew very well she was a fine girl, pretty and clever and respectable, with money in the bank.) Yes, poor Julius; he'd made a great fuss over her, and said he'd gotten himself quite a wife. But there was something she had expected — she didn't know exactly what — and it had never come.

She seemed to be waiting for Fru Lund to say something, as well. She kept thinking of how she would answer when Fru Lund complained of her having to leave, and asked her how she could do such a thing. Helene would reply that she was only human, or something like that. But Fru Lund said nothing about her leaving at an awkward time, nor that she knew why Helene was in such a hurry to get married. She simply said that Johansen was a good-looking man and that Johansen's place looked very nice, and that she only hoped he would know how to appreciate Helene. And the Lunds gave her half a dozen solid-silver teaspoons for a wedding present. Yes, Fru Lund had treated her very generously on that occasion too — and yet Helene felt almost disappointed over the sermon she had never been given and the reply she had never had the chance to offer.

Then Helene was married; it was just before Christmas. She moved to Drøbak and to a home of her own. She told herself that she was sorry and ashamed that it had come about in this way. Yet all the same . . . There seemed so little for her to do in that small house, after all that work at the Lunds' place. She had time to sit for hours making baby clothes at the sewing machine she had bought for herself. During the later months of her pregnancy she slept badly. She sat up late at night or rose early in the coal-black winter mornings. She couldn't use the machine then for fear of disturbing the others, but she sat by the stove doing crochet work or stitching lace onto little shirts and coats. In the stillness she heard the familiar ticking of the alarm clock and the whispering of the lamp, and the burning wood crackling in the stove — and there was the new sound of Julius, sleeping heavily over there in the bed; sometimes she heard the old woman snoring up in the attic. From outside, from the night and the darkness, came the mighty noise of the fjord and the waves breaking on the shore. These new things flowed together in her mind with the feeling of her own changed body and new sensations. She tried to think of what lay before her — of the tiny clothes she held in her hands — clothes she would dress a real live baby in — but she couldn't manage it. She could neither dread it nor long for it; her soul was flooded with serenity. She was calm, as a healthy woman is when she waits for what no one can imagine beforehand or describe afterward — something unlike all the strange and complex events of every day, and remote from ordinary, uneasy, confused feelings; something simple and straightforward, like the miracles of the Lord Himself.

Then the baby came — and went again, before the mother had really grasped the wonder of it; before it had become bound to her daily life by the thousand cares and worries of life. She returned to her house with empty hands.

That was ten years ago. She had nothing to remember of those ten years but the busyness with which she had tried to fill her empty hands. Scrubbing and laundry, sewing and embroidery, crocheting and knitting — busyness that was of no particular benefit to anyone. She moved alone about the scrubbed and shining kitchen; the living room, covered and adorned with her needlework, was occupied by visitors for a couple of months in the summer; the rest of the time it stood empty.

Once she had had an idea of binding Julius to herself with all this activity. But it was now a long time since he had filled her thoughts as she toiled. The notion had slipped from her mind, and she could not bring herself to reason the matter out.

There had been a time when Julius had seemed to her the finest person in the world. She knew very well that she had no right to complain about him. She ought not to complain when she was so well off. It was simply that she had imagined so many foolish things about him and about how their life together would turn out. She tried not to think of this now, for when she did a strange mood came over her, as if she were ashamed of the kind of person she had been back then — as if she pitied herself and envied herself.

———*m*———

She stood outside the garden fence by the little villa at the back of Hægdehaugen. The fog had lifted a little, so that she could see the green light from the lamp shade in the living room shining through the window, with the bare lilac bushes in front. It reminded her vaguely of her own living-room windows at home, staring like black, blind eyes behind her own bare lilac bushes.

It seemed so strange to be calling on the Lunds now, the more so because their place had become so grand. So quiet, so spacious. In Helene's day the children had slept on sofas and cots in every room, but now it was a big apartment for just Fru Lund and Frøken Lovisa. And there were fine new curtains, and new green damask on the furniture instead of the old covers that Fru Lund was forever patching and darning. The grown-up married children had given their mother all these things.

Helene suddenly remembered the day when Fru Lund had come to see her in the hospital. She remembered how those old blue eyes had been full of tears; she remembered the dry, worn, maternal hand resting on her own, and heard the old lady's voice: "Oh, Helene, I was so dreadfully sorry to hear about it! How sad, how terribly sad that you should lose your little girl!"

A strange, warm wave surged through Helene, and all at once, dimly yet strongly, she was aware that in that house sat a mother who had toiled, steadfastly and willingly; who for her children had worn out all the youth and strength bestowed on her for the living of her life. There she sat, rich with all that she had given, while her children flocked about her with their thanks and little presents; now, her work done, she rested, and waited for the night. But out here stood Helene; Helene who had toiled ceaselessly because she couldn't help it; who asked no better than to toil for someone who should be her own heart's love. Like ice the thought ran through her that she couldn't stop working and yet it warmed and cheered no one. She and the lady in there — God had made them in each other's image; yet one was rich and the other poor. It had nothing to do with rank or situation.

She felt as if her heart would break. She *had* a right to complain! All these years she had told herself that she was well off — that she and her husband were well to do for people in their position. Her position was the same as Fru Lund's, yet she was poor, poor, poor . . .

Helene heard the limping step in the hall; Frøken Lovisa was coming to open the door.

"Why, good evening! How nice to see you. Mamma, it's Helene — Helene Østreng, isn't it?" Frøken Lovisa limped ahead into the living room.

"Helene! How nice of you to look in on us again. Now, do take off your things and stay for supper."

Helene murmured that she was staying with a sister-in-law down in Vika and that they kept early hours there, so "thank you very much, but —" She did take off her coat, however.

Once again it seemed somehow unthinkable to talk to Fru Lund about Thjodolf. There was also a strange gentleman in the next room — Frøken Erna's husband — and that embarrassed her. And there was something about Frøken Erna herself that made Helene feel ill at ease, though Helene was unaware that it was because she knew that Frøken Erna was not quite the social equal of the other Lunds: that she was a little too condescending to be quite a lady, and a little too smartly dressed to be well dressed.

But Erna just looked in briefly to say good evening, and then disappeared again into the next room. Henriette, who was now married to a Dr. Rolstad, went back and forth setting the table for coffee over by the window, near her mother's chair; it was the maid's day off.

"The cakes aren't what they were in your day, Helene, I'm afraid. You mustn't be too critical. I'm too old to do much myself these days, and nobody has ever made *fattigmann* as well as you did."

Fru Lund knitted a child's sock, and chatted — chatted about housekeeping and her family, and asked Helene about her housekeeping and her husband. Helene had the impression that these people imagined there were only two or three things she could talk about, and that they were making efforts to keep the conversation centered on those things. Even Henriette, whom Helene had been so fond of, and who had been such a sweet child . . . No, they could never have imagined what was on her mind; and she wasn't able to turn the conversation her way even when Henriette brought out photographs of her children to show her.

It wasn't until she was on the point of leaving, and the son — who was now a lawyer — was holding her coat for her . . . Then it was that Frøken Erna stuck her head in through the curtains: "Oh Helene — how many rooms have you got — to rent in the summer, I mean?"

"We often rent the two rooms downstairs, and Mother's old bedroom in the attic."

"The thing is, I was thinking of taking rooms with you this summer, but that would be a bit cramped — although the children and the nursemaid could sleep in the attic, so that would be — Because then I'd only need to bring one maid; you could give us breakfast and supper, couldn't you, and we'd get dinner at the hotel. What do you think?"

Helene hesitated. "Well," she said softly, "it's just that I don't know whether I could manage it this year. We've been thinking of taking a foster child — that's what I came to town to see about."

"No, really? Are you going to take in a child?" said Henriette.

"A relative, then, or — ?" asked Frøken Lovisa.

"Don't you do it, Helene!" said Erna. "You've no idea what you're taking on — you've never had any of your own. You just don't know what trouble it is — and how little they pay foster parents. It's true, you know. Oh, Helene, don't do it."

"Well, you see, it's sort of lonely being on my own so much. And he's such a beautiful little boy, the one we're thinking of," said Helene. "Such a good baby —"

Old Fru Lund pulled forward a chair. "Sit down again for a minute, Helene. You can't be in that much of a hurry, surely."

And almost before Helene knew it she had told them all about Thjodolf. Fru Lund and Henriette were very attentive, and she saw that they understood. Even the money was easy to talk about; and she never mentioned Julius at all. It was obvious that she would need a little cash for expenses at first, and for something in reserve.

"I tell you what, Helene," said Erna, "you can have my carriage, if you really are going to take this child. It's as good as new — it just needs touching up with a bit of enamel, and your husband can do that."

"Oh, that's very kind — thank you — but I couldn't accept it."

"Nonsense! It only takes up space where it is."

"But you might need it again —"

"God forbid. I'll take care of that. Two's plenty for *me,* thank you."

To her annoyance, Helene felt herself blushing. She felt the blood mounting to her cheeks for shame at the way the other woman spoke.

Lawyer Lund was thinking how odd it was that he had never noticed the beauty of Helene. Hers was a type one most often met abroad; in France and Italy he had seen nuns with that kind of face: pale and pure, hardened and sensitive at the same time.

He walked into town with her.

"Yes, of course; you know I'll help you borrow from the bank. But how is it you want to leave your husband out of it?"

"Oh — well," said Helene slowly. "I somehow thought it would be right for *me* to pay a little to have the boy — I shall have the most pleasure from him, after all."

"Now, listen, Helene. My wife and I give a couple of hundred kroner every year to orphanages and so on — in memory of our little girl who died. But if you'd allow us to give you the money you need — no, no, you know I understand — it couldn't possibly be put to better use for a child. No, you can't refuse — and don't thank me, either. Thjodolf can do that when he's older — after he's thanked you . . ."

3

The evening that Helene brought Thjodolf home there was a fresh southwest wind, so that the steamer was delayed.

She had half expected Julius to be on the dock, for it was the time when he was usually at home. But there was no one. She had to leave the carriage in storage, for she had wrapped it up. Tired and dizzy after the voyage in the hot, nauseating cabin — Helene was not a good sailor — she set off for home with the basket and the child bundled in shawls in her arms. The ground was wet and icy, and she slipped and slid, for the wind was behind her and it was hard to see where she was going; the lights wavered and flickered as the wind tore at the lamps. The roar of the fjord and the rushing of the wind in the treetops in the yards filled her ears. Now and then cold drops of melting snow fell on her, and she drew the shawl still closer about the child and began to run a little through the dark, dissolving night.

It was dark at home. The four windows facing the road were always dark and blind, for they belonged to the two rooms they never used; but whenever there was anyone in, the light from the kitchen window at the gable end shone out onto the bushes. The house was a pretty little white one, standing on a slope; the yard ran right down to the road and ended with a high stone wall.

The slope was like glass, and water was pouring down it. Helene found the key in a hollow of the stone wall where she had put it when she left. And when she let herself in, she felt the chill, raw air from the dark kitchen coming to meet her. Julius probably hadn't been home at all since she'd gone away.

It was too cold here for the baby; she had to take him over to Fru Hansen and ask her to keep him for the moment.

There were three or four women in the little basement shop, and of course they clustered about Helene when she came in with the bundle of shawls and explained that this was her new foster child. They all went into the back room with her and peeked as she unwound the shawls and laid the baby in Fru Hansen's bed. Then they began to ask questions. Helene disliked this; she had always been in the habit of keeping herself to herself. But, "Well, he's a good little fellow," she said, with a smile that was half troubled, half proud.

But the women cried: "Bless my soul — eight weeks d'you say he is? Puny for his age, then. Poor mite — looks like rickets to me. One payment, once and for all, eh? Ah, he'll never make old bones — dear me, no, I can see that from his eyes, mark my words."

Helene's face was flushed and her lips were pressed hard together when she came back to her kitchen. She rattled and clattered the burners of the stove and punched the eiderdowns with her fists when she stripped the bed to get the chill out of it. She would have to have Thjodolf in her own bed tonight, as the carriage was still down at the dock. She took out the clothes that Frøken Erdahl had given her in a basket, and looked at them. How badly washed and ironed they were! She threw them all into a pail, with the things he had wetted on the journey, and put the pail outside on the porch.

Her own baby's clothes lay in her mother-in-law's chest of drawers in the attic passage. Helene picked up the lamp and went to fetch them, and brought down her apron full. Little by little her movements became more as they usually were: gentle, quiet, swift but not hasty, as she rearranged the dresser at the foot of her bed, emptied the bottom drawer, and put the baby clothes into it. Now and then she paused to look closely at some especially finely worked garment, with its pretty lace and tucks. Yes, they were well made; they'd said so at the hospital too; she had taken the whole lot in with her, like a fool, not knowing one mustn't use one's own things there. So none of them had ever been worn.

Ah, that was to have been the christening robe. A pity, really, that Thjodolf had already been christened.

She changed the things around, removing the shirt she had hung up with the other garments to warm in front of the stove. He should have his best shirt on, his first night in the house.

Then she took the last bottle from Frøken Erdahl's basket, stood it in a saucepan of water to warm, threw her shawl around her, and ran to fetch Thjodolf.

When she had locked the kitchen door behind her again and stood in her own home with the child, she had a strange feeling; a feeling almost of embarrassment.

"Peep-peep!" She lifted him up toward the lamp. "Going to live here now, was he? Like it here then, did he? Peep-peep." How solemnly he stared at the lamp. He was perfectly good now, and yet he'd wailed all the time he was over at the shop, Fru Hansen said. "Peep-peep!" said Helene softly.

That it should be so difficult to change a baby! Helene felt all thumbs. And then he began to scream and she couldn't make out why; perhaps the wash water was too cold or too hot; she dipped her hand in over and over again. "Whadda matter den?" she asked, in the same gentle, shy voice, and fiddled with tapes and safety pins. She was drenched right through, apron, skirt, and everything, by the time she had bathed him.

She stayed there on the stool in front of the stove with the baby on her lap, and fed him. He fell asleep before he had quite finished; Helene laid him carefully in her bed and covered him over.

Then she cut bread for herself and poured out some coffee. Thoughtfully she stared at the lamp while she ate. It was just as well, really, that Julius wasn't at home; he'd only have irritated her.

She washed up the few things, and boiled milk and water for the baby as Frøken Erdahl had shown her. Then quietly she undressed.

She'd better leave a light burning tonight, perhaps; she wasn't used to having a child in her bed, and she might crush him. Helene fetched the tiny pale blue lamp from the stand in the living room, filled it, and stood it in a hand basin of water on a kitchen chair, too far from the bed for her to knock it over in her sleep. Then she put out the kitchen lamp and crept into bed beside the baby.

The little night lamp filled the room with a soft, moon-blue dusk and threw a big, round, golden splash of light on the white ceiling. Helene lay still and gazed up at it.

Soon she stole an arm around the boy and drew him to her. He was snug and warm and sleeping soundly.

She lay listening to the intermittent roar of the waves on the shore and the wind rushing in the trees. Tonight there was nothing dreadful in it. It was almost cozy to lie and listen to it; it seemed to remind her of something good that had been, once upon a time.

Twice during the night she had to get up, change the baby, and get a bottle for him. But both times she had the odd feeling that she was waking up to something good: It was lovely to lie down again in the blue glimmer of the night lamp and listen to the southwester droning around the house and the fjord waters breaking along the shore.

4

Thjodolf did well. At first he was a little out of sorts, and Helene took him to the doctor, who said that the child was delicate, but that with proper care . . . And proper care he had, especially when the spring came and he could be taken out into the fresh air; he picked up then, and thrived, so that it was a pleasure to see him. And he was such a pretty child! His light brown hair formed a big curl above his forehead, and what beautiful eyes he had . . . "Ah, he's a good boy, this boy is," Helene told him; but only when there was no one to overhear her. Julius teased her quite enough as it was over this little lad of hers.

All the same, Julius liked having him. He had cleaned up the carriage and enameled it until it was as good as new, and on his Sundays at home he liked to go out with Helene when she took the baby for an airing. On weekdays she usually stood Thjodolf's carriage under the sunny wall at the corner of the house, where she could see him from the kitchen window, but on Sunday afternoons she liked to take him into town; for she was proud enough of the pretty, well-cared-for child. None of the grand families there had a finer carriage; and there were frills on the pillowcase and lace inserts on the sheet, as well as a beautifully crocheted carriage blanket lined with blue satin. The baby's coat and cap were trimmed with swan's down.

Julius and Helene had actually gotten along better since they had taken the baby into their home. Helene might wriggle a little and say "Get along with you" when he grabbed at her, but not so irritably as she had done during the past few years. Julius knew very well that she didn't mean much by it, and that in fact she liked it when he caught hold of her and cuddled her. Now when she struggled it was more as if she were fooling with a youngster — and she turned so pink and pretty, Julius said. Remembering the time when they first knew each other, she couldn't rid herself of that strange aching feeling deep within — they were not like that together anymore. She knew Julius now; poor fellow, he couldn't help being what he was: a big, stupid boy, for all his forty-four years. But there was a lot of good in old Julius; most women had far worse husbands to put up with. If only they'd had children! He might well have been different then; there would have been more life and fun to come home to. And she was fond of poor old Julius too.

He had taken charge of Thjodolf's bankbook. There was nothing to be done about that, and it was better not to think about it. So long as Lawyer Lund didn't get to hear of it, things must stay as they were. Helene had another bankbook for the boy, and into that account she paid what she earned by her needlework. As she worked at her crocheting — she was making a bedspread for one of the ladies of the garrison — she amused herself by planning how she would show Thjodolf the book on his confirmation day. After coming home from church and having dinner — she would make roast veal that day, with cream sauce and many different sorts of jelly, followed by a layer cake like the one the Lunds had had for Erna at her confirmation — and after Julius had lain down for his nap, she would take the boy into the living room and show him his bankbook. "This is for you, from your mamma, my boy," she would say. And she would tell him how she had slaved and scraped it all together for him, ever since he'd lain in his carriage. And she'd sit with him, and they would talk quietly — so as not to wake Julius — about what to do with the money. Helene thought he ought to go to the Treider trade school. She pictured Thjodolf in his confirmation suit as a steady, ambitious young man — something like Fru Sahlkvist's Martin, only much better looking; for Martin wasn't exactly handsome. But he was the kind that got on just by being clever and reliable. Martin was head of a department now, so why not Thjodolf — at the very least?

"Yes, little man," she said, rocking the baby as she took him up to attend to him. "Is you my boy, then — is you Mamma's golden boy?" She pressed him close and smacked his hand against her cheek. "Poor Mamma — poor Mamma —"

But when Julius was at home she never talked to the child like that — never called herself Mummy. And once when Julius took Thjodolf onto his knees and butted him with his head, saying: "Ain't you scared of your daddy, then? Bump him, would you, scamp?" Helene took the boy away from him, saying rather sharply: "Don't act so silly — you know very well he's too young to play games yet, poor little mite!"

She never thought of Julius as Thjodolf's daddy, and didn't know why she disliked it when he called himself so.

—*ᴧᴧ*—

Then came a certain Sunday at the end of June.

Helene was sitting in the sun, at the table by the window. Her arms were folded and she was reading a Nat Pinkerton paperback; Julius sometimes brought one home with him.

She was enjoying herself. She had done the week's laundry; the bedspread and curtains gleamed white, and she had put on the old blue print dress with the white flowers that she liked so much. The food was ready on the stove, waiting for Julius to come in — for he had gone out with some friends. There was an appetizing smell of stew and coffee, which blended with the scent of flowers in the garden and the fragrance of the yellow roses in a vase on the table; Helene found the first blooms on the big bush at the end of the house when she put the carriage out under the sunny wall a little while before.

Then, as she looked up from her book and out at the road after Julius, she saw a bright scarlet silk parasol down by the corner. It blazed against the sun-white water and all the green that was veiled and bleached by dust and sunshine. The parasol was coming up their slope, carried by a lady in a white suit.

Probably it was someone from town coming to ask about a room for the summer, Helene thought. There came a step on the porch, then a knock on the door.

Helene opened it.

"Good morning. Is this where Engineer Johansen lives?"

"Yes, that's right," said Helene.

The lady was young and pretty, fair haired and plump. The parasol cast a faint rosy glow over her face and the upper half of her figure. She wore a white linen suit, rather short in the skirt, and white stockings and shoes.

For a moment she stood there without speaking, and Helene was on the point of telling her that all her rooms were booked for the summer. Then the lady said: "Is it you who have a foster child — a little boy called Thjodolf Erdahl? It's — I'm his mother."

Helene said nothing. The other closed her parasol, rested the tip of it on the floor of the porch and twirled the handle between her hands as she said: "I thought I must come down and see him — I have missed him so. I thought I must come down and see how he's getting on."

"Oh yes. Please come in," said Helene. "Such a state as the place is in —" She tidied the books on the table. The room otherwise was neat as a pin.

The stranger looked about her.

"I've got him outside now," said Helene. "I don't know — most likely he's asleep. He usually sleeps about this time." She went to the door and stepped out, followed by the visitor.

Of course she *had* to come when the baby had on a dirty shirt, thought Helene, and everything about him was dirty. She hadn't wanted to change him until after dinner, when they were going to the park to listen to the band: That had been the plan. His clean clothes lay freshly ironed on the table in the living room.

"Oh, what a charming garden you have," said the stranger; and then they reached the carriage, which stood on the gravel path where peonies and long-stemmed yellow lilies spilled from the old flower bed.

"Oh, how he's grown!" the mother said, and for some time she bent and looked in under the hood at the sleeping baby. "How big he's grown, my little Thjodolf — and how pretty, too!"

The mother wiped her eyes with a little handkerchief as they went in. In the kitchen she sat down in the rocking chair, dabbed her handkerchief over her face, and twisted it in her fingers. Helene sat on the same chair as before.

She wasn't really so pretty, after all. And she had powder on her face — you could see it, now that she'd been crying. She showed her legs almost to the knees, the way she sat — and her feet seemed on the point of bursting out of the white canvas shoes. Under her linen jacket she wore a thin, crumpled white blouse, through which lace underclothes could be seen, with red ribbons strung through them. She didn't look like someone who has learned to be careful after being in trouble.

"How strange it is to see him," she said, looking up at Helene.

"Yes. I expect you notice a change in him since you saw him last."

"I should think so! Poor soul, he was a wretched little thing when he was born. They didn't think he'd live, you know, up at the hospital. And, oh, how ill I was with him — and that time he was with Aunt Lovise — poor thing, she hadn't any idea how to look after a baby. Every time I went and saw him there I thought, that's the last time I shall see *him* alive. And now — !"

"And how like his daddy he is!" The mother's voice shook a little. The childless woman felt something like a stab at her heart. She remained silent.

"Oh yes — yes — yes," sighed the mother.

Helene looked down and rubbed the palm of her hand to and fro along the edge of the table as she said: "No, it can't have been easy for your aunt to have the child — she'd hardly know what to do with such a tiny baby, I expect."

"Oh no, it wasn't easy for her."

They sat quietly for a while.

"You haven't any children of your own, have you? I believe my aunt said —"

"I had a little girl," said Helene quickly. "But she died, and I never had any more." She looked down again.

Then the door opened; it was Julius. He stopped short and looked at the visitor in surprise.

"This is Thjodolf's mother," Helene told him.

"Oh yes? Good morning to you," said Julius, taking the visitor's outstretched hand.

She had risen, and now said: "And you'll be Thjodolf's foster father."

"Ay, that's about it." Julius laughed a little awkwardly. He was better looking when he didn't laugh. He was a heavy, big-boned fellow, with quick brown eyes and a brown, curly forelock, but he had lost some of his front teeth.

"Come down to have a look at your boy then, have you?"

"Yes, I thought — now that the weather's so fine —" She looked up into his face. "You can't help longing, you know. But now I see what a good place he's come to, and what kind people —" and again she put her handkerchief to her eyes.

"Aha, ay." Julius was embarrassed. "Ay, Thjodolf's the lad, all right," he rambled on. "Not that I know anything about such things, mind you — but there's such a fuss made over him you'd never believe. I get to hear it, you know. The wife —" he jerked his head backwards at Helene "— she's a caution. So he does what he's got to do on what he's got to do it on — ain't that so, Helene?" He laughed aloud and winked at them both.

"Ah, get along with you," said his wife. She was taking plates down from the rack. "We were just going to have our dinner; would you care to — ?"

"Well, thank you," said the visitor. "As a matter of fact, I was just going to ask you if there was a restaurant or something — I don't know anyone here, so —"

"An honor, Frøken, an honor. Stay and have a bite with us. Helene, I'll just nip over to Fru Hansen and get another bottle of beer —" and Julius swung out the door.

"If you stay, you'll be able to see him when he wakes," said Helene, and she put out knives and forks.

Julius was in high good humor during the meal. And Thjodolf's mother — her name was Fanny Erdahl — began to liven up. She chattered away about herself — about how horrid and spiteful the other women had always been when she worked in the office of a paper business in Storgaten where she met Thjodolf's father. Now she was cashier at a big butcher shop out Grønland way. And here too it seemed she had quarreled with the rest of the staff. Julius doubled up with laughter at her account of the butcher's fat, conceited wife, and of how Fanny wouldn't be spoken to like that and answered back.

It was while they were having coffee that Helene heard the baby crying, and both women ran out to fetch him.

Fanny Erdahl laughed and wept by turns in delight over her child; she thought he was so sweet. She took him on her lap to give him his porridge; for he had begun to eat porridge from a spoon now. And she laughed because he was so greedy and she herself so clumsy; she spilled the food on the table and down the boy's bib. Then suddenly she lifted the child into the air and stared at the mustard-yellow patch that had appeared on the lap of her white suit — she looked in amazement at Helene and Julius and then at the stain again. Helene couldn't help smiling, and Julius laughed and slapped his thighs.

"That's kids for you! You can't never trust 'em, eh? Hee-hee-hee!"

Helene had to feed Thjodolf. Then she changed him and dressed him in the new white smock and linen hat. There were no bounds to his mother's rapture; he was *such* a beautiful boy.

Frøken Erdahl went to the park with them and listened to the music. Helene had washed out the mess Thjodolf had made and ironed the skirt dry; and Julius was quite proud to be walking out with the charming lady; for charming she was with her red parasol against the afternoon sun. Her face and the top part of her suit looked quite rosy. She and Julius walked ahead, talking, and Helene followed silently with the carriage a step or two behind them.

Helene and Julius went with Fanny to the dock with Thjodolf in the carriage. And she thanked them repeatedly for the pleasant day she had spent with them.

Julius smirked and chuckled all that evening. "One of the right sort, she was," he kept saying. "No flies on *her.*"

"Ugh, I thought she was just a show-off," said Helene.

"Show-off, d'you call her?" Julius laughed even more. He was sitting on the edge of the bed, pulling off his socks. And he threw his arms around Helene, who was just going to get into bed. "Everybody can't be as prim and proper as you, you know!"

"That's the kind you like — I can see that," said Helene tartly, and she broke away from him, adding as she settled down in the bed, "You'd have liked somebody like that for a wife, I expect."

"For a *wife?* No fear. Not *that* one. I wasn't born yesterday. No, you're the sort to marry."

Helene received his caresses, though she was still a little annoyed with him. And just as she was dropping off to sleep she heard Julius chuckling to himself again, "Ay, by golly, she was one of the right sort, that Frøken Erdahl!"

5
_____

For Helene the summer passed quietly and peacefully. She had rented her rooms to two elderly single ladies from Kristiania, who cooked their own meals on a spirit stove and needed no waiting on, so that she had leisure to sit for long spells in the porch and work at the curtains that Frøken Erna had ordered. She had made an excuse not to rent her rooms to Erna — somehow she didn't feel like having people she knew on top of her — and Erna had rented a house farther along toward Husvik. Sometimes her nursemaid looked in on Helene when she was out walking with the two little girls; she was a pleasant, quiet, elderly person, and the children were quite well behaved. The elder one loved to push Thjodolf in his carriage to and fro in front of the porch. They were well brought up, and thanked Helene very prettily when she gave each of them a plate of berries from the garden. One Sunday Henriette came too; she was staying with her sister. She had coffee with Helene and was very friendly; she said that Thjodolf was an exceptionally pretty baby and that he had an unusual amount of hair for his age. None of hers had had nearly as much.

Julius was now working on a boat that made shorter trips, so that during that summer he was more often at home. Not that he stayed about the house much when he was ashore; he went out with the boys and was quite often a little fuddled when he came home. He wasn't as easy to get money out of, either, as he had been, and once or twice Helene had to be quite stern with him over it.

But in general she took her husband's failings fairly lightly now. Julius was a kind fellow at heart and did his best to behave himself at home, even when he'd had a skinful. On the whole they got on pleasantly enough together, and Julius was helpful and handy about the house. He would bring back freshly caught fish, which Helene cooked and served with parsley butter and crisp-bread spread thick with farm butter, and new potatoes from the garden; and with it went a half bottle of beer and a big nip for Julius. Helene would allow no spirits in the house except for the bottle of aquavit she herself bought and kept locked up in the cupboard. She poured out a generous dram for his dinner, and that was that. He submitted to this and never tried to drink any more at home; she'd broken him of that habit.

Only once was there trouble. It was a Sunday early in September, and that woman Fanny Erdahl came to see Thjodolf. Helene had been looking forward to a nice day; Julius had been out the night before and brought back a fine cod, and during the week he had picked raspberries for her. She had made jelly of them, and with the remains had prepared an extra-special dish of raspberry fool, which they were to have for dinner. Then that Fanny arrived, early in the morning when Julius was still in bed. Helene stayed with her at the bottom of the garden while he got up, and then it somehow came about that Julius took Fanny for a walk up to Seiersten while Helene tidied the house and fixed the dinner.

When they sat down at the table, Julius jokingly offered the lady a dram, which she accepted. So Helene had to leave the bottle on the table. Julius took full advantage of this, and Fanny herself wasn't backward either. Helene couldn't make her out. At first she had thought that Fanny claimed to be a lady and imagined herself a cut above them. Not that having a child by a married man was particularly ladylike; but her father had been a primary school teacher and she must have had a decent sort of upbringing. Yet there she sat swallowing drink after drink, saying *skål* and simpering and playing up to Julius — oh, well, she must just be made like that, the hussy, and couldn't help showing off to every man she saw.

After dinner the other two took it into their heads to go for a row in the fine weather. Helene couldn't go with them; she dared not take Thjodolf out on the water, for he had a cold and was a little out of sorts anyway, as he was teething. Frøken Erdahl did say something about Helene finding someone to sit with him for a little, but she could hear from her tone of voice that they weren't eager to have her with them. So off they went, the two of them, while Helene sat at home with the baby, who was whiny and whimpery and snively, and his skin was rough and chapped. She rocked and soothed him in her lap and walked up and down the kitchen crooning to him. And now and then she pressed his little face to her cheek: "Thjodolf's *my* boy, isn't he? My own little boy, he is — mine."

Why that woman kept haunting the place was more than Helene could understand. After all, she had given the boy away. And when she did come, she barely glanced at him; she wanted to swim — go for a walk — pick flowers. But no doubt she liked having a place to go to on Sundays.

Once Fanny mentioned that her aunt wanted very much to come out with her one day to see Thjodolf. Helene said yes, certainly, it would be very nice if old Frøken Erdahl would come. And she bought a roast for the day she expected them; she wanted to have everything especially nice for the old soul: it probably wasn't often she got out anywhere. And then Fanny went and brought a girlfriend instead, saying she hoped Fru Johansen didn't mind, but that she *had* said she might bring somebody. And the friend was another of the same sort.

It was dreadful. Poor Thjodolf, having that mother to be ashamed of when he grew up. For if Fanny didn't go straight off the rails sooner or later — well, it would be a marvel, thought Helene.

"But never you bother your head about that, Toddie," she said to the baby in the carriage. "You're my boy, see, and Helene's your mamma — isn't she, my precious?"

—◦◦◦—

But the last time that Fanny Erdahl came down to see the child, Helene felt quite sorry for her. It was at the end of November and the weather was frightful, but Fanny had on a gray check suit of some sort of thin fabric with hardly any wool in it; an old spring suit probably, out of date in style, and dirty, with several buttons missing. Under it she wore a miserable little crocheted cardigan and a stained, bright red satiny blouse of some thin, sleazy material. She was soaked through, and Helene had to loan her a change of clothes; and when she hung Fanny's things out to dry, she noticed that her boots were split and her stockings full of holes.

Julius wasn't at home that day, so Helene hadn't meant to cook any dinner. But she brewed some strong coffee and boiled some eggs and spread crackers with goat's cheese, and Fanny ate as if she hadn't seen food for days. Tears kept coming to her eyes too, but at first she didn't say much. She asked if she might give Thjodolf his egg, but he had begun to be shy of strangers, and screamed when his mother tried to take him, so that Helene had to set him on her own lap. He sat there fairly contentedly, smearing himself with his cracker, and his mother sat and gazed at him while her tears dripped and dripped. Helene was sorry for the woman and said, "They're all like that for a time, you know —

shy of strangers. When he gets older, and remembers you from one time to the next, like —"

The mother burst into loud weeping. "I just don't know when the next time will be!

"I've lost my job now," she went on eventually. "And it won't be easy for me to get another. I don't dare show myself to anybody even — I've no clothes or anything."

Little by little it all came out. She had lost her position because her accounts were wrong, and the butcher's wife had vowed that wherever Fanny went next her employers should know what kind of person she was. She was wild because her husband had liked Fanny — as if Fanny could help that! Ugh, he was a disgusting old beast; often he'd taken such liberties with her that she felt quite sick; he was an old pig. But she hadn't dared to choke him off too sharply, or she'd have been fired for that. And the old hag had been up telling tales to Aunt Lovise, giving her *her* version, and Aunt Lovise was so furious that Fanny would never dare show her face there again. Now she was staying with a girl — a friend of hers — who rented a maid's room up on Neuberggaten, but she couldn't stop there for long because Selma herself wasn't too well off, poor thing. If only Fanny could have gotten a bit of sewing to do; Selma had a sewing machine.

Helene wanted to comfort the poor woman, but it wasn't easy to find anything to say. So she made more coffee and did some sewing, letting her talk until she grew calmer. And bit by bit Fanny's mood brightened. Thjodolf became used to the unfamiliar face and was no longer afraid; Helene picked him up and made him show off his few little tricks: pat-a-cake pat-a-cake, butt-a-billy-goat, and peek-a-boo through his fingers. He was more than eleven months old now, and had six teeth, and he crawled about when Helene put him down on the floor. He was very sweet, and often so funny that you could die laughing.

Outside, the rain and sleet poured down, so they stayed cozily indoors. Fanny took Thjodolf onto her lap, and he was gentle and sweet; he played with the buttons of her blouse and tried to bite them, and when she poked him under the chin and said "tickle-tickle!" he laughed till he nearly choked.

Helene asked Fanny to spend the night, thinking it would be so miserable for her to set out in that awful weather and not get back to town until late at night — and then to trudge wet and wretched and alone back to the friend's room on Neuberggaten. So Helene got supper and bathed Thjodolf, though he had had a bath the evening before, so that his mother might watch him splashing in the basin. And Fanny laid the fresh, clean, sweet baby in the carriage and sat and rocked him until he fell asleep.

"Oh dear, oh dear!" she said, and wept again. "If only I could have kept him myself. Surely you must understand — if a stranger like you can be so fond of him, what must I feel — his own mother!"

———〰———

The winter went on and Helene heard no more from Thjodolf's mother — not even on the boy's birthday or at Christmas; she didn't even know her current address.

In March Julius took a job as an engineer at a factory in Kristiania. He talked of selling the Drøbak place, so that they could move into town for good; but there was a housing shortage there now, so for the time being Julius was to share a room with a fellow workman and Helene would stay on in Drøbak. He came out there on Sundays, but not every Sunday.

Helene didn't mind very much. She only hoped this arrangement might last, though it meant that she would see even less of her husband than before, for she dreaded having to move to town. For one thing, she was afraid that if she did, Fanny Erdahl would be continually on her doorstep. But apart from that, she had grown very fond of her home and her garden, and marveled that Julius could bear to think of leaving.

The child was now such fun and such good company that she wished for nothing more. He was a little puny, poor little soul, certainly; he had a touch of rickets and caught cold easily, so that she had been afraid of bronchitis and had taken him to the doctor twice. But thank goodness it had been no more than an ordinary chill.

"He's not very strong," the doctor said. "But with all the good care you take of him, Fru Johansen, he'll grow up fine and sturdy yet; there's nothing there to worry about."

And when spring came, for the second time in Thjodolf's life, he could call "Mamma!" and say "b'ead" and "seeze" when Helene put bread and cheese on the table; and when she ran her errands, carrying him on her arm, he pointed to all the animals they met and said "pussy." In the shops she set him down on the floor, for he could stand now if he held on to her skirt. Helene was very proud of her boy. He wasn't as chubby as some, but the doctor said it wasn't a good thing for babies to be too fat — and there wasn't a child in the whole town with such beautiful brown curly hair as little Thjodolf had.

There were big, yellowish buds on the bushes in the yard, and the spirea hedge was a tender, luminous green. Swallows flashed around the house in lightning sweeps and darted with chirps and twitters in and out of their nests under the eaves.

Helene walked along the flower bed in front of the house and saw how big the auricula buds were, and how the daffodils were coming along. She carried the child on her arm and put him down on the sun-warmed gravel of the path; then she ran three or four steps away from him, and crouched down. The child stood for a moment, made a face as if he were going to cry, sagged at the knees and stretched his arms out to Helene. Then all at once he plucked up courage, and with a little squeak like the swallows' he staggered the few steps to the mother and fell into her outstretched arms.

Helene rejoiced and pressed him to her, and the tiny boy rejoiced too, delighted with his own achievement. They did it again and again, and Thjodolf grew more and more enraptured with the new game.

In another six weeks, when the yellow rosebushes were in full bloom, Helene could sit on the lawn with her sewing and keep an eye on Thjodolf as he tottered about fairly briskly, playing with a big wooden horse that Julius had brought back from town. Helene had named it Jakob after a horse they had had at her old home when she was small, but Thjodolf called it Lakel.

———————

One weekday in July when Helene was ironing, the kitchen door opened behind her and Fanny Erdahl walked in.

She was beaming all over her face and was as changed as could be: cheerful and pretty, smartly and stylishly dressed in a tailor-made suit of gabardine, high brown boots of the kind that had buckles high up around the calf, and a pale blue hat of net on her golden-yellow hair.

"Busy as ever!" she cried in greeting; and Helene noticed that her tone was quite different from what it had ever been before. It was guarded — almost patronizing.

"And there's my Toddie! There's my darling boy. How fine and big you've grown — come along to Mamma, then; let me look at you. Give Mamma a kiss."

Thjodolf was no longer frightened of strangers, and he came fairly readily;

but when his mother went on kissing and kissing him he grunted a little and pushed away her face with his little hands. Then, seeing the chocolate and the big teddy bear she had brought him, he settled down quite contentedly in her lap.

Helene folded the ironing cloth, set the iron at the back of the stove, and cleared away the clothes. Then she put on the coffeepot.

"Ah, coffee!" said Fanny Erdahl. "How lovely that'll be. And, oh, how happy I am to be sitting here again — how I've longed for this!" Her eyes sparkled with delight as she looked into Helene's face.

"You'll never guess what great news I have for you this time," she said, as Helene poured out the coffee and put down the pastry that she had fetched. Fanny Erdahl paused for a moment. "I'm going to — I've gotten married!" she said, and bent over Thjodolf, who was dabbling his bun in her coffee cup.

"Well, imagine!" said Helene, and sat still. "Was this recently? Congratulations!" she added hastily.

"Thank you. It was two months ago," was the quick reply. "And you can't think what a nice husband I've got, Fru Johansen! Imagine, he's a foreigner — an Austrian — well, a Hungarian really, I believe. His name's Burg, so I'm Fru Burg now."

"That is," she whispered mysteriously, "that isn't his whole name — I can't say any more just now. But when peace comes — Oh, he's been through a lot, Rudolf has — terribly exciting, you know, but *dreadful* — and *so* interesting! He was in the war, you know, and was wounded and everything, but it was all so ghastly that he couldn't stand it any longer — and so now he doesn't dare go back to Germany — Austria, rather — not while the war's on, anyway. And so he's over in this country now, and has something to do with buying — fish, I think it is — and he writes for the papers too —" and so she went on talking and talking.

My goodness, thought Helene. Might have known she'd get mixed up in something shady.

"Well, the point *is*," said Fanny, squeezing the child to her, "what I really came to tell you — Rudolf, my husband, is mad about children, and what do you think, he wants us to have Thjodolf at home with us —" and she kissed the boy's hair passionately.

Helene sat speechless, incapable of thinking a single thought.

"I expect you'll miss him a bit at first," said Fanny comfortingly, "but you must come and see us, you know — mustn't she, Toddie? Helene tum and see us in town.

"We won't have the apartment ready for another week," she went on, "so I can't take him now. But in a week we thought we'd come down and fetch him — Rudolf and me, I mean."

"But you gave him away for good, to be brought up as our own child," said Helene softly. "So you must surely understand — you can't possibly take him back again just like that." And involuntarily she put out her hand to the child.

Thjodolf was sitting quietly and happily on his mother's lap, playing with her handbag.

"Ah, yes, that was *then,*" said Fanny a little airily. "Why, at that time I was at my wit's end what to do or where to turn. But everything's different now."

Helene sat with her mouth open. "But we took him to bring up as our own," she kept saying, tonelessly.

"But of course, my dear Fru Johansen, I know that — that was how it was then. But surely you realize that you can't refuse to let a mother have her own child — now, can you? — when circumstances are so changed that she can keep him."

Helene said nothing.

"Of course I know you'll feel it at first," said Fanny. "But, after all, you *are* only his foster mother, so it isn't as if he was your own. And being so fond of him yourself, you'll appreciate my feelings as his real mother."

Helene made no answer.

"Naturally I feel for you very much," the mother went on. "But as it's *my* child — And you know," she added brightly, "you'll have no trouble in finding another child — one that's lost his mother. I'd be glad to recommend you to the foster child bureau."

Helene raised her eyes from Thjodolf's face to his mother's.

"I'm just wondering whether it's legal," she said, almost threateningly.

Thjodolf's mother caught the midday boat back to town. Helene still couldn't take in all that had been said, either by herself or by the other woman. She was numb.

The little boy toddled about the room with his toys and Helene could hardly bring herself to touch him, as if she were afraid that every time she took hold of him she would come to love him even more.

That evening, after Thjodolf had fallen asleep, she knocked on the door of the living room. The same two elderly ladies were staying with her as had come the year before. One of them worked in a government office. Helene told them what had happened and asked whether they thought she was required to let the baby go.

Whether she was legally required to do this, Frøken Sand could not say for certain, but she believed that by Norwegian law Helene could not refuse, as she had not formally adopted the boy. Morally, at any rate, she surely could not feel she had the right to withhold a child from his mother.

Helene murmured that there was another side to it — that the mother wasn't all she should be.

"But that's why!" the other lady — a schoolteacher — broke in. "That's it. There have been so many examples — and it's really a miracle to see how an irresponsible — a really *quite* irresponsible — girl can be saved when she's allowed to keep her baby. Nothing guards a woman from going astray so well as being allowed to be a mother to her child."

"And there are so many abandoned, helpless little ones that would give you an outlet for your maternal feelings, Fru Johansen. For every child you can adopt, twenty need your care."

—◦◦◦—

Helene wrote to Julius that evening, telling him he must come home on Sunday, as she had something important to talk to him about.

But Julius said the same thing as the ladies in the living room. If the mother wanted her child back, they couldn't refuse. But mostly he talked about Fanny's marriage, which seemed to amuse him enormously. Whew, that just about suited her! Because of course there was something fishy about that Burg chap — he must be some sort of spy.

They were in the yard, for Julius felt that since he was here, he might as well give the flagpole another coat of paint. He laid it on the ground and went on painting it as he talked on and on about Fanny and Burg. Helene stood by him with Thjodolf on her arm; she was taciturn and stony faced. The ladies leaned out of the window and gave their opinion, and again they said how easily Helene could find another baby in need of her care. Helene crushed the boy to her until he began to cry, and her expression grew even harder.

But Julius thought it was a good idea. This time they'd take care to find a child of decent parents, then there wouldn't be all this fuss. They must get hold of one belonging to a real spinster lady, for one could be sure that people of that sort would never ask for him back.

———∿∿∿———

Helene washed all Thjodolf's clothes, looked them over carefully, and packed them, all mended and neat, in two big cardboard boxes. Day after day went by; every morning Helene woke with the same feeling of tension and went about absorbed in her own thoughts, so that she hardly saw or heard the little boy, and did not answer his prattling.

When the week was up, Helene began to think that perhaps something had happened to prevent it; perhaps the husband had changed his mind. Then again, perhaps not. She dared not dart at the child, talk to him, and play with him as in the days when she believed he was her own. But in the evenings when he had fallen asleep, Helene sat at the kitchen table staring out at the summer night with unseeing eyes, and almost holding her breath with suspense. Suppose it never —

Nearly three weeks passed, and then one day they came — Fanny and her husband. He was a fat little man with curly brown hair, brown whiskers, brown eyes, and a great many white teeth with bluish fillings in them. He looked kind; he smiled all the time and snapped his fingers at Thjodolf: *"Bubi! Bubi! Hübscher Bub!"* Fanny was radiant; so merry and lively that she couldn't keep still a minute.

Helene packed the last of Thjodolf's things and fetched his blue coat with the lion buttons and his sailor cap. Fanny put them on the boy.

"Say good-bye nicely to Mamma Helene, now, Toddie. Go and give Mamma Helene a kiss, Bubi!"

But the boy didn't understand; he had no idea that he was about to leave his home.

"Good-bye, good-bye," said Fanny Burg. "Thank you again so very much — and mind you come and see us soon. Good-bye, good-bye!"

The German bowed gallantly, all smiles. Then he took the little blue-clad figure on his arm. Fanny carried the boxes. And they left.

The window was open. Helene heard the boy beginning to cry; they were at the foot of the slope now. "Mamma!" cried Thjodolf. Helene stood in a corner of the room, pressed against the wall, and didn't look out.

7

Twice Helene went to Kristiania, meaning to go and see how Thjodolf was getting on. But she couldn't bring herself to do it. She walked along Sverdrupsgaten, past the house where the Burgs were living, hoping she might see Thjodolf out on the pavement with the other children. But he wasn't there.

It was just as well, of course, that Fanny didn't let the tiny fellow out by himself; he might easily get run over or something. But when it came to the point, Helene couldn't bring herself to go up and see Fanny; she would have felt like a beggar.

So Helene did the things she had to do, and went home. She started for the cemetery, but turned back. She wondered whether to call on the Lunds, but decided she didn't feel up to it. She would have liked to ask Lawyer Lund a few questions — but then there was this business about the money. Julius had squandered all that they'd been given for Thjodolf, as well as the hundred kroner from the lawyer.

At last, on her third visit to town, she did go and call on Fru Burg. She had dreamed about Thjodolf several times lately, and although she couldn't quite remember the dreams she had the impression that something was wrong, so that she woke with a feeling of dread.

It was a scorching day at the end of August, and the air in the streets was thick with dust. Warm, nasty smells filled the staircase where the Burgs lived. Helene had to wait for a long time after ringing the bell under the little brass plate that bore a foreign name. At last, after she had rung two or three times and was on the point of going away, the door opened a crack: It was on the chain.

"Why, it's you!" twittered Fanny's voice delightedly. She banged the door, undid the chain, and opened the door again wide. "How nice of you to call, Fru Johansen! Come along in. I thought you must have forgotten all about Toddie and me — please forgive the state we're in — I wasn't expecting visitors, as you can see."

She was in a petticoat, corset, and a rather grubby shift; and the same bedroom smell that came from her seemed to fill the room into which she showed Helene. There was a daybed along one wall, unmade; the covers had just been smoothed over it a little.

Apart from the daybed, the room was rather bare, though the few pieces of furniture in it seemed good. There was a very elegant writing desk by one window — one of the American kind that Helene had seen displayed in the shops, with a rolltop to pull down and lock. On one windowsill stood a dead hothouse rose with crumpled tissue paper and ribbons around the pot; in the other window stood an open cardboard box overflowing with sewing things.

Through an open door could be seen a bedroom that had not yet been tidied. Fanny ran in and came back at once with Thjodolf on her arm and a pink bed jacket in the other hand. The boy had evidently been roused from sleep that very moment; he whimpered and rubbed his eyes. His hair was soaked with sweat.

His mother sat him on the floor, put on the bed jacket, and tucked her hair into a little lace cap.

"Who's this, Thjodolf? Don't you remember Helene? Why, I really don't believe he knows you! Poor mite, he's so sleepy. Bubi —

"Everything's in such a state. I've been so dreadfully tired these past few days. We had someone staying here — a friend of my husband's — but now they've gone to Bergen, he and my husband; they left the day before yesterday, so I've been taking it easy since then . . .

"Yes, poor mite, he looks a bit peaky today — yes, you're right, he doesn't look well. Oh, it's nothing serious, you know — just his tummy. It's this hot weather — and then he caught such a cold. We were out at Bygdøn, my husband and his friend and me and the boy, and he got so hot that day, and it's a bit chilly in the evenings now."

She darted out into the passage and came in again with a raincoat over her jacket and petticoat, to look for money behind a few knickknacks on a shelf. Helene said something about not wanting to make trouble.

"Oh, we were going to have something ourselves, anyway. We haven't had dinner yet."

Helene stayed with the child.

"Thjodolf," she coaxed. "Thjodolf, my precious, don't you know me, then?

Have you forgotten your mamma?" she whispered, crouching down before the boy, who drew away from her.

It seemed so. The boy stood mute, with a finger in his mouth, looking at her. And, dear God, how thin he'd become! His face was yellowish white and his dark curly hair clammy with sweat.

"Oh, my precious, precious boy!"

Fanny returned and put three small bottles of beer, a jug of milk, and a bag of pastry on the table.

"There's no coffee left in the house," she explained. "And it would have made it so late if I'd dressed and gone all the way to the grocer's. You'll have to take things as you find them."

Thjodolf toddled along the walls in such a funny way. Now and then he came up to his mother and drank from the cup of milk. Helene thought how he had been in the old days: She hadn't been able to sit down for a bite herself without his rushing to her crying: "Toddie sit Mamma's lap — Toddie taste Mamma's dinner!"

"Goodness, do you give him unboiled milk — when his tummy's upset, too!" exclaimed Helene, horrified.

But Fanny explained that that was just the reason. She had read somewhere that fresh milk was much more digestible than boiled milk, and much more nourishing, she said rather importantly. Though, indeed, there was little enough left of that rather superior air that Helene had noticed the past few times she had seen her. She was more as she had been during her worst period. Poor soul, there must be something wrong somewhere. At any rate she was genuinely delighted to see Helene.

"I think you should take him to the doctor," said Helene, whose eyes never left Thjodolf.

Fanny said that she had thought of it, but that it was so difficult for her to get away. And then the money. The clinic? Yes, but that was so early in the morning. And the money; she found it so hard to make ends meet. Rudolf said that he didn't know any town in Europe more expensive than Kristiania. And his money came in so irregularly; sometimes they had more than enough, and at other times they were very hard up. Fanny went on talking feverishly about her husband and his affairs, and boasting, and she hinted again at some secret about his name: He was a more important person than anyone dreamed. He was so kind; he had such fine manners. But Helene could see that she wasn't saying all this because she felt superior or happy, poor soul; quite the contrary.

At last Fanny came out with what was on her mind. She needed some things for the boy — Bubi, she called him — and she didn't feel she could ask Ruddi — oh, not that he didn't like the boy; he adored him, and Helene mustn't think he didn't — but all the same, *you* know. In short, the bankbook in Thjodolf's name that Helene had once shown her — could Helene loan her the money in that account?

Helene looked at the pallid child — her baby, whatever the world might say, even if the other woman was his mother fifty times over. He was wearing his pretty blue Sunday smock, and it was so filthy in front that it was practically matted. And one underpant leg hung down to the top of his boot. He had an old silk handkerchief tied around his neck, his nose was running, and his eyes were quite swollen from his cold.

Helene said yes, she would send the money the very next day, if Fanny would take Thjodolf to the doctor immediately. When she was leaving she took Thjodolf in her arms, wiped his nose thoroughly — wiped his whole pretty little face — and then kissed him warmly, three or four times.

Some weeks later she went into Kristiania again to see Thjodolf. This time she took Julius along; she somehow felt that this would lend authority to the visit.

The child still had a cold, but he looked better. Fanny said she had taken him to the doctor, who assured her that there was nothing seriously the matter with the boy. The house was tidier, and Fanny was dressed. She was quite radiant with delight at this visit and asked them to stay and have dinner with her. She gave them sausages and beer followed by coffee. In a way it was all quite enjoyable — if only Thjodolf hadn't been so shy; he must have forgotten his foster parents altogether.

Burg wasn't at home this time either; he traveled about a great deal and was in Stockholm now, Fanny thought.

But when Helene rang the bell on Sverdrupsgaten one day at the end of September, no one answered. Burg's nameplate was still there, but when Helene inquired at the apartment opposite, the woman told her that the Burgs had left and that there were some other foreigners in the place now — three or four men whom no one in the house knew anything about. What had become of the Burgs she didn't know; she'd heard they lived somewhere out in Asker, but they didn't seem too keen on people knowing their address. Yes, they'd paid the rent very punctual — it was handy for them, that apartment, you know, whatever it was they wanted it for; there was goings-on enough there, the Lord knew. But they owed money in the shops around about. As to their being married — well, nobody in the house believed *that* tale, the woman said.

—∿∿—

One afternoon in November Fru Hansen at the shop persuaded Helene to go with her to a revivalist family who had a preacher visiting them from Kristiania. They had coffee, and afterward the preacher spoke — very well and beautifully, Helene thought. In general she didn't care for the to-do the revivalists made, but this man Løvstø talked so serenely and sensibly that Helene had something to think about as she went home.

It might have been half past ten when Helene took hurried leave of Fru Hansen at the foot of her own hill. It was nasty wet weather and pitch dark, so there was no temptation to linger in the road. Helene hastened up the slope and was just going to run up the porch steps when she sensed that something dark was pressed against the wall. She started.

"It's only me, Fru Johansen," said a thick, tearful voice, and Helene recognized Fanny Erdahl.

"Dear God — !"

The other stood up. Helene knew without seeing it that she had the child in her arms.

"Dear God," said Helene again; she ran up and unlocked the door. The other woman slunk in like a wet dog and stood just inside the door while Helene lit the lamp. She was holding Thjodolf in her arms, wrapped up in her raincoat.

"Never in all my days . . ." said Helene, and found no more words. But she went over and took the bundle; it was sopping wet on the outside.

"He's asleep," said his mother. "He's slept a long time." Her voice broke. "We've been waiting since six o'clock. I went over to the Hansens', but there was nobody there either."

Helene took the raincoat and the other outer clothes off Thjodolf without waking him. She laid him on the bed and untied his wet boots. Good God, how thin his legs were.

"Take off your things," she said to Fanny softly, "and I'll get some —"

She lit the stove, put on some coffee and milk, and hung out two blankets to warm. Then she went into the living room, lit the stove there, and made up the bed. Not until all that had been seen to and she began fixing some food did she say to Fanny, "You'll spend the night, of course."

"Thank you," said Fanny meekly. She was in the rocking chair, as so often before. Helene couldn't help thinking of a stray cat that finds its way home now and then when it's had too rough a time of it.

"I was thinking — I wanted to ask you whether you'd take Thjodolf again — just for a time. I can't manage to keep him now —" and she burst out sobbing.

Helene poured out the coffee and quietly pushed the food over to Fanny. "Try to eat a little now," she said gently, and just stroked the other's arm.

Little by little Fanny grew calm enough to tell her story, weeping all the time. Burg had gone to Stockholm in September, and she hadn't seen him since. At first he'd sent her money once or twice, and a few letters, but she couldn't read German. He could speak a little Norwegian and she a little German, but she hadn't understood much of his letters. Then some other Germans came — or Finns — who were to move into her apartment, and they made her move out to Asker, where she was to live with a German woman, the wife of one of them. But it hadn't worked; they lived miserably there, and the German lady had been a horrible old hag. Then at last, a few days ago, she had heard that Rudolf had gone back to Germany and the German lady had been insolent to her and thrown her out.

And now at last she admitted that she'd never been properly married to Rudolf. He had told her he couldn't marry her until after the war, because of his papers. But he had promised so faithfully, and he'd been so kind and affectionate, and so madly in love at the beginning — well, all the time, in fact.

Fanny cried a great deal and wallowed in memories of Burg. Now and then she talked about Thjodolf's father too, and her experiences with him. Helene had never known anyone like this: Fanny seemed unable to grasp that men were irresponsible and careless. She seemed to expect that any man who spoke to her would feel obliged to take care of her, as she couldn't take care of herself. What a creature! But it was very hard on her, poor soul.

At last Helene got her settled in the living room. Thjodolf was in the double bed in the kitchen, and he woke up when Helene came in and lay down beside him. She gave him milk and bread, and he ate with a good appetite; and he was warm now, for she had tucked him up in hot blankets. But he wouldn't lie still with her; he cried and called for Mamma, so at last Helene had to take him in to Fanny.

Fanny stayed for three days. She would probably have liked to remain longer, but Helene behaved as if expecting her to leave. Fanny had absolutely no plans for her future; did Helene think she could get a situation in Drøbak? But Helene was sure she couldn't; instead, she advised her to go and make it up with her aunt, and then perhaps she could get some sewing to do, for Fanny had taken a course in dressmaking in the old days.

Two days after Fanny left Helene was down in the garden hanging out Thjodolf's underclothes, which she had mended and washed. They had come back in a shocking state — the few items that did come back.

The boy was toddling about out there, for it was fine weather for the time of year; the air was mild and moist, and a glint of sun came now and then to gild the lawn. The fir trees on the ridge behind the house shone olive-green against the sky, which was a dark gray-blue, with drifting rain clouds.

Suddenly Thjodolf came and pulled at Helene's skirt. He had something in his hand and he held it up to her, his little face alight with smiles.

"Mamma, Mamma, look — Lakel!" he said.

It was his old wooden horse, which he had found somewhere in the bushes. All the paint had come off it; it was covered with dirt, and withered leaves were sticking to it.

The boy stretched his arms up to Helene and said: "Hop-la, Mamma — hop-la!"

Helene sank to her knees on the ground and gathered him in. She hugged him and hugged him to her breast, and the tears came, so that something seemed to have broken in pieces deep inside her, and a wave welled over. She herself didn't realize that never in her life had she wept like this, and that all the tears she had never shed were flowing now.

8

She was not quite aware, either, that during the winter that followed she was different, and her whole life was different from anything that had gone before. Day followed day, full of deep joy and of a hidden, heartrending anxiety.

Tiny Thjodolf began to remember one or two other things from their former life together. One day he stood for a long time looking at the sewing machine; then he touched the shiny wheel, and immediately afterward slapped his own fingers with the other hand: "Ah, mustn't!" as Helene had sometimes done when he wouldn't let her sew in peace. He went over to the stove and put out his hand without touching it. "Ah, ah, ah, mustn't!" And he said "Hop-la, Mamma," and "Sit Mamma's lap" when there was food to be had.

And he was learning all the time: Almost every day there was something, and he was so good and sweet and funny that Helene was dizzy with joy over her child.

He *was* her child. Never again would she let him go. She thought how Fanny Erdahl might come along one day and demand to have him back, and her face went hard and cruel. She thought of what she would say: It wouldn't be pleasant. She would remind her of the two men she had lived with, and of that business of the accounts out at Grønland; she would ask whether Fanny thought that a person who couldn't look after herself was fit to look after a child. Oh no, never again should that woman get her hands on him. She had done the boy enough harm as it was, for Thjodolf had suffered a setback while he was with her.

That was the word the doctor used: A setback, he said. The boy's stomach was in a wretched state, and he had bronchitis. But the doctor said too that good nursing would set him up again all right.

And Helene did nurse him, so she had time for little more than that and her regular housework. Only four kroner had been entered in the new bankbook by February. She made thick carrot-and-kale soup, and water porridge and rye porridge; milk he was not allowed to have for the present, and he was so fond of it and begged so hard for it that often Helene was on the edge of tears at having to deny it to him. She rubbed his back and chest with warm oil, and when his cough was bad she had to lie in bed with him in the daytime, for unless she did he wouldn't stay under the covers. She lay there half undressed, and played with him and sang to him, and stole away to do the housework while he slept. There was no question now of her slipping him a tidbit to keep him quiet; chocolate and sweet things were absolutely forbidden. So when he was whiny and fractious Helene had to play with him and sing to him for hours on end.

He tried her very hard, but grew ever more deeply attached to her at the same time.

Then the spring came. Helene rejoiced, for as soon as Thjodolf could be out every day he would be bound to get stronger. She hummed as she made him a new jacket; the blue one that he had gone back to his own mother in was in such a dreadful state that she decided to make him a new one out of her old winter coat. The fabric was as good as new, though the style was very old fashioned now. It would be nice to make a new coat for herself in the autumn. She planned how she would make it. Navy blue . . . Perhaps she would cut up the old fur stole and use it to trim the coat.

Thjodolf had been coughing again lately. And one night, after a long coughing fit she heard him whooping.

The first, mild days of May had come, and the grass in the lawn was turning green. The rhubarb plants thrust their thick, lacquer-red shoots up out of the soil; the peonies raised their curly brown leaves between the gray, withered sticks of last year's stalks; and in the bed under the living-room window the shoots of the daffodils stood close, like little green knifepoints. Helene saw it all from the window, and her tears ran down for Thjodolf, who lay so pale and wretched in bed when he ought to have been out in the fine weather.

He was really ill, poor little man; he coughed and whooped until he could hardly get his breath, and he couldn't keep his food down. On the doctor's advice she had moved into the big living room with him. She stayed by him night and day, holding his forehead, supporting him during his paroxysms of coughing, and feeding him custard or broth in small helpings in the hope that he might keep it down.

On the fifteenth of May, in the evening, he developed a high fever. Helene telephoned from Fru Hansen's for the doctor, and when he came he told her that pneumonia had set in.

"Do you think he'll come through it?" asked Helene, her terrified eyes on the young doctor's face.

"There's always hope," he said softly, but Helene heard his tone and saw his face, and was inwardly frantic.

For a night and a day and a night and another day Helene fought for her precious boy's life. On the third night he was still alive, and she lay fully dressed beside him on the bed. She renewed the hot compresses on the fevered little body and the cold ones on his burning forehead. Perhaps she ought not to have lain there; it made it too warm for him, but it seemed to soothe the boy to feel her near him. He could no longer speak, but he gripped her hands and arms and clothes and clung there, when he was at all conscious.

During his last struggle he lay in Helene's arms. But in the morning, when there was daylight outside and the starlings were piping in the garden, Thjodolf died.

That evening, when Helene left the beautiful, bedecked little body in the living room, meaning to lie down in the kitchen for a little, she saw that there were blue and green bruises on her arms where Thjodolf's little fingers had clutched her in the death struggle.

—⁓—

Julius came down to the funeral with Fanny Erdahl. The mother looked unspeakably tearstained and wretched under her crepe veil. She gave the impression of being utterly distraught, although she looked well dressed in her new black clothes. She had found a good situation at a seamstress's out at Grünerløkken, it seemed. And once more Helene thought of a stray cat. She realized that Fanny had had something weighing on her mind before Thjodolf's death. Helene looked after her as well as she could, and had prepared the attic room for her, not wanting to put her in the living-room where Thjodolf had died. But she found little to say to her.

On the day of the funeral it rained. The churchyard was dreary in the extreme: The little group of mourners stood under umbrellas around the open grave. When the earth trickled from the pastor's shovel through the wreaths onto the coffin, Helene had to support the mother's arm; Fanny looked as if she would fall headlong, and she groaned like an animal in pain.

Helene herself could not weep. Her soul seemed to have been wrung out of her body during the last days. The mourners came back to the house and Helene got the dinner: roast veal and layer cake, which she had baked the day before. These were the dishes she had meant to prepare for Thjodolf's confirmation party; Helene herself hardly knew why she had chosen to serve them now — perhaps it was to try to bring her pain back to life and to feel that her heart was not altogether dead, that she could still weep to remember all she had dreamed of for her boy. She remembered as she cooked, peeled potatoes, and made sauce, but the tears did not come.

In the evening the rain stopped. There was a heavenly fragrance of birch buds and the sweaty smell of the bird-cherry shoots when Helene stood on the steps of the porch and said good-bye to her guests. Fanny offered to help her wash the dishes, but Helene said no thank you; instead, Fanny and Julius walked a little way with their visitors. Among these were relations of Julius's, who lived out beyond Husvik.

Helene had finished the dishes and tidied the house, and now sat by the window staring listlessly out into the spring night. The fjord gleamed softly under the cloudy sky; the treetops were still transparent, but were beginning to grow denser; everywhere buds were on the point of bursting. A scent of earth and growth wafted in from the garden, where a bird here and there was still awake and singing.

She would divide her auriculas — it ought to have been done this spring, anyway — and plant a thick wreath of them on the grave. Her throat tightened and her eyes smarted, but the feeling passed at once. No tears came when she tried to think of Thjodolf's grave.

Listlessly she rose and stole through the porch into the open. For a time she stood inhaling the cool, damp night air — then wandered about at random. She went over to the corner of the house and looked downhill toward the road and the fjord.

Two people were coming up the slope, walking close together. After a few steps they stopped, put their arms about each other, and stood in close embrace.

Helene glided back into the shadow of the house. Then she ran silently indoors, her knees trembling under her, and sank down on her usual chair by the window. Her shift stuck to her body; she was in a cold sweat.

A little later Fanny and Julius came in.

"You ought to a' come with us," said her husband. "It's a wonderful fine evening."

Helene could not utter a word; she was searching within her mind for phrases bitter enough, sneering and coarse enough. She groped among memories of her distant girlhood in the town for the filthy, vulgar expressions she had learned then — learned but passed by, her nose in the air, pretending not to hear them. They were in her throat, but she bit them back nevertheless.

Julius was over by the stove, shaking the kettle.

"There ain't a drop left, I s'pose?"

Instinctively Helene started to bestir herself, to do her duty as housewife. But her whole body was twitching — she felt she dared not venture across the floor, or she would do something terrible.

"I've washed up once this evening," she said thickly.

"Why, my dear, I can rinse these cups out myself —" and then Fanny met Helene's eyes. She slipped back into the rocking chair, and her face, still blotchy with weeping, turned pale: Helene looked so odd.

"I think I must go straight to bed," Fanny said faintly, a moment later. "I'm so worn out — I'm really at the end of my tether." Her voice was stifled by crying. She felt Helene's eyes stabbing her back as she slunk out, broken and sobbing.

"Ay, ay, poor soul," said Julius, sitting down at the table with a cup of tepid, muddy coffee. "It's been hard for her, all this."

Helene never moved. Her voice was level with suppressed passion as she said without looking up: "It was just an act of charity, I suppose, when you were comforting her just now."

Julius gaped.

"I saw you coming up the slope," said Helene, as before.

"Oh. That." Julius fidgeted in his seat, and his face turned dark red. "*That* —" he said quickly. "You know very well that was just a bit of nonsense. She was in such a state — I had to pat her a little — nothing for *you* to worry about."

The storm in Helene suddenly sank to calm again. Of course. She couldn't think why she had taken it like that. It was just a bit of nonsense, and she ought to be used to that by now — used to Julius fooling with girls. Why should it trouble her anymore? But now that her mind was tired and cold, her voice rang out sharply and excitedly, "I don't know how you can, Julius — what you can see in a creature like that — a flibbertigibbet who's been with one man after another — ugh!"

"Ah, now look here," said Julius in an injured tone. "I wasn't doing it for fun, you know — the poor girl was nearly out of her mind."

"I'm not surprised. She's got something to cry for, and that's a fact. She's in the family way again."

Julius reddened darkly again.

"How can you tell — ?"

Helene sent him a look sparkling with scorn. Misconstruing it, he stood up.

"Ay, ay, Helene — it's a bad business, true enough. It was treating you shabby, I know. But you got to remember this. It ain't been easy for a chap living away from home the way I do — like a lively bachelor. And she was forever hanging about and making up to me like, as coaxing as a kitten. And it's years now since you was so gentle to me — enough to notice, anyhow. Fair's fair, and you got to remember that —"

Helene stood bolt upright; she seemed turned to stone, and her face was so white that it gleamed.

"— Well, I know I done wrong. But you ain't always been such an angel to me, you know. And if you *are* too good for me, you've made me feel it often enough. I always knew the others was nothing beside you, but —"

Helene screamed — a single, long, piercing, animal scream.

"Christ!" said Julius, and moved toward her.

She turned to face him: She was frantic.

"Get away with you, you — you — Go, d'you hear me? Go up to her — go up to your whore, you piece of filth! Jesus Christ, I can't stand the sight of you — I —"

She darted past him, flung open the door of the living room, slammed it behind her, and turned the key. For a time she stood with her hand on it, her whole body shaking. Then she reeled the two or three steps to the bed and threw off the blanket and eiderdown; and as she knelt, twisting and rubbing her head and shoulders into the bedclothes, the weeping came, bitter and burning. She hugged the pillow on which Thjodolf had died, crushed it to her, and in her infinite anguish cried upon Jesus and her child.

SIMONSEN

translated by

naomi WOLFORD

Simonsen stopped in the gateway and dug out his worn, greasy old wallet, meaning to slip into it the letter of reference he had in his hand. But first he unfolded the grimy paper and read it through, although he knew it by heart:

Warehouse worker Anton Simonsen has been with our firm for three years. During this time he has shown himself to be a sober, industrious, and willing man.

N. Nielsen

Hercules Engineering Works.

No, indeed; that reference wouldn't do him much good. Damn the fellow, it was a shabby way to treat him. The boss had never minded pitching the tale to customers about delivery dates and things like that — but write the sort of reference that would get a poor devil a job — not likely! "Well, I can't state that you've carried out your work to our satisfaction," he'd said, the so-and-so. But at least he'd had to put "sober." He hadn't at first, but Simonsen had insisted. "Seems to me I've smelled drink on you from time to time, Simonsen." But Simonsen had spoken up.

"I do take a nip now and again, sir," he'd said. "And I believe you would too, if you had to spend your days rummaging about in that cold warehouse. But nobody can say Anton Simonsen was ever the worse for drink at his work — no, not even tipsy. Not once." So then his lordship had to give in and the secretary lady had to write it out again with "sober" in it. And now here it was — such as it was; no great shakes, but he had nothing better to show.

"Look out, blast you — fathead!"

Simonsen jumped aside against the wall as a cartload of clattering iron girders swung into the gateway. Steam rose from the horses' damp backs as they threw themselves into the collar to drag the sleigh over the bare cobblestones under the arch. The driver shouted something else after him, but Simonsen couldn't hear it for the din of the clashing girders.

He put away his letter of reference and slipped the wallet into his breast pocket. Then he glanced indignantly after the sleigh. It was standing in the yard in front of the warehouse, under the crane that projected with its chain and pulley from a dark hole above the barred windows in the blackish red wall. White steam was rising from the horses' backs, and their coats were matted into little wet, frosty tufts. The driver hadn't put their blankets on them; he was talking to another man.

Simonsen buttoned up his winter overcoat, which was fairly new and tidy, straightened himself up, and threw out his stomach. A sense of his dignity as a citizen arose in him; he was, after all, a respectable member of society, and that ruffian of a driver had bawled at him. And with this feeling something else stirred within him at the sight of the two cart horses, which had hauled their load until the muscles of their sweating loins were tense. He stepped back into the yard.

"You ought to cover those horses of yours, you know. Why d'you let 'em stand in the cold like that, in a muck sweat?"

The driver — a tall lout of a fellow — turned and looked down at him. "Is that any o' your business, fellow?"

"They'd have something to say to you, wouldn't they, if I was to go up to the office and tell 'em how you treat their animals?"

"Just you get out — and be quick about it! What the hell's it got to do with you, eh? Shoving your nose in —" and he took a step toward Simonsen.

Simonsen withdrew a little — but of course the fellow would never dare touch him here in the yard. He stuck out his stomach even farther, saying, "Don't forget they can see you from the office windows, that's all — see how you look after the firm's horses."

With that he turned. And at once the feeling of self-confidence ebbed away. For as he was passing through the gateway a man ran down the steps and shot past him, a gentleman, wearing an astrakhan cap and a fur coat, and carrying a black stick with a silver handle — a red-and-white, fair-haired man, the man he had spoken to when he applied for the job.

Dusk was falling. It was nearly four o'clock. Olga would have something to say about it when he arrived back so late for dinner. Well, he'd just have to tell her he'd been kept late at the warehouse.

Simonsen padded quickly along Torvgaten. He both shuffled and hopped, and with his big round belly and little curved arms he looked rather like a rubber ball rolling and bouncing along. He was a little, short-necked man with a pouchy, fat face and watery eyes hidden far in behind their lids, red-veined cheeks, and a rather blue blob of a nose above the bristly, grayish yellow mustache.

It was a raw Saturday afternoon early in December, and the air was thick with gray frost-fog that smelled and tasted of gas and soot. Out in the street the sleighs swung from side to side over the plowed-up, potholed, hard-frozen snow, while on the pavement the stream of people flowed black and heavy past the illuminated, frosted shop windows. Somebody bumped into Simonsen every moment, and looked back at him angrily as he bumbled along deep in his own thoughts.

Not that many thoughts were stirring in his mind, for he thrust them away. He'd find something, somehow, somewhere. So he needn't tell Olga that he'd been fired at last, and was to leave on New Year's Day. Heigh-ho — the battle of life.

There was no great hurry. He had nearly a month. But if it came to the pinch, he'd have to write to Sigurd. Sigurd would always be able to find him a job. It wasn't too much to ask of one's own son — when the son was in Sigurd's position. Still, he didn't care for the idea; it would be for the fourth time. The fourth time in eight whole years, though — eight years exactly at the New Year, since Sigurd had got him into the office because his smart new daughter-in-law, the bitch, didn't think he was good enough to live with them in Fredriksstad. It was a pity he'd lost all three jobs — but that wasn't his fault. At the office it was the girls who'd done him in, brazen little sluts. As if it mattered to them what he was like so long as he did his work properly — and he had. And he'd taken no liberties with them — as if he would, with such stuck-up, white-faced shrews. And then there was the lumberyard. In those days he'd been really neat and respectable, for it was then he had moved to Olga's. He wasn't used to that sort of job, of course; but if it hadn't been for the foreman's malice he would never have lost it. And then he was taken on by the engineering works. And what sort of situation was that for a man nearing sixty, having to learn about a whole lot of strange new things he'd never heard of, and dispatching and packing and invoicing and all the rest of it. The warehouse boss was a lazy devil; Simonsen was blamed for everything, and they'd always treated him badly — all of them, from the manager and the chief clerk (who kept reminding him that he'd only been taken on temporarily and asking him whether he had anything else in view) to the warehouse boss and the foreman and the drivers — and the cashier; how sour and ill tempered she'd been every time he went up to her to ask for an advance!

All these things went around and around in his head, rolled up in a gray, woolly fog of anxiety and depression: Olga would nag at him when he got home, Sigurd and his wife would make themselves most unpleasant when they heard he'd been dismissed, and he would have to make a fresh start in a new job where he would dither, frightened and uncomprehending and woolly minded, faced with new work that he knew nothing about and would never learn, in a new warehouse or perhaps a new office full of strange, hostile things, cowering under constant correction and rebuke, dully awaiting a fresh dismissal — just as he had dithered and cowered, heavy and old and stupid, through his previous situations.

But Simonsen had had a certain amount of practice in keeping gloomy thoughts at bay. He had dithered through his whole life in just the same way; he had cowered and expected dismissal and reprimand and nagging and unpleasantness as something inevitable. So it had been at sea, so it had been on Consul Isachsen's wharf, and so it had been at home while his wife was alive. She had been ill tempered and sour and strict and cross grained — and his daughter-in-law was not so very different.

Yes, Sigurd had been repaid for marrying that shabby-genteel daughter of Captain Myhre's. What good times Simonsen had had at home after Laura's death! The boy had come along well: He'd been good to his old dad — paid his way and everything. Not that it had been so bad here in town either, for the first few years, when he'd been a merry bachelor again, going out and about and having fun. And since he'd taken up with Olga he'd really been very comfortable — on the whole. She hadn't been too easy the time she became pregnant, but that was understandable, and she had calmed down the moment he promised to marry her. Sometimes she went on at him to keep his word, and of course he fully intended to marry her sometime; he'd have done it long ago if he hadn't known what trouble he'd have over it with Sigurd and his wife. But one day he'd find a good, easy job that he could keep, and when Olga expanded her seamstress business, and her boy Henry went into the office — he was errand boy there now, and shaping up well — they would all be happy and comfortable together. He would sit on the sofa with his toddy and his pipe, and Olga would flit in and out seeing to things, and Svanhild would sit beside him and do her homework. For Olga was a decent, steady person, and nobody should have a chance to call Svanhild a bastard when she started school.

Simonsen had reached Ruseløkveien. The fog lay heavy and raw in the narrow street, and was striped with light — yellowish green light from the frozen panes of the little shop windows. In all of these, visible where gas jet or lamp had thawed a clear patch, hung a cluster of paper Christmas-tree baskets, whether it was a fabric store or a delicatessen or a tobacco shop. The lights from the big windows of the two-story market hall on the other side of the street cast an oily reddish glow out into the fog; the gas lamps on the terrace above could just be glimpsed, but the big private houses up there were invisible; not a gleam of light came from them, though one could sense them like a wall high up in the fog, pressing down upon the street that ran like a ditch at their foot.

Simonsen shuffled and trudged along; the pavement was slippery in many places where the sheet ice had not been chipped away. Children swarmed in and out of the dark gateways, and in the street among carts and sleighs they tried to slide, wherever there was as much as a slippery runner track through the bumpy, brown layer of hard-frozen snow.

"Svanhild!"

Simonsen called sharply to a little girl in a dirty white hood. She had clambered up onto the piled-up snow along the edge of the pavement, and from there slid down to the roadway on tiny skis that were black with dirty snow and had hardly any curve left in them.

The child stood still in the middle of the street, looking up at Simonsen, who had stepped over the heap of snow to her. Her blue eyes were conscience stricken, as she brushed her fair hair up under her hood and wiped her nose on her red-mittened hand.

"How many times have you been told not to run out into the street, Svanhild! Why can't you be a good girl and play in the yard?"

Svanhild looked up fearfully. "I can't ski in the yard; there isn't any slope."

"And suppose a cart came along and ran over you — or a drunken man carried you off — what d'you think Mamma and Dad would say then, eh?"

Svanhild, ashamed, was silent. Simonsen helped her onto the pavement, and they plodded along together hand in hand, her little sticks of skis clattering on the snowless path.

"Do you think Dad'll take you for a walk this evening, when you're such a naughty, disobedient girl, and don't do what you're told? Finished dinner, I suppose, have they?"

"Mamma and Henry and me had dinner a long time ago."

"Hmm." Simonsen trudged in through the gateway. FRU OLGA MARTINSEN. SEAMSTRESS. CHILDREN'S AND BOYS' CLOTHES. 3RD FLOOR. ENTRANCE IN YARD was inscribed on a white enamel plate. Simonsen crossed the courtyard and glanced up at the lit window, where some fashion magazines were propped up against the panes. Then he took Svanhild's skis under his arm and led the child up the narrow stairs at the back of the yard.

Outside Olga's door some little boys were reading a comic by the light of a kitchen lamp that hung there. Simonsen growled something and let himself in.

It was dark in the hall. At the farther end light shone through the glass pane in the living-room door. Simonsen went into his own room. It was dark in there too, and cold. Damn it, she'd let the stove go out. He lit the lamp.

"Run in to Mamma, Svanhild, and tell her I'm back."

He opened the door into the next room. At the table, which overflowed with half-finished sewing, pieces cut out and scraps left over, Frøken Abrahamsen sat bowed over her work. She had fastened a newspaper to one side of the lamp, so that all the light fell upon her yellow little old spinster's face and brown, rat's paw hands. The steel of the two sewing machines glinted a little, and against the wall Olga's and Svanhild's white-covered beds could just be discerned.

"Hard at it, then, Frøken Abrahamsen!"

"Yes, well — you got to be."

"Funny, this Christmas business. You'd think the world was coming to an end."

Svanhild crept into the room. "Mamma says your dinner's in the oven."

"I shall sit here and enjoy your company, Frøken Abrahamsen. It's cold in my room."

Frøken Abrahamsen silently cleared a corner of the table while Simonsen fetched his meal: white cabbage soup and sausage.

Hmm. Good. If only he'd had — Simonsen rose and knocked at the living-room door. "I say, Olga —"

"Why, good evening, Herr Simonsen! How are you keeping?"

He opened the door and looked in.

"So it's you! Another new dress, Frøken Hellum?"

Olga was standing with her mouth full of pins, fitting her customer. She arranged the folds at Frøken Hellum's breast, in front of the wall mirror.

"Like that, I thought." Olga took the lamp from the nickel stand beside her and held it up.

"Ye-es. You're sure it's not lopsided at the back, now, Fru Martinsen?"

Two girls who were sitting and waiting in the half-light over on the plush sofa put down a fashion journal, glanced at each other and smiled, looked at Frøken Hellum and smiled at each other again. "Gracious!" one whispered audibly. They were dressed almost exactly alike, in three-quarter-length coats with a little strip of fur at the neck, and respectable felt hats trimmed with a bird's wing. Simonsen paused in the doorway; he was a little shy of them.

"What do you think of it, Herr Simonsen? Is it going to look nice?"

"How well that color suits you, Frøken Hellum! But to beauty all is becoming, as they say."

"Ah, get on with you!" Frøken Hellum laughed. Pretty girl, that. Olga was cutting around the neckline, and her customer bent her head a little and shivered at the touch of the cold scissors. She had a pretty, plump neck with curly yellow hair growing low on it, and soft round arms.

"I expect this costs a bit," said Simonsen, feeling the silk — and then feeling her arm, as Olga went to fetch the sleeve.

"Shame on you, Herr Simonsen!" laughed Frøken Hellum. Olga looked annoyed; she shoved him aside and pulled on the sleeve.

"What was I going to say? . . . Oh, yes, Olga. Do you think Henry could nip down and borrow a couple of beers?"

"Poor Henry had to go back to the office; there was an estimate to be copied, he said."

"Oh, did he? Too bad. It's the same every Saturday evening nowadays, seems to me. Yes, it's a grind all right. And it was nearly four before I could get away from the warehouse. Oh, to be young and lovely, Frøken Hellum!"

Svanhild looked in.

"Come along, Svanhild. Do you remember my name today?"

"Frøken Hellum." Svanhild smiled obediently.

"Would you like some sweets again today?" Frøken Hellum looked into her handbag and brought out a paper cornet.

"What do you say now, Svanhild? Your right hand, mind, and a pretty curtsey."

Svanhild whispered thank you, gave her right hand, and curtseyed. Then she began breaking apart the camphor-drop sweets that had stuck together in the paper bag.

Frøken Hellum dressed and talked and laughed.

"I'll be along for the final fitting on Tuesday, then, at the same time. You won't let me down, Fru Martinsen, will you? Good-bye, then. Good-bye, Herr Simonsen. 'Bye, Svanhild."

Simonsen gallantly opened the door for her, and she swept out with waving feathers, the muskrat stole flung stylishly back over her shoulder.

"Gosh," said one of the young girls on the sofa. "Not bad."

"Hee-hee! No, she's a one, all right."

Simonsen went back to Frøken Abrahamsen and his dinner, which had grown cold. Olga came in soon afterward, fetched the coffee, and poured it out.

"I don't understand you, Anton, playing the fool like that! What can you be thinking of — in front of other people too."

"Who cares about those little baggages?"

"It was the pastor's daughter from the Terrace and her friend. You make things hard enough for me as it is, without carrying on so foolishly with Frøken Hellum. Yes, that's given them something to talk about — as if they hadn't enough already!"

"Ah, go on — it wasn't as bad as that."

The front doorbell rang. Frøken Abrahamsen went to answer it.

"It's Frøken Larsen."

Olga put down her cup and laid a tacked-up dress over her arm.

"Never any peace —"

Frøken Abrahamsen bent over her sewing again.

Fru Martinsen and Frøken Abrahamsen sat sewing all that Sunday. They put off dinner until it was too dark to work; afterward Olga lit the lamp and they started again.

"That lace insert for Frøken Olsen's dress, Frøken Abrahamsen — you were working on it just now, weren't you?"

Frøken Abrahamsen buzzed away at the machine. "I put it on the table."

Olga searched, and looked about the floor. "Svanhild, you haven't seen a little piece of white lace, have you?"

"No," said Svanhild from the window. She crept out and began searching too — but first she laid her doll on the upturned stool that was its bed, and covered it up well.

"Astrid's asleep — she's got diphtheria and scarlet fever," Svanhild protested, as her mother hunted through the doll's things. But relentlessly Olga lifted the patient — it was wrapped in white, pleated lace fastened carefully with safety pins.

"Good gracious! The child must be out of her mind! And I do declare you've torn a hole in it with the pins — you naughty, wicked girl —" she smacked her "— oh, what shall I do? Frøken Olsen's expensive lace . . ."

Svanhild howled.

"Haven't I told you never to take anything that's on the floor? You're a wicked, mischievous little girl!"

Frøken Abrahamsen inspected the lace insert

"I can undo the pleats and press it and pleat it again so's to hide the tear in a fold. I don't think it'll show —"

Svanhild was yelling at the top of her voice. Simonsen opened the door a crack.

"What on earth's the matter, Svanhild — screaming like that when you know Daddy's taking his nap?"

Olga explained, vehemently.

"Oh, what a bad girl, Svanhild, to play such a nasty trick on your mother. You're not my Svanhild anymore."

"I think you might take her out for a bit, Anton. It can't be good for you to lie in bed and sleep all day."

Simonsen scolded the child vigorously as he set off with her. But when they got as far as the hall and he helped her into her outdoor things, he comforted her.

"Don't cry anymore now — oh, what an ugly noise! We'll go and toboggan in the palace park. It was very wrong of you, you know. Blow your nose now — there. You and I will go off and toboggan now — come along, Svanhild love."

Olga was really too strict with the child sometimes. Not that children shouldn't be punished when they did wrong — but Svanhild took things to heart so. There she was, still sobbing on the sled behind him — poor little mite.

The evening sky was dark purple above the towers and spires of the Terrace. The weather had cleared, and only a thin, sooty frost-haze hung in the streets around the lamps when Simonsen trudged uphill dragging his daughter on the sled.

It was so pretty in the park. Thick white hoarfrost lay on all the trees and bushes, so that they sparkled in the lamplight. But what crowds of children everywhere! On every little slope they were sledding or skiing; in the big avenue were swarms of big, rough boys, five or six of them on a fish sledge, yelling and shrieking as they whizzed down over the frozen snow with a long, thin rat's tail of sticks behind them. But Simonsen knew of a nice, quiet little slope; he and Svanhild had often tobogganed there in the evenings. It was fun for her there; Daddy stood at the top and gave her a shove, Svanhild shouted, "Make way!" till her thin little voice nearly cracked, and Simonsen roared: "Make way down there!" from the very depths of his stomach, although the only other people around were two little boys in ski runners' shoes and woolen caps. Simonsen spoke to them; their names were Alf and Johannes Hauge, and their father was head of a government office and lived on Parkveien. Simonsen gave all three children a shove — they were going to see whose sled ran fastest — but he shoved Svanhild hardest so that she won. Then he trotted down after them and helped Svanhild up again, for otherwise her feet broke through the frozen crust of the snow and she got stuck.

But presently Svanhild began to whimper. "Daddy, my feet are so cold."

"Run then, my dear — come along, we'll go up onto the path and run."

Svanhild ran and cried; her toes hurt her so.

"Come now, you must run faster than that — much, much faster, Svanhild. Try and catch me!"

Simonsen bounced along with little tiny steps, like a rubber ball. And Svanhild ran after him as hard as she could and caught up to him — again and again until she was warm and cheerful again, and laughing.

But then they couldn't find the sled. Simonsen hunted above the slope and below the slope and in among the bushes, but it was gone. Alf and Johannes had seen it standing over by the big tree near the path a little while before, but that was all they knew. Yes, and some big, rough boys had passed — Simonsen remembered that. They must have been the ones who took it.

Svanhild cried bitterly. Simonsen thought of Olga — oh, she really ought to be kinder; she was so snappy all day. Nasty, bad boys to steal a poor little girl's sled. How could children be so cruel.

"Don't cry, sweetheart, we'll find it again, you'll see."

Simonsen trotted about from slope to slope asking if anyone had seen a little blue sled. Svanhild went with him, holding his hand and crying; Alf and Johannes came too, clutching their sled ropes as with wide eyes they told

Simonsen all the dreadful things they had heard about big, nasty boys who stole sleds and tobogganed into little children and threw lumps of ice in the palace park.

There was no sign of the sled. And up in the main avenue they met a grand, angry lady who turned out to be Alf's and Johannes's nanny, and she scolded them for not having come in half an hour before, and promised them they would catch it from Mamma and Daddy. She wasn't a bit interested to hear that the little girl was called Svanhild and that she had lost her sled; she went on scolding and scolding as she shuffled away holding the little boys' hands in a nurse's iron grasp. And Simonsen nearly got a steering stick in his eye and the tip of a sled in his shin.

"Well, I'm afraid they've taken your sled, Svanhild; I don't think we shall see that again." Simonsen sighed dejectedly. "Hush now, don't cry so, my darling. Daddy'll give you a fine new sled for Christmas. There! Come along, we'll go down Karl Johans Gaten and look at the shops — they're wonderful tonight — and perhaps we'll see a fine new sled for you there," he said, brightening.

So Svanhild and her daddy went and looked at the shops. And when they came to a window where the crowds had halted and clustered in a big, black, jostling mass, Simonsen lifted her up on his arm and wriggled and shoved until they got right up to the shining window, and there they stood until there wasn't a single thing in it about which they hadn't talked and wondered how much it cost. In some places there were decorated Christmas trees with electric lights on their branches — and Svanhild was going to have a tree too, on Christmas Eve. In one shop there was a Christmas party, with tremendously grand lady dolls — just like Svanhild would be when she grew up. And in a shop where they sold trunks and suitcases, there was a tiny, tiny crocodile in a tiny, tiny pool; they had to wait a long time — could it be alive? And at last it blinked one eye the teeniest bit. Imagine, it *was* alive! A little crocodile like that would grow up to be so big that it could eat up a whole Svanhild at one gulp — "But this one can't bite, can it?"

"No, this one can't do you any harm."

Up at Ekertorvet there was a movie camera in the window, among advertisement photographs. And Svanhild had been to a movie with Daddy — three times — and they had to go over all they had seen there: the two little girls who had been kidnapped by kidnappers in an automobile, and a lot more. The lost sled was quite forgotten — and so was Mamma, sitting with pursed lips at her sewing until she grew tired and ill tempered — everything was forgotten except that Svanhild was Daddy's little girl and that in seventeen days it would be Christmas.

There was a sports shop with sleds in the window, sleds large and small — but the finest of all, the scarlet one with rosemaling on it and a bronzed iron backrest — that was the one Daddy would give Svanhild on Christmas Eve.

But after all this they needed something hot inside them. Simonsen knew of a snug little temperance café; it was Sunday, so the licensed ones were closed. There were no other customers, and the lady behind the counter was not insensible to Simonsen's gallant conversation while he had his coffee and sandwich and Svanhild a cream cake and a sip from Daddy's cup now and then.

"Not a word to Mamma!" Simonsen said with a wink. But Svanhild knew better than to tell Mamma when she and Daddy popped in one place or another on their evening walks, and Svanhild had a stick of barley sugar although Mamma believed it gave little girls worms in their teeth, and Daddy had something to drink that Mamma thought gave him worms in the stomach. But Mamma was always busy and it made her very grouchy — and Daddy was busy too when he was in the warehouse, and Henry at the office — When people were grown up they had to work terribly hard. Svanhild knew that.

———

But after Sunday came Monday and five other gray weekdays. Svanhild sat on the floor in the sewing room and played, for Daddy came back so late in the evenings now that he had no time to take her for a walk. Daddy was grouchy too, now, she noticed; perhaps because he had so much work to do at the warehouse, or because Mamma had so much work that she hardly had time to get dinner or supper until late. And Henry was grouchy as well, for ladies had fittings until late at night in the room where he slept, so that he couldn't get to bed. But Svanhild consoled herself with the thought of the wonderful sled she was going to have for Christmas.

On the fifteenth Anton wrote to his son. He was sick of running after jobs in vain. After that he took a calmer view of the future, and had time once more to go out with Svanhild in the evenings and drag her along on her skis in the park; and they talked about the fine sled she was going to have.

But on the morning of the eighteenth, as Simonsen was nailing up a crate of machinery parts, the warehouse boss came to tell him that he was wanted on the telephone. It was Sigurd; he was in town. Would his father drop in at the Augustin for coffee — take a couple of hours off that afternoon so that they could have a talk?

"How's Mossa and the children?"

The children were very well. Mossa was in town too; she had a bit of Christmas shopping to do.

"I've just remembered, son — I haven't a chance of getting even an hour off now, with Christmas coming on."

Sigurd said he'd have a word with the manager.

Well, thanks. Love to Mossa.

How like her! Ask him to dinner? Not on your life! Damned if he wouldn't get himself a skinful before he went to that *party*.

———

"Do you think that's necessary?" Fru Carling asked her husband, who was uncorking a bottle of punch.

"Yes, I do think we should offer the old man a glass of punch."

"Well, well, just as you like, dear." Mossa Carling displayed all the double chins at her command. She was not pretty: Her eyelids thickened toward the temples, so that her piercing little gray eyes seemed to creep toward the bridge of her nose; her face was fat and fresh colored but her mouth was small and pinched, with thin lips. Her chest was narrow and cramped, but the lower half of her body was broad and bulky.

She sat in the middle of the plush sofa under the electric chandelier, whose three lights splendidly illuminated the hotel room with its two iron beds, two mahogany washstands, two bedside tables, the wardrobe with the mirror, and the two armchairs in front of the table, on which an ashtray stood on a mat in the middle of the chenille cloth.

There was a timid knock on the door, and Simonsen stepped warily into the room. He shook hands.

"Well, Sigurd, nice to see you again, my boy. How are you, Mossa? Glad to see you again too — young and pretty as ever, I see."

Mossa rang for coffee and poured it out while Sigurd filled the glasses.

While he talked to Sigurd, Simonsen glanced at his daughter-in-law, who sat mute with a pinched mouth. Slowly and deviously the conversation turned toward the purpose of the meeting.

"We may smoke, mayn't we, my dear? Here, Father, have a cigar. Now, about what you said in your letter. I went up to the office this morning and had a word with your boss. He agreed with me: You don't fit in here in town. The work's too hard for a man of your age. And I can't get you anything else."

Simonsen said nothing. But Mossa took over.

"You must remember that Sigurd's in a subordinate position himself — in a way, that is. The board of directors wouldn't like him to keep bothering their business associates to give you a job. He's done it three times now, and each time you've lost your position. I must tell you that Sigurd was in quite serious trouble after getting you into this last place, which it seems you've now lost —"

"Yes, I was. No, as I say, you don't fit in here, Father. And you're too old to start anything new. So there's only one way I can help you. I can get you a job at the Mensted works up in Øimark — it's nice easy work. Of course, the wages aren't high: sixty kroner to start with, I believe. But, as I say, I can get you that."

Simonsen was silent.

"Yes, well — that's the only way I can help you," said Sigurd Carling.

"Do you want me to get it for you then, Father?" he asked after a while.

His father cleared his throat once or twice.

"Yes. Well, now. There's one thing, Sigurd — I don't know whether you've heard anything about it, but I'm engaged to be married — to the lady I've been lodging with these past six years. So I shall have to talk this over with Olga first and see what she thinks. Her name's Olga," he explained. "Fru Olga Martinsen, a widow."

There was a horribly long pause. Simonsen fidgeted with the tassels on the armchair.

"She's a real, good, respectable, decent person in every way, Olga is. And she's got a big, expanding seamstress business here in town, so it's questionable whether she'd care much about moving into the wilds. Her boy's got an office job here too."

"Is that the lady —" Sigurd spoke very slowly "— who's said to have a child by you?"

"We've got a little girl, yes; her name's Svanhild — she'll be five in April."

"Oh." This was Mossa. "So you have a daughter by the woman you lodge with — the woman who's such a good, respectable, decent person in every way."

"And so she is — decent and respectable. And hardworking too. And kind."

"Then it's odd, father-in-law —" Fru Carling's voice was very sweet and gentle "— that you didn't marry this wonderful Fru Martinsen long ago. You had every reason."

"Well, I'll tell you, Mossa my dear." Simonsen perked up as he thought of what to say. "I didn't want to see any wife of mine toiling and slaving so hard, so I waited until I could find something better. But marry her I will. I've promised her that all along, and I'll keep my word as sure as my name's Anton Simonsen."

"Ye-es." Mossa grew sweeter and gentler. "Sixty kroner a month isn't much to marry on, and keep a wife and child. And Fru Martinsen can hardly hope to build up much of a seamstress business in Øimark."

"The worst part of it is this child of yours, Father," said Sigurd. "But no doubt Fru Martinsen can be made to understand the situation, so that we can come to some arrangement."

"You must remember this about that little sister o' yours — about Svanhild. I don't want her to suffer for being illegitimate, and I think you're taking on a big responsibility, Sigurd, if you interfere in this."

Mossa snatched the word from him, and now there was no trace of gentleness in her voice.

"Responsibility! For *your* illegitimate child! You must be joking! Here's Sigurd offering to get you a position — for the fourth time — in Øimark. To find one here in town is out of the question. If you don't think you can leave town because of your private affairs, you're perfectly free to stay. And if you can find a job and marry on it, we certainly won't interfere. But naturally Sigurd can't help you in any other way. His responsibility, first and foremost, is to his own wife and children."

—⁓—

Fru Carling had put on her silk petticoat and draped herself in her new set of furs when on the following morning she climbed the stairs to Fru Martinsen's seamstress establishment in the courtyard off Ruseløkveien. She placed a determined first finger on the bell under Simonsen's dirty visiting card.

The woman who opened the door was small, plump, and dark. She had pretty blue eyes in a face that was pale and washed out from sitting indoors.

"Are you Fru Martinsen? I'm Fru Carling. I wanted to speak to you."

Rather hesitantly Olga opened the door of the nearest room. "Please come in. I'm sorry there's no fire in here; we work in the other rooms."

Fru Carling sailed in and seated herself in the only armchair. The room was furnished as rooms for rent usually are. On the chest of drawers, which was covered with a white cloth, stood conscientiously displayed photographs of the late Fru Simonsen, of Sigurd and herself — their engagement photos — and two group pictures of the grandchildren.

"Well now, Fru Martinsen —" Olga was now standing over by the chest of drawers, observing the speaker "— there are one or two things I'd very much like to talk to you about. Won't you sit down?"

"Thank you, but I really haven't much time. What was it you wanted, Fru Carling?"

"Quite so. I won't keep you. We understand that Herr Simonsen, my husband's father, has certain obligations toward you. I don't know whether he has made the present situation clear to you?"

"About the new job in Øimark? Oh yes."

"Oh. Well, as you know, it's quite a modest position, so that for the time being he won't be able to fulfill his obligations to the child — his and yours. My husband and I have therefore decided to offer you —"

"Thank you very much." Olga spoke quickly and curtly. "We don't want to trouble you with our affairs, Fru Carling. We've agreed about it, Anton and I. We've agreed to get married now, right away."

"I see. Fru Martinsen, I must point out that Herr Simonsen cannot expect any assistance from my husband — none whatever. He has a large family himself. And for four people to live on sixty kroner a month — I understand you have another child besides Herr Simonsen's —"

"My boy will stay here. I have a sister on Trondhjemsveien he can live with. Our plan was for us to live in Fredriksstad; I could carry on my seamstress work there, and Anton could come down to us on weekends."

"Yes, well, that sounds a very sensible idea. But you see, there are more than enough seamstresses in Fredriksstad already, so it's doubtful whether it would pay for you to give up your connection here and start all over again there, *Frøken* Martinsen!"

Olga jumped.

"*Fru* Martinsen, I beg your pardon. That's what you call yourself, of course. Yes, you see my husband and I have been making a few inquiries. You can't be surprised that we should want to know just what sort of person it was he'd taken up with."

Olga gave a snort. "And it's the same thing for me, Fru Simonsen — I beg your pardon, Fru *Carling,* I mean. But it so happens that Anton thinks none the worse of me because my fiancé ran away to America, leaving me to support myself and my boy the best way I could. And he's told me, Anton has, he's said it over and over again: 'I shan't let you down, Olga.' So it don't seem to me it need concern you at all, Fru Carling. We won't trouble you and come running to you — and as your husband hasn't even kept his father's name —"

"My dear Fru Martinsen." Mossa waved her hand and displayed all her double chins. "I beg you not to get so excited. I hadn't the least idea of meddling in your affairs. Quite the contrary — I came here with the very best intentions. I simply wanted to make it quite clear to you — in case you imagined that Herr Simonsen was any sort of catch — that if you do marry him, I believe all you'll gain will be the pleasure of supporting both him and his child. Just think for a moment. My dear father-in-law has never been exactly a model of efficiency, has he? We have no guarantee that he won't be dismissed again as usual. Yes . . . Do you think it will be easy for a man of his age — with a family — to keep on finding new situations? I've come here in a perfectly friendly way to bring you an offer from Herr Carling. Look, my dear Fru Martinsen, up to now you've managed very well without a husband. Herr Carling offers you a sum of money — we thought five hundred kroner — to compensate you for losing your lodger so suddenly. Without conditions. You understand that if later my father-in-law is in a position to marry we won't stand in the way. As you very rightly say, it doesn't concern us. And as for your little girl, we're prepared to offer her a home with us —"

"Never!" Olga flashed. "Let Svanhild go? That's one thing you can be certain I'll never do."

"Well, well. That's entirely as you wish, of course. You and my father-in-law will naturally do as you like. If you want to marry on sixty kroner a month — give up your livelihood here and try to start a seamstress business in Fredriksstad, which I assure you will never succeed . . . What baffles me is why you should want Herr Simonsen at all. To *marry* him! In your circles people surely aren't so particular as to whether or not you've had some little affair with your lodger. How you could take up with him in the first place . . . You must forgive my saying this, but it's no recommendation in my eyes. Frankly, he's a nasty old man —"

Olga broke in, "Please say no more, Fru Carling. But I'll tell you just why I wanted Anton Simonsen. Maybe there *are* one or two things against him. But it didn't take me long to find out that he's a kindhearted man — and there's not too many of that sort about. And as soon as he saw I wanted to make things snug and comfortable for him, he took to me and tidied himself up and behaved himself; and he'd a' done it before, I say, if he'd had any kindness or comfort where he come from. Kind and grateful always, Anton's been. And so taken up with Svanhild — almost too much of a good thing, it is — he quite spoils her. I'm fond of Anton, let me tell you, Fru Carling."

Mossa stood up and put the tips of her gloved fingers between the lace edges of her muff.

"Ah, well. If you *love* Herr Simonsen, that's another matter."

——◁∿▷——

Sigurd Carling had a high opinion of his wife's cleverness — he'd heard about it so often that he'd come to believe in it. As Frøken Mossa Myhre she had urged him on and made him the man he was today. Nevertheless, he had his doubts of her being the right person to come to an understanding with Fru Martinsen. She had very strict views, and this Olga creature had had two children in a rather irregular manner. And Mossa could make herself most unpleasant. So afterward he regretted allowing her to go: It had been a stupid thing to do. For an arrangement of some sort there must be. If his father were to move to Fredriksstad with a wife and child whom he couldn't support, it was as clear as daylight what would happen: Sigurd and his wife would never be safe from appeals for help, along with all the other kinds of bother his father always caused. And endless trouble with Mossa.

The matter had to be settled, and at once, before the old man had time to play them any tricks. Sigurd went to the Hercules works and ordered two new turbines, and in passing said a word or two about his father. It was arranged that Simonsen should leave for good on Christmas Eve, so that he might go home with them for the holiday.

Afterward, he too went to see Fru Martinsen.

Olga's face was tearstained when Simonsen came home at dinnertime. Carling had been there. He'd been quite nice; he had asked to see Svanhild and taken her on his lap, and told her she should have something special for Christmas. Afterward he had talked to Olga. It was about her debts: She owed rent, as well as sums here and there among the tradespeople. And she had accepted his money. Besides that, he had promised her fifteen kroner a month for Svanhild; that meant something steady coming in, and she had Henry too, who wouldn't be able to support himself for a while — fifteen kroner a month, he'd said, for the time being, "until my father has become self-supporting and can marry you." Olga sat on Simonsen's knee and cried; he was in the armchair in that cold room, in front of the chest of drawers with its family photographs. She cried, and he patted her.

"Oh, Anton, I don't know! What else could I a' done? If he won't help you there's nothing else for it. And I could see he wouldn't — not in any other way. If they set themselves against us, we should never make a go of it in Fredriksstad, you see —"

She blew her nose and wiped her eyes. And had another fit of crying.

"We got to accept it — you got to accept a lot of things when you're poor."

—*⁓*—

But to go home with Sigurd and Mossa for Christmas was one thing Simonsen would not do. They tempted him with a Christmas tree and grandchildren and goose and beer and spirits and headcheese, but the old man stood firm: He wanted to spend Christmas with Olga and the children. The most they managed to get from Simonsen was his promise to come the day after Christmas Day. Sigurd had given him twenty-five kroner, so it was as well to get him out of town rather than let him loaf about there with money in his pocket until the New Year. Far better for the old boy to have his Christmas drinks with them, under supervision.

When Simonsen came home the evening before Christmas Eve, he had the new sled under his arm. Humming away in a deep bass voice, he lit the lamp in his own room and unpacked his parcels.

There were drinks — aquavit and punch and brandy, and sweet port for Olga; so with a drop of beer they'd do all right. A pipe for Henry — it hadn't cost much; it was really just to show the boy he hadn't forgotten him, and it was a manly sort of thing to have. All the same he was pretty well broke now; the blouse material for Olga cost only one krone, forty-five øre, but then he'd bought her a brooch too, for three seventy-five, which looked more like it cost ten kroner. Simonsen took it out of its little box; he was sure she'd like it. He wanted to buy some little trifle for Frøken Abrahamsen too — just a souvenir. Something quite small — he could afford that.

And then the sled, of course. Simonsen took the cloth off the table, unpacked the sled, and put it on display.

"Come and have a look, Olga love," he called into the sewing room.

"What is it? I'm busy."

Simonsen moved the lamp over to the table. "What do you think Svanhild will say to this, eh, Olga?"

"Mind the varnish, Anton!" and she spread newspaper under the sled and the lamp. "Yes, that's lovely — that's a beautiful sled."

"And look!" Simonsen unbuckled the cushion so that Olga could see all the rosemaling. "The cushion was extra."

"Hmm. Must have been expensive."

"Five kroner and twenty-five øre with the cushion," Simonsen answered briskly.

"Yes, well, that's a lot of money to spend on a thing like that, Anton. For such a little girl — she'd have been just as happy with a plainer one." Olga sighed.

"Oh, but now we got a little ready money handy, it's fun to give nice things. You've settled your debts and that. I bought something for my sweetheart too —" and he nudged her. "Run and fetch a couple of glasses, Olga — I've got some port. You must taste it and see how you like it — I bought it on your account mostly."

Olga glanced at the many bottles on the chest of drawers and sighed a little. Then she fetched the glasses.

—◦◦◦—

It was late on Christmas Eve when work finished at Fru Martinsen's. But at last all was done. Henry had gone off to deliver the last of the completed sewing, and Olga and Frøken Abrahamsen had cleared away everything else, heaping it on the chairs and table in the sewing room. Before she left, Frøken Abrahamsen was given coffee and pastries and from Simonsen a bottle of eau de cologne.

Then Olga went into the living room. She cleared the magazines off the table, and materials and half-made garments off the chairs, and picked up pins and buttons to drop them into the glass bowls on the console table. And she lit the candles on the Christmas tree, which she had decorated the night before.

Svanhild and Henry and Simonsen came in; the grown-ups sat down on the plush chairs, but Svanhild skipped and danced and rejoiced; she caught sight of the sled and shrieked with delight, then ran back to the tree again, not knowing what to do with herself for joy. Simonsen beamed and Olga smiled, though her eyes were sadly red; Simonsen had glanced at them several times during the afternoon. If only she wouldn't start to cry on this of all evenings, when they were going to have such a nice time.

He fetched his presents, smiling mischievously: She wouldn't think the blouse material was much of a gift. Then he brought out the eau de cologne; for he had yielded to the temptation of doing things in style when he went into the fifty-øre bazaar to find something for Frøken Abrahamsen. There was also a cup to hold Olga's ball of wool when she knitted, and a little matchbox that looked like silver for Henry. The boy shook hands and laid pipe and box down by the window, where he had been lounging in a chair. But then came the brooch.

"All those was sort of practical things, Olga; you must have a little trifle just for pleasure, too."

Olga picked up the brooch and her eyes filled with tears. "Such a lot of things, Anton!"

Simonsen threw out his hand in a magnificent gesture. "You must think of me when you wear it, Olga love."

"Oh, I will, Anton."

"And what about that box that came for Svanhild?"

Olga fetched it. On it was written: TO LITTLE FRØKEN SVANHILD, C/O FRU MARTINSEN'S DRESSMAKING ESTABLISHMENT. Olga opened it. The card inside bore the inscription: MERRY CHRISTMAS! It was Sigurd Carling's card. With it was a doll — but what a doll!

It had curly yellow hair and eyes that opened and shut. It was dressed in a white coat and white fur cap, and carried a little pair of skates over its arm — that was the most marvelous thing of all. Svanhild was speechless, but Simonsen talked and talked; he and the child were equally enraptured with the doll.

"Mamma must keep it for you — you'd better only play with it on Sundays."

"He's a good fellow, you know, Sigurd is," he said to Olga, who was bringing in the glasses and the jug of hot water. "It's what I always say: Sigurd's all right at heart — it's that damned hag of his who puts him up to things, for he's a good chap."

Simonsen mixed a toddy and Olga had port. Even Svanhild was given a little drop of the sweet wine in her own glass as she sat on Daddy's lap.

"Come along, Henry, and mix yourself a toddy. You're a man now, you know."

Henry rose rather reluctantly, not looking at Simonsen. He had hard, pale eyes in a white, freckled face, and he looked thin and slight in his grown-up clothes.

"Well, *skål,* everybody! Isn't this jolly! Eh, Olga love?"

"Yes," she said, and bit her lip. Tears came into her eyes. "If only we knew what next Christmas was going to be like."

Simonsen lit his cigar. He looked troubled. "Aren't you going to try your pipe, Henry, my boy? You'll find some tobacco on my chest of drawers if you haven't any yourself."

"No, thanks," said Henry.

"Yes, next Christmas," said Olga, fighting back her tears.

"Hard to say when you don't know," Simonsen said. He leaned back in his chair. "Good cigar, this. Drink up, Olga. Yes, well, perhaps we'll all be celebrating Christmas together among the country bumpkins. I hear they have great goings-on at Christmas up in Øimark. I think you'd like the country, Olga. When you want a Christmas tree, all you got to do is walk out of the door and cut one. Not bad! How'd you like that, Svanhild — going out into the woods with your daddy to cut down a Christmas tree — and then drag it home on your sled, eh?"

Svanhild nodded, radiant.

"And Henry would get time off from the office and spend Christmas with us."

Henry smiled slightly — scornfully.

"Wouldn't that be fun, Svanhild — going to the station to meet Henry? Would you like it if you and Daddy and Mamma lived on a big farm with cows and horses and pigs and roosters and hens and all? And then kind Sigurd, who gave you your doll — he's got a little girl about your age, and a boy just a bit bigger, and a tiny, tiny baby; you could go into town and play with them."

"While I have tea with that stuck-up daughter-in-law of yours, I s'pose! That's the idea, eh, Anton?"

"Oh, well — I don't think that would be necessary —"

"How can you go on talking such nonsense!" Olga laughed — and then burst out crying.

"Oh now, Olga, what are you crying for, love? Why do you take it like that?"

"How do you expect me to take it? Am I supposed to be pleased when that woman throws it in my face that Henry's father made a fool of me, and that now you're leaving me too? And me and my children — my castoffs — we're left with the disgrace. Perhaps you think like they do — you think it serves me right to sit here and make clothes for all the girls you have fun and games with. Just as if it was all right for people to treat me as they choose. Yes, yes — good enough for me. I ought to a' known what you was all like; soon's you get your own way with a poor woman it's love you and leave you — thanks and good-bye!"

"But Olga, my dear!"

"Ah, it's nothing to you. No, you can move out into the country, you can, and start all over again with your sozzling and your girls — like you was doing when I found you. And my God, a nice fool I was to give in to you."

"Olga, Olga — remember the children!"

"Ho, they hear enough about it, you may be sure, in the yard and on the stairs. So they might just as well hear it from me too."

"It's Christmas Eve, Olga. Remember that, please," Simonsen said solemnly.

Olga wept quietly with her head on the table. Simonsen laid his hand on her shoulder.

"Now Olga, you know very well — you know very well how fond I am of you. And there's Svanhild — d'you really think I'd forget my own, innocent little girl? Trust me, Olga; I won't let you down or deceive you — I'll keep my promise to you."

"Why, you poor man —" Olga sat up and blew her nose. "That's not for you to decide."

"But you must remember one thing, Olga —" Simonsen laid one arm around her neck and held Svanhild with the other, straightened himself, and stuck out his stomach. "There's One Above — one greater than either Sigurd or Mossa — who does decide — for us all.

"Now I think we ought to sing a carol," he said a little later. He took a gulp of toddy and cleared his throat. "'The Joy of Christmas' — let's have that; Svanhild knows it, I know. Sing out, now, Svanhild love."

Svanhild sang joyfully, and Simonsen growled too, leaving off when the notes went too high, but beginning again with every verse. Soon Olga joined in with a voice hoarse from weeping. Henry alone did not sing.

Then came the last morning. In Olga's room the alarm clock rang, but Simonsen lay dozing on in the darkness — it was so cold getting up. And everything was dreary and comfortless. That he should have to get up in the cold and go away — away from everything.

Never, in any place where he had lived, had he had so comfortable a bed as this, with eiderdown both under and over him.

Olga opened the door, and by the light shining through from her room she set down the tray she was carrying, lit the lamp, and took the tray over to the bed; on it were coffee and rolls.

"You'll have to get moving now, Anton."

"Yes, yes — I s'pose so."

Simonsen sighed. He drew her down onto the edge of the bed and stroked her — stroked her cheek and arm and breast and hips, as he drank the coffee and dunked the rolls in it.

"This is splendid coffee, my love. Won't you have a drop too?"

"No, I'd better go and get a bit of breakfast ready for you."

Simonsen crawled out of bed, dressed, and packed the last of his belongings. Then he locked both his boxes and went into Olga's room.

He stood by the bed where Svanhild lay asleep, looking down at her with his hands in his pockets. "My Svanhild . . ."

He peeped into the living room too; it was pitch dark and icy cold. Henry had gone off to Nordmarken with some friends on Christmas morning. Simonsen pottered about in there for a while, and in the darkness knocked against Svanhild's Christmas tree, so that the little tinsel balls tinkled together. Who knew — who knew whether he would ever come back here again?

He returned to Olga's room; it was nice and warm in there. Places were set at the lower end of the long table where Olga and Frøken Abrahamsen worked during the day. On the white cloth were headcheese and beer and spirits and all the rest, and over it the lamp shone peacefully, humming softly as it burned. A light fell on Svanhild, asleep in her little bed, with her pretty hair spread over the pillow. His little, little girl . . .

There was a sweet, cozy warmth from Olga's bed, which was unmade, the covers thrown back from the hollow where she had lain. How good his life had been here with Olga and Svanhild! His eyes filled with tears; he let them run without drying them, so that Olga would notice. His pouchy, bluish red cheeks were quite wet when Olga came in with the coffee.

"We'd better have breakfast," she said.

"Yes, we'd better. What about Svanhild? D'you think she'd like to come to the station, just for the sleigh ride?"

"I thought of that, Anton, but it's so dark and cold outside. But I might wake her now, so she can have a cup of coffee with us." She went over to the bed and gently shook the child.

"Svanhild, would you like to get up now and have coffee with Mamma and Daddy?"

Svanhild blinked, sitting in her nightgown on Simonsen's lap. The coffee had aroused her a little, but she was still quiet and subdued because the grown-ups were.

"Where are you going, Daddy?"

"Why, to Fredriksstad, don't you remember?"

"When are you coming back?"

"Oh, well — I expect you'll be down to see me first."

"In the country, like you talked about?"

"That's it."

"You'll be able to toboggan with me again there, won't you, Daddy?"

"Yes, that's right — I'll be able to toboggan with you again there."

The doorbell rang. Olga looked out: The sleigh had come. The driver's boy took Simonsen's boxes and went.

Simonsen kissed Svanhild, and having got up, he stood for a moment with her on his arm.

"Now you must be a good girl, mind, and do as you're told while Daddy's away!"

"Yes, I will," said Svanhild.

Olga went into the kitchen to turn off the stove, as Svanhild was to be alone at home; then came in again and stood with her hand on the lamp screw. "Well, Anton —"

He gave Svanhild a smacking kiss, laid her down in her bed, and covered her up. "Bye-bye then, Svanhild love."

Olga put out the lamp, and they left the room. In the hall he put his arms around her and pressed her to him. They kissed.

In the sleigh they sat in silence as they jolted down through the darkness of early morning. And they still had nothing to say to each other as they wandered together around the cold, bleak station hall. But she followed at his heels when he bought his ticket and dispatched his trunk; she stood behind him, a small figure in black, bulky in her thick outer clothes.

Then they wandered into the waiting room and sat looking up at the clock.

"We started in good time, didn't we?" said Olga.

"Yes, we did. Best thing when you're going on a journey. Shame you had to get up so early, though, when it's a holiday."

"Oh, well," said Olga. "Perhaps we'd better go along and take a seat for you on the train."

Simonsen put his things into a smoking compartment. He stood at the window while she remained down on the platform.

"Mind you, write often, Olga, and tell me how you're getting on."

"Yes — and you too, Anton."

Porters began slamming the carriage doors along the train. Olga got up on the step, and they kissed again.

"Thanks for everything, Olga love."

"And thanks to you, Anton. Good journey!"

The engine whistled — the train gave a lurch, and it began to move. Olga and Simonsen pulled out their handkerchiefs and waved to each other for as long as the handkerchiefs could be seen.

The train rushed along in the first pale light of dawn — past the Bekkelag villas, past Nordstrand and Ljan. There were lights in the windows here and there. Below the railway line the fjord could be glimpsed, ice-gray, with black islands on it.

Oh, it was dreary . . . Simonsen was alone in the compartment, smoking his cigar and looking out of the window. Farms and woods came up and swam past — gray-brown fields with strips of snow along their edges — black woods.

By now Olga would be back at home. What would she be doing? Dressing Svanhild, probably. Olga had to work today, so she'd said. Svanhild would sit on the floor by the window, playing with the leftover scraps. Now she had no Daddy to go tobogganing with in the palace park.

The snug room with its two warm, white beds. And the lamp, and the sewing everywhere, and the scraps on the floor that one waded through. Svanhild over by the window — his own, precious child. He could see her sitting there so quietly with her little affairs. Now and then a Frøken Hellum or someone came in and gave her sweets. She'd miss her daddy, Svanhild would.

It was wrong. It was all wrong.

For a moment the wrongness of it struck a spark inside him and smarted and burned through all that life had left of Anton Simonsen's heart.

"Svanhild love, my own little Svanhild . . ." he whimpered.

But he thrust the thought aside.

That innocent little girl, who was so good — so very good. Surely life would turn out well for her?

He wiped his eyes. There must be One Above who decided these things. That must be his consolation: that there was One who decided . . .

LETTERS

translated by

TIINA NUNNALLY

TRANSLATOR'S NOTE

In the spring of 1898 sixteen-year-old Sigrid Undset became a member of a Swedish pen-pal club that she had seen advertised in the magazine *Urd*. A few months later she received a letter from Andrea (Dea) Hedberg, and thus began a correspondence that lasted more than forty years. Only four months older than Sigrid, Dea was the daughter of a Malmö bookseller and an ardent reader. She also shared Sigrid's dreams of becoming an author, although her talents would lead her to journalism rather than to fiction writing. The deep friendship that developed through their letters was further strengthened by their first meeting in 1903. Although they met only a few more times over the years, they continued to confide their hopes and yearnings to each other through their letters.

The following is a selection of Sigrid Undset's letters to her friend Dea, which are now held in the Manuscript Department of the National Library in Oslo.

Much of the information used in these notes was taken from the biography *Menneskenes Hjerter: Sigrid Undset, en livshistorie* by Tordis Ørjasæter (Oslo: Aschehoug, 1993). Additional information was derived from commentary written by Christianne Undset Svarstad for *Kjære Dea* (Oslo: Cappelen, 1979), the letters from which these translations were made.

Kristiania
April 3, 1900

Dear Dea!

Thank you so much for your last two letters. This time I've truly outdone myself, since it must be more than 2 months ago that you heard from me, but I really couldn't bring myself to take pen in hand during all this time, and tonight I'm sending you only a few words so that you'll at least know I'm alive — you mustn't even think about my rudeness in not answering your letters, but I'm in a mood that's as black as pitch, and it just keeps getting worse and worse. Lucky you for finding some work that catches your interest and enthusiasm — the very thought of the office makes me sick. Although I know it would be just as bad no matter what I started, but I can't overcome my loathing for work, any sort of regular, routine work. The trouble is, you see, I have an artist's tempera-ment — give me a minute and I'll try to explain what I mean . . . First of all, this isn't meant as an excuse, I'm not saying this out of vanity, but it's the bitter, sad truth, which I have only recently dared admit to myself. There's nothing I have greater contempt for than artists, especially those useless creatures who have the type of artistic temperament that produces nothing, who are artists for their own sakes, which means that they possess only the "introspective" characteris-tics of the artistic temperament: egotism, a lack of ability and desire to work, a lack of interest in and love for others, as well as a wild imagination, so they dream away their time, and that's exactly one of my bad habits, which I've been giving in to more and more. Because I can no longer rein in my desire to dream, nor do I have any wish to do so. I spend all my spare time wandering along the country road and playing with my fantasies, scraps of made-up novels, images from my dreams, and memories of landscapes from past summers. Dreaming, I've walked along the same roads so many times that it's as if spiderwebs hung from the trees and my own selves from all the past years are still sitting along the culverts — and I yearn so much for summer! Because that's the joy of being a dreamer; no one else can enjoy as ardently all the sunshine and loveliness of summer. Because that's when I understand; when the sun shines on me I can feel that I was taken from the earth and to the earth I will return, and it's a sacred act for me to place my hand on the sun-warm soil, and for me, child of the earth, to embrace my own lineage when I wrap my hand around the stem of a flower. It's a sinful thought, but I can't help it, I wouldn't want any eternity but to glide forever through the chiaroscuro of my dreams. I'm only happy when I'm alone in the woods or in . . . well, I can't find any other word for it than nature, but it's not what other people call nature: a scenic view or anything like that, but rather the hypnotic immersion in the corolla of a rose when you've stared at it for so long that all outlines are erased and you become dizzy with crimson: to disappear into nature so that you cease to feel or think, but with all your senses you greedily draw in the light and colors, the rustling of the leaves and the trickling of underground streams, the sun and the shifting shadows — that is happiness, nirvana.

Sometimes I want so much to write a book. The way I envision it in my mind, both the plot and the characters are good, but I'm afraid I'll never have the skill to portray any of them — let alone be capable of writing it all down. I've started a few times, but nothing comes of it, and I burn it at once. But it's supposed to take place in 1340, and the novel will be called *Svend Trøst,* or *Svend Ungersvend,* but the story is anything but historically correct or dull, and there isn't a single romantic scene in it. It's about two young people — of course — Svend Trøst and Maiden Agnete, whose unhappy story . . . an unhappy marriage that I won't bother you with right now. You must have had enough of my outpourings, but you see it's so good to write things like this to someone I can trust and rely on, things that I don't think another living soul ever suspects about me, and that I could never bring myself to talk about with anyone.

So I beg you to write to me soon. The best of luck with your work — do you know, Dea, I'm almost jealous after all!

I'll be expecting a letter from you every single day and longing terribly, so I beg you again to write soon!

Your devoted
Sigrid Undset

Kristiania
January 2, 1901

Dear, dear Dea!

Finally I've retreated here to my cell. Your letter arrived on New Year's Eve while I was waiting for Mamma and the girls to finish dressing to go out, and on New Year's Day we have that ungodly institution of paying visits. But I thought about you, poor thing, as I stood outside on the Winter-Hjelm* family's veranda and waited for the new year. I wanted to write and tell you so many consoling things — but why should I do that? There's no medicine for sorrow, you have to grow beyond it, and then it will recede as you change — or develop, I suppose it's called. And surely it's deeply satisfying to feel how you're changing, how impressions of what you've seen and felt and dreamed and thought and read are all building up — to sit still and sense the calm growth of your soul inside. You're familiar with those lonely hours, aren't you?

God's joy in creating, which is enjoyed by everyone who creates in words, in colors, in notes, and in clay, maybe even every craftsman when he creates the smallest object that pleases him — that joy *can* be won by anyone who secretly shapes his own self and opens his eyes; so often we keep them closed — eyes that look inside the workshop of our lives. Life, isn't that a lovely word? Do you know, I was in such despair, such boundless despair, about living and yet not living, standing in a corner and watching life pass by without being allowed to participate. At times it seems to me unbearable to take the same road to work each day and then back home, with those same three faces year in and year out, so that by now, with all my 20 years, I feel like a ghost with no power to live. Because I have no ability to win people over or to find any joy in what gives joy to others. I don't think it's amusing to go dancing or to stroll with my girlfriends along Drammensveien or to spend time in the company of gentlemen — other girls live under the same circumstances and are happy. Yet I still say to you that life is wonderful. If it should turn out that I couldn't bear life anymore and voluntarily decided to go, I would say in my last hour that life

---

*Organist Otto Winter-Hjelm, his wife, and their eleven children lived on the first floor of an old villa at Lyder Sagens Gaten 10 in Kristiania. Sigrid and her sisters became friends with the Winter-Hjelm children when the Undsets lived on the second floor of the same house 1886–90.

is a miracle, that it was my fault, not life's. Oh, Dea, Dea, whatever you may see when you look at people — look at their work!

Look at your dress, look at your shoes, and think of the hundreds of weaving machines and dyeing machines and sewing machines; all of them, with all their wheels and rims and tiny little patented details, are the sum of the concentrated energy from thousands of human souls. All the thinking, all the brooding and energy that is put into every single little thing we have around us! I sit in the office* and write up estimates for motors and wires that will bring electric light and power to a master cabinetmaker or a lathe operator in some remote corner of the country — and I had written hundreds of them before it occurred to me what exactly it was: one enormous fairy tale. Up in Nordmarken, in the middle of a black spruce forest, the waters of Skjærsjø plunge between the wet walls of the mountains, making the foam splash up into the fringe of the spruce trees — and it has splashed and churned like that in the mountain cauldron for thousands of years; until one day some people come padding along and force the waters out of their ancient course and into huge pipelines and through turbines and machines and via axles and wheels through cables as thick as arms, through the armatures of dynamos that are braided from copper wires as fine as a thousand-petal flower, and into thick cables through the silent forests of the wood nymphs, through the outskirts of the city, some hung from slender posts, some buried in the ground, carrying electricity to the delicate carbon filaments of thousands of little lightbulbs and arc lamps — isn't the mere thought enough to make you drunk and dizzy? Dea, if you try to *comprehend* the sum of everyone's lifeblood and the work of their fervent will and minds and thoughts behind every small part that the Skjærsjø waterpower passes through. When I go out at night and see the white beads of the arc lamps up in the golden evening sky, oh, it feels as if my heart could burst when it tries to think about what *human work* is. It's all the misery and deprivation, the workers' conditions, that have created this miracle; yes, but all the same, all the same! Life is glorious — whether or not it holds happiness for you or for me.

---

*Sigrid's beloved father died in 1893 at the age of forty, leaving his widow with three young daughters and only a small state pension to provide for them. To help support her family, seventeen-year-old Sigrid went to work as a secretary for the Wisbech Electrical Company, a subsidiary of a German firm, the Allgemeine Elektrizitäts Gesellschaft. She worked nine-hour days for a starting salary of thirty kroner per month, and she held this position for ten years.

I suppose it's something new this year that I'm preaching in this tone — while I'm the one who has been poring over books and pictures and dreams, and even I don't understand how the two streams happen to have run together in my mind. I don't even know why I woke up to this new point of view, but I do know that I've never before felt such joy at seeing life around me, although my own path in life is still so impoverished. I can see that there is beauty and there is joy in perceiving this beauty, whether it's a rose or a locomotive or a meadow, whose green contours are sketched against the sky, or a soulful painting or a Shakespeare sonnet or a cloud of smoke from a factory chimney in a gray winter sky or a pair of handsome eyes that meet mine in passing. I think it's possible to find beauty everywhere — and there you have my creed. Good night for now!

—⁓—

January 3. I congratulate you on your decision to study languages — and also that you're going to Dresden. The Germans as a people are so different from us that whether you like them or not, you're bound to learn something. And it's Dresden, after all. You must write to me often in the new year and tell me all about how you are and what Dresden is like — and whether there's anything amusing in the German theaters. I can keep up with all of it so splendidly because I read the German newspapers at the office in the morning, even the Reichstag debates. Good Lord, a person ought to be interested in as many things as possible, and you can certainly expand your knowledge of human beings by reading about a tariff debate. Give my greetings to the Madonna Sistina and tell me whether it looks like a box of chocolates. Otherwise I'm not very fond of Raphael — well, I know it only from photographs, but I don't think he's particularly interesting. My idol is Botticelli. I think it was Georg Brandes* who said that you can read more in paintings [than?] in books, and he's right. Now you'll have the entire Dresden gallery as your library. How do you go about learning a language? Is it mostly by studying grammar? There's one good thing about studying languages: You don't have to stick to the well-known authors but can go off on adventures. I've read old English writers from Chaucer to Shakespeare — and I can tell you it was fun! You hear a

---

*Georg Brandes (1842–1927) was the foremost Danish literary critic of his day. His landmark lecture series in the 1870s titled "Main Currents in Nineteenth Century Literature" launched the Modern Breakthrough in Scandinavia.

name, and then it's a matter of tracking down his books and you start reading, without any kind of guidance from a literary historian beforehand, struggling your way through peculiar language and old forms of expression, through affectation and bombast and listening for the speech of that era and the thoughts of those people, until you find what is universally human. It's such a pleasure, let me tell you, to make the dead speak. That's why I want to learn Latin and Greek too. I love what I know of translated Greek literature, and all the glory of the entire Middle Ages and the Catholic Church can be found in Latin. Do you know the letters of Abelard and Héloïse?

No, Dea, you see, when you work and put all your thoughts into *understanding,* then gradually you end up with nothing left to grieve about, at least while you're *working.* God knows there will be time enough for grieving. But in truth, from what I know of you, that's what you'd most like to be: a whole person who understands as much of life as you can — and I salute you for that. *Happy* New Year, Dea.

Your
Sigrid

Have a good trip! You must write and tell me if I've understood your address correctly:

Østre (?) Allé 28 1

Here is my photograph. It's a good likeness, although my neck can't possibly be that short.

Kristiania
November 6, 1901

Dearest Dea!

At last I'm making a serious effort to write to you — it's been such a long time, and I have so much to write that this letter may take on the dimensions of a sweetheart's letter. God knows how I'm going to manage to get it all written — or how you'll find time to read it. First of all, I've managed to get a room of my own — which I've never had before, you see. If you've been used to having your own room ever since you were a child, you can't imagine how lovely it is. Although I'm not going to sleep here; Mamma wouldn't allow it. But the room is twice as comfortable because there's no bed in it. I had it painted the exact blood-red color that I wanted, and since the walls are wood paneled, and the furniture of the simplest kind — which I painted a brilliant green color — and since there's plenty of space from one wall to the other, it has all turned out so charming. A "corner sofa" draped with an old Italian rug, one of Father's old curved bookshelves, and over by the stove a lovely "peasant bench" where I wish you were sitting right now with a cigarette so we could have a good chat, instead of me having to write down every word that I would have said to you. And I have my books and flowers and shelves with ceramics and pots and lots of pictures — all of them pictures that I either bought myself or took from Mamma's huge collection of photographs of Renaissance paintings — so you see, everything has a *personal* meaning for me and suits my own taste. It would have been pure torture if I had been forced to fill the room with all those sorts of knickknacks that girls love to decorate their chambers with — "artistic" embroideries and porcelain cats and vases with embossed landscapes and bowls painted with courting couples wearing Empire or rococo attire. Thank God, I say, looking at my Botticelli-like Madonna as she takes a child in her thin hands, closing her lovely, heavy, curving eyelids as sobs tremble on her delicate, childlike lips.

Oh, if only you were sitting next to the stove and the two of us could have a good talk. Then we could have tea and smoke our cigarettes and afterward go to the theater and see Bjørnson's splendid *Paul Lange and Thora Parsberg** — it's

---

*Norwegian author and playwright Bjørnstjerne Bjørnson (1832–1910) played a central role in Scandinavian cultural life in the nineteenth century. He was awarded the Nobel Prize for Literature in 1903. His play *Paul Lange and Thora Parsberg* dates from 1898.

splendid and captivating the way BB's [Bjørnstjerne Bjørnson's] plays seldom are, and my old idol, Fru Dybwad, is just as she was in her heyday — enchanting.

Well, I came in here yesterday. Now it's already late in the evening. After lunch I came in to continue writing, but first had some coffee and opened the book lying on the table. Then I started on Shakespeare's "Venus and Adonis," and read through the entire long poem, so by now it's almost suppertime. Do you know it? It's radiant with a sensual splendor of colors, more luminous than Titian. Apropos books: I have now read *Inga Heine* and *Gunvor Thorsdatter.** But I can't share your enthusiasm. Both books are so sincerely well meaning. And they're alike in that neither of them deals with visualized, felt, or living human beings but with ideals — heroes and heroines. And I can't summon up any interest in the incomparable *Gunvor Thorsdatter of Hærø.* The mere fact that no Norwegian village shopkeeper's daughter would ever have such a name; and besides, the woman doesn't have a single ordinary human quality — in particular, not a single female one — or at least not this one: the petty, cunning shyness that all women possess to a greater or lesser degree, and which men so scornfully point out, but which is nothing more than a mother animal's weapon of defense against the male and protection for her brood — that which has branched and split off and been faceted for both good and bad, as the living conditions of women have developed over thousands of years, from the naked prehistoric humans up until the present day — all of this Frøken Prytz ignores. But isn't what almost all women writers do a betrayal of their own sex? If they moralize, they take the man's point of view and by brute force try to make the ideal woman the same as the ideal man. But then the character follows suit. A woman's courage and pride and fidelity and veracity are completely different from a man's, more personal — at least, for example, as far as a woman's honor is understood to mean something purely personal, physical, a faithfulness to her own body or to the one who possesses it; while a man's is almost something external, conventional. At any rate many men sacrifice their own personal honor, "their heart's honor," for the concept of honor, while the best women, to preserve their heart's honor, disregard the accepted concept of honor. But if you melt the "slag" out of a woman and try to fuse maternal love, tenderness, and domesticity all together with a large portion of the male ideal, you end up with nothing but

---

*The novel *Inga Heine* by the Danish author Jenny Blicher-Clausen (1865–1907) was published in 1898. *Gunvor Thorsdatter of Hærø* from 1896 was a highly popular novel by the Norwegian author and feminist Alvilde Prydz (1846–1922).

hash, and in my opinion the glorious, sterling Gunvor falls completely apart with the choice of qualities given to her. And in conclusion, I want to say that Frøken Prytz's Nordland could just as well be on the moon. *Inga Heine* is a little better. But even Inga is constructed, not visualized. Fru Clausen apparently admires her characters too much for her to have experienced their emotions. That the youth speaks in a manner that no youths in reality would ever use is insignificant; that all of them are artists to some extent, that the grandmother was in love with an artist, is something we have to accept from women authors — even the fact that Gunvor falls in love with a man because he is artistic; there can't be anything else that attracts her to that spineless fellow, Falk — but women authors like to cultivate artists and doctors. The fact that the doctor simply has to be a doctor — well, there's no shortage of them in Denmark, but never mind that. Oh, but that sort of love, Dea! He, who has envisioned her in his mind and loves her at first sight — and if he hadn't imagined that she was destined for him from the time the constitution was written, there wouldn't be any story. All that nonsense, that fervent nonsense about a deep and absolute understanding. God forbid that a man and a woman should know each other through and through. Know each other so well that they can respect what they don't understand, as a condition for those qualities they love, that's the ideal that very few ever attain; anything beyond that is a bad idea. I think most marriages run aground because the two people have tried to know each other too well, and have tried to find nothing but happiness — and love dies as they come to know each other's [. . .] shirts and underwear and corsets and garters and all those dismal things — the prosaic that we have unfortunately come to call reality. And I wonder, my Dea, if you would have regarded your acquaintance from the summer in exactly that way if you hadn't read *Inga Heine*? Forgive me if I'm wrong, I can only judge by a few lines in a letter, but it did strike me.

And forgive me if you think I'm talking in a much too self-assured and conceited way about books that you like and admire. You might find it odd that I speak so boldly about art. I'm used to it. I can speak fervently about some cause, pronounce my judgment with firm conviction, and at once a couple of little girls, smiling with superiority, say: "My dear, are you so sure you know what art is?" "Well, you certainly don't have a small opinion of yourself." If I just had even the shabbiest little story or poem published by the Luther Foundation, those same girls would probably never question it, oh no, then I would be an authority; but try to make them understand that someone can have so much love for art and such understanding of what art is that in the morning she burns what she fever-ishly wrote the night before because she hasn't been able to blow the breath of life into the people who haunt her heart. That's the reason, the only reason, why I am sad and tired, and the only reason why I plague you and others with sadness and jeremiads about my lonely life; that's why I long to live life, because I need to cre-ate art, but I don't know life well enough — from my own mind and from books, I don't want to write books about dreamed-up characters who float off into wild blue ideals. Ideals for life — bread for stones . . . what wretchedness! All these females who make books like woolen stockings and fabricate images that are supposed to resemble those of men. And yet there *are* women who can be artists. Your own wonderful Selma Lagerlöf* — she sees life through the soul of a woman so it glitters, too distinguished to imitate men; and Amalie Skram;† and then here in town there's poor, frail Fru Anna Munch‡ — in the midst of the glo-rious days of the women's movement she tried to be a woman, and was jeered at by men and feminists alike. And the images of Agnes Slott-Møller§ and Minka Grønvold! Oh, if only women would be women — try to find themselves and try to live accordingly, and refuse either to compete with men or to let them decide what is eternally feminine or what they ought to do. And then, above all else not be so afraid to admit that we belong to the ranks of mammals — dear God, at least we can console ourselves that we are in the forefront.

—◊◊◊—

November 9. I wonder when I've ever going to be done with this epistle! The more I write, the more I think I must write. I had thought of condensing for you the project that I'm working on, but now I'm going to put it on a page all

---

*The great Swedish author Selma Lagerlöf (1858–1940) won the Nobel Prize for Literature in 1909. Her best-known work in English is *Gösta Berlings Saga,* first published in Sweden in 1891.

†Norwegian author Amalie Skram (1846–1905) was a prominent and controversial literary figure who is today recognized as a major voice in the feminist literary canon. Her works include *Constance Ring* (1885, English translation 1988) and the chilling autobiographical novels *Professor Hieronimus* and *Paa St. Jørgen* (1895, translated in one volume as *Under Observation,* 1992).

‡Anna Munch (1856–1932) was a Norwegian writer who made her literary debut in 1889 with the story "Kvinder" (Women).

§Danish painter and sculptor Agnes Slott-Møller (1862–1937) devoted her art to the depiction of figures from Scandinavian folk ballads. She and her husband, the painter Harald Slott-Møller, visited Sigrid Undset at Bjerkebæk in 1923. There he painted the famous portrait of Undset that now hangs in the foyer of Aschehoug Publishing Company in Oslo.

by itself so you can read it when you feel like it, but I would awfully like to hear your opinion, so you're not going to be able to escape your fate.

But I will try to keep it brief. I'm "working," you see, on something; in fact, it's a big, heavy novel. It's the same beast I've been thinking about for years. Inside old books or folders I occasionally find a page from my childhood describing the escapades of Svend and Agnete. Though there's nothing much left of the old story but the names. And the outer circumstances, of course. Unfortunately, I'm using the names and fates of historical figures as a framework. The first time I read Ingemann* — you do know Ingemann, don't you? — I was deeply intrigued by the hearty young Svend Trøst, who wins Agnete, daughter of the noble Marsk Stig — wins both the princess and half the kingdom. The music of their names captivated me. I wrote a continuation of their fates. And whatever I saw or thought I put into their stories. That must be 8–10 years ago now. My admiration and respect for the "hero" and "heroine" have subsided as I became acquainted with the people and got to be on a first-name basis with them. Now I no longer know whether to regard them as good or bad. They're definitely not admirable. But I think I know what they're like. Svend wins the princess, but he doesn't win half the kingdom. Their dowry is a child. Their love, which has carried them beyond all other considerations, cannot adjust to marriage. She is practically a child herself; deathly tired, she longs for a man who can give her peace and protection. She sees that her husband, who loves her and would do anything to make her happy, is a boy who truly doesn't know how to act because he's incapable of understanding why they have grown so unhappy. Their life together becomes a torment, more and more bitter with each day that passes — until in the end they realize that for both of them only one thing exists in life: the love that has destroyed them both, but which neither of them can relinquish. They find some sort of happiness, but it comes too late. She is exhausted by the long struggle, and she dies, while life has rendered him powerless; he is left behind, worn out, weak, and despondent, and he slips further and further until a few years later he dies too.

I have written it over and over, changing and reworking it, but now I want to make a serious attempt, once and for all. Because now I'm convinced that I can see both of them clearly. So it's a matter of whether they're people with both feet on the ground, or figments of my imagination, shadows, hovering in

---

*The historical novels of Danish writer Bernhard Severin Ingemann (1789–1861) had a strong influence on Sigrid Undset's early aspirations to write stories set in the Middle Ages.

the blue! If only you could see how hard I've worked on this, Dea! I have a few short chapters that are just the way I want them. That's the result of two years of effort. And there are plenty of faults that I can see for myself. First of all, the characters are historical. If instead they were, for instance, a Lieutenant Graah and Frøken Hvide, or an office manager or engineer and a wholesaler's daughter, or anyone else — the deadly Niels Ebbesen and all that. And my fear that they will turn out pompous, declaiming instead of talking. And that they will think in modern terms and be nervously reflective instead of letting their nerves work in the dim realm of the instincts as was the case with people in the year 1340. Not to mention the historical color. *Orate pro me!* Alas, yes. But now I have to get busy!

And there's still a swarm of projects, ideas, names, and subjects distracting me. They sit one behind the other, the way the poisonous fangs of a snake supposedly do — if one is broken off, the next one immediately appears in its place. By the Devil, if I ever get rid of these two who have plagued me for so long, a new lady and gentleman will no doubt force their way forward. And probably not a single one of them is worth a sour herring.

My sister Ragnhild* sends you her greetings. She has come in "to take care of me." She's such a tiny thing, Ragnhild is, petite and plump and silky soft and neat as a kitten, graceful and chirpy like a bird, with shining eyes and a rosebud mouth that never utters anything but the most loving words, but her little, innocent-looking hands are as solid as a boy's, and God only knows how things will go — everyone dances to her beck and call. She has an unbelievable way of making people happy when they can please her. And she has so many talents. She graduated this spring at the top of her class, and has as many private students as she wants. Seventeen years old and she's tutoring an older teacher in mathematics, a bank clerk in French; 6 downright idiot adolescents have learned good manners after 8 hours' treatment; a disobedient 12-year-old boy who was expelled from school has become a lamb who voluntarily writes term papers and brings her flowers and hand-drawn maps; her friends, both male and female, adore her; Pappa's old friends came over after the matriculation ceremony and welcomed her to the university, and Professor Brøgger went around exclaiming that if she wanted to continue her studies, she would be a boon to scholarship. In addition, she dances like an elf, embroiders enormous

---

*Sigrid Undset's sister Ragnhild was born in 1884.

lace pieces, and helps Mamma with the house — "She's the only one of you who's any good at helping," my mother says. Here in my room she has installed herself in the most pleasant way, allowing me to read aloud, steeping the tea, buying cakes, and rolling cigarettes; and for me to refuse Ragnhild anything she might ask me would be just as impossible as for me to give you a kiss, Dea, when you're sitting in your clinic down south in Germany. In terrible downpours I go over to the university and stand in the corridor to wait, letting all the students stare at me, until Ragnhild appears at last! Her hat and curls and veil all have to be properly arranged — "When I go out with you, I have to look nice." If she's cold, I'm happy to offer the young lady a cup of cocoa; if she's in need of a fan, ribbons, gloves, dancing slippers — it's sheer delight to be able to give them to her. And it's through no merit or worthiness on my part — but when Ragnhild thanks me as we walk home together, and gently kisses me on one of the lanes through the park, or when we're sitting here and she nods and smiles at me, "It's so lovely that the two of us mean so much to each other!" — that's so splendid!

I think Ragnhild's secret lies in the fact that she genuinely admires everyone.

Sunday, November 11. Now I'd better see about finishing this letter so I can put it in the mailbox on my way to the office. This must be the longest letter I've ever written to you — or to anyone else in ages. But I think it's awful that the two of us have drifted so far apart; a large part of the blame must be mine, of course — I haven't corresponded with you properly for almost half a year, but now I'm determined to do better. I don't suppose you will have much time for writing, but my dear, let me hear from you as soon as you find time and as often as you can. I long to hear how you like it at the clinic — many greetings and a kiss, my sweet Dea, from

your devoted, truly devoted
Sigrid Undset

p.s. My address is Pilestrædet 49 (the same as before)

Kristiania
March 8, 1902

My own dear Dea!

Es ist die alte Geschichte — die wird doch immer neu. [It's the same old story, yet there's always something new.] If everyone else in the world stopped having good intentions, mine alone would provide enough material to pave the road all the way to Hell — no matter how wide it is. The fact that this afternoon, just as on so many other afternoons, I sat down to write to you but nothing came of it until now, at 8:30 at night, that's something that has happened at least once a week since I got your last letter, almost two months ago. But all excuses aside — I can never find the energy to carry out my intentions.

It's really quite odd. I take out your letter and every time I read through it, I know exactly what I want to tell you, but when I put pen to paper, it's all gone.

—⁓—

Monday, March 10th. Oh no . . . all of my plans are falling apart. I've told you that I want to be an author. I can't get it into my head that it won't happen. Because I know what I want to write about, and how I want to write it, but if I manage one page in four hours, by the next day it's only worth burning. Just like when I want to write to you — I know what I want to say, but the words here on the page look so strangely faded, and I'm afraid that it often ends up being something different than what I meant. To you it must seem like some kind of madness on my part, since my letters are often unbearably pompous and affected, and if there's one thing I'm afraid of, it's affected, insincere books; affectation is the skerry on which most women authors run aground, but I still want to. It's the only way I can see of getting anything out of my life. Going to the office and then being a good girl here at home; reading books, walking around imagining and dreaming and longing to get away, not knowing a single person who belongs to the same race as I do or who has a single emotion in common with me — in general, not accomplishing the slightest thing in life — I don't find that very amusing. And on top of that, to hear constantly that things are actually just fine . . . Mamma is convinced that I'm basically leading the life that suits me best. God help me, I think she seriously believes that I'm meant for this nun's life with three women whom I've known all my life, with visits to other women every other Sunday. As you can see, I'm quite pretty — I don't mind admitting that. The picture I sent you is not overly flattering; on the contrary. I like it because the expression is typical, and that's the countenance I've most often turned toward you in my letters, but I'm much prettier than that. I'm tall and sturdy, with beautiful hands, splendid light brown hair, quite lovely eyes, and a mouth that's so beautiful that many times when I look at myself in the mirror, it astonishes even me. I also know exactly what my faults are. My face is too round and my hair too thick to pin up properly. I walk on the edges of my boots. I can carry myself gracefully if I move slowly, and I have a nice smile, but laughter doesn't become me, and I simply cannot dance, and to flirt or bat my eyes or do anything like that would suit me so horribly, it would be ridiculous. And because I hate everything that is unattractive and ridiculous, Mamma thinks I have a natural aversion to dances and amusements and youth. Furthermore, those ordinary modern dresses don't suit me. A fitted black dress, an old-fashioned linen collar with lace trim and big cuffs, a silver pin in my hair and a rose at my bodice — that's what suits me. But Mamma is always insisting that I wear "youthful colors"! She truly cannot understand that there's something called virtue by necessity. I'm not content with fashions in pictures and books and in exhibitions; of course I can see that a red walking dress is pretty — yes, I'm even grateful to the women who wear them because they look so charming when there are lots of them, for instance in the spring sunshine with the green trees. But if they don't suit me . . . Dance music can make my breast ache with feeling — but I'm too old to learn to dance, and since I don't dance well, I'd rather not dance at all. And just because I say that the love of my life is a Florentine portrait bust in the gallery, Mamma actually believes that I don't want any young men to admire me or court me. Dear God, just because none of [. . .] the students or cadets or engineers or bookkeepers or idiots whom I've met so far has ever inspired me to wish to see him again or to spend more than 5 minutes with him, Mamma actually believes that I'm destined to fantasize away all my best talents on a plaster head in a gallery or on some imaginary character in a poem! And yet all I ask is a tiny bit of intellect and wit and charm in a man's thoughts; I don't mind if he's as ugly as sin — my beloved, Gentile della Luna, is ugly too. Dear God, you must tell me, Dea, do you think any real men exist, or are they all just menfolk? I'm so tired, so very tired of people for whom life is nothing more than the daily bread with a little "fun" added, and art is merely an "interest" — or else it's all meaningless and life is something that starts after death. I think that's so sad. That people either slave for God, whom they have created in their own image, and do everything they possibly can for payment and advancement after the grave — or else they would stop asking about good and evil as soon as they didn't have our Lord above with a whip in one hand and sweets in the other. I think it's so wretched that it practically makes me cry! I was quite young when I began to believe in people, in life as God. For me, God became a sacred image before which we should offer flowers to life, the way the Greeks and the Chinese, all the mature, thinking races of humanity, once did — instead of crawling and trembling like savages before their stone idol. Life, the eternal, was in every-thing, "in suns, in violets," I've never believed in any other eternity. But I thought life was so vast, so great, and so beautiful, that we should shape our-selves into a work of art, pure and glorious, as if it were created for eternity. The great power that makes the flowers bloom doesn't care that they will wither one day. The Greek masters didn't ask whether their statues might someday be crushed; no artist asks about the fate of his creation; he creates the most beautiful thing he can — and yet a human life is the greatest work of all. My life, one day I want to be able to place it in the hands of death, and perfect or imperfect, it should be a work that I can be proud of, whether death oblit-erates it or preserves it. That's my belief, what I have believed and still do — but I know if death came today, I would have nothing to give him and I would say, "Look here, my life, my work." But I love and honor both life and death so dearly that I would grieve bitterly if I had nothing to give to death.

Oh, Dea, Dea . . . I must become something, I must work. I am screaming inside for work. Maybe I should be content with helping my mother — she cer-tainly deserves as much from me, but everything on earth wants to be some-thing more than just life in another life, everything wants its own life, as surely as the seed will survive after the flower falls, otherwise the plant would die. It may well be that I would gain little joy, and no honor or benefit if I could real-ize all my dreams, but they do exist, and surely I must have some talents. It's not that I want to be talked about, that's not it, or to be included in a more "interesting" or "amusing" group, or to become an artist, reviewed, critiqued, disparaged, gossiped about, or to have the privilege of dressing differently, or to ignore all the middle-class rules — if they ever start to bother me, I don't intend to respect them anyway. It's not even the possibility of leaving home and traveling, of meeting people who are like me, of escaping a job that bores me

— not even that is what entices me. I have too many faults of the artistic person for that — shamelessness, suspicion, the urge to unravel the finest fibers of joy that would be best left in peace, the wish to illuminate and investigate the most hidden corners of the instincts, which are best and most healthy when left lying in the dark — to want to live among artists, but *I want to create art.* That's the only thing I want. But it's an *artist* that I want to be, a *woman* artist, and not a pen-wielding lady. Instead of sinking down and becoming a diligent book producer, who publishes a certain number of printed pages each year, I would rather live and die in my office chair — but fortunately, there's no risk of that. The work, the toil of putting down on paper what I've composed is so loathsome to me that I have to be profoundly moved before I can feel [happy?] at dipping my pen; and before I can bring myself to write about the images in my mind, I have to be haunted by nightmares, practically tortured by their fates or sorrows.

Here I meant to comfort you in your sorrow and I end up giving you this long speech about my artistic dreams — perhaps it will make you smile and think it's all the figment of someone's imagination who has never truly, personally experienced what sorrow is. Oh Dea, I would be eternally grateful for a true sorrow that my heart could feel and that my mind wouldn't immediately try to dissect. And don't get married unless you're so in love that you would rather be with your sweetheart in Hell than alone in Heaven. Even in happy marriages — I assume that they do exist, although I haven't seen any that I would call happy — happiness is assuredly paid for with one's most precious possessions; or, even worse, with the other person's. And remember that most people, at some time in their lives, have wished that their mother had never given birth to them. Furthermore, marriage makes most women stupid, or they dilute their demands on life, on their husband, and on themselves so much that they can scarcely be counted as human, or they become uncomprehending, vulgar, coarse, or unhappy.

Yes, my dear Dea, I certainly hope you will take great joy and comfort from this edifying epistle. I'm keeping one consolation for my own use: I *will!*

I will hold my head high, I will not buckle under.

I will not commit suicide — will not waste my talents. If I have any, I will also find them and use them. I will be whatever I can be.

If I can't be what I *want* to be, then I will be what I *can* be.

And if things go wrong, the blame and the punishment will be mine alone.

It will not be because of our Lord or the Devil, life or death, my father, mother, grandparents, great-grandparents, or anyone else, either living or dead.

And a child ought to treat others as he would wish to be treated himself. But he should be responsible for his own deeds, both for his own sake and for all those who understand him.

Because two things are certain: I'm alive, and I'm going to die. And it's not good to live if you have no joys.

Amen.

And you should regularly, morning and night, conjugate the verbs: *should, can, will, ought to,* and *must* in all the languages you can master. It's a most beneficial exercise.

Many kisses, dear Dea, and write soon to your babbling fool.

Sigrid Undset

Kristiania
April 23, 1902

My own dear girl!

To think you've been composing poetry in all secrecy — I have long had my suspicions, otherwise I wouldn't have dared confide in you what I have been secretly hoping. Besides, many years ago I had a taste of something you wrote. You had written a little play and then burned it; that was just after we first started writing to each other. As for this verse, I would like to tell you my opinion, but I truthfully have no opinion except that I think you're good at making up rhymes. I came to this conclusion because you don't seem to have had such a strong urge to write about the theme — a mother's prayer — that you were *compelled* to do so, despite the struggle and difficulties of composing the verse. To put it bluntly: If it had been a hard and painful struggle to shape your thoughts into a poem, I don't think you would have written it — and if you did, I also think you would have found a more vigorous and concise means of saying what you wanted to say — something more personal. For if I'm going to tell you my most heartfelt opinion, and that's exactly what I'm doing because, as I said, I do believe that you *can* write poetry, then an expression such as "you, my radiant star in the cloud-shrouded night" isn't especially personal. Don't ever write anything, not a line, not a word, not a comma, that doesn't belong, that isn't carefully considered and weighed and found to be essential. "You must sacrifice for the king the reddest of blood" — what do you mean by that, for example? This is something that in our time would only apply to officers — and hardly even to them. I can accept that a man defends his nationality and his fatherland, for all of a nation's potential for development lies in its independence. That South Jutland, for example, where children of Danish extraction learn to think in a foreign language and are brought up in a foreign culture with foreign ideals — that South Jutland* will ever make any contribution to culture is as likely as a dead tree sprouting blossoms. But to sacrifice blood for a king . . . Who would do that today? Should a German woman, for

---

*Conflict over the control of South Jutland, also known as the duchies of Slesvig and Holstein, erupted in two German-Danish wars in the mid–nineteenth century, with the border shifting several times. In 1866 both were annexed by Prussia, and it wasn't until a plebecite in 1920 that the northern part of Slesvig was returned to Denmark.

example, teach her child to sacrifice blood for one of Kaiser Wilhelm's whims? Blood of her own blood! Then I'd rather see him shot as a rebel, so he would die for a cause that he himself had carefully considered, a son who dared to die for what he believed in — that's someone I could be proud of. For heaven's sake, Dea, think not only twice, but ten times before you write, and remember that it's worse to reinforce children in their old, established, and authorized delusions than to preach new ideas to them — the new, which they must first fight for and prove to be viable — and besides, there are never very many who believe in the new teachings.

Well, dear Dea, now I've disposed of your poem so you're probably quite annoyed with me. But since you want to write, I don't think it should be just a game; you should do some honest work — that's why I'm telling you my honest opinion without embellishment.

—∿—

May 4, 1902. I'm sure that you won't misunderstand me, and I beg you to send me whatever examples of your work you can; I would so terribly like to read them all. You must tell me something about your poems, what you intend to do with them, and about all your plans in general.

Inspiration — yes, that's all well and good. But sometimes a person writes things due to an "inspiration," which shouldn't be included, if he wants to write something bigger, that is. What a job it is to hammer together a story so that the characters develop and *live*. And if you're interested in a minor character, to keep that character in his proper place so he doesn't emerge too much in the foreground. Not to give in to the temptation to embellish him from the inside. And yet you would like to make him as vivid as possible, and I can tell myself that the story is going to be long enough as it is, ergo, the character in question can't be elaborated on, but will have to be defined by what he says and does, and the way he intervenes in the book. I would like to describe Anders and Folkvar very clearly, but it will have to be done with a few strokes. Anders, for example, is the brother of the young girl, Agnete; I'm struggling to fit in the relationship between the two siblings. I've written page after page about his feelings regarding her situation — but it will have to go. It falls outside the framework, gives the story unnecessary breadth, and I have to refuse myself the pleasure of developing Anders. He must be portrayed solely through his appearance in the key scenes, meaning after his sister's marriage, where he brings about the decision. Etc. — one favorite scene after another I have to cut out, but new ones emerge that are necessary because they help define the main characters and motivate the action — so some are deleted and others are shortened — one sentence has to be as clear as the previous ten — and it goes on forever like that. There is no doubt that this is the method for writing a good book — but whether I can write a good one, whether I can write at all?

The setting: northern Jutland. The time: 1339–1347. Thus: "On a bright sunny spring day in the year 1339, a solitary horseman rode through the great forests which at that time covered most of northern Jutland, along the sunken road that leads west toward Hald Lake [?]. The horseman, a tall, slender youth of about nineteen, was wearing . . . etc."

Oh, it's almost silly to tell you that this is not how I want to write. Because there's probably no one who writes like this anymore. Everyone has gone to the other extreme nowadays. I want to write in a painterly way — and I'm well aware of the danger. I'm afraid of borrowing, of painting with someone else's colors. Oh, if only I could master the language in such a way that I could simply and naturally, and yet using words that are new and fresh, make the reader see the springtime. In 1339 the Danish forests were composed mostly of oak trees — ergo, springtime in the oak forests — in the grove, leaves and fine grass, new brown leaves and blue anemones — bright and cool, with big open crowns and lush underbrush. The whole time, you see, the reader should know where he is, how the land looked, as well as the houses and the people and the animals and the clothing and the weapons and saddlery, and you should quite naturally and easily enter into the life, see and understand why these people *are* this way, how they feel and why they behave as they do; and all of this without pedantic lectures about the era and the spirit of the times and all that muck that can make a story so inartistic because it's historical. No grand gestures, fancy words, or "romantic" events. It should be written in such a way that whatever might seem romantic to us — murder, violent scenes, etc. — becomes ordinary and alive. And so all this merely for the simple story of a man and the people who intervene in his life.

These are not trivial matters, you understand. Whether anything will ever come of it, I don't know. It's tempting; I've made several drafts and attempts, and the plan is good and well constructed, the plot simple and plausible. That's the reason why I have no peace. And I've dreamed of the characters for so long and worked with them until in my mind they are alive, flesh and blood — and yet! Even so, I'm often about to give up the whole thing. I don't think I'm familiar enough with the fourteenth century to venture into an intimate description of daily life on an estate in Jutland — and I'm not capable of mastering the language either. I can't even think of letting the people speak the colloquial language of the day, but on the other hand, there has to be an old-fashioned tone to the whole book, so that the language throughout, both in the speech of the characters and in the description and narration, excludes all words and expressions that are not of Old Danish origin. But it's not easy, let me tell you, to get by without foreign words or to make the old words sound natural, without affectation, and without sentimentality or excessive formality. *Summa summarum* — if I ever manage to get a grip on this lad, it won't be this year. And if I ever get him finished, I'll never find a publisher for this big, lengthy monster, unless I manage to have some lesser pieces published first — but we'll cross that bridge when we come to it! As long as I myself am pleased, that's the important thing right now.

This has turned into a long opus about an unwritten ditto, and I don't feel like talking any more about myself. Are you going to Sweden this summer? Write to me soon and tell me your plans — I'm just like a little child, going around and dreaming about important works to be done. Oh, but Dea, you must know how it is — so tempting. That's really the hope that keeps the life in me or rather, keeps me alive.

Farewell, dear Dea — write to me *soon*. Remember, I'm hoping you will send me something soon!

Your devoted
Sigrid Undset

Give your sister my thanks for her greeting!

Kristiania
October 28, 1903

Dearest Dea!

I don't feel like starting off with a few sentences about how long I've been waiting for your letter; that it has been a *long* time, you know as well as I do, but I
was terribly glad when it finally came. I hope you'll write again soon, so please
note that my address is now *Eilert Sundts gade 52,* or A.E.G.,* *Tordenskiolds Gade 1.*
   The new office is nice. That's where I'm sitting now and writing to you. It's
5:30. The room faces the street and it's big and almost cozy. Right now the sky
is quite a dark violet-blue, and on the other side of a little park is Karl Johans
Gaten with all its glittering beads of light. The electric arc lamps are lavender
colored and white, and the shop windows are gleaming reddish yellow, but the
Auer lamps burn with a greenish tinge. In the mornings I stand at the window
and watch the people: I mean, early in the morning, because otherwise I have
other things to preoccupy me. The park forms an oblong rectangle between the
city's two main streets; at one end of the rectangle stands the National Theater,
and at the other the parliament. Actors on their way to rehearsal, parliament
members, shop clerks, well-dressed pretty young girls, and clumsy, dreary-
looking men stream steadily past; but in the park children are playing — not
the well-to-do, with their nursemaids, but poor children and mostly middle-
class children, in rather threadbare clothes. I'm beginning to recognize the various types — the messenger boys running errands for the big stores, what a
comical lot they are. It would be fun to peek inside the mind of one of those 12-
to-16-year-old boys . . . Then there are all the old men who sit smoking their
pipes on the benches. Some are old and poor and feel they're enjoying a sorrow-
free old age. They sit there, gentle and smiling and at ease. Others have no
doubt "seen better days." Not long ago an old man asked me for fifty øre to buy
lunch, and he wanted me to recommend him to my friends as a mathematics
tutor — he had been a teacher, he told me. Today I saw him down in the park;
he was filling his pipe next to an old, ragged man with a kind, rosy face and
venerable white hair. Then there are all the cripples. I've never seen so many
lame and blind people [here?] before. An old woman wearing a gray shawl,

---

*The Allgemeine Elektrizitäts Gesellschaft, parent company of the firm where Sigrid Undset
worked.

with bandages covering her whole face, led by a lovely, pale, half-grown girl in a faded velvet hat. They come here every day. Then there's a man on crutches who stops every third or fourth step with a grimace, as if it were very painful for him to move. And in the evening, after it's dark, I meet a tall, straight-backed young man who is led by a little boy. He's a former lieutenant, who went blind several years ago. There are various intriguing stories about him, the other ladies in the office tell me . . .

I stand at my window and feel a compassion, at a distance, for all of them, and I wonder what will come of the fact that I never meet anyone who interests me in a truly warm and personal way when I come close. It feels as if life has no use for me. Mamma and my family, I'm sure they love me, but it's not for my own sake — they would love me just as much if I were the exact opposite of "what" I am. I've lain in bed and wept night after night and listed everything I thought was rich and good inside me, examined and grieved over those things, because they couldn't buy me the love of a single human being. You have often told me that you're fond of me, and I do believe you — for that I'm much, much more grateful to you than I can ever say. I could only do so if I had you here and could kiss you — and yet I don't know whether you would still love me if we were always together or even just for a longer period of time. I think of everything and all the people you've written to me about that have disappointed you — that's something we have in common, you and I; we demand that things happen according to our dreams, but they never do, and I wonder if the two of us will ever have the strength to say to life: Don't happen the way *I* want, but the way *you* want.

But I'm awfully glad that I was able to see you this summer, because you were all so sweet to me, both you and your family. And I can't even tell you how fond I've become of you, sweet, sweet Dea.

Say hello to your sister for me and give her my congratulations. I think it must be so strange to love someone who speaks a different language. But maybe it's a good thing; then you won't be tempted to talk your love to death. Talk has no doubt killed more happiness than silence.

—∿—

November 18. That's how far I got a month ago. And ever since, I have almost daily thought about writing to you. I've been straightening up my room; this afternoon I put the finishing touches on the task: cleaned out the drawers and arranged my "papers," read through your old letters, and burned and sorted my "manuscripts," read a little of Edgar Poe's works. Do you know his poems "For Annie," "The Raven," "Ulalume," "To Helen," "The Sleeper," "The Conqueror Worm," "Dreamland"? It's useless to list them all — they're masterpieces, every single one. Actually, I haven't felt like reading much besides my own old books, from which I've practically memorized the poems: Danish folk ballads as well as English and German, and Shakespeare and Keats and Christian Winther,* and Adam Oehlenschläger† and Heine. And I've also read Verner von Heidenstam's *Hans Alienus,*‡ which I hadn't read since I was a child, not understanding a word. I actually think it's rather obscure, but there's much in it that seemed to be directed especially at me. Have you read it? And now I've started on Byron's *Don Juan* in English, but I'm reading it in bits and pieces.

I wasn't sure which of the pictures you sent me I could keep. So I'm sending them all back to you except for the ones of you and your room. The one of you wearing the Vingåker dress and the most "heavenly" is in a frame in my room, and here on my desk, under Shakespeare and Cæsar *(sic)* Borgia, is the one you sent me this summer, with the roses in your hair. It's the loveliest of them all — the only one that's as sweet as you are, when you look at me with your clear, somber eyes.

Keep well, Dea, write to me soon! I kiss you in effigy.

Your Sigrid
who loves you more than you know.

P.S. Please give my greetings to your parents and sisters.

---

*Danish writer Christian Winther (1796–1876) was particularly known for his love poems.

†Poet Adam Oehlenschläger (1779–1850) was a key figure in the romantic movement in Danish literature.

‡The novel *Hans Alienus* by Swedish author Werner von Heidenstam (1859–1940) was published in 1892 and became a kind of "aesthetic bible" for an entire generation.

Kristiania
September 4, 1908

Dear Dea!

Thank you for your letter — it was forwarded to me up at Høvringen. No, I
don't think I'll be taking any trips south this year. I was so tired and nervous
that I didn't think I was fit to go traveling or visiting. I've been staying at a
mountain farm in Gudbrandsdalen, most of the time alone with the farm girls
who have taught me to milk cows and churn butter . . . and I've spent hours
roaming around alone across the mountain plateau, playing cards in the
evening with the girls and their sweethearts who come up from the village, or
sitting alone at the hearth, smoking cigarettes and dozing. I am and will continue to be tired and overworked, and it probably won't get any better until I
quit my office job, but that won't happen before April or May — by then I'm
counting on having some money so I can take a proper trip abroad. First to
Denmark for a couple of months and then to Italy, I think, or southern
Germany. Then I'll come and see you if you want to and are able to have a visitor at that time — I have often longed *terribly* to see you and to get to know
you properly — and to see your home and your little girl — tell her hello from
me. She must be big and lively by now, your little Elisabet. Of course I would
love to have you translate *M. O. [Fru Marta Oulie]** to Swedish — it was written to be read, after all, and it would be fun to tell my precious publisher† about
it — although I have to admit he has been nearly beyond reproach in his behavior toward me, but I would dearly love to impress him a little. So far he has sold
531 copies of my book, so he has made money from it, no doubt more than I
have. That's why I was relatively confident today when I went over to talk to
him about the new book. And he was quite amenable, admitting that *M. O.* had
been an unusually successful debut, etc. My new book will be almost twice as
long: *The Happy Age: Stories about Children and Women.* I look forward to sending it to you; I think you'll like it. In my opinion, it's much better than *Marta;*
if it's not better written, then at least it has much more interesting themes,
although one of the stories is unfortunately terribly "daring," by our standards.

---

*Sigrid Undset's first published novel, which appeared in October 1907.

†Sigrid Undset's relationship with publisher William Nygaard eventually developed into a
warm friendship, and she later took to calling him affectionately "Sir William."

Well, nothing ventured, nothing gained, and if it's as good as I think, then I should gain much from it. There are two short stories and two longer ones.

I'm longing so much to see what you've written, and especially to receive a proper letter from you; the last one was all too brief. How are you, anyway? You must see about finding time to write a real letter to your Sigrid soon!

Now I ought to be taking a rest, but I don't think I have time: I have at least three books in mind that I'm longing to write, and sometimes I have the feeling that I should hurry up. The doctor says that my heart is very frail and if I can't abstain from sports and strong tobacco, it won't get any better. And I can't bear to give up either one . . .

You asked me to write about a wife who is faithful to her husband — I have a story like that in mind, but first will be two stories from the Middle Ages and a novel, *Outside of Wedlock* — for a change about a married man whose wife doesn't understand him and who finds consolation elsewhere, with the consequence that he ends up shooting both his lover and himself. For the wife, I have someone in mind as a model — for a change — whom I'm going to enjoy butchering; the "respectable" woman who possesses no heart, no sensibilities, or anything else besides selfishness and vanity.

I hope this won't be a boring letter for you to read; it seems to deal mostly with my literary concerns. You will have to forgive me, but, as I mentioned, I paid a visit to my publisher today and I'm still thrilled at my unexpected good fortune. A royalty of about 600 kroner and a friendly reception by Herr W. Nygaard. Not bad, by our standards, let me tell you.

Now I hope to hear from you soon — and a bit more than you usually write. By the way, I have to admit that our friendship by correspondence could soon use a more solid foundation, but we've been friends in this way ever since we were little girls and became grown-up women — I look forward to seeing you again, my dearest Dea!

Your devoted friend
Sigrid Undset

Kristiania
November 7, 1908

Dear Dea!

Thank you for your last letter and for the articles; it was fun to read them. I'll be sure to send them back, but right now I'm staying indoors, purporting to be ill — although it's not so bad that I can't sit up and feel like having a good talk with my friends. But perhaps you've given up that art, Dea?

I look forward to hearing — or rather, I can't wait to hear — what you think of my new book. I think the best one is "A Stranger," and the two shorter stories. I'm *very* anxious to hear what the critics have to say this time. I do hope I get the stipend. It's rash of me to think of giving up all security and running out into the world with almost no money, but I can't bear to keep on going this way; I'm so overwrought from work and cigarettes that I can tell I won't be able to continue like this much longer. Good Lord, surely I can stand to starve for a while, just like other authors. How I long to be out in the world someday. And to meet you in the springtime.

You ask why I'm interested in the marriage problem — I can't say that any "problems" interest me, just people, and it's most often marriage that is a person's fate, at least for women. It would never occur to me, for example, to write a book in order to portray an ideal "marriage of conscience," as I've seen young Swedish writers do — I've never seen this in practice and I'm absolutely convinced that it wouldn't make things any better. But as I've told you, I'm thinking about a story of two people who *have to* live their lives outside of marriage, and then things happen the way they usually do in real life with that sort of relationship, which almost daily collides with societal rules and institutions. Not the rebellion of "free souls," but two quite bourgeois individuals who try to maintain an outward decorum, who adapt and constantly have to conform and comply and keep encountering new obstacles, new humiliations — until their love is worn out and they are worn out too — worn to death. Although my next book might be the one about the "wife who is faithful to her husband"; I'm not sure. There are also some themes from the old, bloody days that I've been thinking about. And when I go traveling, maybe I'll think of something entirely different.

Have you read *The Heart** by Egge? I see there was a review of it in your magazine. It's a brilliant, solid book.

You ask about my family. Nothing much has changed here. Mamma toils with the house, Signe works in an office, Ragnhild is a teacher. She's engaged, by the way — secretly, for the time being. I'm glad . . .

[rest of the letter missing]

---

*A novel by Norwegian author Peter Egge (1869–1959).

Kristiania
December 22, 1908

Dear Dea!

Merry Christmas again! Now it's your turn to celebrate Christmas at your own hearth and light the Christmas tree for your own child — and I suppose you've had plenty of housework, so you're quite aware that it's Christmas! Yes, bless you . . . I hope you have a cozy Christmas.

    I am so looking forward to visiting you in the spring, and to leaving here, free as a bird — "lighthearted and glad, but owning little," as the ballad says — out into the world — not because I'm particularly happy or lighthearted, but maybe that will come. I have now given notice that I'll be leaving my job as of May 1st, and I'll take off as soon as I can. If only I would get the stipend . . . The other authors swear that I'll be awarded one of the smaller state grants, but I have to see it before I'll believe it. I've had a few inquiries about translations from Germany, and I've given a Rhea Sternberg the rights to "A Stranger," but it could take a long time before she finds a publisher; I'm trying to place a one-act play* with Fahlstrøm, where Fru Wettergreen is. They would probably take it at the National Theater, but they always let things lie around for years before they stage them, and besides, they don't have a decent actress. No, Dea, it's not much fun being an author, but I can't help myself. I don't expect to have an audience for years to come — for that I would either have to write trash à la Alvilde Prydtz or Bernt Lie,[†] or be inveterately deaf to criticism and the public and persist in doing what I think is right, and then I would no doubt win success one day, if I lived long enough and persevered long enough — and had talent, of course. Oh no, sacred innocence, learn from the criticism! Good heavens, I've had praise enough, and that's quite nice, especially for my publisher, who of course must want me to succeed, but when such a well-meaning and uncomprehending woman as Fru D. K. is allowed to write for our foremost paper . . . I'm sending you her review; she's nice enough, but she certainly hasn't understood much. Still, I can thank her for some of my books being sold.

---

*Sigrid Undset's only attempt at a serious dramatic work, the play *I graalysningen* (In the Gray Light) was not published until 1926 and was first performed in 1954.

†The rather sentimental novels of Norwegian author Bernt Lie (1868–1916) were very popular at the time.

What has pleased me is the genuine approval that I've received from the older authors, whose works I admire. I have a few other reviews that I'd rather show you, but I have only one copy of them and I don't dare ask for them back, since I've kept your magazines for such a shamelessly long time, but I'll send them after Christmas because it wouldn't be right to tax the post office more than necessary.

Thank you for your last letter. I look forward to receiving a picture of Elisabet when you have the little lady photographed, and even more to seeing her in person.

Now here I've written another Christmas letter all about myself — I'm starting to take on all kinds of bad habits of an artist, and it's a little early for that. To mend my ways a bit, I've made a buffet tablecloth for Mamma, with English embroidery, 1½ meters long, and thank God that today I took the beast off to the laundry, so she'll have it on Christmas Eve.

Give my greetings to your mother and sisters, if they still remember me. Take care, and have a good Christmas, you and all your family.

Fondest greetings from your devoted old friend

Sigrid Undset

Kristiania
March 8, 1909

Dear Dea!

Thank you for your last letter. Yes, I'm so looking forward to seeing you, and to setting out on my travels. I'm sure that I'll leave sometime in May — my last day at the office will be the 1st or the 15th, and then I'm off as soon as possible. I won't find out about the stipends until after I've left, but I have a little money and will probably receive more in the fall for my new novel.* I don't dare expect it to be as successful as the first two, because I'm sure I've been very lucky, you know; at least I've had nothing but fair winds. Meaning that neither of the books has sold in great numbers, but recently there was a survey of the year's books in *Samtiden,* and I was given a long, insightful review by a young and very stern critic, who named me as the most important and noteworthy of last year's author personalities. The thing is, you see, that when I started to write about what was right under my nose, I discovered something completely new — without fully realizing it myself. Kristiania has never really been described before except by outsiders, who have poured the bitter cup of their anger over our poor provincial town and all the young people who struggle and toil here alone — never by someone who has been part of the toil herself. But this time I'm not writing about Kristiania, so I suppose I'll hear enough criticism that I'll end up going back to my special forte. But I have to write what I want to write and the way I want to write it. It would be fun if you could get a translation published — I'm most fond of "A Stranger," and "The Handkerchiefs," and no doubt they're also the best; at least that's what the other writers say, the ones whose opinions interest me most. Well, enough about that; I'm trying to keep my writer's vanity in check as best I can, and when people talk about my books, I lower my eyes and look pious, as if I had never even read them.

Today I was at the office from 9 until 2:30. At lunch I did some embroidery — I'm sewing for my little sister who is engaged; she goes skiing and to lectures with her sweetheart and has no thought for serious matters such as buf-

---

*Undset is here referring to *Fortællingen om Viga-Ljot og Vigdis,* translated into English as *Gunnar's Daughter.*

fet tablecloths and napkins. I read a little of Sven Lidman's poetry* — how wonderfully he writes! — and was back at the office from 5 to 7, came home and ironed a blouse, and now I have to work some more; but God, how lazy I'm going to be this summer!

Many greetings from
Your devoted
Sigrid

Hope to hear from you soon! Don't forget to send me anything that Fru v. Kræmer† writes! I'm waiting for a family picture of all of you.

---

*Swedish poet and novelist Sven Lidman (1882–1960).

†The Swedish translator Vera von Kræmer translated Undset's *The Happy Age* in 1912.

Kristiania
June 3, 1909

Dear Dea!

It has been so long since I heard from you — how are you and your family? Are you still home, or are you thinking of going away for the summer?

On Tuesday — I think it's June 8 — I'm leaving for Denmark, and now I'm going to take you at your word and visit you at once, provided that you want to and are able to receive me. Please send any letters after Tuesday morning to: *Wholesaler Leop. Gyth, Strandboulevard 60, Copenhagen Ø.*

Finally I'm my own boss — after 10 years. And now all of a sudden it looks as if I'm being flooded with good fortune. I was prepared to set off into the world with 1000 kroner and to have my publisher grumble because I'm threatening to produce a novel set in the year 1000 — but now he seems remarkably receptive to my plans, and I've been nominated for the biggest grant that we have here in Norway. If I get it, I'll be able to live on it for more than a year if I'm careful, and they say there's no doubt that I'll get it. So you can understand that under the circumstances, it's not surprising that I think things are wonderful right now.

I was quite touched and melancholy about my farewell from A.E.G. It took place with all manner of honors and tributes, which I would never have imagined 10 years ago, when I made my less-than-sparkling debut there. Roses in a crystal vase next to my typewriter — that was from my colleagues; a farewell letter with a piece of jewelry from the manager; supper in a private room with the ladies; and endless leavetakings. And now I'm free, and I roam around town in the mornings, preparing to leave.

It's good for a person to be lazy for a while — but I'm looking forward to settling down in some peaceful place to finish my new book* — in Denmark, or I've given some thought to Falsterbo (you once talked about it many years ago when I visited you in Malmö). Until I head farther south, that is.

Now I'm looking forward to seeing you and your little girl — I hope it will be soon, or in the fall. Take care until then!

Your old friend
Sigrid

---

*Undset was working on a volume of poetry titled *Ungdom* (Youth), which was published in Norway in 1910.

Via Frattina, Rome
December 13, 1909

My Dear Dea!

At last I've settled in a bit and am feeling good. This morning I sat on my own sofa and drank tea, which I had made for myself, wearing my nightgown and enjoying the warmth of the sun and my view across the old gray rooftops of Rome with their terraces — terraces with palm trees and orange trees — and agaves and broken washbasins and laundry hung out to dry — and above everything the statue on the Piazza Martiri — Maria Immacolata with a crown of stars; she stands on a pillar and towers just above the rooftops. And beyond it all a glimpse of the evergreen oaks on Monte Pincio.

I live in a garret room on a street that is supposedly neither very healthy nor very fine, but it's a comfortable room and my new friends find their way at all hours of the day up my stairs, which are little more than a chicken-coop ladder. For the first two weeks, you see, I lived in a Norwegian boardinghouse. It was cold and noisy, but I met quite a few pleasant people, and unfortunately I've fallen into the habit of carousing the whole night away in tavernas. One day we didn't get home until breakfast, but on that occasion we had been to a morning mass and watched the sun come up over Monte Pincio. I think I last wrote to you from Bolzen, didn't I? I was in Florence for nearly 3 weeks, but I stayed in an appalling boardinghouse, filled with stupid old ladies who annoyed me terribly, and it was cold and I was miserably tired and depressed. So it's not until now, afterward, that I can truly see what a wonderful city Florence is. I traveled through Germany in a semi-doze. But now I'm beginning to feel like a human being again, and I'm thinking of starting on a new work.

My last book *[Gunnar's Daughter]* has again won success; it looks as if it may be the most successful of all. And I'm traveling on a grant, so I ought to pull myself together and be happy. But I'm filled with dread every time I start on a new work, because I want it to be better than the last one. And in my opinion it's dangerous to be successful. But inside I'm cursing to myself, and it won't make me any less attentive to every word I write down.

How are you, Dea? I now see that it's been 3 months since I last heard from you. And you must be about to fulfill woman's destiny once again. Oh yes, that's what the rest of us are missing, you know. A few days ago, around three in the morning, five or six of us were sitting in a wine taverna; a little child, about seven years old, came in and wanted to sell us newspapers. Her name was Elena, a tiny, pale, dark-haired Italian girl. She went from one person to the next. Sitting with us was an unmarried woman in her 40s. She's quite beautiful, especially on a festive evening when we've all had a great deal to drink of the marvelous wine they have here, which doesn't make you drunk or stupid or tired, just warm and happy and in a good mood. Oh, you have no idea what it's like, this delightful Roman wine. And this woman, in her 40s, on such a night she's beautiful and elegant and radiant and lively; warmth streams from her smiling, big brown eyes. She put her arm around little Elena and slid the black shawl back from the child's forehead and spoke to her in Italian — and her voice sounded so strangely anguished, and her smile looked so odd and wistful as she poured coins and candied fruit into the folds of the little girl's dress. And as I watched, I felt the same way as when beggars down here display their crippled limbs and hideous sores.

Strangely enough . . . we've all found for ourselves a cheerful little clique — Norwegians and a single Swede, a Dr. Brising. But . . . most of them are very young lads and girls. And the others — I think they all have some wounded place in their souls; they've come here to forget about something.

Let me wish you at once a Merry Christmas and a Happy New Year. I suppose you'll be lighting the Christmas tree for your little girl. For the first time I'm going to spend Christmas among strangers. God knows how that will be. It's odd to think that there's snow and winter back home right now. Here the oranges hang on the trees and the camellias are blooming in the Protestant cemetery near the city wall — in the cypress woods. Imagine huge camellia trees, as tall as lilac trees back home, covered with red and white rosettes!

I hope you will write to me at Christmastime. Don't forget that I'm all alone among strangers! Give my greetings to Elisabet, and a thousand greetings and a Christmas kiss for you, Dea.

from your old friend
Sigrid

Kristiania
January 18, 1912
Eil. Sundtsgate 52 1

Dear Dea,

Thank you for your letter. I was very glad to hear from you — at long last. Yes,
I've often felt sorry that we write so seldom to each other — but that's how it
goes. In the old days, when we were little girls, we had the time and energy to
fill letter after letter with our innocent confidences and little moods. Now that
we're grown women and both of us are intensely involved in our own lives —
you have your house and your home and your children and your work — I
have my work and my life — I suppose it's only reasonable that there's less time
for letter writing, and no doubt if we started writing a proper letter about ourselves, it would be much too long. But my old friend Dea, isn't it true that we
both know that we won't forget each other, and that we think about each other,
and now and then we will send each other a little greeting and sign of life?
Happy New Year, and I want to give you my thanks for the past year and for
all the other years too. And to thank you also for the tray cloth. I was so touched
and so happy to receive something that you had made for my home. I don't
think I'll be getting many more things like that because our relationship is very
secret,* and we won't be making it official until we're married somewhere
abroad — maybe in May. But I've been quietly doing a lot of sewing, and my
sisters have sewn a few little things, but it doesn't add up to much. My sisters
don't have a great deal of time, and I'm sewing all my own trousseau, every single piece. I had such a yearning to find myself an old "bridal chest" like your
sister Maggi showed me the first time I visited you in your old home in Malmö
— but I couldn't find one, so instead I bought myself a small old birch dresser
in the Empire style. Both my sweetheart and I have bought quite a few pieces of
beautiful old furniture from antiques dealers whenever we could, and I've managed to collect a number of lovely old glasses and pieces of porcelain, but everything will have to be stored in a warehouse for the time being. We're going
abroad, to be married and to stay for perhaps a few years, so it's impossible to

---

*Sigrid Undset fell in love with the Norwegian painter Anders Castus Svarstad while in Rome
in 1909. Svarstad was thirteen years her senior and a married man with three children back
home in Norway. They kept their relationship secret until Svarstad could arrange for a divorce.

know what kind of home we'll have. For that matter, I suppose I'll have a little child with me by the time I come back here. I often feel such a longing to
have a child with my dear, blessed boy, and after we're married, I don't think
I'll wait any longer. You can understand that, can't you?

Anders and I are both so happy and love each other so much. And during
these past two years we've become more dependent on each other so that we
can't bear to be apart. He was in Stockholm this fall and was supposed to stay
there for 3 months, but he came back after 5 weeks, and admitted that it was
mostly because he was longing for me. "There's no one else I can have a sensible conversation with," he says. "You mustn't think it's just because I can't do
without your kisses and such, but you're the only good friend I've ever had."
Which reminds me that in April he's going to Stockholm again for an exhibition there, and I'm terribly tempted to go with him, but I don't know whether
I dare. Mamma is very strict and old-fashioned — alas, I've had to lie to her
more often during the past year than in all the rest of my life put together. And
she wouldn't like it much if I went to Stockholm while he was there, especially
if it led to any sort of gossip. Otherwise she's very fond of Svarstad, who in turn
admires her and courts her in every way: "Because she's your mother, after all,"
he says to me, "and she's the one you take after."

At any rate, I'll be going to Copenhagen in April, and from there probably
on to London. If it can be arranged, we'd like to be married there and spend
time together in England. I've received another grant and have also made quite
a lot of money from *Jenny,* which to my enormous surprise was one of the year's
biggest successes and is now in its 3rd printing. If you want to translate it, I
would of course be very happy — that's one book for which it should be possible to find a publisher, since Norway isn't the only place it has been praised; it
has also been reviewed in the Danish newspapers, and even *Tilskueren* gave it
quite a lengthy review. I've sent my other books to Fru v. Kræmer, but haven't
heard anything from her.

I was sorry to hear that your mother is so ill. Give her my greetings, if she
still remembers me. Here at home everything is fine, although we all have
plenty of work and toil.

I look forward to seeing you, as I hope I will when I come to Copenhagen
soon. I hope to see both you and your children and to have a nice long talk with
them. I wish you could meet my betrothed. You would probably think him
frightfully ugly, since most people do — but I think he's the handsomest man

on earth with his oddly irregular, lean face with its thousands of shifting, sparkling, lively expressions.

Well, so long until we meet again this year, my dear Dea. And if you should find time to write to me before then, you know it would make me happy.

Many greetings
your devoted Sigrid

Hotel Kong Frederik, Vester Voldgade
Copenhagen
June 12 (1912)

Dear Dea!

Now that I'm once again so close to you, I would dearly love to see you. I'm here in town, passing through — on my honeymoon, of sorts, although alone for the time being; my sweetheart will follow as soon as he can. We're headed for Antwerp and have made arrangements to be married there at the Norwegian consulate — and will then travel on to London and later out into the world for as long as our money lasts. Hopefully for at least a year.

As things stand, it would be difficult for me to come to Åkorp. First of all because I don't know exactly when Svarstad will arrive, and secondly because I'm not feeling very well — I keep throwing up, etc. Under the circumstances you must understand that I wouldn't want to be anyone's guest. But aren't you planning to come to Copenhagen anyway? Or if you're going to Malmö one day, just let me know and we could meet there.

Otherwise I am well — and happy, very happy. I miss my "betrothed" terribly, but I know he won't linger in Kristiania without me any longer than is absolutely necessary. I wonder if you can imagine what it's like for two people who can't bear to be apart — who, for more than two years now, have had to steal all our time together, and tell lies, and often had to be separated when we most needed to be together — finally, finally to be allowed to live together in peace and quiet. You see, we almost can't believe that at last it's going to come true, that we're going to meet and will never have to be parted even for an hour unless that's what we want ourselves.

My sweetheart had a big exhibition in Stockholm in April, and it was a great success — maybe you saw something about it in the Swedish newspapers.

Fru v. Kræmer has begun translating *The Happy Age* into Swedish and has found a publisher. I won't get more than 50 kroner in royalties for the whole thing — but I mostly just wanted to be published over there.

I hope to hear from you soon — and preferably see you too. Give my greetings to your husband and children.

Your devoted old friend
Sigrid Undset

October 2, 1912
64 The Grove
Hammersmith
London W.

Dear Dea,

It was such a long time ago that we were together in Copenhagen, and I haven't yet managed to write to thank you for those days. I'm doing so now, because it was terribly nice to see you again and to say hello to your sweet children — but it was a shame that I couldn't meet you after Svarstad arrived. I did try to call you several times, but without any luck — and besides, my family was there and completely monopolized our time. By the way, my aunt didn't care much for Anders until the last day. That's when he got a telegram saying that the portrait he had painted of me had been sold for 2000 kroner to a gallery in Bergen — and that fact changed my aunt's feelings about him so unbelievably that in her parting words — this was in the ladies' room at the train station, to be quite frank — she was very enthusiastic about my betrothed.

Well, at least from the postcard sent from Brussels you saw that we actually did get married. It was very simple and straightforward: Anders delivered our papers at 10 o'clock and at 5 we were married by a young man whom we politely addressed as Herr Vice Consul, although he apparently held a much lower rank. He behaved with all the dignity of an archbishop and the following day invited us to dinner, whereupon we were forced to invite him to breakfast, and he kept chasing after us the whole time we were in Antwerp, no doubt wanting to fill in for our absent families. He was inexpressibly kind — and just about the most boring individual I've ever met. It was only by the skin of our teeth that we escaped having him as a third wheel at our wedding dinner, but we managed it and had a delightful celebration all to ourselves — with champagne and toasts to both the born and the unborn family members in a lovely restaurant out at the zoo. Otherwise our wedding trip to Belgium was not as successful as our other wedding travels — it rained constantly, the hotels were dreadful, and I wasn't well — although we did have several charming evenings in Brugge, which *is* marvelous. In fact, all the old Flemish towns were, but steady downpours and nausea always detract a bit from the mood — and both of us had a feeling of moving on to a more amusing chapter when we sailed away from Antwerp and our consular friend — me loaded down with roses and candy, all compliments of Herr Vice Consul.

We've liked being here in England from the moment we set foot in the country — in fact, it started on the wharf in Harwich. The porters, conductors, and hansom cab drivers — who are a nuisance everywhere else in the world — took such good care of us and our belongings that we felt as if we were under the protection of angels. And even the awful boardinghouse in Bloomsbury where we first landed couldn't dampen our spirits. London was too lovely in the sunshine at the height of summer — and after some searching we found this place in Hammersmith, where we've lived for two months, and where we feel utterly comfortable — that is, the weather is terrible, but we've simply given up all hope of seeing any sunshine or warmth until we reach Italy, and the house is cold and drafty, but all buildings in England are that way, unless you can live in a palace. Otherwise, we're living here as cheaply as is possible in England, and our landlady, Mrs. Tarner, is the kindest and friendliest and dearest person you could imagine — outside of England she would probably be inconceivable. Because the English *are* so enchanting to deal with, and England is wondrously beautiful; if you ever come over here, as you once talked about doing, you must go out to Middlesex. It's not a tourist place; it's just pale green farmland with green meadows and old oak trees and sunken roads and paths through the fields and blackberry brambles along the hedges and lovely old farmsteads and villages — practically the same wherever you go. Lately we've taken to going out there every Sunday — getting off at some randomly chosen railway station and wandering around all day long, having a bite to eat in a little old inn with gardens full of chrysanthemums and dahlias and lavender hedges. Fortunately I've felt completely well the whole time we've been here and can manage to wander around for several miles without difficulty. And besides, I'm so happy and content that even if I feel sick for a few days now and then, it doesn't have the slightest effect on my spirits.

To be quite blunt, I'm enjoying all the legitimate benefits of marriage — without yet having any of its obligations or troubles. No housekeeping — it wouldn't pay over here, where a furnished room with board costs about the same as one without board. We each have a big, pleasant room, my husband and I, and both of them face the small villa gardens and green trees, which have lost nearly all their leaves by now. Even though this is a boardinghouse, we have our meals served to us privately in a little room downstairs. And my husband doesn't demand that I do so much as sew on his buttons or darn his socks — on the contrary, I think he regards it as a tedious inconvenience if I rummage in his dresser drawers and carry off any of his tattered clothes — although afterward he thanks me with the utmost courtesy for my "trouble." And best of all, he's the same dear, sweet, loving boy he has always been toward me, and nothing is any different between us now from what it was years ago in Italy or in Paris.

Until lately I've been working on my new book,* but a few days ago I sent off the manuscript. At least I didn't have a sense that it was any more difficult for me to work now than before — but I'm looking forward to putting all that aside for a good long time and devoting myself to other activities. When we get to Italy — and unfortunately that probably won't be until November, at the earliest, and no matter how happy I am here in London, I would still like to go south soon and I'd also like to have the traveling behind us before too long — but when we get to Italy, I'm going to start cooking and keeping house. (So at that time please do send me the cookbooks you promised; God knows I'll need them!) For the time being I have enough to do trying to see everything [. . .] that I still haven't seen in London, and which I'll probably see mostly on my own, because Anders is working like mad in the daytime on a huge painting — twilight on the Thames — and I'm making a serious effort to study English literature. My mantelpiece is already weighed down with heavy volumes; it's the old dramatists, Shakespeare's closest predecessors, contemporaries, and successors that I've especially immersed myself in, and my God what splendor and wealth they hold. In general, what a wealth of everything there is in this country. What treasures there are of ancient art, of scenic beauty, of riches and luxuries — as well as want and misery — and how dizzyingly sumptuous life is here. I know I will always long for England — just as I will always long for Italy, but never for France or Germany, for example.

And now I must start sewing baby clothes. But if you happen to write to me sometime soon, please remember to tell me: Do you think it's right to dress an infant in wool — "woolen flannel" — next to the skin? You see, I've been to a doctor — an enchanting, sweet, and maternal old miss, about whom I later found out that she is quite famous and a specialist in . . . the bubonic plague in India!

---

*Undset was finishing her new short-story collection *Fattige skjæbner* (Fates of the Poor), which she dedicated to her husband. The volume was published in the fall of 1912, and in her letter dated December 21, 1912, Undset noted that the book was already in its third printing.

She lived in India for a decade or so, making various discoveries regarding the plague, and she has a house filled with the most delightful Oriental rugs and metal objects, so that I was about to turn into a kleptomaniac when I was there. Well, it wasn't about the plague that I consulted her, and she gave me, among other things, some patterns for very practical little garments — but she kept on preaching about "woolen, woolen, woolen." There might be good reason for it here in this barbaric country where it's always cold and damp and the houses are drafty and they don't have any other heat than these wretched fireplaces that you have to huddle close to in order to get a little warmth. But I don't know if it would be suitable in Rome. Of course I'm sewing woolen clothes as outer garments, but I think the child should wear linen underneath. We're going to stay in Italy over the summer, and after a couple of months anything woolen would be downright cruel, and it must be easier to take off a woolen outer garment than to exchange woolen underclothes for linen, don't you think? What would you advise?

With this I've found an excuse to expect a letter from you sometime during the winter. Many greetings to Elisabet and Gösta — I hope that they are well and lively, and that you are too.

Your devoted
Sigrid

Via Frattina 138
Rome
December 21, 1912

Dear Dea,

Thank you for your letter. This will probably arrive too late for Christmas Eve, but I wish you and yours a Merry Christmas and a Happy New Year all the same! It must be fun to have two little children for whom you can light the Christmas tree.

I'm not in much of a Christmas mood right now. We're staying in an awful hotel room — arrived here three days ago — and the exciting question is whether we'll have other rooms by Christmas Eve. If we do — well, then everything will be fine. We're staying in the same place where my husband and I first met on Christmas Day three years ago. But the room is cold and unpleasant. The rooms we had rented are the same two that we lived in back then. They're the only ones on the top floor (6th floor!). They have all the sun Rome can muster, and a terrace filled with roses and orange trees outside. If we can move up there — and early enough for me to decorate the place with candles and flowers — and if the sun will only shine, then we'll have the kind of Christmas Eve that our first and hopefully last Christmas Eve alone should be. But it all depends on an old English spinster — I wish I could pray to God for her to leave. But the landlady — our wonderful old Signora Lehmann-Lucronesi — has promised to do what she can. She was delighted to see us again as a married couple — there have been a total of 4 couples who became engaged up on her terrace. And she has promised to take care of the wash and to find me a nurse and everything else for my confinement, and I'm so happy — she is kind and clean, the rooms are very private, with their own entry and water and sink and petroleum stove. They're cold, the way all Roman rooms are — but I'll just have to put warm clothes on me and the baby at night — and by the time the child arrives, the worst of winter will already be over. And when the sun shines, there's no place in the whole world as charming as Fru Lehmann's terrace — sunlight from dawn until dusk, with all the bells in Rome ringing for vespers, and a view over the old brownish gray rooftops and church domes and towers and spires, and with the stone pines and cypresses on the distant ridges black against the clear blue sky, unsullied by scarcely a single column of smoke. Oh yes . . . I'm healthy and happy, and I'm dreaming about how wonderful it will be to sit outside on that blessed old rooftop belonging to me and my sweetheart, and let the baby lie there and bask in the sun all day. You can't possibly imagine how lovely it is up there — except that it makes a person much too lazy, so you hardly feel like going down the six flights. And the weather has been so glorious here in Rome these past few days. Yesterday we went up to Monte Pincio as soon as we woke up, and we had lunch at a *latteria* up there, in the middle of a green meadow among magnificent old stone pines, while the big brown, half-wild cattle grazed between the tables. And we walked all day, up there among the lovely fountains and along the grand lanes of holly oaks.

Oh, I'm so glad to be here again. I was very happy in London — but to Svarstad's glee I had to admit on the first morning we awoke in Paris, that the sun, the sun full and bright with no veils of fog, that was something I hadn't seen in all those months in England. Dry, clear air — I had actually forgotten what it felt like. It's beautiful, that soft misty air over there, the milky sunshine and the grayish blue shading on the horizon — and I love London, but the change seems dazzling. Even though it was bitterly cold in Paris — and even colder in Milan, where we stayed for two days — it wasn't until Florence that it started to get warm. Here it's full summer; the trees are filled with oranges, and the daisies are blooming in the Protestant cemetery. We haven't yet been out to the *campagna*.

And then there's the marvelous Italian food and wine. During the last months in London I was utterly miserable with a burning in my chest — the food was all mutton, mutton, mutton, and terribly heavy pies and puddings; ever since I came south to salads and oil and fried little octopuses and artichokes and omelettes, I've felt completely well. In fact, I have to admit that I've experienced so little of the unpleasantness that arises from being pregnant, that according to the doctors, I'm one woman out of a hundred. But I'm still looking forward to being done with this.

My book is selling — it's now in a third printing. And that's wonderful; next year, of course, there won't be any writing . . .

Well, this has turned out to be all about me and my family. But there are some things that I can't talk about with my husband, you know. He has three little children back home who were not received with joy, but he still loves them deeply and worries about them. They were brought into the world under unfavorable circumstances, and yet they are half siblings to the little one we're expecting. And it's so strange to think that my child has two little sisters and a brother in Norway — God only knows how things will go later on . . .

I wish you a Merry Christmas and Happy New Year. I hope you will write to me soon. I send you many, many greetings, and I am so happy — even though I don't yet know whether I'm going to be cheated out of a Christmas Eve this year.

Your devoted
Sigrid

Rome
January 30, 1913

Dear Dea,

On the morning of the 24th I gave birth to a son — a big strong boy — 5 kilos. It was quite a dreadful experience, but I've quickly recovered my strength. Of course I'll spend another week in bed; I've taken lodgings with a midwife who is half German and half Italian, and I'm doing fine here.

It won't do any good for me to tell you what I think of the boy. But everyone else who has seen him says he is truly unusually beautiful and healthy and well formed — so maybe it's not just my imagination. His name is Andrea, after you. Actually, all children who are born here in the city have to be registered by the father within 5 days, under the name they are to be given. I had decided from the first day I knew of his existence, that if the baby was a boy, he would be called Anders, like his father. But at the Municipio they refused to accept it and demanded that the name be translated into Italian. So now the documents we have for the child list his name as "Andrea Castus Svarstad."

Many greetings to you and your sweet children,

Your devoted and happy
Sigrid.

DATE DUE